Russell Andrews is the pseudonym of Peter Gethers, a novelist, screenwriter, author of several bestselling works of non-fiction, and an editor for a large New York publishing house. He divides his time between his apartment in Lower Manhattan and his houses in Long Island and Sicily.

APHRODITE

RUSSELL ANDREWS

timewarner
paperbacks

A *Time Warner* Paperback

First published in Great Britain in 2003 by Time Warner Books
Published as a Time Warner Paperback in 2004

A CIP catalogue record for this book is
available from the British Library.

ISBN 07515 3351 3

Typeset in Minion by M Rules
Printed and bound in Great Britain by
Clays Ltd, St Ives plc

Time Warner Paperbacks
An imprint of
Time Warner Books UK
Brettenham House
Lancaster Place
London WC2E 7EN

www.TimeWarnerBooks.co.uk

D E D I C A T I O N

To Esther Newberg. I definitely owe you big-time for this one. Oh, okay, I might as well go all the way! Not just for this one but for a lot of other things, too. It's hard to be a better friend than you are an agent, and somehow you even manage *that*. Thank you. But if anyone asks me about this, I'll deny everything.

ACKNOWLEDGMENTS

As usual, the list is a long one: To Bill Goldman, for the obit, the readings, the guidance, and, as usual, everything else; Hilary Hale, for being a great and supportive editor; Jamie Rabb, Sarah Ann Freed, Beth DeGuzman and Larry Kirshbaum for their enthusiasm, support and savvy; the Zigmeister for putting me in touch, yet again, with the right people; John Boris, for his insight into the pharmaceutical/financial world; Bill Borbidge, for his amazing knowledge of explosives; Ron Malfi, for his inside info; Alicia Goldsmith, Susanna Green, Dina Dillon and Sonam Wangmo for all things to do with yoga, Buddhism, massages and fun; Janis, for everything.

To her father white
Came the maiden bright:
But his loving look,
Like the holy book,
All her tender limbs with terror shook.

William Blake, *A Little Girl Lost*

APHRODITE

PROLOGUE

February 21

She knew there were no monsters.

And yet, when the lights were out, she also knew that there were.

It's why she screamed when she heard the footsteps. There was a quick flurry, someone running – no, *darting*, that's the way it sounded, definitely darting – and then there was a crash, glass being shattered, a piece of pipe, perhaps, swung against the ugly overhanging fluorescent light. Everything turned shadowy; the whole room was suddenly fifty per cent darker than it had been. Then, almost before she could register what was happening, there were more footsteps, on the other side of the garage – how did he get over there so fast? It didn't seem possible – and another crash, another light smashed, and then it was dark. Not just darker this time, but completely dark. She couldn't see her hand right in front of her face.

It was absolutely quiet, too. Black and silent.

And suddenly there it was.

The feeling.

Even under normal circumstances, when things were

3

calm, when she was tucked up safely in bed, under the down-filled covers with the lights out, Maura Greer was overwhelmed by the dark. Even in her own room there was nothing she could do to stop her imagination from running wild. To stop her heart from beating madly and her throat from drying up and that thing inside her head from saying: *Be afraid. Something bad is coming. Something really is there, inside the blackness* . . .

And now something really *was* there.

Footsteps again.

She could hear someone breathing.

She thought she was going to faint. Her whole body was shaking and, despite the freezing temperature and dankness of the garage, hot, clammy sweat was starting to drip down the back of her neck.

Maura had lived with this fear for so long. Maybe her whole life. As a child she needed a night light. When she went away to college, got her very first apartment, she used to leave the light on in the hallway outside her bedroom. She told her roommate it was so she could find the bathroom when she woke up in the middle of the night but that wasn't true at all. It was because the darkness terrified her. Filled her with numbing, paralyzing dread.

That's what she was feeling now. She was stuck in the underground garage of her apartment building with some madman who had shattered all the lights and was, she was positive, going to stalk her and catch her and rape her. So the dread was deep in the pit of her stomach. A physical sensation. A pain. As if she'd been injected with a drug that was quickly taking effect, moving upwards from her feet, through her legs, clenching her

4

stomach, wrapping around her throat, choking her. It's not fair, she thought. Not today. Not now. Not when, in less than an hour, her whole life was about to change. And it *was* going to change. She *knew* it. Today he was going to tell her he loved her. He was going to tell her they could be together. Finally. And she was going to comfort him and assure him that everything would be all right, and make him understand he'd made the right decision, and . . .

More footsteps!

To her left. He was all the way to her left, maybe thirty feet away. There was a door there, leading up to her apartment building; it was the way she'd come in. But there was another way out. An easier way. The driveway. That was maybe fifty or sixty feet to her right. The metal door, the one that rolled slowly down from the tracks on the ceiling and guarded the ramp the cars came up, was shut. It shouldn't have been – it was supposed to stay open until 7 p.m. She didn't have the clicker that opened it, either. She would have, normally, but she hadn't brought her purse. He didn't like her to carry any ID when they met. He didn't want them to be seen together in public, and they always took extra careful precautions; he didn't want her to have any identifying papers in case anything happened, so she just took to leaving her purse and her wallet at home when she saw him. She could picture her bag, sitting on the kitchen counter. And in it was the goddamn clicker. She'd thought about taking it, decided it wasn't important, she wouldn't need it, not before seven. So she left it. Her ticket to freedom sitting on the goddamn kitchen counter . . .

But there was another way out, she realized. Another door that led out to the front of the building. All she had to do was beat him to that door by the driveway and she could make it up to the street. There'd be people there. Someone to help her. There'd be light . . .

But she didn't know if she could make it. She wasn't dressed for running.

She had wanted today to be so perfect. She wore his favorite blouse, a flowery Donna Karan, very flimsy and practically see-through. She had tried on two different pairs of pants in her apartment, then decided that pants weren't right, she really wanted to go sexy, so she wound up with a short black skirt. Straight, no pleats, linen. It came down to the middle of her thighs and she knew he really liked her thighs; even in public he could barely keep his hands from brushing up against them at dinner, sometimes being as daring as he could be, squeezing them under the table and lingering.

The bra had been easy. It came from the Bra Store, in Manhattan, on Madison in the East 60s, practically her favorite place on earth. The perfect store. Today's choice was very daring. It was flesh-colored and revealed a lot of cleavage. Under the Donna Karan, it would look, at first glance, as if she was naked, and she knew he'd really, really like that. Leaving her apartment, she'd thought about how he'd look at her in mock disapproval, shake his head, and say something like, 'That should be illegal.' She'd look concerned and maybe say, 'Do you want me to go home and change?' And, of course, he'd grab her then, because he couldn't help himself, and she'd let him hold her, touch her, for a long time, and she'd kiss him, once or twice, slowly lick the inside of his upper lip, he loved that so much, and when he groaned with pleasure, she'd say, 'Did you do it? Did you tell her?' And this time she knew the answer would be yes. Because this time she really had something for him. She had some real information. She would show him once and for all that she was not just a piece of fluff or merely the object of his lust. She had a brain. A good brain. And she was important to him. Useful.

Because this time she could give him what he wanted, something besides the sex.

He said he had a name: Aphrodite.

But he needed more. He needed information.

Now she had that information. She knew what Aphrodite was.

She could, even in the darkness of the garage, picture his eyes, the way they'd shine when she told him what she'd discovered. And she pictured his voice when she'd finally hear the words she'd been dying to hear for so many months now.

Yes, I told her. Yes, we can be together.

Yes. I love you.

Yes . . .

It was going to be exactly the way she'd dreamed about it, that's why she'd had to get the shoes just right, too, of course. He liked spiked heels, all men did. God, men were fools sometimes. It was still the middle of the afternoon and she didn't want to look like a hooker but what the hell, she'd decided to go for it. She wouldn't wear them when he took her to the White House – and he *was* going to take her to the White House, he'd all but promised –

but today wasn't for meeting presidents and senators. Today was supposed to be for something altogether different, so she went for the Jimmy Choo eggshell-colored heels. Why not? They showed her ankles off so perfectly and that was the best part of her body, she knew. She might be ten pounds on the plump side . . . okay, fifteen . . . but her ankles were perfect. So that's what she was wearing with her tight skirt, and that's why she was not dressed for running.

Her ankles just might get her killed, she thought . . .

Where was Hector? Why hadn't that occurred to her before? He was *always* in the garage during the day. He complained about it all the time. *Sunny outside but I'm underground all day long*, that's what he constantly said to her. He'd leer at her a little bit, especially when she looked like she did today. He'd leer and complain about being inside and underground breathing in car fumes. Where was he now?

She screamed out his name.

Hectorrrrrrrrrrr . . .

No answer. Was Hector the one doing this? It seemed inconceivable. But still, the way he looked at her sometimes. Had she ever told him she was afraid of the dark? She might have. Everyone said she was too gabby. She might have told him and now here he was, wanting her and knowing she'd be terrified . . .

There was another noise, a *sssssttttt*. A match being lit. Then a tiny speck of light. She saw something. A man. Not Hector. Nothing like Hector. A tall man. Tall and thin with short-cropped, white-blond hair. Handsome and pale . . .

8

Then the match went out and the light was gone. And so was he.

Back in the dark.

That's when she realized that if she couldn't see him, he couldn't see her. So as terrified as she was, her brain began to work. It told her to crouch down and kick off those eggshell high heels and move quietly, quietly but steadily, toward the door by the driveway . . .

She wondered if they'd realize she was late checking into the hotel. She told them she'd be there by five. They knew her there by now, at the Marriott in Virginia. The desk clerk no longer bothered to take her credit card imprint when she checked in, he'd just wave her away and say they'd take care of it on her way out. Then she'd pay cash. Her story was that she was from out of town, coming in repeatedly on business. She said she lived in East End Harbor, on Long Island, in New York, and that wasn't really a lie. More like a fib. She also told him she was a lobbyist for the Nature Conservancy and that *was* a lie. She didn't know why she'd said it, maybe because that's what she wished she were. That's what she *would* be, one of these days. But the clerk certainly remembered their conversations because when he saw her he always called her Ms Greer, he always asked how her lobbying was going, and then he'd hand her the key to her room, always the same room, 1722. He knew not to bother to call a bellhop, she had made it clear she preferred to carry her small overnight bag herself. The only question he ever asked was 'Early or late checkout?' and after she told him she'd smile to show she was very satisfied with the service, then head straight for the bank of elevators that went to the seventeenth floor. All she'd have to do after that was wait for the love of her life to arrive. She always arrived on time, she was never late. So maybe they'd realize that something was wrong, maybe they'd come looking for her . . .

Another *sssssttt*. Another flash of light. He was far from her now, the blond man. He was guarding that door all the way to the left, and she'd moved maybe fifteen feet closer to the driveway. She could make it. He was looking around, he didn't see her, but she could see he was wearing a khaki suit with an open-neck blue shirt, and now she thought: I can do it. I can make it. He's not even looking in my direction and, okay, I see the clearing, I see the door. As soon as the match goes out, just run like hell. I can make it . . .

Then the match went out and she took off.

She banged her knee into the corner of a car, the darkness was disorienting, but that didn't really slow her down. She was hauling ass and there was no way he was going to get her. She didn't even hear footsteps, he wasn't even trying. He knew it was impossible, knew that he'd lost, and she reached the door, grabbed for the doorknob and started to turn it, started to yank the door open and yes, there was the crack of sunlight, she had made it . . .

And that's when she felt the hand on her arm.

She looked up and there he was. The light from the crack in the door showed the short blond hair, the khaki suit and the blue shirt. But it wasn't possible. She'd seen him, knew he was all the way on the other side of the garage. She hadn't heard him running. He *couldn't* have beaten her to the door. It was not humanly possible . . .

10

She felt a pain in her wrist now, realized he was twisting it, pulling her away from the door. She heard it shut with a click and a quiet whoosh. She started to scream, maybe someone could hear her on the other side, but his hand was over her mouth, and she couldn't scream. She couldn't move and she couldn't make a sound and she couldn't even see him anymore. She couldn't see anything. She was back in the dark.

There was a strange and overwhelming pressure on her throat now and she was having trouble breathing. She felt her head twisting and it hurt, it really hurt, and then she heard a little snap and started to fall to the concrete floor. She was vaguely aware that the man was holding her up, that he was dragging her to the back of a car. She felt herself being lifted up, realized that the trunk of the car was open and she started to squirm.

And then she felt another tug at her neck and heard another crack and then she didn't feel anything.

Maura did not hear the trunk of the blond man's car close on top of her. She did not know that the Donna Karan blouse she was wearing now had a long tear under her right armpit or that the Jimmy Choo spike-heeled shoes were streaked with grease and carelessly tossed, inches away from her bare feet. She did not see or feel the body of Hector, the garage attendant, that was already stuffed in the trunk next to her.

As the blond man's car slowly pulled out of the parking space and moved toward the exit ramp, Maura felt like she was floating, like she was drifting off into space, weightless. She was surrounded by blackness, blacker than she'd ever imagined. She tried to make herself come

11

back, tried to stop herself from fading into the dark, but she couldn't. And as she floated farther and farther away, she thought: *It's not fair. It's not fair, it's not fair, it's not fair. He has to tell me he loves me. He has to take me to meet all the famous and powerful people. And he has to know about Aphrodite.*

I have to tell him about Aphrodite.

And then the terrible feeling that had been with Maura Greer her entire life disappeared. There were no more shadows. No more terrifying shapes. And no more fear.

There was only a new and different kind of darkness.

LONDON, ENGLAND

March 2

The lecture hall was packed.

The turnout was more than a little surprising to Joseph Fennerman because over the past twenty-four hours a steady stream of cold, hard rain and a numbing winter dampness had re-arisen and the combination seemed to permeate not just every English person's clothes or even skin but *life*.

Fennerman was delighted with the event. For one thing, the size of the crowd guaranteed that his lecture fee would remain at the exceedingly high level he now commanded for an appearance. For another, he was autographing and selling the hardcover edition of his latest book, *The Morality of Numbers*, already a bestseller on the other side of the Atlantic, and judging from the buzz in the room he'd sell every copy on hand. Finally, prior to taking the stage he had been approached by a rather awestruck grad student, a somewhat bony brunette wearing a man's rose-colored collared shirt, a short black skirt and black leggings. She was not particularly attractive but, after a remarkably easy ten-minute conversation, she not only seemed charmed by his awkward demeanour – facial tics and all – she agreed to meet him after the lecture to continue their discourse over a late supper at his favorite London restaurant, Rules. Fennerman was astonished by his successful pick-up, and he was so eager to meet up with her, he did something that went totally against his normal behavior pattern: he rushed through his material, knowingly omitting several salient and key points, trying to get to the end of his speech as quickly as possible. When the moderator opened up the floor for questions, the 48-year-old Dr Fennerman, for the very first time in his distinguished career, was wishing that his audience would stop making him the center of their world, and let him get off the damn stage.

'Of course, we are just beginning to explore the complicated questions of limits,' he heard himself saying in response to a rather smug, long-winded comment from someone in a corduroy jacket and beard sitting in the third row. 'By limits, I am referring to our own population, to the extension of human life into prolonged senescence, as well as limits to our own consumption and exploitation, both of resources and our very nature. The question of limits is probably our most difficult one to grapple with because biologically we are designed to increase at will and acquire whatever is available. The matter is complicated further because any kind of thorough historical perspective shows that people will exploit anything they can as completely as their technology and force permit.'

Another question. This one from a singularly unattractive woman near the back. He barely let her finish her sentence before he roared into his answer.

'You must understand the difference between what is visible – and thus easy to ascertain and comprehend – and what is underneath the surface, which is, in almost all cases, far more defining than something that can be touched and seen. When it comes to the question of human existence, understanding that difference is essential. All of us carry a unique genetic profile in our cells. That profile includes expressed genes, those things easily recognizable such as eye and hair color, size of various features, etcetera, and that is called a phenotype. But we also have genes that are not expressed, recessive if you will, that make up an individual's genotype. If I can use a mundane but clear example: Think of a birthday present, nicely wrapped and handed to you. The wrapped package is a phenotype. You can tell something about what is inside by the size and the weight and possibly the sound. But you can't tell exactly what it is, you can't define it, until you open it. The contents – in many ways, the essence – are the genotype.

'What I hope you take away from our conversation this evening is the complexity of the ethical dangers inherent in tampering with either phenotype or genotype. Does it really matter to the moral structure of the universe if we use transgender engineering to produce perfect-looking strawberries? No, of course not. But does it matter if, because of our interference, we create something that looks beautiful but has no taste? That is no longer functional nor serves the purpose for which it was

15

originally created by nature? That's what each of us must decide.

'Thank you and good night.'

Joseph Fennerman practically raced off the stage, sat at a small desk off to the side where he impatiently signed books for half an hour, then threw his coat and muffler across his shoulders and, waving away his well-wishers and admirers, rushed outside to his stretch limousine that was waiting in front of the University of London's urban campus. He tapped on the dark, tinted window to alert the driver to his presence, and jumped into the back, a good six feet away from the front seat, rubbing his hands together to brush off the cold and the rain. The driver didn't bother to turn around.

'I'm waiting for a young woman,' Fennerman said, smothering his nervousness with an awkward cough. 'She'll be here momentarily.' He tried but was unable to make out some of the man's face in the rearview mirror. He remembered from the initial pick-up that he was handsome and young, with smooth, pale features and well-groomed blond hair. Not the sort of face that would be surprised or anxious at the thought of having dinner with a too skinny woman.

'She was already here, Dr Fennerman,' the driver said. 'She said she'll meet us a couple of blocks away, at the corner of Melton and Euston Square.'

'Why?' Fennerman asked. The little twitch in his left eye was suddenly back and doing its work. It occurred to him that the driver had an American accent. Not a very refined one, either. Broad and harsh. He hadn't noticed that earlier. 'Why didn't she just stay here?'

'It's where she parked her car. I guess she had to get something out of it. I told her I could drive her but she didn't want to wait.'

Fennerman grunted and nodded, said, 'Fine, fine,' and kept rubbing his hands together as the driver took him two blocks away. When the long black car pulled up to the curb at Euston Square, the back door opened. Looking up in anticipation, Fennerman was more than a little annoyed when a man slid in next to him.

'You've got the wrong car,' Fennerman told him with an exasperated sigh. When the man didn't move, he added an impatient, 'You've made a mistake.'

'I don't think so,' the man said. Then, turning to the driver, he said, also in a jarringly harsh American accent, 'Have I made a mistake?'

Fennerman, facing the front seat, demanded to know what was going on.

'Just taking on another passenger,' the driver told him. 'It won't be for long.'

'This is unacceptable,' Fennerman said. 'In my hotel room I have the name of the event organizer who booked your car service and I will definitely make a complaint. Now take me back to the lecture hall.'

'You flying to Washington tomorrow?' the man in the back seat now asked.

'How do you know that?'

'I'm a psychic.' The man held his hand over his eyes as if envisioning the future. 'Three o'clock meeting at the Hubert H. Humphrey Building. Two hundred Independence Avenue. Southwest. You want the room number?'

'Take me to the lecture hall,' Fennerman told the driver again. 'Take me back immediately and let me off.'

'Meeting your young lady?' the man next to him said.

'Yes.' It only took Fennerman a moment to make an unpleasant and frightening connection. It's what he did for a living: make connections between thoughts. 'How do you know about her?'

'Move forward. There's something up there I want you to see.'

Fennerman hesitated, then slid toward the driver and jutted his chin out until it almost touched the glass shield that separated the front seat from the back. Slumped all the way forward in the seat, unmoving, her head resting limply between her knees, he saw the woman he had talked to at the lecture hall. He also saw the large, ugly wound running from her spine around to her ribs and the pool of blood that was still accumulating under her body.

'Oh my god,' he said, his eye blinking furiously and uncontrollably. He looked at the driver's face in the rear-view mirror now. Turned to stare at the face of the man sitting beside him. 'What's happening?'

'I read one of your books. The one about actions and consequences,' the man said. 'You should have realized. You made that appointment, now there are consequences.'

'What consequences?' Fennerman asked, his voice hoarse and his throat dry.

'We're gonna have to fuck with your genotype,' the man said and moved so quickly that Fennerman barely saw what happened. All he knew was that there was a sharp stinging at his throat and the black leather car seat was suddenly splattered with red. Fennerman felt himself choking, heard a loud and harsh gurgling noise, like a clogged drain trying to disperse its contents or a neglected fountain struggling to increase its water pressure.

Dr Joseph Fennerman, physiologist, scientific ethicist, and internationally esteemed observer of the complexity of human life, was dead before he could even realize that his throat had been cut. The man whose reputation was made by connecting abstract theories to form precise and practical applications did not even have time to make the connection that the unpleasant noise he was listening to, the last thing he would ever hear, was the sound of him drowning in his own blood.

LONG ISLAND, NEW YORK

June 14

Up until 9:15 this morning, Susanna Morgan had loved everything about her life. She adored her work, she was crazy about where she lived, and since the two things were so intertwined on a day-to-day basis, she felt safe in assuming it was the combination that made her so content. Some might say *too* content. Two of her best friends recently broke it to her that being around her was a little bit like going into diabetic shock. They told her if she didn't cut down on her sugary disposition, they'd have to come over and slap some sense into her. This conversation came after she'd explained to them why she didn't mind staying at the office until ten o'clock at night sometimes and why she wouldn't think of asking for overtime. It was after she said, 'I'd pay *them* to let me work,' that the whole slapping issue came up.

She'd come to New York from Dayton, Ohio, to be a writer and while she was toiling away at her first and sure-to-be epic novel, she decided she'd do what she'd done in Dayton, which was work at the local paper. So she went to the New York *Times* and waited for them to be impressed by her perkiness and her extremely literate application form. After several months of waiting, she decided they had indeed been impressed but they were not going to be hiring her, so she started looking elsewhere. In a couple of months she'd been turned down by both New York tabloids, several small papers in New Jersey, and an Upper West Side give-away. In the meantime, she went to a temp agency, and they sent her from ad agency to publishing company to, while they lasted, dot com start-ups. At one of the ad agencies, she met a guy whom she dated for a while. In their third week of dating, he took her for a weekend to the Hamptons house he shared with six other people and within an hour of driving and strolling around she fell in love with that part of Long Island. She and the guy broke up at the end of the summer but she couldn't get Long Island out of her mind. She decided it was the perfect place to write her novel so she gave up her city sublet and rented a small two-bedroom apartment, half of an adorable Victorian house, right on Main Street in the center of the town of East End Harbor, which was a bit more blue collar and not quite as chic as the Hamptons but was only a few minutes away. And what do you know: her first week there she went to a yoga class, just two doors down from her new digs, and not only was the yoga instructor the woman who rented the other apartment in Susanna's house, but one of the people in the class was the man who owned and ran the local newspaper. Two days after that she began working on the East End *Journal*. A dream come true.

She started out at the low end of the totem pole and

did a little bit of everything at the paper: editing, writing, rewriting, reporting, making coffee. It was only a staff of five. Four years later, she was still writing the same novel but she was no longer at the bottom of the pole. She practically *was* the East End *Journal*. She'd added a food page and now traveled all over Queens and Long Island looking for quirky ethnic restaurant stories, interviewed all the top chefs who were gradually opening upscale eateries in the area, and from time to time even tossed in some recipes of her own because she was not a bad cook herself, thank you very much. She reviewed the local summer stock theater, which wasn't very good, but she did get to have a drink with Alec Baldwin to discuss the local writing talent. At the drink she happened to mention that she was working on a novel and that it would make a terrific movie if she ever actually finished the damn thing, and he told her he'd love to look at it – if she ever did finish it. Susanna also wrote about local gardens and covered the twice-yearly house tours of the town's old homes and, as of three months ago, she was even writing the obituaries. She didn't tell this to many people, but the obits were her favorite thing to work on. She didn't mind that she was writing about dead people and talking to bereaved relatives several times a week. She loved digging into the family histories and hearing about the community roots that went back years and years. There was a wonderful graveyard in East End Harbor, some of the tombs went back to the early 1700s, and she had even begun to think about doing a book based on all the history she'd uncovered from talking to so many grief-stricken people.

Yes, everything was absolutely wonderful.

Then, two days ago, it all began to unravel. She didn't understand how life could get so screwed up in a mere forty-eight hours.

Wednesday afternoon she'd been in the office working on a piece about an athlete, the only local football player who'd left East End High and gone on to play in the NFL. He used to play for the Green Bay Packers in the mid-80s and once ran an interception back 102 yards for a touchdown. But after he retired from football he got into crack, was arrested for armed robbery, and spent several years in a homeless shelter. Earlier that morning he'd jumped off the roof of a building in Dallas, Texas, leaving behind a note that said, 'A hundred and two yards my ass.' Except that 'two' was spelled 'too' and 'my' was spelled 'mi.' She was trying to decide whether or not to mention that the player had gone through four years at a Texas college when she looked up and saw that Harlan Corning, the owner of the *Journal*, was standing over her desk. He looked like he'd been standing there for several seconds. And he looked uncomfortable, she thought. He looked as if someone had died.

'I got a call,' he told her. His voice was softer than usual and gentle in that way that people spoke when they thought they had to be gentle. 'Bill Miller died.'

Susanna didn't swear very often, but the first thing that came out of her mouth was 'Oh, damn,' and she turned her head down toward her desk because she felt her eyes welling with tears and she didn't particularly want to cry in front of Harlan.

She composed herself, nodded, accepting the news she'd

23

heard, and instead of crying, said, in as clear a tone as she could muster, what she thought a good journalist should say: 'I'd like to write the obit.'

Which she did.

Susanna did not have to do a lot of research for her obituary on Bill Miller. Over the past two years, she had gotten to know him extremely well.

Since working nearly twenty-four hours a day clearly wasn't enough to keep her busy, twice a week Susanna did volunteer work at the East End Retirement Home. The Home was a series of small apartments, near the bay of the Long Island Sound, around which the town was originally built. The apartments had been built as a condominium project but, in the mid-70s, the developer had gone broke. Before the 80s boom struck, another developer, a local this time, bought the half-finished building on the cheap and turned it into an assisted-living complex, mostly so his grandmother would have a nice place to live out the last years of her life. Susanna, who spent her two afternoons there talking to the inhabitants, reading to them, mostly just showing them that someone cared, soon got very personally involved. She got to know many of them intimately. She loved hearing their stories about the old days – it all fit in with her growing interest in the town's history – and she never tired of their fascinating, often odd perspectives on the world. She had always liked old people. Her attitude was, *I'm going to be one of them someday, might as well find out what I'm going to be like.*

Her absolute favorite was William Miller, who had been living there for quite some time, as long as anyone could remember, and who was friendly and garrulous and had extraordinary energy. Susanna often would start out reading to Bill only to have him take the book out of her hands, explain to her about the need for dramatic inflection, and end up reading to her. She would try to entertain him with stories about her most recent date or something crazy that happened at work, but he would usually interrupt with far more compelling reminiscences about a woman he'd dated when he was a teenager or anecdotes about a lunatic boss from fifty years ago, and Susanna would find herself sitting, sipping ice tea and listening to his yarns, their roles once again reversed. Bill Miller had been an actor and he was a marvelous storyteller. He entertained her with Hollywood tales and stories of his days on Broadway. She was not a showbizzy-type person, it all was new and fascinating to her. Soon she knew his credits by heart, and was a little in awe of the fact that Bill, when he was young, had been nominated for an Academy Award for Best Supporting Actor. It was for a movie called *The Queen of Sheba*. Susanna had tried to rent a tape of it once – she wasn't ready for a DVD player, she had just figured out how to work her VCR – but the kid at the local video store said they mostly kept new stuff on hand. One of these days when she went back in to the city, she figured she'd get a copy. In the meantime, she'd been content to listen to Bill yak away. Particularly when he spoke about Cowboy Bill, the character he'd played on TV in the early 50s. It was a series for kids and Susanna's mother got extremely excited when she heard that her daughter had met the real Cowboy.

'I used to watch that as a little girl,' she gushed. 'I can

still see it, on the black and white TV my parents used to have in the living room. It was the only "boy" show I liked, mostly because Cowboy Bill was so handsome. My god,' she said, finally coming up for air, 'how old is he? He must be a hundred.'

'Eighty-two.'

'You're kidding? That's amazing. I remember him as being so old. Of course,' her mom laughed, 'I was seven, so anyone older than sixteen was an old man to me.'

Bill had been very pleased when Susanna told him about her mother's reaction. That night, he'd asked her to dine with him, which she did. They ate in the Home's common room, in front of the TV. After that, they'd even had dinner outside the Home a couple of times. She tried taking him to Sunset, her favorite seafood dive, thinking he'd love it, but leaving the apartment complex seemed to disorient him. When he talked, he got his dates all mixed up, forgot a lot of details of his career, and mingled dubious fact with obvious fiction. So after two unsuccessful attempts they went back to their twice-a-week afternoon chats in the comfortable if somewhat musty complex.

As Susanna wrote Bill Miller's obit for the East End *Journal*, she found herself getting tearful. She was sad for Bill, yes, but she was even sadder for herself, she realized. She was going to miss him. His stories. The way he used to poke fun at her. His advice about men and her career. She liked Cowboy Bill Miller, she was sorry he was gone, so she decided she'd write the best obituary she'd ever written. She'd give him a proper send-off. A tribute.

So that's what she'd done. Or what she *thought* she'd done.

The obit had come out in that morning's paper and she picked it up to read for perhaps the twentieth time in the past half-hour.

COWBOY BILL DEAD AT 82

William Miller, best known for the three years he spent riding the TV range as the poor man's Roy Rogers and folksy star of 'Cowboy Bill,' was found dead in his room at the East End Retirement Home this past Wednesday. Miller, one of East End Harbor's most beloved and colorful citizens, began his career as a serious actor, receiving an Academy Award nomination for Best Supporting Actor when he was just a teenager, in the 1939 costume drama, The Queen of Sheba. He was too rebellious to fit into the Hollywood studio system however and his film career stalled. By 1953 he found himself starring as Cowboy Bill in the television series of the same name. Cashing in on the popularity of western shows starring Roy Rogers and Gene Autry, Cowboy Bill lasted three seasons and is fondly remembered by many Baby Boomers.

Mr Miller's credits are spotty after that. He appeared in one low-budget horror film, The Vampire's Bite, in 1966. In 1968, he appeared in a lead part in the acclaimed off-Broadway revival of Clifford Odets' Golden Boy. His final stage appearance was in 1971 in another Odets revival, Waiting for Lefty.

Mr Miller's wife, Jessica Talbot, an actress, died in 1972. He is survived by his great-nephew, Edward Marion, of Wilton, Connecticut.

Susanna Morgan

When she first saw it, she had been a little disappointed with the way the piece had come out. There was a space problem and Harlan had cut a lot of the personal touches she had labored so hard over. She felt as if she hadn't done what she promised herself she'd do – make the town proud of Bill Miller and make Bill proud of her. But after the conversation she had with Harlan first thing that morning – all about the conversation *he'd* had with some nut who was incensed about the obit – her disappointment was fading. It was being replaced by confusion. And a strong feeling of embarrassment.

As soon as she strolled into the office that Friday, Harlan had come over to her desk. He said that he'd gotten an irate phone call. In fact, irate didn't even begin to describe it. Some guy in Middleview, a mid-Island town about an hour closer to the city, had erupted on the telephone. The guy's name – 'Get this one,' Harlan had said – was Wally Crabbe and he was a movie fanatic. So fanatical, in fact, that he'd flown into a rage because all the information in the Bill Miller obit was wrong. While Harlan held the receiver away from his ear, Crabbe had ticked off the long list of errors that he'd spotted. Susanna's boss held up a yellow legal pad, almost apologetically. He tore off the top page, which was covered with his scribbling, and handed it to her. 'This is everything Mr Crabbe said was wrong with your story,' he said softly. 'Actually, it's not everything. He was still going on when I told him I had to get off the phone. When I hung up, he was screaming at me that he wanted a free subscription to the paper to make up for our incompetence. Why is it that people want something for free if they think it's not good enough to pay for?'

He grinned, to show her that his question was meant to prove that he didn't take this all that seriously, but she didn't return the grin or give an answer, so Harlan told her, still in that uncomfortably gentle tone, to get to the bottom of things. If her facts were wrong, he said, they'd have to print a retraction in next week's paper. Susanna knew the way the town worked and she colored a deep red at the idea of admitting in print that Bill had lied about himself. If she had indeed screwed up, she would not have immortalized her friend Bill in town lore. She would have permanently humiliated him.

She herself had been surprised at one thing when she was researching the story. She had called over to the Home to confirm certain facts, and found one she didn't know: Bill had had a nephew. A great-nephew to be exact. She was certain Bill had told her, several times, that he had no living relatives. But Fred, who managed the Home, had told her about the nephew – great-nephew – who came and visited Bill every three months, like clockwork, stayed no more than five or ten minutes, and always paid for the next three months of Bill's stay. Fred said that he had called the nephew right after he'd found Bill, slumped in an easy chair in his room, to give him the sad news. The man had said he'd take care of all funeral arrangements and, in fact, that very night Fred called

Susanna at home to say that Bill's body had been picked up by ambulance and taken away. The nephew – great-nephew – made it clear that the funeral was going to be small and very private.

Everything else in the obit she'd gotten from Bill when he was alive. She'd taken it all on faith because she'd heard it so many times and she realized now that even if one were a cynic – which she most definitely was not – repetition was a subtle form of brainwashing. If you heard something often enough, especially from someone you trusted, it became true. Whether it was or not.

She told herself that Bill Miller was not a liar. She told herself that there had to be a misunderstanding. She told herself that what she'd put in the obit had been correct.

Only deep down she didn't believe it so she decided to find out for herself.

If there was a mistake, it was her mistake, not the paper's, so she didn't want to do this work on the *Journal*'s time. That's why, at lunchtime, three hours after Harlan told her that she'd screwed up, Susanna walked over to the East End Harbor Public Library.

After conferring with the librarian, Adrienne, a surprisingly snippish and impatient woman, Susanna took a seat in front of the computer that sat in the lobby to the right of the checkout desk. She pulled out the piece of yellow legal paper that Harlan had handed her, looked down the list of errors that angry Wally Crabbe had called in. She went on-line, wound up going to the Askjeeves.com web site and typed in the question: *How do I find out who was nominated for the 1939 Academy Award for Best Supporting Actor?*

30

It didn't take long. Within seconds she had her answer. She had to admit that she hadn't heard of any of the nominees – no, wait, Basil Rathbone, he was English, wasn't he? He played someone famous ... oh yes, Sherlock Holmes, she was pretty sure that was it, and Walter Brennan, he was in some show on *Nick at Night*, he played a farmer or something like that – and she also had to admit that William Miller wasn't among them. She tried looking at the awards for 1938, then 1940, and then going back earlier, year by year, until 1930. She decided to stop searching then. Bill might have gotten the year wrong at his age but she doubted he'd miss the entire decade.

She wondered how much further she should pursue this. Decided – out of duty and curiosity – she had to keep going. After several false starts, she got to the site for IMDB.com – Internet movie database – and looked up the career of William Miller. It took her over an hour of staring at the screen and reading and scrutinizing photos and double-checking, then triple-checking, on other movie web sites before she began to accept what she was seeing.

By the time she was done, she had a splitting headache and a steady wave of nausea flowing in the pit of her stomach. She practically fled the library, gasping in warm, fresh air once she made it to the sidewalk outside. Leaning up against a lamp post for support, she flicked open her cell phone, called Harlan's number at the *Journal*, and told him she wasn't feeling well, wouldn't be coming in for the rest of the afternoon. He told her to go to the doctor, started to ask if there was anything he could do, but she just clicked the phone off and hugged the lamp post until she had the strength to walk.

When she got home, Susanna paced nervously around her living room, picking at her cuticles, and tapping the fingers of her right hand against the knuckles on her left. Finally, she looked at the notes she'd jotted down from the conversation with Fred, the manager of the Home, saw the phone number she was looking for, picked up the phone and dialed it. After the fourth ring, she heard a man's voice on the phone machine, giving a bland out-going message. After the tone, she took a deep breath, it was suddenly hard to talk, and then she said, 'Hi . . . uh . . . Edward Marion? This is Susanna Morgan. I was a friend of your uncle's . . . uh . . . great-uncle's . . . and, um . . . well, I wrote his obit for our local paper and I'm very confused about a few things . . . I need to . . . well . . . know a few more things about Bill . . . I know this doesn't make any sense and I'm probably wrong . . . I've *got* to be wrong . . . But I really need to talk to you.' She left her phone number on the tape and then said, 'Please call me.' Then she hung up, took three aspirins and, even though it was three o'clock in the afternoon, got into bed and pulled the covers up over her head.

Edward Marion called back around six o'clock that evening. Susanna was still in bed, although she hadn't slept a wink, and the sudden noise of the phone made her shudder. When she answered it, her voice sounded thick to her, as if she'd been sedated.

'Ms Morgan?'

'Yes.'

'This is Ed Marion. Bill Miller's nephew.'

'Great-nephew.'

'What?'

'You're his great-nephew.'

'Yes. That's right.'

There was an awkward pause. Now that she had to convey the news to another person, now that she had to say it out loud, Susanna didn't know how to begin.

'Listen,' she said. 'I'm very sorry about your loss.'

'Thank you.'

'I was pretty close to Bill, I used to—'

'I know. He talked about you all the time.'

'I wrote his obituary for our local paper and I used a lot of information that your uncle had told me, you know, over the years.'

'Great-uncle.'

'What?'

'He was my great-uncle.'

'Oh. Right.'

'Ms Morgan, I'm afraid Bill was a bit of a . . . how should I say this . . . fantasist?'

'You mean he made things up?'

'I mean I think he probably believed them when he said them. And the more he said them, the more he believed them, if you know what I mean. I'm sorry if he told you things that weren't true. I hope it wasn't anything important. Or embarrassing.'

'The thing is, Mr Marion . . .'

'Call me Ed. Please.'

'The thing is, Ed . . . Somebody called, some movie

nut, and he was pretty angry – we don't get too many angry calls at the *Journal* – and he said that things I'd put in the obit weren't true. So I did some research.'

'You did?'

'Yes.'

'What kind of research?'

'I went on the Internet and checked out the things Bill told me about his career.'

'You researched my uncle?'

'Yes. And it turns out, this guy, this movie nut, he was right. Well, not about everything. Some of the things Bill told me *were* true. Only they weren't *really* true . . . This is going to sound kind of crazy . . .'

'Ms Morgan, may I make a suggestion?'

'Sure.'

'Let me meet you for lunch tomorrow. I was going to call you anyway because my uncle left you something in his will.'

'He did?'

'Yes. He was very fond of you. I've been wanting to meet you, so this is a good excuse. I can discuss the will with you, I think you'll be very pleased with what I've got to say, and you can tell me whatever it is you need to tell me.'

'Well, yes, it might be better to do this in person. But, listen, I have to tell you, this is pretty disturbing . . .'

'I can't imagine anything too disturbing about my uncle. He was such a sweet old guy. But let's talk about it at lunch.'

'It's an awfully long drive for you, isn't it?'

'Three hours. And I don't mind. From what I've heard about you, it'll be well worth it.'

She told him where to go, that she'd meet him at Sunset restaurant at 12.30. He said he was looking forward to it. She didn't say anything.

She'd have more than enough to say over lunch, she decided.

Susanna didn't fall asleep until one o'clock in the morning, which was incredibly late for her, two hours past her normal bedtime. And then she woke up one hour later. Two-oh-five to be exact, according to her new Bose clock radio.

At first she thought she'd awakened because she was hungry. She was so shaken by the experiences of the day she hadn't been able to eat dinner. She had heated up some soup, toyed with it with her spoon, then poured it right down the drain. She'd tried reading, couldn't concentrate. Tried watching TV, couldn't even do that. At 9.30 she gave up and got into bed, tossing and turning until one. Now she was awake again, her stomach growling.

And then she realized that she wasn't awake because she was hungry.

She was awake because there was a noise at her front door.

A noise like someone fiddling with a lock.

And then there was a noise like someone turning a doorknob. And opening a door.

And coming inside.

There was somebody in her apartment.

All of a sudden, Susanna was having trouble

35

swallowing. She felt her throat constricting at the same time as a rush of bile shot up from her stomach, choking her. She closed her eyes and ordered herself to be calm. Willed herself to keep her eyes closed an extra second until her throat relaxed. She took a deep breath, it helped to clear her head, but right in the middle of that was when she heard the creak of a floorboard in her living room and Susanna jumped out of bed, flailing at the covers, stumbling for just a moment as her foot was still wrapped in the sheet, and she lunged for the door to her bedroom, threw her shoulder against it and slammed it shut and locked it.

She stood still, one hand on the door, in total silence except for her own heavy, rhythmic breathing. After a few seconds, she began to feel silly. Maybe she'd been dreaming. Maybe everything that had happened that day was just ganging up on her to make her edgy and paranoid and . . .

And there was a scratching noise on the other side of the door.

There was no mistaking this one.

He was picking the lock.

She was in her nightgown and bare feet and she was pretty much frozen with terror and her heart was pounding so loud she thought she might actually be having a heart attack and six inches away someone was picking the lock to her bedroom door.

Was about to come in and do god knows what . . .

The air conditioning was on full blast but she was sweating through her nightgown. Beads of salty water dripped down her forehead, into her eyes, stinging them into a series of erratic blinks. Susanna looked around the room, searching for something, *anything* that could help her, but there wasn't a damn thing. No cell phone even, she'd left it in the living room, where she kept the cradle for the charger. She thought about racing to the regular phone, it was just by the bed, but something told her she wouldn't have time to call, something told her it was a matter of seconds now . . .

She took her hand off the door and turned, told herself not to look back, no matter what, and sprinted toward her bedroom window, the window that led to the back of her building, to the back of Main Street.

The window that, because she lived in the middle of the town's one-street-long business district, had a fire escape right outside.

She went to throw the window open, forgetting it was locked, wrenching her back because she'd yanked so hard, then she fumbled with the latch – *stay calm, stay calm, don't panic* – and then it was open and she jumped through, made it onto the landing just as her bedroom door burst open. She didn't want to look but she had to, it was instinct, and she saw a blond man barrel in, look up, and then charge the window. Instead of going down, she went up – it was easier to elude his grasp that way. Even so, he managed to grab hold of her foot. It sent a terrible shock through her entire body. The physical contact terrified her way beyond any level she had ever experienced. It made everything all too real and too close. And it brought her imagination into play, turning danger into something she hadn't let herself think of – pain. She was phobic about pain. The thought of what might be done to her made her freeze for a moment, paralyzed her. She felt herself go limp but then her anger took over. *No panic*, she told herself again. *You cannot panic!* She felt the man's grip tighten and her hysteria disappeared, replaced by fury. So she kicked as hard as she could, shook her leg and kicked again, and his fingers let go and she scurried up the fire escape, climbing away from him as fast as she could. She got to the flat roof and even before she hoisted herself over the top, she knew she'd won. She'd been up here many times. She kept a beach chair there, used to come up and sunbathe and read on weekends when the beaches were too crowded. She knew this roof and knew that all she had to do was hop over to the next building, maybe a one-foot jump, no big deal, and there was another fire escape there, at the back. All she had to do was get there and climb down and then it was over. He couldn't possibly get there as fast as she could. Couldn't even know which direction she'd go.

It was easy now.

She was safe.

So before she pulled herself onto the roof she looked down. Saw that he wasn't even trying to follow her. He was just looking up at her. She stared straight into his eyes, studied his face so she could remember to tell the police exactly what he looked like, was startled because he was smiling. Looking up at her and smiling.

She swung her legs up onto the tarred rooftop. Started running over to the next building. But she only got a few steps before she stopped cold. It was impossible.

What she saw was physically impossible!

He was there. The blond man. He was on the roof, smiling at her. The same smile she'd just seen.

38

But it couldn't be. He couldn't be here! He *couldn't* . . .

She was going to scream. That was her only chance. She could scream and hope that someone would hear. Hear her and help her.

But she didn't scream.

The blond man moved too quickly and the thing she feared more than anything, the pain, was too great. When the blond man spoke, it was quietly, as if he was being respectful of the early morning silence. 'I need to know a few things,' he said.

So she nodded. She wanted him to understand that she'd be happy to tell him anything she could. He said, 'Aphrodite,' and she looked confused, even through the pain, so he said, 'What do you know about Aphrodite and who did you tell?' She said she didn't understand what he was talking about; it was more of a whimper really. He asked her three times and after the third time she couldn't even answer, she could just moan, very, very quietly and shake her head, and he was convinced she was telling him the truth. Then he said, 'I need a name,' and she knew the answer to that one, so she told him, she was so happy to tell him, and then he took a small step away from her.

'Is it over?' she asked, barely able to get the words out. 'Do you need anything else from me?'

'It's almost over,' the blond man told her. 'There's just one more thing.'

There were details to be attended to inside Susanna's bedroom. First her body was carried down the fire escape, put inside and arranged on the floor, by her bed. Then her nightstand was tipped over, the contents of the one drawer allowed to spill and spread on the floor, the clock radio tumbling and breaking. The sheet and summer quilt were wrapped around Susanna's feet and legs. From the kitchen, a drinking glass half-full of water was brought in, then thrown down. The glass shattered, the water spilled. Soon, it was safe to assume that anyone finding the body would make the reasonable assumption that Susanna Morgan had gotten out of bed in the middle of the night, tripped, fallen, and broken her neck.

Outside, Main Street was absolutely empty. It took less than a minute to reach the car, which was parked in the alley behind Susanna's apartment. It took less than four minutes for the car to pass the sign that read, 'East End Harbor, Town Limits.'

It had been a totally satisfactory professional hit. There was, in fact, no trace that a crime, much less a murder, had even taken place in the town of East End Harbor.

Nothing had been overlooked.

Except for one thing.

That thing was still up on the roof of Susanna Morgan's building. And it wasn't exactly a thing. It was a person.

It was a woman who had been sitting quietly, as still as could be, cross-legged, in the corner of the flat roof, as she often did in the middle of the night when she couldn't sleep. She had been sitting peacefully, breathing in, breathing out, appreciating the misty night and the hazy, half-moon. She had been thinking about life in general and her life in particular, and what direction it might be taking in the next few months. Up until the blond man had appeared on the roof, she was thinking that her life could move in just about any direction she decided to move it in. After the man had climbed down the fire escape, after she'd looked down to see the car drive away, after she'd seen her friend Susanna murdered, she had a terrible, sickening feeling that the decision had just been taken out of her hands.

BOOK ONE

CHAPTER ONE

The breeze floated in off the bay, bringing in the faint odor of brine and fish and gasoline fumes. Justin Westwood tilted his head ever so slightly, taking a deep breath. His eyes closed, shutting out the world for, at most, a second or two. But it gave him just enough time to think, once again, how nice it would be to shut that world out for a much longer time. Like forever.

Half of his face caught the full impact of the hot morning sun, half was cooled by the soft wind off the water. A vague confluence of words began to float through his brain. Then they crystallized and he realized it was a rock lyric. Elvis Costello. *What shall we do with all this useless beauty?* The plaintive music that went with the words also began to play silently inside his head. That's what was usually playing inside him: haunting, mournful songs; rough, ragged rock and roll. Harsh, melancholy words, often blunt and full of undiluted rage. Driving music that fueled his anger and overpowered him with sadness. He pushed the song out of his thoughts. Told himself to force some silence until he could get home, smoke a joint and let some scotch slide down his throat, then let some real music overwhelm him. He told himself to wait. It's the word he repeated more than any other throughout his days: *Wait* . . .

His eyes fluttered open. Squinting directly into the harsh glare, through a heat-distorted haze that made it seem as if he was looking into some other dimension, he could see the glittering outline of a sailboat glide away from the dock that jutted out from the end of Main Street.

'Hey, Eastwood! What the hell do you think you're doing?'

Westwood allowed himself to slowly come out of his self-induced fog and shifted his gaze in the direction of the two cops twenty yards away from him on Main. *Cops*, he thought, with contempt. *They weren't cops. They were children. Summer help. They were lifeguards let loose on unsuspecting motorists who might, heaven help us all, back up several feet to try to catch a precious parking space or, even worse, park in a public space for one second longer than the allotted two hours.*

'Eastwood! Seriously, man. What the hell's goin' on? There're *two* cars that've been here more than two hours and you didn't slap a ticket on either one! What's up with that, man?'

Justin Westwood was thirty-seven years old. These summer cops were maybe twenty-three or twenty-four and they not only thought he was duller than shit, they thought he was a total loser. *They* wouldn't be handing out parking tickets in a half-assed, middle-class resort town when they were thirty-seven. *They* would be police

46

chiefs somewhere where there was real action. Or retire early and own a great bar that served fish and chips and had two big-screen TVs for Monday Night Football and March Madness. Or they'd be working in their daddy's business, knowing that, thanks to the time they spent on the EEPD, they could bully with impunity any neighbor who dared complain that their music was too loud and that they were drinking too much beer. They wore Keanu Reeves sunglasses and walked with a swagger and a smirk. They liked nothing better than writing up tickets and lecturing drivers who were making somewhere around fifty times their salary. Although they had holsters – cool, black, shiny leather holsters – they didn't carry guns. They kept cell phones in their holsters, because that would be the single most helpful tool they could carry in case there was ever an emergency.

Which there wasn't.

East End Harbor did not have a lot of emergencies. The occasional case of food poisoning. Plenty of arguments about the level of noise and the amount of garbage generated by the club in the back of the town's public parking lot. Constant and heated council meetings about the difference between a roundabout and a traffic circle. Politicians came to the Hamptons to raise money and they'd sneak into East End Harbor for a photo op, which raised the town's blood pressure. A few months ago the Vice-President had come, along with several cabinet members. They had to shut Main Street down and it caused a hellacious traffic jam and several storeowners went ballistic over the lost business. But that was the extent of it. There were no real emergencies.

47

Justin didn't carry a gun, either.

He did have one, though, back at the station. And it was at times like this – when they tauntingly called him 'Eastwood,' because he was always looking to avoid confrontation, because he shied away from anything remotely violent and was, let's face it, out of shape and as far from being a Dirty Harry-type cop as they could imagine – that he was glad he didn't have his gun handy. He had not kept up on the latest mandatory prison sentences, but he was fairly sure it would still be a lot of years for shooting his fellow police officers in cold blood.

He took a step toward the two cops – one was named Gary; he didn't have any idea what the other one was called, even though they'd been working together for at least six months – but he was interrupted by the shrill beep of a car horn. Justin turned back toward the honk and saw an old lady, her car stopped in the middle of the street, frantically waving for him to come over. When he reached her, he tried to say, 'Can I help you,' but she didn't give him the chance.

'There was a truck on my street this morning!' the woman screeched, when he was still several feet from her car. There were two cars behind her now. Justin knew they'd wait patiently for all of about one minute. Then they'd start honking or sticking their heads out the window to roll their eyes impatiently or ask what the hell was taking so long.

'I'm sorry to hear that,' he said as politely as he could.

'I'm in a no-truck zone!' she yelled. 'There shouldn't be any trucks in a no-truck zone!'

'What street are you on?' he asked. 'If I know where you are, maybe we could—'

'I'm on Harrison Street! And no trucks are supposed to cut through on Harrison Street!'

'You're Mrs Dbinsky,' he said.

'How'd you know that?!'

'You call us every day to complain about the trucks on Harrison Street.'

'Yeah? Well, a fat lot of good it does! Every day there's another truck!'

'The thing is, Mrs Dbinsky, even though it's a no-truck zone, that doesn't mean that no trucks are allowed. They can come to make deliveries.'

'These trucks weren't making deliveries! They were just driving around, making noise! You know how little my street is? And you know how big those trucks are? The *walls* are cracking in my house from those goddamn monsters!'

There were six cars behind her now. Any second now, one of them would start getting pissed off and the chain reaction would set in. He started to ask Mrs Dbinsky if she'd mind pulling over against the curb, but he knew that would set her off again, and he had a feeling there was more on her mind than just trucks today, so instead he said he'd come by her house later this afternoon, how would that be? He'd come by and they'd discuss what he could do about the trucks . . .

'What you could do and what you're gonna do are two different things!' she said. 'You *could* put up signs, you *could* give 'em tickets. You *could* get the damn trucks off my street. You're *gonna* do absolutely nothin'!'

The first horn honked now. It came from one of the nine cars backed up behind Mrs Dbinsky. But now Justin Westwood wasn't concentrating on the honking. Or Gary and the other idiot-boy cop who were smirking at him, enjoying the whole thing. He wasn't even concentrating on Mrs Dbinsky. Because from the middle of Main Street, from inside a building somewhere, it sounded like it was near the yoga center, there was a scream. A loud, frightened and frightening scream.

People were coming out of their stores now, looking around for the source of the noise.

Gary and What's-his-name were running, sprinting toward a small house in the middle of the block.

Westwood was running, too. His hand instinctively went to his belt. Even after all these years that instinct hadn't left him, and he was shocked when he realized that. But of course there was no gun there, so he dropped his hand, trying to pretend it hadn't happened, that those instincts were long dead and buried, and just ran.

And he thought: *Son of a bitch.*

East End Harbor has an emergency.

The girl's name was Susanna Morgan and Westwood knew her, of course. Everybody in town knew her. She was bubbly and friendly and curious. She had interviewed him a couple of times, nothing serious, she didn't know anything about his background, hadn't done any probing before they talked. It was just human-interest type stuff. Wanting to know the way the local police force worked and thought. Basically, he had told her that the force worked hard and didn't think much and Jimmy Leggett, his boss, had not been too happy with that quote so that was the end of the interviews.

He'd bumped into Susanna a few times after that. It was hard not to bump into people in East End. There were only so many bars and restaurants. Once he'd seen her at Duffy's. He hadn't pegged her for a Duffy's girl. Not that it was hardcore, nothing was hardcore out there, but it was fairly serious for East End Harbor. Duffy's didn't have any real food, just nuts and pretzels in red straw bowls and sometimes sandwiches that were wrapped in plastic and looked like they came out of a vending machine. They served a lot of beer and straight liquor, didn't keep cranberry juice as part of their stock, and there was a dartboard off to the side, which was about all the atmosphere the place had. It wasn't a pick-up place or a place to take anyone you wanted to impress. It was a place to drink and to be lonely, if not alone. So he'd been surprised to see her there one night. She was with a girlfriend and they drank a couple of beers. He was sitting at the bar when she came in and they nodded at each other. He was still sitting at the bar when she left. She had smiled at him on her way out.

She was twenty-seven years old, he knew.

Well, she'd *been* twenty-seven years old.

Now she wasn't anything because she was goddamn dead.

The woman who'd found her body was Regina Arnold. She worked with Susanna at the paper and when ten o'clock rolled around and Susanna hadn't shown up for work, everyone got worried. She called Susanna's apartment, got no answer, then called her cell phone and got nothing there, either. She had a spare key – several people had keys, according to Regina; Susanna tended to lock herself out periodically – so she went over because she knew Susanna had called in sick the day before and wanted to make sure she was okay. She wasn't okay. Regina found her sprawled on the floor by her bed. That's when she screamed.

They'd talked to Regina for ten minutes or so, got everything they were going to get out of her, then they told her she could go. Justin couldn't decide if she was so anxious to leave because she was so upset by this experience or if she simply wanted to get back outside and start telling everyone what had happened. She was going to be the center of attention for the next couple of days. She'd be talking about this for the rest of her life. Justin knew that from now on, at every dinner party that Regina Arnold went to, she'd find a way to tell all about the time she found her friend's dead body. He wondered how the story would be embellished over time. Would Susanna be still breathing when Regina arrived? Would she have tripped over the body. There'd be something. Something that wasn't true. There always was.

Justin almost had his breath back. Jesus, he'd only run maybe forty, fifty yards but by the time he got to the first-floor apartment he was actually wheezing and was practically doubled over with cramps. He had to sit down in the living room, right after he checked the body. Now the two assholes were coming in from the bedroom, grinning. Justin sucked in a big rush of air, hoping he didn't give the two cretins the satisfaction of watching him have a heart attack.

'You ever see a dead body before, Eastwood?' the non-Gary asshole asked. There was a slight taunt to his words. 'Makin' you a little sick?'

Justin didn't answer. Death *did* make him sick, and more than a little. There was nothing that made him sicker than its finality and its total lack of discrimination. Its ability to strike anywhere and anyone, no matter how undeserving, at anytime. It also had rattled his two fellow cops. He'd seen their faces when they walked into Susanna's room. He'd seen the way they shrunk back, the way they hesitated before touching the body. Now that they were protected by twenty feet and a closed door and several minutes of getting used to being in death's presence, their swagger was returning. Their snide bravado was their way of covering up the fact that they'd been just as frightened as he'd been.

'You should cut out the smoking,' Gary said now.

Westwood, still breathing hard, looked up, waiting for the punchline, the taunt, but there was none.

'My dad died of lung cancer a couple of years ago. It sucked big time. You can barely breathe right now,' Gary went on. 'You're gonna wind up like him. Like' – he jerked his head towards the bedroom door – 'her.'

Westwood looked at the kid, thought, *I hate when assholes show signs of being human*. He didn't have to respond, though, and pretend to appreciate the thoughtfulness, because that's exactly the moment Jimmy Leggett, the East End Harbor chief of police, picked to walk through the front door.

'Fill me in,' he said. He was looking at Westwood when he said it, but it was Gary's partner who spoke up.

'It's pretty cut and dried,' he said. 'Her name is Susanna Morgan, the one who works for the paper, you know, and it looks like she was getting out of bed in the middle of the night, go to the bathroom we figure, and she trips . . .'

'And kills herself?'

'Breaks her neck, it looks like.'

'Jesus. You call Doc Rosen?'

'He wasn't in his office. Nurse is trying to find him. We left a message on his home machine, too.'

Leggett pursed his lips and thought about this for a moment, turned to Westwood and said, 'That the way you see it? She trips and . . .' He waved his hand vaguely, as if vagueness was the best way to deal with what had happened.

Justin Westwood didn't say anything. He sat, staring straight ahead, sucking in a few more deep breaths.

'Jay?' Leggett said. 'You look things over and you agree?'

Westwood squinted and scratched his forehead and contorted his face as if he were going to say something, but it took him a few more seconds before he said, 'Yeah, I guess so.'

Leggett turned to the two young cops. 'Okay, you guys, you can take off.'

'What about him?' Gary said, nodding at Westwood.

'He's staying here for a minute.'

'We got here first, Jimmy.' This was from the other one. 'We were the ones, you know, checked things out and . . .'

'Fine. You checked things out. I'm happy for you, Brian. Now get the fuck out of here.'

The two cops scowled and started to leave but before they got to the door, Gary stopped, turned back to Leggett and said, 'Eastwood didn't do shit, Jimmy. We got here, we did what we were supposed to do.' Then they both went out the door.

'That right?' Leggett asked, when he was alone with Westwood. 'You didn't do shit?'

'His name's Brian?'

'What?'

'Gary's little friend. I didn't know his name was Brian.'

'Jesus Christ, Jay. You been workin' with the guy for almost a year.'

Westwood shrugged. Leggett realized that was all he was going to get on that matter, so said, 'Wanna go back in there with me?'

The chief opened the bedroom door and stepped inside. Nothing had changed since Justin had first gone in. The room was still a mess and the girl was still dead on the floor.

Leggett let a long breath escape, a faint whistle creeping into it, said, 'The only time I ever saw a body was in a casket.'

'They seem a lot more dead when you see 'em in real places.'

'Yeah,' the chief said. 'So what's bothering you?'

'Nothing,' Westwood said.

Leggett waited. Westwood scratched at his cheek, then he said, 'It's funny, though. Look at the broken glass.'

'What about it?'

55

'She got out of bed, tripped, knocked the glass over. It was probably on the nightstand, right? Next to the clock radio.'

'Yeah?'

'It's just strange. She must've knocked it over first, you know, flailing around when she realized she was falling, trying to grab hold of something. So she knocks it over, it breaks, and then she falls. But she doesn't fall *on* it. I mean, you'd think she'd fall on some of the broken glass. It's all around her.'

'How do you know she didn't fall on it?'

'There's no cuts. No blood. Even if she died almost instantly, she should've been cut. She couldn't've died *before* she hit the floor if she died of a broken neck.'

'What else?'

'Look at this.' Westwood bent down, pointed to the girl's left knee. 'A scrape. And it's fresh. How do you scrape your knee while you're sleeping?'

'Maybe she did it before she went to bed.'

'She would've put something on it. A Band-Aid. That stuff that stings like hell . . .'

'Mercurochrome. Okay, maybe she did it when she fell.'

'No. This floor wouldn't do it, too smooth. A bruise maybe. A bump. But this is like she rubbed it against something rough.'

'So what are you saying, Jay? You saying it's not an accident?'

Westwood closed his eyes for just a moment. He remembered being on Main Street, not much more than half an hour ago, with his eyes closed the same way. He

56

remembered the feeling of locking the world out and he remembered how much he liked that feeling. Another song began to rattle inside him. Roger McGuinn. King of the Hill. *It's sunrise again. The driveway is empty. The crystal is cracked. There's blood on the wall . . .*

Justin Westwood opened his eyes. He walked to the window, the one that had the fire escape outside. He fiddled with the latch, opened the window, and looked at the ledge. Then he closed the window, flipped the latch so it was locked.

Then he looked at the chief of the East End Harbor police department, such as it was.

'It's an accident,' Westwood said. 'Has to be an accident. There's no other explanation.'

CHAPTER TWO

Justin was in Duffy's again, sitting at the bar. It was the third night in a row he'd planted himself there. He was almost finished with his third Pete's Wicked Ale and was thinking about polishing it off with a scotch. He wavered. Right now he had a pleasant buzz, was reasonably relaxed. The scotch would put him over the line. Well, the one scotch wouldn't but once he started he knew he'd have more than one. Tonight he'd have three or four. Or five. Which is what he'd had the night before. And the night before that. He watched a young woman sitting in one of the four booths and for a moment he thought it was Susanna Morgan. Then he realized that it couldn't be and decided he wanted that scotch.

Donnie, the bartender, brought the shot glass over, with some water on the side. Westwood took a sip and enjoyed the burn as it went down his throat and into his stomach. It warmed him instantly and he polished off the rest of it in one more gulp. He signaled for another even as his head was tilted back, drinking. When he'd finished the second one, the buzz wasn't quite as pleasant. It was more of a hum and the hum was saying to him the same thing it had been saying ever since he'd examined Susanna's body. *Stay away from it*. Don't *touch this one*. *Just stay away*.

After the third scotch, he realized he wasn't getting drunk. But the hum was getting stronger. The fact is, it had been getting stronger with each passing hour.

Leave it alone, it was saying.

You know better.

Just leave it alone.

It had been saying that for three days now.

Justin nodded to himself, nodded to the hum, agreeing with it. Knowing he should listen to it. Knowing that he *had* to listen to it.

Then he put down money for his tab, got up from the bar and headed to the door. When he was out on the street, the hum kept telling him to go home. It was an easy walk, maybe half a mile. The previous two nights he'd paid attention and followed instructions. But now he found himself walking toward Main Street and the center of town. He found himself walking back to Susanna Morgan's apartment.

When he got there, when he stood in front of the two-story building, looking up at the top floor where the girl had died, he thought, *What the fuck am I doing?*

Then he walked around back to the alley, went to the building next door, the one with the fabric shop in the front, and he jumped up so he could grab hold of the bottom rung of the building's fire escape. He pulled it down so he could step on it comfortably, then he began to climb up to the roof, telling himself it was no problem, he knew how far to take it, he was just going to play his hunch, then he was going to leave it alone.

Halfway up, he stopped. Told himself he'd already gone too far. If he went any farther he'd get sucked in, might never be able to disentangle himself. His right foot stepped down one rung lower, but his left foot hovered in the air. He muttered the word 'shit' out loud. Then, telling himself nothing, doing his best not to think at all, he put his left foot back on the fire escape and began climbing back up to the top.

Westwood stood on the roof for a few moments, taking in the scene. He wasn't trying to focus on anything in particular, just wanted to get a feel for his general impressions. He slowly turned his head, taking in the shadows and the view of the town. He listened, didn't hear much. One bird. Then another, answering. From somewhere, probably several blocks away, the steady drone of a car engine.

He didn't exactly see or hear the girl. But he did feel her presence. When he turned to the corner of the roof, spotted her sitting there, then took several steps closer and was able to see the expression on her face, he realized that what he had felt was her fear.

'Don't hurt me,' she said. Her voice didn't quiver, which surprised him. It was steady and strong, if extremely soft.

He held up his hands, to show he meant no harm. 'I'm a policeman,' he said, making his voice match her hoarse whisper. 'I'm not going to hurt you.' He flashed his ID, peered in closer at her, tried to smile in as friendly a manner as he could muster, and said, 'You're the yoga teacher. I can't remember your name. I'm Justin Westwood. We talked once, remember? You had the guy who kept exposing himself outside your class.'

She didn't say anything but she nodded slowly. Justin said, 'You live in this building?' When she nodded again, he said, 'The other apartment? The other half from Susanna?' and once again her head moved almost imperceptibly up and down.

'I'm just looking around,' he told her now, keeping his tone gentle. 'Nothing serious. Just to satisfy my own curiosity. I'm going to go down Susanna's fire escape, just for a minute. Will you wait here for me, until I get back?'

The woman nodded. Westwood thought about saying something else, she seemed to need some more reassurance, but he didn't know what else he could say, so he walked across the flat roof until he got to the fire escape that led to Susanna Morgan's apartment. He stepped down a few rungs. When his eyes were level with the ledge of the roof, he stopped, squinted, looking for something, then resumed his descent. When he got to the landing outside the bedroom, he examined the exterior wall and the outer window sill. He scratched his cheek and climbed back up to the roof, expecting the woman he'd left there to be gone. But she was right where he'd left her. Sitting cross-legged in the corner. He walked closer to her, putting the smile back on his face and saying, 'See? Nothing to worry about.'

'I don't want to get hurt,' she said when he was a few feet away from her.

'I told you.' He was out of practice at being sincere, but he did his best to keep his body language as non-threatening as possible. 'I'm not going to hurt you.'

'I have a daughter,' she said. 'A little daughter. She's seven years old.'

'That's nice,' he told her. 'What's her name?'

She didn't answer him. It was as if she hadn't heard him. It was as if she was listening instead to some kind of voice within her.

'I saw something,' she finally said.

'Something about what?' He tried to keep his voice level but he could hear his heart pumping and he could feel his blood racing through his body. Suddenly, he knew he should have listened to that damn hum, should have stayed the hell off this roof. What did he think was going to happen by coming here? Nothing good, that's what. Nothing remotely good could possibly come from this.

'I know why you're here,' she said. 'I know what you're looking for.'

Nothing remotely fucking good.

'You don't have to tell me,' he said. 'You don't have to tell anybody if you don't want to.'

'I saw something.'

And if you tell me, I'll have to do something about it. It won't just be pretend any longer. I'll have to do something.

'Don't tell me,' he said again, and he was surprised at how desperate his voice sounded. 'Please. Don't tell me what you saw.'

'I have a daughter,' she said. 'And I'm afraid.'

Please . . .

'But I saw Susanna. Here on the roof.'

Don't . . .

'She didn't trip and fall like everyone says,' the woman said now. She still hadn't moved. She still had her legs crossed and she was breathing in and out, slowly and steadily, in an easy, perfect rhythm.

Don't tell me . . .

'He killed her,' she said, her voice still firm and steady. 'He murdered her. And I saw it.'

He didn't know how long the silence lasted. A long time. She was trembling now. She looked like she was going to cry.

'It's okay,' Westwood said slowly. 'It's okay that you saw it.'

'I have to tell somebody. I need to tell somebody. But I'm afraid.'

'Let's go somewhere and talk. You can tell me.'

She was relieved, he could see it. And reassured by his smile. She stood up now, in one graceful movement, not even using her hands to prop herself, just rising in one corkscrew-like motion until she was on her feet. He took her hands and led her to the fire escape at the back of the roof, the one leading down to the alley.

As she put one hand on the railing and placed her foot on the first step, she said, 'You won't let them hurt me, will you?'

Westwood did his best to smile again, and he squeezed her hand more firmly as she stepped down. But he didn't say anything.

He didn't think there was anything he *could* say.

You should have left it alone, the hum said.

And then it said one more thing, the thing that scared him the most, the thing he knew was all too true:

Too late now.

CHAPTER THREE

The dream didn't come every night. Not anymore. It had for years. Every night like clockwork Justin Westwood awakened with a scream, trembling, drenched in sweat, the sheets wet and sticky. Now it just came sometimes. There were nights he wanted it to come because he didn't ever want to forget. Other times he prayed for it to stay away because the pain of remembering had long ago become unbearable.

It came that night.

It began as it always did, in a time when he was happy. When he and Alicia were in love, even before Lili was born. In his dream he felt Alicia caressing him, felt her naked body melt into his as it always did in bed. Then there was Lili. The perfect child. Sweet right from the start. He could hear her cooing and gurgling as a baby. And he saw her take her first step. Heard her speak. Somehow the dream always let him see her in school, in first grade, maybe because he always thought of her as so smart. She should have been beautiful, Lili, like her mother, but she wasn't. She had Alicia's body, thin and athletic with long, coltish legs that, right from the beginning, seemed to go on forever. But she got his face, poor kid, so she was slightly goofy-looking, at least that's what she felt. He would always tell her how beautiful she was, how perfect, how smart, and in the dream he'd hear what she always used to say: 'Daaaaddddy, it's no good if *you* think I'm beautiful. It's the *other* ones who have to think I'm beautiful.'

The dream changed from time to time. Jumped around. Tonight it jumped to when Lili was eight years old and things had started to go bad. His father usually came into the dream now, his face, big and close, stern and frightening. His father never spoke in the dreams, just looked at him, that look, so bitter and angry and disappointed. Then there was a jumble of images. Everything rushed in at him, like a train swooping through a tunnel: Alicia harping at him, saying *What's wrong with you, why are you doing this?* and then the arrest and everyone patting him on the back, telling him he'd done a great thing, and in the dream his chest puffed out, he was so full of pride. He could see Lili looking at him like he was the most important man in the world. He handed her his medal, his shiny gold medal that glistened like a precious jewel. And then . . .

And then in his dream he heard a noise. In real life there had been none. Other than normal noise. Alicia at her desk, riffling through papers and paying bills. Lili padding around the living room. The TV. Everything was normal. But in the dream he heard something. A warning. And then suddenly they were there. Inside his home. And there were shots. Screams. He was on the floor. They thought he was dead. He heard laughter and felt someone touch him and then there was another noise, an explosion of heat and fire, and there was blood everywhere. Thick and red. Dripping. Flooding. Red, everywhere . . .

Justin Westwood woke from his dream, breathing hard. He grabbed for his chest, feeling the physical pain as if it had all just happened. His hands quickly probed his stomach, then his neck and thighs. There were no fresh wounds, only raised scars, reminders of the raw, scorched flesh that had once been there. His breathing eased a bit and he resisted looking at the empty half of the bed across from him. Justin reached for the glass of water he'd put on the nightstand. He gulped it down, was still thirsty, didn't want to move, though, to get any more. Didn't want to disturb the images of Alicia and Lili that were still with him, still so real.

He looked at his watch. Four a.m. In another hour it would start getting light. He didn't bother closing his eyes, he wouldn't be going back to sleep. He never did after the dream. He'd stay up and wait for dawn. Then he'd wait until he could see Jimmy and the girl, the yoga teacher. Then he'd see what they were going to do. They'd hear her story, ask questions, see what was real, what was fake.

In his own life, Justin knew what was real and what wasn't.

His wife and daughter were dead and it was his fault.

He was alive. And wishing he wasn't.

That's what was real.

Everything else was fake.

CHAPTER FOUR

'What were you doing up on the roof?' Jimmy Leggett asked. He was not comfortable with the conversation. It wasn't going well. He didn't want to believe what he was hearing because, if it was all true, he didn't know what the hell he was supposed to do about it.

'I told you, I was meditating. I go up there a lot late at night. When I can't sleep. It's quiet. Peaceful. At least, it usually is.'

'And you just leave your daughter in your apartment?'

'I leave her bedroom window open. It's right below me. I can hear if anything happens. And if she wakes up and I'm not in my bed, she knows I'm up there. It's not like I'm off partying. I'm only a few feet away.'

'Why couldn't you sleep that night?'

She shrugged, starting to look annoyed. 'You want to hear about all my problems? I'm single, I'm a mom, I don't make enough money, what's going on in the world scares the shit out of me . . .'

'Did you hear anything?'

'Before I went up there? No.'

Chief Leggett took a deep breath. He looked at Justin. The chief didn't say anything but Westwood knew him pretty well. So he stepped in.

'Tell us exactly what you saw up on the roof . . . uh . . . Deena.' It took him a second, but she'd finally told him her name last night, when he'd walked her back to her apartment. Deena Harper. He'd watched her look in on her sleeping daughter, then he'd said goodnight and told her he'd see her at eight.

'I told you already.'

'One more time. Sometimes when you repeat things, you remember new facts, little details.'

'I was up there for about half an hour. It was a little hazy. I was very relaxed, almost in a meditative state. I heard something. I don't think I opened my eyes at first, sometimes your imagination kind of takes over when you're meditating and you hear things. You know, like if you're thinking about a river, you can hear the water . . .'

'The roof,' Justin said. 'What did you hear on the roof?'

'I guess it was the door opening. The door that opens onto the roof from the attic of the house. It's usually locked. We weren't supposed to use it to go up there. Some kind of fire hazard or something.'

'We?'

'Me and Susanna. The landlord told us both to stay off the roof.'

'But you went up anyway?' That was Chief Leggett interrupting.

Deena rolled her eyes and nodded. 'Yes, I'm sorry. I'll do my time and try to make my re-entry into society a productive one.'

'Okay, so you heard the door open,' Justin said.

'There was this blond guy there. Really handsome. I described him. Blond hair, pale skin . . .'

'Pale like no sun tan?'

'Yeah. Hardly any tan at all.'

'You didn't tell me that before.'

'I didn't? Huh. Well, he was really pale. Hair was medium, casual but done. Robert Redford kind of hair. Maybe six feet tall. Not thin, not fat. I couldn't tell what kind of body he had, he was wearing a suit.'

'A fancy suit?'

'Not a pinstripe, if that's what you mean. Khaki. He had a T-shirt underneath. But not a crummy T-shirt, not Fruit of the Loom. A designer T-shirt.'

'You have good eyes. It was hard for me to see up there.'

'I'd been there for a while. My eyes were used to the dark.'

'Okay, good point. What kind of shoes was he wearing?'

'Shoes?' She thought for a minute, scrunched up her face. 'I don't know. I don't think I saw them. They must have been some kind of sneaker, though. Something soft. He didn't make any real noise when he moved.'

'Good. Then what happened?'

'Then I heard this . . . I don't know what . . . commotion. I could hear something going on. A window opening or closing. Then I saw Susanna. She pulled herself up onto the roof and she was frantic. Breathing hard. She started to run, then she saw the blond guy. She stopped short when she saw him. She looked like she'd just seen a ghost.'

'She was surprised to see him?'

'Shocked, I'd say.'

'And then?'

'He moved really slowly. At least, it seemed to be slow, but it couldn't have been. Susanna tried to dodge him, run around him, I guess trying to get to the fire escape over on the other roof, but he caught her really easily. He said something to her, I remember that he said something, kept asking her questions . . .'

'You didn't tell me that either,' Westwood said. 'What did he say to her?'

'I can't remember exactly. He was quiet, talking really soft. He kept asking her something and she didn't seem to know the answer. He wanted to know what "amfer" was. Or "afro," I couldn't really tell, something like that. Then he said something like, "Give me . . ." He said, "give me" something . . .' She shook her head in frustration. She had dark blonde hair that had been permed and it slithered like it was alive. She was not trying to be sexy when she shook her head but Justin noted that she simply couldn't help it.

'It's okay,' he told her. 'Relax. Think about something else. You want some more coffee?'

She shook her head, her curls jumping around again. One of them snaked over her forehead, covering her left eye and she brushed it away with her hand.

'Did he want money?' Justin said.

'I don't think so.'

'Something she had on her? Drugs?'

'No!'

'Information? A phone number, an address . . .'

'I don't know,' she said.

'Did she give it to him?'

'I don't know. I think so. He hurt her, he snapped something here' – she pointed to her neck – 'and he twisted her arm. I thought he broke it.'

'Did you hear what she told him?'

'She was crying. Sobbing, quietly, like it hurt too much to really cry. I couldn't really make out what she told him. It didn't make sense to me, I'm sure I heard it wrong. It sounded like "walrus" or something. Walrus and something else. But it's what he wanted to hear. Because once she told him, he got real calm.' Deena shuddered, her shoulders hunching up toward her chin. 'Then he just leaned over and broke her neck.'

'What happened after that?'

'I didn't move a muscle. I was terrified he'd see me. I could have made it over to the other roof, I mean, I was a lot closer, but I don't know if my legs would have worked. But he never even looked my way. He picked Susanna up, like she weighed nothing, this guy was strong, and he carried her down the fire escape.'

'Did he come back up to the roof?'

'Uh uh.'

'So he must have gone into her apartment, through the window.'

'I guess so.'

Justin looked at Leggett, spoke to him now. 'While he was in there, he arranged the bed and the sheets so it would look like she fell. He smashed a glass, knocked over the table so it would look even better.'

'Jesus.' That was Deena. She wiped her eyes, which had started to fill with tears.

'Did you see him leave?' Justin asked her now.

'No. I was too afraid to move.'

'So you didn't see the car he drove away in?'

She nodded. 'I did. When I heard it start up, that's when I went to the edge of the roof, the back edge. I guess I felt safer. Thought I should try to see something, you know, like the witnesses on *Law & Order* or something. So I saw it pull away. But I don't know cars. I don't know what it was.'

'Do you remember anything about it?'

She thought, closing her eyes as if that would help her picture it. Then she frowned and shook her head. 'Not much. It was kind of boxy. Not sleek or anything. Not a sports car.'

'Color?'

'Dark. Not red. Black maybe. Or dark green or blue.'

Justin exhaled a long breath. 'Deena, you've been incredibly helpful. I'm sorry you had to go through it, but maybe it'll help us find the people who killed Susanna.'

'Can I go now?'

Leggett looked at Justin, who nodded and said, 'You can go.' As she stood up, he said, 'Where's your daughter?'

'At the yoga center. She hangs out there. I've got another teacher who watches her.' Deena smiled now, for the first time since Justin had seen her on the roof the night before. 'Her name's Kendall. She's going into second grade in a couple of months. In September.'

'Do you want someone to drive you home?' Justin asked.

'I can walk. It's just a few blocks.'

'Do you want someone to walk you home?'

She smiled again and nodded. Chief Leggett opened the door to his office and called out, 'Brian, I want you to walk Ms Harper home.'

Brian sauntered over and stood in the doorway.

Justin saw Deena Harper look over at the young cop, then back over at him. She smiled at him one more time and walked over to her escort. Justin wondered if he was reading too much into her expression. He also wondered at the feeling of pleasure it gave him.

When she realized that Brian would be the one walking her home, Justin was certain she looked disappointed.

CHAPTER FIVE

After Deena Harper left the police station, Westwood and Leggett huddled behind closed doors for almost half an hour. The first thing the chief had asked was, 'Do you believe her?'

'Don't you?'

'I don't know. Why'd she wait so long to say anything?'

'She was terrified, Jimmy, that's why.'

'Pretty weird, being up on that roof and all.'

Westwood chewed on the inside of his lower lip. 'That girl wasn't lying.'

'What about the roof thing? Maybe she's the killer.'

The briefest of smiles crossed Westwood's face. 'She's about thirty pounds too light to be a viable suspect. If that girl killed Susanna Morgan up close, which is how Susanna was killed, there would have to have been a struggle. She'd be scratched, a couple of nails would be broken, there'd be some physical sign.'

'How do you know there isn't?'

'Because when I saw her up on the roof she was

wearing a T-shirt and shorts, no shoes. Not a scratch on her. And I made sure to take both her hands in mine when we were climbing down the fire escape. Nothing there either.'

Jimmy Leggett bent his head forward and shook it. His back was stooped, as if the weight of what was happening had already aged him. 'Jesus, you actually checked her hands? I *never* woulda thought of that.' He kept quiet for a few moments, fidgeting, his fingers tapping nervously. 'Should we do an autopsy?' he finally asked. 'You know, on this Susanna Morgan?'

Justin tilted his head, as if to say 'good question,' but then he shrugged and said, 'Too late. Unless we want to dig her body up.'

'She's buried already?'

'Yesterday morning. Turns out she was Jewish. They bury quickly.'

Leggett puffed out his cheek with his tongue and looked embarrassed about something. Finally, he said, lowering his voice, 'I've never been involved in a murder investigation. To be perfectly honest, I don't have a fucking clue where to even begin.'

'I know.'

'What about you?'

'I know where to begin.'

'That's not my question,' Leggett said.

'I know that, too.'

'Maybe we should call in the Southampton boys.'

'Good idea,' Westwood said. 'I'm sure they have a crack homicide department.'

'Goddamnit, Jay! I've been covering your ass for six

76

years! You haven't had to do anything harder than run down some high school shitheads making obscene phone calls. Now, what, you wanna play macho cop again, all of a sudden?'

'I don't want to play anything, Jimmy.'

'Then what *do* you want?'

'You ever have a homicide in East End?' Westwood asked.

'Not since I been here. We had one vehicular manslaughter.'

'I know how to get started. I know what questions to ask. So let me ask them. Hopefully, it won't be that complicated. Most homicides aren't. There'll be a boyfriend or someone she fired or a crazy ex-husband. I can handle that.'

'And if it *is* complicated?'

When Westwood didn't answer, Leggett said, 'If it is? Can you handle *that*?'

'I don't have a fucking clue.' Westwood let loose with a quick laugh. It didn't have a hell of a lot of humor to it. 'If you want a guess, however, I'd say the answer is no, I can't.'

Leggett didn't say anything for a while. Then: 'Is there anything anyone else can do?'

Westwood snorted. 'Like who? Gary and what's-his-name?'

'It's Brian, for Chrissake.'

'No, Jimmy. There's nothing Gary or Brian can do.'

'We have other people.'

'We have three other people. And they make Gary look like Serpico.'

'They're gonna ask questions, you know. They're gonna want to know why you're all of a sudden turning into Supercop.'

'Let 'em ask.'

'What do I tell them?'

'The same thing you tell anybody who ever asks about a homicide investigation: not a damn thing.'

The first thing he did after leaving the chief's office was go to the computer on his desk in the station. He opened up a file, labeled it 'Susanna Morgan' and began typing in information. His brain was working logically and objectively. It all felt surprisingly natural.

He typed:

> Roof – Blond guy – pale skin.
> Well dressed. Casual.
> Victim (Susanna) shocked to see man on roof.
> He wanted info – she gave it to him. Name of person? Place? Thing? Code?
> Info wanted: 'Afro' or 'Amfer'????
> 'Walrus'????
> Broken glass, staged accident. He's clever.
> But not as clever as he thinks.
> Dark color car. Probably stolen or rented.

He saved his notes on a disk, stuck the disk in his desk drawer, told Gary to check and see if there were any reports of a dark, non-sports car stolen over the previous two days within 40 miles of the town. When Gary looked blankly at him, Justin said, 'You're a cop. Use some cop stuff to figure it out.'

And the next thing he knew, he was headed over to the East End *Journal* office because that was the logical starting point. You could start with family, boyfriend or office. Susanna's family was back in Ohio, which is where the body had been shipped for burial. She didn't seem to have a current boyfriend. The office was four blocks from the police station. It was an easy call.

The atmosphere in the *Journal* office was solemn and subdued. Not surprising, Westwood decided, since everyone who worked there was still in mourning.

'What was she working on?' Harlan Corning repeated Westwood's question. He leaned back in his chair, Justin thought, his best Perry White impression. 'She was in the middle of a lot of things, as always.'

'Can you be a little more specific?'

'I just don't see the relevance, that's all. I don't think Susanna was killed – *if* she was really killed – because she panned Steven Spielberg's new movie.'

'Is that the last thing she wrote?'

'Is Spielberg a suspect now?' When Westwood didn't answer, the newspaper editor just said, 'No. The last thing she wrote was an obituary. A horrible coincidence, isn't it?'

'What was the obit?'

'One of the local old-timers passed away. Bill Miller, used to be an actor. Susanna was quite attached to him. She used to do volunteer work at the Home.'

'The old age home on the bay?'

'Yup. The old boy died on Tuesday or Wednesday and she did the obit.'

'Anything special about it?'

'Yeah. She screwed up.' Westwood raised an eyebrow and the editor said, 'She was too close to Miller and it turns out he was a gasbag. He exaggerated about his career and she printed it as if it were the gospel. It happens. We ain't the New York *Times*, you know what I mean? But we got a crazy phone call from some guy, a movie nut, who caught the mistakes. Demanded a retraction. I sent Susie back to do some fact checking. That's what she was doing, I think, when she got sick the other day.'

'Sick?'

'Yeah. She went out to lunch, didn't come back. She called in sick. That was the day she . . . you know . . .'

'Do you know where she called from?'

'No. It wasn't her apartment, though. Probably somewhere in town. I could hear street noise. Cars. She must've been on her cell phone.'

'How crazy was the phone call, Mr Corning? The one about the mistakes in the obit.'

'From the movie nut? You don't think—'

'I can't imagine killing someone because she got her facts wrong in an obituary. But I'd like to talk to him anyway if you have his number.'

'I gave it to Sue, but I've still got it somewhere. That was her punishment, she had to call the guy when she found out what was what.'

'Did she?'

'I don't know if she found out and I don't know if she called him. I never got the opportunity to ask her,' he said sadly.

80

Harlan Corning rooted around in his desk, shuffled through a stack of yellow Post-Its. While he was looking, Justin said, 'I'd appreciate it if you wouldn't put anything in the paper about this.'

The editor looked up, surprised. 'About what?'

'The fact that we think Ms Morgan's death might not have been an accident.'

'I have a responsibility—' Corning began.

'I know you do,' Justin cut him off. 'But so do I. If I'm right.'

'So if you *are* right, you want whoever did it to keep thinking he's home free.'

Justin nodded. Corning went back to rooting through his desk until he found what he was looking for. 'Here it is. Wally Crabbe.' He held up a scrap of yellow paper with a name, address and phone number on it. 'He lives mid-Island, about an hour from here. The town's called Middleview.' The editor wrote down the information for Westwood. 'You know,' Corning said slowly, 'I also have a responsibility to report the facts. You don't know if your theory is fact, do you, Detective?'

'No I don't,' Justin said.

'And Susanna was a good friend. I have a responsibility to her too, don't you think?'

'Yes I do.'

'Then it would be irresponsible of me to say anything. At least for now.'

'Thank you,' Justin said.

'But you will let me know one way or the other, won't you? When you have the facts, I mean.'

'You'll be the first, Mr Corning. I promise.'

Harlan Corning handed Justin the piece of paper with the scribbled information. As they shook hands, he said, 'Good luck with this guy, Detective. You're in for quite a treat.'

CHAPTER SIX

Wallace P. Crabbe was irate.

This was nothing unusual because Wallace P. Crabbe was almost always irate. But he always kept his anger deep inside him. Always. On the surface – at work dealing with incompetent co-workers, on dinner dates with women whom he found unattractive and uninteresting, at meetings with authors whose manuscripts he copyedited, catching the most minute grammatical and factual errors – he was civil and polite, hard working and trouble free. He was never the life of the party. About that he had no illusions. On the other hand, he was always invited to the party because he was appreciative of good food, could talk about the latest novel, was a very good listener and almost always had a benign smile on his soft and pleasant-looking face.

That was the surface.

Inside, he hated smiling while he was bombarded with a constant stream of drivel. He hated all the novels he read and all the food he forced himself to eat at obnoxiously trendy restaurants. He hated almost everything and everyone. Inside, Wallace P. Crabbe was a roiling storm. Had been since he was twelve years old and Tony DeMarco knocked his school books out of his hands into a big patch of mud, then shoved him into the same mud patch and left, laughing, with his arm around the beautiful and bewitching eleven-year-old Abigail Winters. Wallace was just about to ask Abigail, who had the most appealing ponytail, to go out to the movies with him. Instead, she went to the movies with Tony DeMarco, and that's when Wallace decided that life was basically unfair and that he was one of the unlucky majority who was going to get screwed over and over again by that very unfairness. But he saw no advantage to griping about it. The more he complained, the greater the chance, he figured, of being shoved into ever deeper and ever dirtier patches of mud.

By the age of forty-nine, Wallace P. Crabbe had managed to do everything he could to quietly prove his theory to himself and show that he had zero chance of achieving the slightest bit of happiness. And with each additional proof, Wallace got angrier and angrier.

Inside.

He'd been married once, some years ago, and it had lasted six years, until his wife came home and told him she'd been seeing his best friend on the side. Wallace was not happy about losing his wife, she was fairly quiet and easy to be with, but he had to admit he was even unhappier about losing his friend, since he didn't have all that many of those to spare. On the outside, he was understanding and rather gracious during the entire divorce process. Inside, he began having fantasies of his ex-wife and ex-friend in combinations with such things as meat grinders and crossbows and hunting rifles. At age fifty-two, after his publishing company was absorbed by a huge German conglomerate, he was offered – and told to accept – early retirement. He accepted it gratefully and unhesitatingly and was well paid off. But ever since, he had dreams about the Human Resources Director who gave him the bad news, in which his own hands were wrapped around her pale, too-thick neck and he choked the life out of her.

Since he'd been laid off, he'd sold his one-bedroom Upper West Side apartment, making a tidy profit, as it was nearly mortgage-free, and moved out to Long Island. Not one of the chic places, one of the suburban areas half an hour from the chic places. He got a small ranch-style house with a patch of a backyard and set himself up. Why not? What was in the city for him now? That was an easy one to answer: not much. The move didn't affect whatever work came his way. He could still get his occasional freelance copyediting assignments, that was no problem. There was less noise, less hassle, less pretension in suburbia. His social life had suffered, no question about that; it was a lot harder to meet people, especially women, but even in the city his social life had been moderately successful at best. Currently, he was seeing a woman who worked at a magazine geared for home gardeners. He found her too angular to be attractive and too obsessed with various sub-species of day lilies to be interesting, but he saw her two or three times a week. Either she cooked a bland meal that he didn't like or they went to a restaurant where the maitre d' kept them waiting too long before seating them. Through it all, Wallace P. Crabbe kept smiling. But slowly, he began retreating into the world within his 1950s, split-level, two-bedroom ranch house.

His routine there was very consistent. Every morning, Wallace had all three New York newspapers, the *Daily News*, the *Post*, and the *Times*, delivered. As well as *Newsday*, the Long Island paper. On Fridays, which was the day it came out, he also read the East End *Journal*. He tried to break himself of this end-of-the-week habit several times but was unable to do it. He felt compelled to read the inane gossip about famous people he despised and the police reports about thieves stealing left-over chicken out of refrigerators and the idiotic letters to the editor about the new speed-bump controversy. He particularly was unable to resist the obituaries about the barbers who'd been cutting hair so many years they refused to use electric razors and the old biddies who'd been there so long they thought they'd come over on the *Mayflower*. So over three cups of strong black coffee, he read his papers, always in the same order – *News*, *Post*, *Times*, *Newsday*, on Fridays the *Journal* – and always cover to cover. Nothing made him angrier than reading about crooked politicians and slimy rich people who broke all the rules and got away with it. On almost any given day, Wallace would rant and rave – silently, to himself – about national politics, local politics, the heat, the cold, the lack of quality on TV, obscene music lyrics by gangster rappers, the price of groceries, the low level of water in the reservoirs. Later that day, right before lunch, when he'd speak with his girlfriend on the telephone or with someone calling to ask him about a possible copy-editing assignment, he would bring up a story he'd read earlier, one that had knotted his stomach and caused his throat to constrict. When it provoked no anger on the other end of the line, he would let it drop and say, in an absolutely even tone, *Yes, you're right, it's just the way of the world. It's nothing to get excited about.*

After lunch, he usually spent a couple of hours at his computer, in chat rooms, talking to his new circle of anonymous and mostly pseudonymous friends. In the late afternoon and, if he had no plans, at night, Wallace P. Crabbe would retreat into his one passion that elicited no anger and that never let him down: the movies. He rented at least one tape or DVD a day, sometimes two or even three. He read every book he could about Hollywood: celebrity biographies and autobiographies, critical analyses, books on how to write screenplays, behind-the-scenes *Making Of* books. He was obsessed with Hollywood movies. Not all of them, not the silents, he couldn't care less about those, but everything from the late 30s on up. Screwball comedies. Melodramas. Noir thrillers. The Astair and Kelly musicals. Mushy romances. He loved them all. At night he was usually awake until two or three in the morning watching his rentals or old films on cable. He thought he knew everything there was to know about the movies; he could tell you who directed what and who the cinematographer was and even the theme song that played over the credits and who wrote it. Watching a 1940s Clark Gable picture or a 1950s Ava Gardner was the one thing that transported him into a state of relative inner calm.

All in all, Wallace didn't mind the fact that he was almost always angry. Something inside of him had long ago told him to be afraid of what was in there, to never let it out, and since he hadn't, he was fairly proud of the way he'd dealt with things. He was not all that unhappy with the way he'd organized his life and he felt he had things pretty much under control.

Until this past Friday, when Wallace's two main obsessions had come together to drive him into a state of barely controlled fury.

At first he didn't even realize what the problem was. He had finished all the real papers and was aggravating himself with the East End *Journal*. He made a mental note to remember how much money the school board was trying to gouge the town for and he checked out the diagram of a house that some Israeli was building in the Hamptons that was supposed to be the largest private residence in the world. There were several decent obits, too, so while sipping his final half-cup of coffee, he read quarter-page summations about the life of one man whose hardware store had been on Main Street since 1957 and the history of another who'd invented some kind of special lawn-mower blade that had revolution-ized the lives of gardeners everywhere. The third obit was about an actor, William Miller. It was longer than the others and somehow it seemed more personal. Wallace paid particular attention to it because it was about Hollywood.

At first, Wallace P. didn't know what it was that was bothering him so much about the obit. One thing that annoyed him was that he'd never heard of William Miller and he was convinced that he'd heard of everybody. But it was more than that. It was the 1939 costume drama, *The Queen of Sheba*. And William Miller's Academy Award nomination for Best Supporting Actor. Even now, days later, Wallace felt the bile rising in his stomach. Nobody had ever been nominated for an Oscar for some historical piece of shit like that. And definitely not in 1939. Best Supporting Actor nominations that year were Gene Lockhart for *Algiers* . . . no one even remembered *him* . . . John Garfield for *Four Daughters* . . . Basil Rathbone for *If I Were King* . . . and . . . oh yes . . . Robert Morley for *Marie Antoinette*. Walter Brennan won for *Kentucky*. No goddamn William Miller. Nobody who had the word 'cowboy' in the headline of his obituary! He didn't even have to look it up! Christ!

The Friday he'd read the article, Wallace had tried to calm himself down. He knew that the rage within was starting to spill over onto the outside. But he couldn't contain it. *Fucking small town papers! How could they make a mistake like this? How could they not know?!* And then Wallace P. realized he wasn't just thinking those thoughts, he was speaking them aloud, yelling them, actually, although there was no one else in his house. For the first time in a long time, Wallace P. Crabbe also realized that he wanted to tell someone – no, *needed* to tell someone – about this horrible thing. This inexcusable error that seemed to him to spell the end of modern civilization. This was something he could not push away and ignore with a happy smile on his face.

He tried calling his girlfriend but all he got was her office voice mail. He left a message saying that it was important and she should call him. He then called one person who still worked at his old publishing company, a fairly precise production guy, but although this person sympathized with Wallace's opinions about the world's ineptness, he didn't see what the big deal was. After he hung up, he decided that this emergency called for some *real* action, so Wallace P. stormed to the phone book, looked up the number he wanted, once again grabbed the telephone that hung on the wall of his small kitchen and called the East End *Journal*. Amazingly enough, the person who picked up the phone was the man who owned and edited the paper and he said he'd be more than happy to listen to Wallace's tirade. The owner did indeed listen, although not nearly as long as Wallace would have liked for him to. And he kept calling him 'Wally,' which infuriated Wallace even more. At some point, the owner thanked him for spotting the errors and promised that he would take care of it. He asked for a phone number and address so someone could let him know when to look for the correction in the paper. The editor told him it would probably be printed in next Friday's issue. Wallace gave him the information – but only after insisting that the editor write his name down as Wallace, not Wally. He made him spell it back to him and still, when the man hung up, he said, 'Thanks for calling, Wally.'

Wallace was certain that no one would ever call, sure that the guy was lying to him. If there was something of which Wallace was positive, it was that he did not trust anyone who insisted on calling him Wally. He was sure that the owner was listening to him just the way Wallace listened to everybody else: patiently, smiling, nodding, and paying absolutely no attention. Wallace P. was as sure about this as he'd ever been of anything in his whole life.

So he was particularly surprised when someone from the police department called and asked if he'd be home in the afternoon. The policeman said that it was about the obit that had run in the paper.

Wallace said he'd be home and he'd be happy to talk about it.

He was delighted that someone had, in fact, been listening to him.

That delight turned to anger once again when, before hanging up, the policeman said, 'I'll be there in about an hour, Wally.'

The first thing Wallace Crabbe noticed about Justin Westwood was that he was sloppy. No. To be precise, it wasn't sloppiness. It was a certain disdain for his own appearance. It seemed almost deliberate. The man's hair was a little too long and unruly. How difficult would it have been to run a comb through it? He wasn't fat but if he didn't start working out soon he certainly would be. This man did not turn down that extra cookie after dinner. Which was fine, but when was the last time he'd done a sit-up? And his clothes! They were nice clothes. Not cheap. But the shirt could have used a little starch. Not too much, but some. And the pants could be creased. Oh yes. Those pants could absolutely be creased. Plus: brown loafers. Puh-lease.

The first thing Justin noticed about Wallace Crabbe's

house was how extraordinarily clean it was. There seemed to be absolutely no dirt. Or clutter. Or *anything* personal except for the second thing he noticed, which was that there were at least several months' worth of newspapers stacked up in his kitchen. Crabbe saw him eyeing the stack, immediately got defensive and said, 'I use them as sources of reference. I save them for four months exactly. Then I throw them away. Each day I throw out the ones from four months ago.'

Justin nodded casually, as if it weren't the weirdest thing he'd seen in a long time. 'Did you save Bill Miller's obituary?'

'What's so damn important about this obituary that you had to come all this way to talk to me?'

'The woman who wrote it was murdered.' He watched Crabbe's face, waiting to see the reaction. The news seemed to barely register. 'You don't seem too upset by that.'

'Didn't know her,' Crabbe said. 'And she certainly wasn't a very accurate or competent journalist.'

'So you couldn't care less?'

'I couldn't care at all.'

'Nice.'

'Mr Westwood . . .'

'*Detective* Westwood. As long as we're being concerned with accuracy.'

'Detective Westwood. Did you drive all this way so you could impugn my character?'

'No. I'd like you to tell me what got you so upset about the obit.'

'Who said I was upset?'

'Weren't you?'

'Yes. But it was hardly irrational, if that's what you're implying.'

Westwood didn't say anything, waited to see where this guy was going with it.

'I had every reason to be upset,' Wallace Crabbe said. 'There are standards to be kept up.'

'And this obituary violated your standards.'

'The obituary violated everyone's standards. First of all, it said that this . . . this . . . Miller person . . . was nominated for an Academy Award in 1939. Preposterous. This man was never nominated for an Oscar. Believe me. Not in 1939, not ever.'

'He was an old man. He exaggerated.'

'He didn't just make up the award. He made up the movie.'

'*The Queen of Sheba*?'

'Didn't exist.'

'How do you know?'

'Detective, I assume you know all about clues or evidence or whatever it is you do. I know movies.'

'There was no movie called *The Queen of Sheba*?'

'Not since a little thing I like to call "talkies" came in.'

'Speaking of evidence, Mr Crabbe, when I called you earlier you said you'd been away.'

'Yes. That's right. I went away with my girlfriend for two days.'

'Where'd you go?'

'I don't see that it's any of your business.'

'It kind of is,' Westwood said. 'I'd like to see if you can account for your whereabouts when Susanna Morgan was murdered.'

'I have no idea when she was murdered, but whenever it was, I most certainly can account for my whereabouts. The two days I'm referring to, I was in the Poconos. At a small lodge called Pococabana.'

'I assume you can prove that.'

'Whenever you'd like me to.'

Westwood nodded. He hadn't really expected this little guy to be involved in the murder. He was lingering now just because he felt like being as annoying as possible.

'Was there anything else?' he asked. 'In the obit, I mean. Anything else that bothered you.'

'Other than the writing style? All the other credits were TV and theater. I don't watch TV and the theater's irrelevant in today's world, it doesn't concern me.'

'So the answer's no?'

'The answer,' Crabbe said, starting to get angry all over again, 'is that getting something like an Academy Award nomination incorrect in a newspaper, even a newspaper like the *Journal*, is an egregious sin. And to make it worse, they were supposed to call me. The editor I spoke to said they'd call me when they discovered the truth. But like everyone else, they lied. I haven't heard a word.'

'They've been a little distracted.'

'By this woman's murder? It's no excuse for their lack of professionalism. If you see them please tell them I said that.'

'I'll do that,' Westwood said. 'As soon as I see them, I'll be sure to pass that along.'

As Justin walked toward the front door, Wallace Crabbe cleared his throat. 'I'll still accept a free subscription.'

Westwood stopped, turned, faced the balding little man with the smug expression on his face. 'Excuse me?' he said.

'When they finally get back to work and they find out I was right about this Miller fake,' Wallace P. Crabbe said. 'I told them I'd accept a free subscription as an acknowledgment of my contribution. I still will. And make sure it's in the name of Wallace P. Crabbe. *Not* Wally.' Then he added with a sniff, 'Make sure you tell them that, too.'

This time Justin didn't say a word. He didn't even nod. He just left the very clean house and was extremely relieved and happy to sit behind the wheel of his very dirty car.

CHAPTER SEVEN

Justin went to bed early that night, fell asleep with the TV on and was out by 10:30 p.m.. The dream came again, earlier than usual. He'd been asleep only an hour or so.

There were more details than the night before, the violence was even more vivid, the pain even deeper. This time the dream forced him to remember lying on the floor, and that the red was his own blood. He saw the man standing over him lift his leg to kick him, felt the impact of the shoe into his chest. He saw himself turning over, saw the look of pleasure on the man's face, then the look of shock. This time Justin knew that the explosion came from *him*. And then there was more red . . .

When he awoke there was no lingering haze. He was wide awake, his brain was going at full speed. This time he did not want the images to stay, so he flung the blanket off and swung his legs out of bed. He turned off the television, went straight to the laptop computer he kept on his kitchen table, inserted the disk he'd copied earlier that day at the police station, and looked at the notes he'd typed up.

He stared at the line that just said: '*Walrus*'????

'It sounded like Walrus,' Deena had said. The blond man had wanted something, some information, and Susanna Morgan had given it to him. Something that sounded like Walrus.

'Goddamn it.' He said it out loud, got up and ran to his pants that he'd tossed on the bed post, stuck his hand in the left front pocket. He found the crumpled Post-It that Harlan Corning had given him, the one with Wallace Crabbe's phone number on it. Corning had written 'Wally' on it. That's what had thrown him off. The man had even said that he preferred to be called Wallace, but Justin was thinking Wally all the way.

Justin Westwood glanced at his watch. 11:45.

'Fuck it,' he said, also aloud, and quickly dialed the number.

Wallace P. Crabbe was trying not to let his anger overcome him. His girlfriend had brought that subject up during their two days away. She'd told him that she thought it was unhealthy the way he got so upset over little things, that he'd make himself sick. He was surprised that she had noticed. He'd thought he kept his emotions so far below the surface that they were undetectable. But she'd taken his hand in hers, said she knew that's what he thought, but that she had gotten to know him well. Possibly even better than he knew himself. So she could see what was going on below the surface. This scared Wallace. But it also made him happy, in a strange, disconcerting way, and he told her he would try to work on this problem.

When he went to the door to answer the doorbell, his first instinct was to erupt. And he had plenty of reasons. First of all, he was watching a DVD of *The Third Man*, certainly in his top ten of all time, maybe even the top five. And he was nearly at the moment when Orson Welles appeared for the first time, the shot in the shadowy doorway when he was so handsome and so mysterious. He hated being interrupted when he was watching a movie, especially this movie and especially at this moment. Second, it was nine o'clock. That was way too late for anyone to be ringing his doorbell. Third, he was not expecting any more visitors and he was in no mood to entertain anyone he knew or talk to any other policemen or listen to the ranting of a proselytizing religious fanatic, and those were the only three options he could envision.

When he opened the door, he was surprised to find a fourth option.

'Are you Wallace P. Crabbe?' a blond man, quite handsome, asked. He didn't seem to notice that Wallace was trying to contain his fury. Or if he did, he certainly didn't care. The stranger seemed perfectly at ease. 'The Wallace P. Crabbe who called the East End *Journal* about the obit?'

Wallace P. was stunned. So they actually *did* do something. Maybe that police officer really had passed along his message. Amazing. They even sent someone to apologize. What was the world coming to?

'You're from the paper?'

The blond man nodded.

'I was right, wasn't I?' Wallace couldn't help crowing. It came out smugly but that's okay, he thought, I deserve to be smug. But then his anger crept back into the smugness, and he said, 'Do you have any idea what time it is? This is an outrage!'

'You *are* Wallace P. Crabbe?'

His ego won out over the lateness of the hour. 'I told them they screwed up, didn't I? I was right about everything, wasn't I?'

'You were right,' the man said. 'Congratulations.'

Wallace vented then for thirty seconds or so. He couldn't help himself, no matter what he'd promised about trying to remain calm. He just started spouting off. About the state of the newspaper business, about the state of the world, about the lack of work ethic in just about everyone. About the fact that no one takes his job seriously anymore . . .

'I take my job *very* seriously,' the man said. 'May I come in? I know it's late but I'd like to ask you a few questions.'

'About what?'

'I'm curious how you discovered the errors.'

'Is this for the paper?'

'Well, it was such a serious screw-up, I think we're going to do a story on it.'

That set Wallace off again. By the time he was finished spouting about his knowledge of movies and his awareness of history and the fact that the errors in the obit were so blatant he hadn't even needed to check them against a reference book, he was sitting in an easy chair in his living room and the blond man was comfortably ensconced on the couch.

'Wow,' the blond man said, 'you really do know your movies.'

'It's something I take quite seriously,' Wallace Crabbe said.

'Me, too,' the blond man said. 'I'm kind of obsessed with movies.'

'Well, I don't like to use that word, I think it has a slightly negative connotation, but . . .'

The blond man nodded toward the TV and DVD player. 'What were you watching when I interrupted you?'

'*The Third Man.*'

'A classic. I probably listen to the soundtrack more than any other one. You know directors and writers and cinematographers, too?'

'And the editors and the cameramen and the composers.'

'Can I test you out?'

Wallace was eating this up. It could have been four in the afternoon as far as he was concerned. The paper was writing a story about his diligence and knowledge and he had a fellow movie connoisseur in his apartment. Heaven.

'Okay,' he said, nodding. 'But I warn you . . . I'm very good.'

'*Extreme Prejudice.*'

'I beg your pardon?'

'It's one of my favorite movies. Who directed it?'

'Oh, I didn't realize you were starting.' Wallace couldn't

help his superior smile. 'Walter Hill. Nick Nolte and Powers Booth were the stars.'

'Wow. How about *The Hand*?'

The same condescending smile. 'Early Oliver Stone. Michael Caine is a cartoonist whose hand is severed.'

'*The Big Heat*.'

'Fritz Lang. Glenn Ford is the policeman whose wife is killed and he goes after Lee Marvin.'

'Do you remember the actress who gets the hot coffee thrown in her face?'

'Gloria Grahame. A marvelous performance.' Wallace put his hand over his mouth to stifle a cough. 'The films you're asking about, they're all extremely violent.'

'I guess that's true,' the blond man acknowledged. 'It's what I like, though. I wonder what that says about me?'

'This has been extremely entertaining,' Wallace said, 'but I guess we should get on with it. What am I receiving?'

'Receiving?'

'From the *Journal*. I assume that in addition to the story, the very least I'm getting is a free subscription. Although that still doesn't make up for the sloppiness, you know.' Wallace worried that, because he was in such a good mood, his rebuke wasn't as harsh as it should have been. 'That doesn't make up for the kind of mistake this was.'

'Do you think I could get a glass of water? Before I tell you what you're getting?'

Wallace stood up, not bothering to hide his annoyance, and went into the kitchen to get the drink. The blond man didn't even look up when he heard a glass drop and break and his host begin to splutter. In a couple of seconds, Wallace came storming back into the living room, staring at the blond man, then turning back toward the kitchen, his mouth open.

'I'm not giving you a free subscription,' the blond man in the living room said.

'I'm not either,' the second, identical-looking blond man in the kitchen said.

'What is going on here?' Wallace whispered to the second blond, who now stepped through the kitchen doorway into the living room. 'Who are you? How did you get in here?'

'You were really angry about that obit, weren't you?' the first blond man said.

'I'm not now,' Wallace said, stuttering. 'It d-d-doesn't really matter.'

'What's the P in Wallace P stand for? Pissed off?'

'You know,' the blond who'd been in the kitchen, who was still lingering in the doorway, said, 'sometimes when you're angry, it's better to just keep quiet.'

'Yes.' Wallace nodded quickly. His head bobbed up and down several times. 'I understand that now. And that's what I'm going to do. Keep quiet.'

'We know,' the first blond said. And, smiling politely, he pulled a SIG-Sauer with a silencer attached out of his jacket pocket, pulled the trigger once and shot Wallace P. Crabbe right in the middle of his forehead.

'He sure was surprised to see you,' the first blond said.

'They're *all* surprised to see me,' the second one said.

Then the two men smiled at each other and, professionals that they were, began to clean up.

Justin was holding the phone to his ear, gripping it tighter than was necessary. It had rung ten times now. He was hoping that the little shit in his spotless, impersonal house would answer the phone, irate at being awakened. He was hoping that Wallace P. Crabbe would give him living hell and then call the East End Harbor police station to register a complaint against him.

He let the phone ring twenty times before burying his head in his hands and bending over in despair. He only hung up when he was certain that Wallace sounded enough like Walrus that Wallace P. Crabbe wasn't ever going to answer the phone again.

CHAPTER EIGHT

'**H**ey, Eastwood.'

Justin was sitting at his desk, his eyes closed, doing what he liked best, which was drifting away into his self-created cloud of darkness. The voice jarred his eyes open and he glanced over at the cop at the desk next to his. *What the hell is his name again?* Westwood thought. *Oh yeah. Got it. Chalk one up for my side.*

'What do you want, Brian?'

'I just want to tell you I think you're an unbelievable fucking pussy.'

Justin nodded wearily. 'Is that right?'

'You let those guys from Middleview push the shit out of you.'

'No I didn't. I just didn't push back.'

'You think that missing guy is dead. I heard you with the chief. You convinced him you were right.'

Justin shrugged. 'Well, they didn't believe me. And there was nothing I could do to convince them.'

'Bullshit. You just rolled over and played dead.'

'Maybe it's because I don't know if *I* believe me.'

Brian didn't say anything to that. He didn't have to. The look of scorn on his face said more than enough.

'Eastwood.'

This time it was the other one, Gary. Justin looked up at him but didn't bother to respond.

'What's the deal with the chief and you?' Gary said. He didn't seem to care if Justin was ignoring him.

'What deal is that, Gary?'

'It's like he thinks you're . . . I don't know what. Like you're special. Like you know stuff.' He looked at Justin, took off his silly-looking ultra-cop sunglasses and took a long look. 'What is it you know?'

'He don't know shit,' Brian said.

Gary kept looking. 'Is that right?' he asked, but he wasn't asking Brian. He was asking Justin.

'That's right,' Westwood said. 'It's the first smart thing I ever heard your little friend say.' Then he got up and walked out the door of the station, onto the East End Harbor streets.

As he walked, he thought about the conversation he had with the Middleview police.

He'd called them the night before, right after he gave up on reaching Crabbe. He explained his fear and the department dispatched two men to check out Crabbe's house. He wasn't there. The house was empty. But there was no evidence of B and E. No blood. No sign of theft or a struggle or anything violent had occurred. The sergeant at the desk called Justin back, asked him to explain his suspicions and then said he thought it would be best if they could talk in person. Next, Justin called his chief, filled him in on what was happening. Leggett was nervous. Justin could tell that he wasn't wild about the call to the Middleview force but he agreed to back Justin, said he'd be at the meeting in the morning. And he was. Two cops from Middleview showed up at the station around nine o'clock. They went into the chief's office and Justin did his best to explain his thought process as calmly and cogently as he could. But as he spoke he realized he didn't have much. Yeah, he had a witness saying that Susanna Morgan had been murdered. But there was no motive and very little physical evidence to back it up. There was a connection between Susanna Morgan and Crabbe. But it was a tenuous one at best. And there was absolutely no proof that anything had happened to Wallace Crabbe other than the fact that he might have decided to stay at his girlfriend's house for the night. Halfway through his explanation, Westwood could feel the two cops tune him out. They weren't buying it. Not enough proof. Too much of a stretch. Absolutely no evidence. And it was all coming from a schmuck walking a one-street-long beat in a basically crimeless town.

So he clammed up. The passion that had come out when he'd explained his theory to Leggett was gone. He finished his story in a quiet monotone, listened as the cops politely said they'd check up on Crabbe and keep Justin informed as the investigation progressed. They both had glanced at each other and smiled at the word 'investigation.'

It was over. Without Wallace Crabbe's body there was nothing.

As the two cops left, he heard one of them say to Brian,

'What's the story with that guy?' Brian responded, too low for Justin to hear. Then he heard them all laugh knowingly. One of the cops also said, 'Hey, isn't this where that intern's from? The one who's missing in D.C.?' And this time it was Gary who answered, 'Maura Greer. Yeah. She was a townie.'

'You know her?' one of the Middleview cops asked.

'Went to high school with her,' Gary said. And Brian said, 'Me, too.'

'She looks like a babe,' the same Middleview cop muttered.

'A little porky,' Brian said. 'But not too shabby.'

'Hell,' the Middleview cop said, '*that's* who you guys should go out and find. Be a couple of heroes. Don't waste your time on *this* bullshit.'

And they all laughed again.

Then, when he came out of Leggett's office, Brian had accused him of rolling over. Had he? Yeah, probably. He'd spent so many years rolling over that he couldn't tell the difference anymore. But what the hell could he have said that would have made any difference? *I have a hunch? I give out parking tickets in a resort town now but my hunches used to mean something?* Yeah, that would have worked. He told himself that he gave up trying to convince them because he had nothing. Somewhere inside him was the thought that he was wrong. That his instincts had dulled and atrophied and his hunches no longer had validity. That the unpleasant and compulsively tidy man hadn't been attacked, that he did actually have a girlfriend and he was probably just spending the night with her. That's why Wallace Crabbe hadn't

107

answered his phone. Because he was simply leading a normal life, something Justin Westwood hadn't led in six and a half years.

Justin made the turn onto Main Street. So what now? Too early to get drunk. Besides, he was on duty. He thought about saying he was sick and going home, smoking as much dope as he could and blaring some R.E.M., drowning out the world and shutting his eyes for the rest of the day. But he knew he wouldn't do that. Couldn't do it. If he did, he'd stay there a lot longer than one day. So he had to ask himself the same question he'd asked himself almost every hour of the day and night for the past six-plus years: What do I do to get through the next sixty minutes without blowing my brains out?

Much to his surprise, Justin Westwood decided that what he'd do was go see about a yoga lesson.

Deena Harper's class was just ending. Justin peered in from the street, through the tinted plate-glass window that separated Deena's studio from the sidewalk. She was wearing a pair of black tights and a black tank top. No shoes, just a pair of thick gray wool socks. He saw two middle-aged women doing their best to unfold their legs and stand up. And one young man – Justin thought it was the guy who ran the computer store a couple of buildings down – who seemed amazingly fit and remained in a sitting position, legs folded, breathing deeply in and out. Finally, the computer guy stood up and all three people handed Deena some money. She thanked the two women and kissed the guy lightly on the cheek, then the three students emerged onto the street in front of Justin. He nodded at them, hesitated, aware that they were all watching him as he stepped through the doorway into the yoga room.

'Hey,' he said, casually.

Deena looked up, surprised. But she smiled when she saw him.

'I'll be with you in a second.'

She dashed into a back room and Justin had time to survey the studio. Not all that much to survey, really. A few gym mats on the floor, several more rolled up and propped against a corner. One whole wall was a mirror. There were a couple of bulletin boards with strange, non-English words on them: *trikonasana* and *sirsasana* and *parsvakonasana*. Across from the mirror was a small poster, hand-made, that said, 'My religion is kindness. – Dalai Lama.' The room was clean and clutter free. But somehow it radiated a degree of warmth and serenity that pleased him.

Justin looked at himself in the mirror, bent down to see how close he could get to touching his toes. He got just about to his knees, heard himself grunt. He decided he should look up, check out his form. It wasn't pretty, that much was for sure. Made less pretty by the nerdy East End Harbor police uniform he was wearing. It looked more like a Boy Scout uniform than something that should be on a cop. And it was all made even uglier when, unfortunately, Deena chose that moment to return from the back room. Justin looked up at her, his arms dangling in front of him, his legs bent, his head cocked, his uniform sleeves snagged a few unsightly inches above

109

his wrists. He straightened up as fast as he could, felt his back wrench, decided there was no way in hell he was going to acknowledge the pain and show this woman that he was barely capable of bending over.

'Ever do yoga?' Deena asked.

'Can't you tell from my expert technique? I used to be a black belt.'

'Wrong discipline,' she said. 'No belts in yoga. Other than that you were totally believable.'

He winced now, wanting desperately to stretch his back, but that's when he noticed that standing behind Deena, as if hiding, was a small girl. She looked like a miniature duplicate of the older woman.

'This is Kendall,' Deena said. 'This is Mr Westwood. Or is it Officer Westwood?'

'Justin,' he said. 'It saves a lot of confusion. You can even make it simpler and call me Jay.'

The little girl poked her head out, smiled shyly, a charmer of a smile, then ducked behind her mother again. Justin knew what he should say. He used to be good with kids. *Why is such a beautiful little girl hiding?* that's what he should ask her. *If I were that beautiful, I would definitely not be hiding.* But nothing came out of his mouth. He just stood there awkwardly, looking at mother and daughter.

'So,' Deena said finally. 'Is there news?' He looked startled, his brow furrowed in confusion, so she said, 'You know. About Susanna and . . . everything.'

'Oh,' he said. 'Not exactly.'

'I thought maybe you'd come to give me an update. Thought maybe you'd caught them.'

'I'm just passing by.'

'Is anything happening?'

'Sure,' he said, but it didn't sound convincing, even to him. 'Lots of stuff.'

'That's very reassuring. I'm sure I'll sleep soundly now.'

'Aren't you sleeping?'

'No,' Deena said, 'as a matter of fact I'm not.'

'Bad dreams?'

She looked as if she wanted to say something, but glanced down at the little girl and thought better of it – why put bad dreams into *her* head – and just nodded. All she said was, 'Are there any other kind?'

'They don't know you were there,' he said.

'What?'

'You might have reasons for your dreams, what you saw. But whoever those guys are, they think they got away with it. They don't know there was a witness.'

'And you're telling me this because . . .?'

'Because sometimes when people have bad dreams, it's not just the things they've seen. It's not just what's real. It's the things they're afraid might happen to them. So I thought I should make it really clear that nothing's going to happen to you. There's no *reason* for anything to happen. They don't know you exist.'

Deena was silent for a moment. Then the right side of her mouth flickered upward in a half-smile. 'I guess I should have thought of that myself, huh? Could've helped out my beauty sleep.'

Justin was surprised to hear himself say, 'I don't think you need too much help there.'

The rest of her mouth managed to smile. They stood,

facing each other, Justin shifting back and forth on the balls of his feet, feeling slightly foolish.

'Well . . .' she said.

'Well . . .' he said.

'I have to take Kendall over to the library. They're having a special kids' book thing. Somebody from *Sesame Street* or *Between the Lions* or one of those shows. A story-telling hour.'

'Is it all right if I walk you over there?' he asked, directing his question to the little girl, who was still clutching her mother's waist and trying to remain unseen. 'I'd really like to.'

Again, a quick dart of the head, an even quicker smile. 'Okay,' the girl said. 'It's okay with me.'

Deena patted her on the head, looked up at Justin and added, 'It's okay with me, too.'

CHAPTER NINE

The library was three blocks further down Main Street, tucked into a residential area. It should have taken them no more than ten minutes to make the stroll. But they were slowed down when a blue Jaguar, driving on the other side of the road, passed them by, stopped suddenly and began honking its horn. Justin peered across the street, heard someone call out, 'Jay? For Chrissake, Jay, is that you?' He knew he had to do something, the guy was getting ready to hop out of the car and Justin knew that he'd dash across the street to meet them, so he held up his hand and walked slowly, lumberingly, over to the driver.

'I can't believe it,' the guy behind the wheel said. He looked comfortable in the Jag, like he belonged there. His clothes were casual but very expensive and he was wearing a watch that probably cost two grand. He lifted the arm with the watch and waved his hand at Justin's police uniform. 'Is it Halloween?'

'Can I help you?' Justin said.

'It's me! It's Jordy. Chris Jordan! I know I put on a few

pounds, but from the looks of it so have . . .' He hesitated, now sounding unsure of himself. 'You *are* Jay Westwood, right?'

Justin didn't say anything. He adjusted his sunglasses, tipping them a fraction of an inch higher on the bridge of his nose.

'Look,' the driver of the Jaguar said, 'I heard about Alicia. I tried to get in touch with you, a lot of us did, but you kind of disappeared . . .'

'I'm sorry,' Justin said. 'I don't remember any Chris Jordan.'

'What?' And as Justin turned away, started heading across the street, the driver called after him. 'Jay! What the hell are you doing. Jay, for god's sake! You're just gonna walk away? You walk away from college, you walk away from your friends, now you're going to walk away from your old roomie . . .?'

But Justin didn't turn back. Even when the driver said, 'Jay, I've got a place in Southampton. I'm listed. If you want to, call me.' He just crossed the street, didn't turn around until he heard the car speed away. Then he went back to stand beside Deena.

'What was that all about?' she asked.

'Don't know,' Justin said. 'I guess he thought he knew me.'

'Sounds like he did know you,' Deena said. 'Sounds like he knew you from college.' When Justin didn't say anything, Deena asked, 'Where'd you go to school?' When she didn't get an answer, she said, 'Justin, where'd you go, a local college? That's nothing to be ashamed of, you know. I mean, if you're embarrassed because you didn't go to a good school, or you dropped out, come on . . . I bet a few of the guys on the force here didn't even go to college. Or maybe they went to a junior college. Hey, I didn't go to the world's greatest school either.'

'I don't like to talk much about my college days,' Justin said.

Deena chewed on her lower lip for a moment. 'He looked pretty successful,' she said. 'The guy in the Jaguar. But being a policeman is nothing to be ashamed—'

'I don't like to talk about that either,' Justin said.

Then he nodded his head, jutting his chin forward, indicating that they should continue on their way to the library.

When they arrived, Kendall – whom Deena sometimes called Kenny or Ken – went running in ahead of them. By the time Justin and Deena got up the steps and to the librarian's desk, the little girl was comfortably settled amidst a horde of six-, seven- and eight-year-olds in a room directly behind the foyer. The room had a sliding door separating it from the entry hall but the door was open. A middle-aged man with a large monkey puppet on his hand was already addressing the excited children.

As they sidled in closer to the doorway, the librarian looked up from her desk and saw Deena. Justin realized he'd never been in the East End Harbor library before. Out of habit, he glanced down at the librarian's nameplate. Her name was Adrienne.

'Terrible thing, wasn't it,' Adrienne whispered to Deena. By the way she said the words, Justin knew immediately that she was one of those people who got extraordinary pleasure from gossiping over terrible things.

'You mean about Susanna?' Deena asked and Adrienne put her hand to her mouth. 'Sshhh,' she said and pointed toward the kids nearby. Then she nodded vigorously, quietly saying, 'Yes, I mean Susanna,' and Deena whispered back, 'Terrible.'

'She was in here the day she died.'

'Really? Checking out a book?'

Adrienne shook her head. 'Using the computer. This one right here.' She tilted her head in the direction of a large desktop, probably three or four years old. It sat to the left of the front door, in the foyer. 'She was very mysterious about it. Didn't want me looking over her shoulder. Not that I would anyway.'

Justin stepped forward now. 'What was she working on? Did she say?'

Adrienne put her finger to her lips again. 'Who are you?'

'I'm with the police department here.'

Adrienne nodded vigorously again. 'I can see that. Ohhhhh yes – I've seen you directing traffic. Seems to me you slow things down rather than speed things up. What kind of crazy system is that?'

Her quiet rant was interrupted by a chorus of laughter from the kids in the room behind them. The monkey puppet was singing a goofy song. You could see that the actor who had the puppet on his hand was really doing the singing. He was making no effort to hide that fact. But none of the kids were even looking at him. They were

116

all staring delightedly at the fuzzy creature on the end of his arm as if he were a totally separate entity.

'Do you know what Susanna was doing on the computer?' Justin whispered.

'Don't have a clue.'

'She went on-line?'

'She did. I collected the eight dollars.'

'But she didn't tell you what she was looking for?'

'Didn't tell me a thing. All I can tell you is she looked pretty intense and excited, like it was something important. And then when she left, she was kind of wobbly. Like she suddenly got sick.'

'She was,' Justin said slowly. 'She called in sick to her office.'

'Well, I can vouch for that. She could barely walk when she left here.'

'So she was here at lunchtime, then.'

'Around twelve or twelve thirty, I'd say. Stayed for forty-five minutes or so.'

'Have a lot of people used this computer since she was here?'

'Three or four. Is that a lot?'

He shook his head. 'You mind if I use it?'

Now Deena spoke up. 'You gonna trace what she was looking at?' She realized she'd said it too loudly. The man with the puppet on his hand gave her an annoyed glare from the adjoining room.

'If I can,' Justin said softly.

The librarian looked skeptical. 'You know how to do that?'

'I'll have to see.'

'It's four dollars for every half-hour on-line.'

'I'll spring for it,' Justin told her. Then he sat at the computer, waiting for Adrienne to return to her desk before he began tapping away.

The first thing he did was click on the Start button, then he went to Programs and clicked on that. He double-clicked on Windows Explorer, ran the cursor down until he came to the Windows program and tapped on the mouse. He ran the cursor down again until he came to a file that read Temporary Internet. He clicked twice and a window appeared with small files inside it, six to a row, each one labeled directly underneath.

'These are all the recent routes people have used to get on to sites,' he said to Deena, making sure his voice was kept low enough to disturb no one and draw no attention.

'I'm impressed,' she acknowledged. 'But how do you know which ones were Susie's?'

'We'll go chronologically. Or backwards, really. See if anything seems logical.'

He began clicking down the long list of locations. There were a lot of things that were impossible to decipher – letters that didn't form words and numbers that seemed meaningless – as well as phrases like *e-mail* and *AOL* and *outlook* and *cookies* and *sportsdata*.

'Adrienne won't be happy,' he murmured.

'Why not?'

'Someone's been logging on to porn sites.'

'How can you tell?'

'Here's a string of three: tiffanyphoto, titsgalore and fatasspix. I'm just guessing, but . . .'

'Seems like a pretty fair guess. You think Susanna was checking out porn?'

'No, I'd put my money on a horny thirteen-year-old boy.'

She looked at the list of sites on the screen and frowned. 'Can you really tell anything from these little things?'

'No,' he confessed. 'I was just hoping to see if anything struck me.' He started to click the escape button, but then hesitated. 'Huh,' he said. 'Here's one: Oscars.'

'What's that mean?'

'Not sure. Could be somebody looking for people named Oscar. But I think your friend Susanna was checking out some information about an actor. Someone she thought won an Academy Award. So maybe there's a connection.' He stared off into space, collecting his thoughts, then clicked out of the window. 'Let me go on-line and check something else,' he said.

As soon as he was connected, he moved the cursor to the address window and clicked on the arrow to its right. Approximately thirty Internet addresses appeared and Justin leaned forward, squinting to read them.

'Listen, will you do me a favor?' he asked.

'What?'

'Do you have the last issue of the *Journal*? The one with the obit Susanna wrote about the actor in the old age home?'

'Probably.'

'Will you go home and get it?'

'Will you keep an eye on Kenny?'

Justin glanced back at the room full of enthralled

children and nodded. Deena said, 'I'll be back in fifteen, twenty minutes.'

As she walked out the door, Justin felt a twinge of guilt. He didn't need the obit, he'd practically memorized it and remembered all of the key details. But he didn't want her privy to what he was searching for. And as soon as he'd seen the sites in the address window, he knew he was on the right track.

Two or three people had used this computer to log on since Susanna Morgan had used it. So he skipped the first three addresses. The next four entries were, in order: William Miller, Supporting Actor, Oscar Winners, and Internet Movie Database. He wanted to see things in the order that Susanna had seen them, so he let the cursor linger for a moment, then clicked on International Movie Database. Immediately, the address came up: http//www.imdb.com. Then he was connected to the site. He ran down the list of categories. You could get daily movie grosses and reviews and updated show business news. He tried to retrace Susanna's thought process, so in the window that was labeled 'search,' he typed in: Oscar Winners. When that site came up, he could hear in his head – clear as a bell – Wallace P. Crabbe ranting and raving about the 1939 Oscar winners, so he typed in the year 1939, just as he was certain Susanna had done. When the list came up, sure enough, William Miller's name was not among the nominees. He remembered Crabbe screaming about Miller's movie, *The Queen of Sheba*, so he typed that in the search window and double-clicked. Crabbe had been right again. There was no 1939 movie with that title. There was no talkie with that title, either.

There was one Hollywood film called *The Queen of Sheba* and that was obviously not the right one. It was a silent film made in 1923. Miller would have been two years old.

Impatient now, Justin decided to cut to the chase. He typed the name 'William Miller' into the search window and clicked. Moments later, Miller's bio appeared on the screen. Justin Westwood began to read. And as he read, his mouth dropped open. This was wrong, he thought. This couldn't possibly be correct. He went back to the home page, typed in just the name Miller. He thought there'd be another William Miller, maybe with a middle initial, or there'd be a Bill Miller – something to differentiate the actor who'd died in East End Harbor from the man whose bio Justin had just seen on the screen. But no, there was only one William Miller and the details of his life and career reappeared on the screen. Justin read through all the information, tried to absorb the specifics, then read through it all again, still not convinced he was seeing what was right in front of his eyes. He tried to imagine what Susanna Morgan had done when she'd reached this page on the web site. He tried to imagine her forcing herself to believe that what she saw could possibly be the truth. Just as he was doing.

In William Miller's filmography there was a string of films with titles Justin had never heard of. The titles were followed by the dates the movies were made and the names of the character played by Miller. The first few titles read:

> In the Land of Plenty (1922) . . . Charles Robertson
> The Runaway (1922) . . . Police Chief

The Safest Place (1922) . . . Professor Allen 'Smitty'
Smith
Blue Boy (1923) . . . Roger Darris

Justin felt disoriented. The dates made no sense. But he kept scrolling, and there it was, just as it had been the first two times he'd scrolled through the info. The next film on the list:

The Queen of Sheba (1923) . . . The Prince

He blinked. Rubbed his eyes to make sure they were clear and that he was reading correctly. He barely noticed the rest of the credit roll. There were several films in the 30s, just a couple in the 40s. In the 50s there was a sub-head that read TELEVISION WORK and listed from the years 1953 through 1955 was the series *Cowboy Bill*.

Justin began to scroll faster. He scanned the mini-biography. Saw the highlights of Miller's life. Saw that he'd been married. Saw the date his wife died. He saw – and read the line over three times – that the couple had never had any children. Saw that for *The Queen of Sheba* he had not received an Academy Award – the award hadn't even come into existence yet – but he was voted *Screen* magazine's 'Favorite Non-Leading Man of the Year.' *Screen's* honor would certainly have been a memorable one for the young actor. Was it memorable enough so, as he got older, it led the old man to tell people he'd won the Oscar? Maybe. One more crazy maybe to add to the growing list.

Miller's theater credits were listed, too. Justin

remembered that the obit had said he was in a 70s revival of two Clifford Odets plays. William Miller had indeed been in those plays. But not in the 70s. In the 30s. In the original productions.

It was impossible.

But there were other matches, too. The Miller he was reading about was married to an actress named Jessica Talbot. She'd appeared with him in *Queen of Sheba* and she died in 1972. Exactly as Susanna Morgan had written in her obituary. Exactly as Bill Miller must have told her.

He scrolled back up, read the line one more time: No children.

No Bill Miller, Jr.

This had to be the guy that Susanna Morgan had known and written about. It *had* to be. There were too many details that connected. But how *could* it be? The answer was that it couldn't. That was the only thing that made any sense at all. It simply couldn't be . . .

Justin got to the end of the bio. Saw that William Miller had been born in Pittsburgh, Pennsylvania. Saw that there was no date of death yet listed.

For what seemed like the hundredth time, he read the date of William Miller's birth.

'Jesus Fucking Christ!' Justin Westwood said and he said it slowly and clearly and very loudly.

When he realized that his words were reverberating throughout the library, he turned around, saw twenty small children and one grown man with a monkey puppet on his hand all staring at him in shocked silence. He saw Deena Harper, clutching a newspaper, freeze as she stepped through the front door of the building. And he watched as Adrienne the librarian's eyes opened as wide as they could possibly open.

The oppressive silence lingered as Justin turned back to the computer screen. He forced himself to read, one more time, the last line of William Miller's biography.

Justin thought of the headline in Susanna Morgan's obituary. The obituary he was more and more certain had gotten her killed.

COWBOY BILL DEAD AT 82

One last time, he stared at the line on the screen in front of him:

Date of birth: 1888

Impossible, inconceivable and illogical.

But there it was in black and white. The proof was staring him right in the face. And there were only two possibilities.

One: the guy who died wasn't Bill Miller. But what sense did that make? Why would he lie?

Which left possibility number two: the guy who died wasn't 82.

Because if the old man in the retirement home was who he said he was, Cowboy Bill Miller lived until he was 114 years old.

CHAPTER TEN

Justin Westwood knew exactly how Susanna Morgan had felt when she left the library only a few days earlier. His legs were wobbly and his head was spinning. His mind kept racing around in circles, but there was no logical end to the race. He could come up with no reasonable conclusion or pattern to any of the information he had just gathered. He wanted a drink as badly as he'd ever wanted anything in his life. And even more than that, what he really wanted was to step back in time. He wanted to go back to the moment he'd seen Susanna's lifeless body on the floor of her bedroom, to ignore the various signs that had pointed to her murder. He wanted to shut out the voice that had told him to go up to Susanna's roof and wipe out the fact that he'd seen Deena Harper, heard her describe the murder. He wanted to forget the fact that he'd ever met anyone named Wallace P. Crabbe and, more than anything else, he wanted to eradicate from his brain the fact that he'd just verified the impossible on an out-of-date computer in the rinky dink East End Harbor library.

He wanted to close his eyes and make everything disappear.

Everything.

But he couldn't. His eyes were open and everything was right in front of him, in absolutely plain sight. Even if none of it made any sense.

So in the still silent library, Justin shut off the computer, dropped a ten-dollar bill on Adrienne the librarian's desk, told Deena that he was leaving, that if she wanted to come she should go get her kid, now, no questions asked, just go, which is exactly what she did, striding into the children's room, swooping Kendall up under her arm, and then Justin walked them both home. He didn't say a word the entire ten minutes. She asked a couple of questions, he just stared, didn't even bother to shake his head. He walked them back to the apartment on Main Street, didn't say goodbye. As soon as they were inside, he continued walking straight ahead, kept going until he reached the end of Main, where he made a left. Five minutes later, he was in the East End Retirement Home, talking to Fred, the home's longtime manager.

'Sure,' Fred said. 'Just like I told Susanna when she called. Bill's nephew's name is Ed Marion. Nice guy. Always was. Even when he came up the last time. *Helluva* nice guy, considering the circumstances.'

'What circumstances were those?' Justin asked.

'Well, you know, his uncle being dead and all.'

'Oh. Those circumstances. So you'd met him before that?'

'Well, sure. He used to come pretty regularly, four, five times a year, to see Bill and to pay me.'

'He paid for Mr Miller's stay here?'

'Every penny of it.'

'Why didn't he just send a check?'

'I guess he liked to visit his uncle. And he didn't pay by check.'

'How did he pay?'

'Cash. Every three months, for the next three months in advance.'

'Do a lot of people pay cash?'

'Hell, I wasn't even sure it was still legal to pay in cash.'

'So he was the only one.'

'Unfortunately.'

'Did Mr Miller talk about his nephew, talk about Ed?'

The manager shook his head. 'Nah. Hardly ever. In fact, I don't think they got along all that well. Old Bill, he used to tell everyone he didn't have no relatives. One time I heard him say that and I said, 'What about that nephew of yours? He's a relative, isn't he?'

'And what did Bill say?'

'Didn't say much of anything, as I recall it. He could be a stubborn old coot.'

'Tell me something, Fred, how long have you worked here?'

'Me? Six, seven years now.'

'And how long was Bill Miller here? Before you?'

'Oh sure. He was a carryover. He's been here a while.'

'Do you know exactly how long?' Justin asked.

'Pretty close. But not exactly.'

'Don't you keep records?'

'Duhh, yeah, we do. But the day before I started work, literally the day before, we had a robbery. They took some office stuff, a computer, a phone machine, you know, stuff like that. And a bunch of files. God only knows why they wanted that stuff. One of the things they took was Bill's file. Don't think they got a lotta dough fencin' that, I'll tell you what.'

Justin stood up to go.

'You wanna tell me what's goin' on here?' Fred asked.

'I wish I could,' Justin told him. 'I really wish I could.'

Back at the station, Justin went straight to his desk, was already dialing Ed Marion's phone number before he was even seated in his chair. For some reason, he wasn't at all surprised when he got a recording, telling him that the number he'd dialed was no longer in service.

He wasn't surprised either, when he got Susanna Morgan's phone records faxed to him slightly less than an hour later and saw that, on the last day of her life, at 2:07 p.m., she had placed one call to Ed Marion's number and, at 5:54 p.m., received one call from that same number. A number that no longer existed.

The first call had lasted twenty-seven seconds. Long enough to leave a phone message. The return call had lasted just over four minutes. Plenty of time to have a substantive conversation.

But what was the substance?

So a senile actor was mind-bogglingly old. So what? What made that something other than a piece of fascinating and astonishing trivia?

What made it a fact worth killing over?

Justin checked the information he received from the

phone company. The address that belonged to Edward Marion's number was 2376 Old Post Road in Weston, Connecticut. It was a valid address. He could take the car ferry over, be there in three hours.

He could . . .

'Hey, Eastwood.'

It was shithead Brian. Justin didn't bother to look up at the young cop.

'What are you doin' playin' policeman all of a sudden?' Brian said. 'It's a little late for that, isn't it?'

Justin stood up now. Took three careful steps over to Brian's desk. But before he did, he palmed the heavy stapler from the corner of his own desk.

'You're a tough guy, aren't you, Brian?'

Brian smiled up at him from the seat behind the desk. An arrogant and confident smile. 'I'm tough enough.'

'You could kick my ass in a fair fight, couldn't you?'

'I could kick the shit out of you. And I wouldn't mind doin' it, either, if you want to know the truth.'

'I believe you. The thing about life, though,' Justin said calmly, 'is that it isn't very fair. Maybe you're too young to have learned that lesson yet.'

Brian put his hands down on the desk, spread his fingers apart, ready to use them to push himself up from the chair. 'Then maybe you should try to teach me,' he said.

'I think that would be a good idea.'

Brian went to stand up but before he could rise more than an inch or two, Justin slammed the stapler down on the fingers of his right hand. As Brian yelped in pain and looked down at his smashed knuckles, Justin picked up the telephone that sat on Brian's desk, swung it back, and slammed it into the young cop's mouth as hard as he could. Brian toppled over backward in his chair, blood streaming down his chin. Justin was certain he'd loosened three or four teeth. Maybe even knocked them out completely.

The younger cop groaned now from his prone position on the floor, looked up at his attacker. Justin could see the hate in his eyes, even through the pain. It wasn't over yet, he decided. Not quite yet. So he lifted the phone above his head, threw it down with all his might into Brian's groin. That was the end of Brian's resistance. He lay on the floor, moaning and twisting in agony, spitting blood, his hands shoved between his legs.

'Let me explain something to you, Brian, now that I've got your attention.' Justin was surprised how calm his voice sounded. 'My name is Westwood. Justin Westwood. I'd like to hear you say it.'

Brian did his best. Through his broken teeth, it came out, 'Ussin Esswood.'

'If I hear you call me anything but that again,' Justin said, 'here's what's going to happen. Because you're such a big, tough guy, I'm not going to fight fair with you ever. You're going to be walking down the street, nice and relaxed, maybe even with a girl if you can get one to look at you again now that you're uglier than shit and your dick's gonna be broken for a while. And what I'm going to do is take my gun out, the gun I'm going to carry at all times now, and bring the butt down on the back of your head and crush your fucking skull. Do you understand?'

Brian managed to nod his head and say, 'Ah unnersan.'

'Good,' Justin said. 'I'm glad.'

Chief Leggett came rushing out of his office then, saw Justin standing over one of his young cops, saw the other young cop, Gary, standing several feet away, paralyzed, his mouth open in dumb shock.

Jimmy Leggett looked up at Justin Westwood, looked back down at the floor.

'You better clean yourself up,' he said to the terrified Brian. 'You're a pathetic mess.' And to Justin Westwood he said, 'Maybe you should take the rest of the day off.'

'I was just leaving,' Justin said.

As he gathered up the papers off his desk, shoving them into his small satchel, and took the gun out of his drawer, making sure that Brian saw it, Justin realized something that surprised him. Since his wife and daughter had died, he had felt, almost every minute of every day, as if he were choking to death. There was a weight on his chest and his breaths came in short, shallow bursts. He could not take in much air. When he went to that first shrink, the one the force had insisted he go to, he had told her that he hadn't been able to breathe since it had all happened. She asked him what air meant to him. That was her exact phrase. At first he hadn't understood what she was asking, he wanted to say, 'This isn't a fucking abstraction here, I can't breathe!' But he thought about her question for a few seconds, then he said, 'Life. Air is life.' She had nodded and said, 'That's right. That's exactly why you're having trouble breathing. You can't let any life back in to you.'

He accepted what she said. It made sense. It didn't help, though, not a bit. But he believed that she was right.

What surprised him now, as he walked back out onto

the streets of East End Harbor, was that, for the first time in so many years, he did not feel that heavy pressure in his lungs. His chest was rising and falling in a slow, deep rhythm, letting air in, easing it out.

Justin looked down at the knuckles of his own right hand, saw that they were speckled with drops of Brian's blood, and he thought: *I'm breathing again.*

CHAPTER ELEVEN

Justin drove into Weston, Connecticut, exactly three hours and fifteen minutes after he left East End Harbor. On the ferry ride across the sound, he sat in his car, never even got out to lean over the railing and take in the fresh air. While he sat, he didn't listen to the radio, didn't read the newspapers. He just stared at a small spot on the windshield, stared through it really, trying to make sense of all the pieces of information he'd managed to put together. William Miller's age. The murder of Susanna Morgan. The disappearance of Wallace Crabbe. He tried to keep his thinking as linear as possible, tried to keep his mind open to any and all possibilities that might pop into his head. None of that mattered. He came up with no connections, no logical conclusions. When the ferry landed on the Connecticut side of the water, he had exactly as many explanations as he'd had when the trip started: none.

He consulted his fold-out map, basically figured out how to get to Old Post Road, but when he filled up the gas tank of his four-year-old Honda Civic, he decided to play it safe and ask for specific directions. It didn't take him long after that before he was on the rural-sounding Old Post Road, which turned out to be a decidedly suburban-looking thoroughfare. A few blocks later, he was in front of the address he had for Edward Marion. It wasn't a house or an apartment building. It was a fairly large office building in the middle of a small strip mall. Although it was not what he was expecting, he realized he was not surprised.

There was no Edward Marion listed on the tenant directory in the lobby. Nor did the security guard know the name. The phone company information showed that the number that Susanna Morgan had dialed was in room number 301. The directory had that office being occupied by a company called Growth Industries, Inc. Justin asked the security guard what he knew about the company and the answer, also unsurprising, was absolutely nothing. Justin then asked the guy what his name was. He half expected the same answer: I don't know. But this one the guard knew. He said that his name was Elron.

Justin wondered why Elron was called 'security' guard because when he asked if he could go up to the third floor and Growth Industries, the answer was, 'Why not?' So he took the elevator up, walked down the hallway until he came to a door with the right number and the name of the company on it. He rang the buzzer and when nobody answered, knocked loudly. Still no answer. Justin stuck his ear against the upper part of the door, which was beveled glass, but heard nothing. There didn't seem to be anyone there. At 3:30 in the afternoon on a weekday. Either

Growth Industries was not a very well-supervised company or . . .

Or what?

Justin decided his imagination was running away with him. The various answers to his question all suddenly seemed foolish. *Or* it was a front. *Or* it didn't really exist. *Or* . . .

Stop it, he told himself. *This is exactly what you don't do as a cop. You don't imagine. You go for logic. You latch on to what's real and understandable. There are no 'ors' in police work. You eliminate them. That's your entire job. You eliminate them and that's how you find what's real.*

Justin went back down to Elron who, miraculously, knew how to reach the building manager, a man named Byron Fromm. Byron Fromm turned out to be puffy and pale and maybe forty years old. When Justin showed him his badge and explained what he wanted, Byron Fromm got even puffier and paler.

'Well, have they done anything wrong?' he wanted to know.

'What I'm trying to do, Mr Fromm, is actually find out who *they* are.'

'You mean Growth Industries?'

Justin nodded. 'What do they do?'

'Well,' Fromm said, his voice rising a notch above its normal pitch, 'they're in market research.'

'For whom?'

'Don't know. For whoever hires them, I guess, but that's really none of my business.'

'Do you know how long they've been here?'

'They were our very first tenant. They've been here

since we opened in 1972. You know, at the time, we were the only mall in town. This was a very classy address then. It still should be but they've kind of let it run down a bit.'

'And who is that?'

'The real estate company that built it. Alexis. The Alexis Development Company.'

'Why do you think they've let it run down?' Justin asked.

'Why? Why does anybody do anything? Or rather, not do anything? Money. Either they don't have it or they have it but don't want to spend it. Those are the only choices, aren't they?'

Justin had to agree with him. But those choices weren't what interested him. 'Do you know who owns this building?'

'I work for the people who manage the mall. That's who I know. I deal with the individual tenants. I'm responsible for upkeep, within a budget, and day-to-day stuff like security and tenant complaints. The owner deals directly with my contact at Alexis. Bert Stiles.'

'Growth Industries,' Justin said, 'they pay their rent on time?'

'Never been a minute late.'

'Why do you think there's no one there right now? This is prime business time, right?'

'It should be. Although, I gotta say, this place hasn't had a prime business time in quite a few years.'

'Mr Fromm,' Justin said, slowly, 'how'd you like to let me into room three-oh-one?'

'Detective, I would be happy to. Except I quite like this job. It's easy and they pay me really well. And, aside from the fact that you don't have a warrant . . . *do* you have a warrant?'

'No.'

'You're not even local. So I can't see as there's anything in it for me at all if I let you in. Except trouble.'

Justin decided he'd hold off on his answer, give himself a few seconds to see if he could think of something other than trouble that just might be in it for Mr Byron Fromm, but before he could come up with anything, his cell phone rang.

'Yeah?' he said, answering it.

It was Jimmy Leggett. 'Where the hell are you?' the chief said. 'Actually, I don't care where you are. Just get the hell back.'

'I thought it was my day off,' Justin said.

'Not anymore,' Leggett said. 'The shit's hit the fan.'

'What happened, Jimmy?'

'We got another body, that's what happened. We got another goddamn body.'

'Who?'

Leggett told him who it was and Justin heard his own sudden intake of breath.

'Where?' he said. 'When?'

'I can't give you any details over the phone. Just get back here.'

'All right,' he told the chief, glancing over at Byron Fromm. 'I just need about half an hour here to—'

'No half-hour,' Leggett cut him off. 'I've been ordered to get you back asap.'

'You've been ordered?' Justin asked. 'Ordered by who?'

'By me,' a strange voice said over the phone. Justin

could hear the receiver being wrested away from his boss.

'Who the hell are you?' he demanded.

'Special Agent Leonard Rollins. FBI. And that's the end of your little Q and A, Detective. Get your ass back here. Now.'

Justin heard the receiver at the other end of the line click off. His cell phone went dead. He stared at the pale, overweight man standing in front of him. Another harsh rock song blared into his head. Nick Cave. *Is there anybody out there, please? It's too quiet in here and I'm starting to freeze. Under fifteen feet of clear white snow . . .*

The words and music felt as if they were going to smother him. It's exactly the way he felt: freezing and isolated, buried under an unbearable weight.

'Something wrong, Detective?' Byron Fromm asked.

'Yeah,' he told the building manager, and he thought the man looked a little too gleeful, as if whatever information had just been transmitted over the phone had somehow gotten him off the precarious hook he was on in his shabby and getting shabbier suburban sanctuary. 'Life's about as wrong as it can possibly be.'

CHAPTER TWELVE

efore leaving the Weston mall, Justin went into a Barnes & Noble, strode over to the magazine rack and stared at the rows of new magazines. By his count, eight of them had a picture of Maura Greer on the cover. Maura Greer, the one-time East End Harbor townie turned Washington intern who'd been missing for four months. The girl whose body, according to Justin's frantic boss, had just been found floating in East End Bay.

Justin flipped through several of the magazines, read a page of Dominick Dunne's theorizing in *Vanity Fair*, checked out what Mark Singer had to say in *The New Yorker*. He bought them both, along with a copy of *Jump* magazine. He drove back to the ferry and, as it cruised across the sound back to Long Island, he read the piece in *Jump*. Then he read it again. And then a third time.

And he began to wonder if East End Harbor would ever again be the quiet little town it had been just a week before.

From the July issue of *Jump* magazine; cover story:

Health, Wealth and . . . Death?
by
Leslee Carter Reese

On the day her daughter Maura disappeared, Rachel Greer had a psychic experience.

It had never happened to her before, not like this. Before this particular Thursday it was just the usual I-knew-who-was-on-the-phone-the-moment-it-rang or I-was-just-thinking-about-you-exactly-when-you-called kind of thing. But on February 21, at 4:15 in the afternoon, she felt a chill sweep through her entire body. The feeling was both disturbing and enthralling. It was as if a ghost had plunged inside her, filling her with the frigid sensation of death and the glowing power that she is now convinced came with her brief foray from this world to the next and back again.

There is little question in her mind that a ghost did, in fact, plunge inside her.

There is also little question in her mind that the ghost was her 24-year-old daughter, Maura Devon Greer.

Maura, who has been living in Washington, D.C. for the past eighteen months, interning at the Food and Drug Administration, has been missing for four months. She has, in essence, disappeared off the face of the earth and her disappearance has not only caused scandal, it has disrupted the political landscape in a way not seen since the emergence of Monica Lewinsky or Chandra Levy. It has stirred widespread national debate from both the left and right about the nature of the media. In our post-September 11 world we were all going to be focused on the serious and pressing issues that swirl around us. The emphasis on celebrityhood was over, as was our obsession with scandal, sex and frivolity. Yet, since this young Jewish girl disappeared, newspapers, magazines, television and radio call-in shows seem to have done little but speculate about the sordid details of Maura Greer's life and presumed death.

It is essential to the well being of the United States and our efforts to cope with the potential threat of biological warfare that the Secretary of Health and Human Services, Frank Manwaring, function without distraction. Instead, the search for Maura Greer has damaged Secretary Manwaring's credibility, possibly beyond repair, and put a stranglehold on his effectiveness.

But most of all, Maura's disappearance has caused heartache for her family. In the midst of our global obsession with terrorism, it is easy to forget that there are other, smaller tragedies in life. Unless, of course, you happen to be living in the middle of such a tragedy.

Maura Greer left her one-bedroom apartment in Washington, D.C. at approximately four o'clock in the afternoon on Thursday, February 21. It is presumed that she went to pick up her car, a three-year-old Silver Honda Accord, in the underground garage beneath her apartment building. Although she was not spotted there, the garage was vandalized and the attendant, Hector Diaz, has also been missing since that day. (For a time, Mr Diaz was a suspect in the disappearance but police have since ruled out that possibility.) According to a neighbor who saw her in the hallway on her way out, there was nothing about Maura's demeanor that struck him as strange. He did say that she was dressed rather provocatively but Maura usually dressed provocatively. She had never been a shy girl and that aggressiveness carried over to her sexuality. She was never afraid to voice her opinions or take over a room with her personality or use her body to give her an advantage. There was only one area of her life about which Maura seemed to turn inward, reticent to reveal details even to her closest friends: her relationship with the current man in her life.

'For the longest time, she would talk about it only in vague generalities,' said her best friend since childhood, Gay Chilcott. 'I'd ask her who she was seeing and she'd get this beatific smile on her face and say things like, "You'll meet him soon," or "It's going really well but I can't talk about it yet." It didn't take a genius to figure out she was going out with a married man. From a few hints that she dropped, it was pretty obvious it was also an older married man. Then, about two weeks before she died . . . I mean, disappeared . . . she became a little more open. Started revealing a few details. She told me that he was fifty. And that he was a great lover. She also told me he was very important and she made it pretty clear he was with the government. One of the last times I talked to her on the phone she said that there was a decent chance she'd get to go to the White House and meet the President soon.'

According to friends and family, Maura's affair had been going on for at least six months, probably closer to eight. Those who knew about the affair also knew that she expected her lover to leave his wife – and marry Maura.

'She was certain that she was going to be the winner in this relationship tug-of-war,' Chilcott says. 'I told her that men do sometimes leave their wives – but I sure as hell wouldn't count on it. But people believe what they want to believe in situations like that. And Maura believed that everything would end up happily ever after.'

So far, things have ended up anything but happily. Whether that unhappiness is forever depends on two things. Will Maura Greer turn up alive? And what will happen to her married lover – our current Secretary of Health and Human Services, Frank Manwaring?

Manwaring has denied any role in Maura's disappearance. For weeks he also denied that he and the young intern had been having an affair but recently, as incontrovertible evidence of the affair was publicly released by the Greer family, the Secretary made a televised confession and apology. Maura's parents do not believe the confession went far enough. And they most certainly do not accept the apology.

'He denied his relationship with Maura until we

forced him to admit it,' says Maura's father, Marcus. While Rachel is strong and definite in her belief that their daughter is the victim of foul play, Marcus can't speak about Maura without weeping and he says he prays every day for her safe return. 'Everything Frank Manwaring says has been a lie – until someone forces him to tell the truth.'

Having an affair, of course, is a far cry from committing murder. And while it's not been proven that everything Secretary Manwaring has said about his relationship with Maura Greer has been false, many of his statements have been reticent and incomplete. Police feel he has been less than forthcoming. Maura's parents believe he has not only hindered the investigation, they are convinced that he should be at the center of it.

On Friday February 22, Maura was supposed to come visit her parents in East End Harbor, a small town on the outskirts of Long Island's chic Hamptons. It was Marcus's birthday on Saturday and Maura was going to spend the weekend celebrating. Marcus had reserved an hour of tennis at a local indoor court on both Saturday and Sunday because Maura loved to play tennis and they had a friendly competition going back to Maura's teens. Rachel made a salon appointment for both mother and daughter on that Saturday afternoon. They were going to get facials, manicures and pedicures. 'She loved being pampered,' Rachel says. 'And I loved being able to pamper my daughter.'

Marcus went to the train station to pick up

Maura. She was supposed to arrive on the 4 p.m. train. But when the train pulled away and the platform was cleared of people, there was no Maura. 'At first I wasn't too concerned,' Marcus says. 'Maura was not always the most responsible person in the world, at least when it came to her parents. But when I called Rachel to see if Maura had called, she started talking about how she'd had a premonition. Rachel said that something bad had happened, that she'd felt it the day before but didn't say anything.' So when he got home, Marcus called the Washington, D.C. police and said that Maura was missing. The D.C. police asked a few questions and, according to the Greers, basically dismissed their concern. 'She hadn't been missing long enough to be "missing,"' Rachel says, her voice tinged with anger. 'We couldn't get them to do anything for forty-eight hours.'

When the police finally did decide to act, they went to Maura's apartment. What they found was a spotless home with alphabetized CDs, a closet full of designer clothes, and nothing but two cans of Diet Coke and two cartons of unflavored yogurt in the fridge. Oh yes. They also found Maura's purse. In it was her driver's license and all of her credit cards.

'Why would she leave her purse?' Rachel asks. 'We think it's because she was told to leave it behind. We believe that Secretary Manwaring didn't want her to meet him if she was carrying any identification. From the things that Maura said about the relationship, the man she was seeing was obsessed with secrecy. He had all sorts of rules for her to follow when she met him. We believe that this was one of those rules. It's why we believe she was on her way to meet him when she disappeared.'

Manwaring did indeed try to keep the affair secret. Not only is he married with two college age children, he is in a highly visible and sensitive cabinet position, appointed by a president whose popularity is partly based on his constant reaffirmation of his belief in and the country's need for faith and traditional family values. He is the tough, honest, anti-scandal leader. That is the image he ran on, it is the image that has kept his poll numbers higher than any president in recent memory, and it is the image he insists on maintaining for himself and his advisors. Manwaring's affair does not conform to that image. It is not just damaging to the President on a political level. According to several advisors, it offends the President's personal sensibility.

Although Manwaring at first denied that he was meeting Maura the day she disappeared, the Greers also forced him to admit the truth about that. Maura had a reservation at a local Marriott Hotel and was due to check in the afternoon of February 21. Manwaring admitted, nearly a month after Maura went missing, that he was supposed to meet her there and spend the afternoon and evening with her in the suite they regularly frequented.

Two weeks after Maura's disappearance, the D.C. police had uncovered no clues and had no leads in the case. They had not made a connection to Manwaring at this point. That came after the Greers got their phone bill. While scrutinizing it, Marcus Greer noticed that there were several long distance calls made that month to a Washington number he was unfamiliar with. He realized that the dates of the calls coincided with the last weekend that Maura had visited East End Harbor. He mentioned this to Rachel, who immediately went to the phone and dialed the number. It was a pager. Fifteen minutes later, the Greer's phone rang. The call to the pager was being returned. The person who returned it was Secretary Frank Manwaring.

The Greers asked Manwaring if he knew their daughter. He was nonplussed, they say, and evasive. He refused to speak to them. They immediately took their information to the Washington police. It took the police another four days before they contacted Manwaring. They came to his D.C. apartment, interviewed him for half an hour, then released a statement that the Secretary knew Maura Greer, they were friends and nothing more, and that he had absolutely nothing to do with her disappearance. The police announced that he was not a suspect.

The media immediately jumped on the story. Two days after it was made public, a woman named Eva Grey called a press conference. Ms Grey is a lap dancer at a Washington club called Privates. At the conference, she revealed that several years earlier she had had a four-month-long affair with Secretary Manwaring. The affair ended, she said, when she confronted him about his promise to leave his wife. According to Ms Grey, the Secretary got violent during the conversation. She alleges that he choked her until she almost passed out and told her that if she ever brought up the subject of his divorce again, he would make sure she disappeared. Secretary Manwaring immediately called a press conference to say that not only was Ms Grey's story untrue, he had never met her or heard of her.

In the weeks that followed, two other women came forward with similar stories. One woman, Esther Forrester, is a secretary at a Washington insurance company; the other, Felicity Black, is an out of work advertising executive. Both said that when their affairs with Secretary Manwaring became serious they talked to him about his promise to leave his wife and he became enraged and violent and ended the relationship.

At this moment, the various mysteries remain as such. What will happen to Frank Manwaring? He denies having ever met Ms Grey or either of the two other women. He did – nearly a month after Maura's disappearance – admit to the affair with her but denies knowing anything about what has happened to her. There has been a tremendous public outcry for Secretary Manwaring to step down from his cabinet position, something he has thus far refused to do. There is also great political pressure being put on him to resign. The head of the Food and Drug Administration, where Maura Greer was interning and where she met Mr Manwaring, is Chase Welles. Mr Welles is the man most often rumored to be Mr Manwaring's replacement. Welles has a close relationship with the President and his positions are often much more in line with the President's. Manwaring and the President have differed publicly on the question of stem cell research. The President has signed a bill restricting such research and is on record as opposing it on religious and moral grounds. Mr Manwaring is a vocal proponent of the need for such research. Mr Welles has stated that he believes the President is on the side of the angels when it comes to this issue.

Welles and Manwaring have also clashed repeatedly and angrily over the past several months, particularly over the potential ban of Rectose 4, a new drug that passes fat through the body without being absorbed. Since Rectose 4 appeared on the market just over twelve months ago, there are reports that sixteen people who have taken it have died. Secretary Manwaring infuriated lobbyists and drug companies, particularly the KranMar Corporation – which has donated large sums of money to the President in the past and which holds the patent on Rectose 4 – by demanding that the product be taken off the market. Mr Welles has opposed Secretary Manwaring's demands, saying that the drug is safe and has been properly tested and approved. He has implied that he believes Manwaring's decisions are suspect and steeped in corruption. He has not accused Mr Manwaring of taking bribes from KranMar's competition but it has not been difficult to read between the lines of Mr Welles's criticisms.

Secretary Manwaring did not return phone calls

asking for a comment for this article, but a close friend has said that, 'He feels that his mistakes have been of a personal and private nature. He has committed no crime and has told no lies. In this time of perpetual national crisis, he feels he is the best man to hold his position and he intends to hold it until he is asked to step aside by the President of the United States.'

At the heart of it all is, of course, the question of what has happened to Maura Greer. Is she dead, as her mother believes? Or will she suddenly return home, safe and sound, as her father so desperately hopes?

Right now, there are no answers. There is only the missing 24-year-old woman, whose disappearance reminds us that tragedies do not only happen on grand and global scales.

They happen to everyday people in everyday life.

When the ferry docked, Justin Westwood drove straight to the East End Harbor police station. During the fifteen-minute drive, he tried to figure out how Maura Greer's body had wound up back in her home town. Had she come into town without telling her parents to see some-one? A lover? That didn't make sense, not if the stories about her relationship with Frank Manwaring were to be believed. So why would she come back without telling anyone? And if she hadn't come back, how did she wind up in the water there?

When he arrived at the station, Justin quickly learned

that several of the mysteries he'd just read about surrounding Maura Greer and Secretary Frank Manwaring had now been solved.

He learned that at 4:30 that morning Hank Lobel, a local resident who made his living installing sprinkler systems, had taken two buddies out on his 26-foot Hunter 260 for a day of sailing, beer and fishing in the waters of East End Bay. A fishing line had snagged on something in the water. Under the influence of many cans of Budweiser, the men refused to cut the line, determined to haul in whatever was causing the problem. After a lengthy struggle, they dragged in the decayed and gnawed-upon body of Maura Greer. By the time Justin returned from Connecticut, the coroner had determined that Maura had not drowned but rather had been killed – her neck broken – before being put in the bay. The lengthy investigation into her disappearance was now a murder investigation.

As soon as the news had leaked out about the discovery of Maura's corpse and the ensuing coroner's report, a CNN report revealed that Frank Manwaring had been in East Hampton, just several miles from where Maura's body had been found, soon after she disappeared. That was four months ago – the approximate length of time the coroner estimated the body had been in the water. Minutes after that report aired, the Secretary of Health and Human Services was asked by the President of the United States to resign. Chase Welles, head of the FDA, was immediately named as Manwaring's replacement and there was expected to be no trouble with his confirmation. The President called a press conference and read a

151

prepared statement that said: 'I wholeheartedly believe in Secretary Manwaring's innocence. I believe his statements that he had nothing to do with the tragic death of Maura Greer and I accept at face value his rejection of all the other charges and accusations that have been leveled at him. However, in these very dangerous times, the fact that the Secretary is now involved in a murder investigation, however peripheral his involvement, will be such a major distraction that I no longer feel he can fulfil his duties in a timely and competent manner. I am confident that Chase Welles will be a superb Secretary, more than capable of handling this crucial Cabinet position.'

At his own press conference, Frank Manwaring declared his innocence in Maura Greer's murder. He also reiterated the fact that all the other women who had revealed their relationships with him were lying. 'For what reason, I don't know,' he said. 'I assume that greed enters into it and it is a sad day when greed overcomes any and all sense of morality.' He refused to comment on his replacement other than to warn against changes in current policy. Secretary Manwaring also said that he would no longer comment publicly on the Maura Greer situation. He had been told to keep silent from this point forward. When asked who had told him to keep silent, the Secretary declined to comment.

Rachel and Marcus Greer held a press conference, too. They tearfully expressed gratitude that they at last had some closure but said that, of course, their gratitude was tainted by their sorrow. They stated that they did not believe Secretary Manwaring's declarations of innocence and ignorance and they demanded that he take a lie detector test. When that demand was relayed to Frank Manwaring, he nodded and said that he would be happy to take such a test, but before he could finish making a commitment, he was hustled away by two aides.

Justin learned all this from Special Agent Len Rollins of the FBI. He learned from his boss, Jimmy Leggett, that the Maura Greer murder now took precedence over the investigation into Susanna Morgan's death.

'Since when is one murder more important than the next?' Justin asked.

'I thought you said he wouldn't be any trouble,' Agent Rollins said to Leggett, not even bothering to look at Justin.

Leggett, slowly shaking his head, said, 'The media's going to be all over this, Jay.' Leggett sounded rattled. Scared. 'I'm sure I don't have to remind you that we're not exactly the New York City police department and that this is not our area of expertise. I'm not telling you to forget about Susanna Morgan, I'm telling you there are priorities.'

'What are the priorities?' Justin said, looking straight at Rollins. 'You guys covering your ass because you didn't do shit for four months and now you've got a body so you're looking kind of stupid?'

Rollins smiled and nodded. It was not a friendly smile. It was the smile of someone who was acknowledging that he'd do whatever it took to fight back and win. Rollins looked as if he knew a lot about winning, too. He was six-one, maybe six-two, a muscular two hundred pounds. Justin guessed that he'd played college football. Or had spent a few years in the marines. He had the aura of someone who didn't shy away from physical contact. He was in his mid-forties with dark hair that didn't show any signs of thinning. Justin decided that this guy was a player. His instinct was immediately proven correct.

'I know all about you, Westwood,' Agent Rollins said. 'We checked you out. You may have been a hot shit guy at one time in your life, but that doesn't mean fuck all right now. I'm not looking to be a hard-ass but it won't bother me, either. There's shit going on that you don't know anything about and my guess is you never will. But Maura Greer is my priority. It's the government's priority. You don't want to go along with that, fine. You want me to get you put on permanent leave, no problem, that can be arranged in about a minute. You want to stay on the job and collect your paycheck and do what you've been doing for the last six years, which is getting drunk and handing out parking tickets and feeling sorry for yourself, what you do is say, "yes, sir" to me whenever I tell you to do something and otherwise you stay the fuck out of my way. Is that understood?' When Justin didn't say anything, Rollins took the hard-ass edge out of his voice and said, as if they were best friends talking about nothing more important than borrowing a lawnmower for the day's chores, 'I can use you, Jay, you mind if I call you Jay? I know you know what you're doing, you've got more experience than anyone else. I value that. I can use you here. But if you don't want to be used, say so now, because I promise you, if you fuck around with me I'll step on you like the frightened little bug that you are.' The smile came back on the FBI agent's face and so did the edge in his voice. 'Now is that understood?'

Justin narrowed his eyes and tried to take a deep breath. He felt his lungs contract, realized his breathing would only come in short, quick gasps. He exhaled twice, ran the fingers of his right hand through his hair. Out of the corner of his eye he caught the two idiot cops, Gary and Brian, looking in at him from the other room, waiting to hear his response. Brian's mouth seemed to be stitched together. Two teeth were missing and the lower half of his face was as swollen as a balloon. Despite that, Justin could see the smirk there. He could see the pleasure Brian was getting from his eavesdropping.

Justin thought of many things he wanted to say to Special Agent Len Rollins. He ran through all of them in his mind, which is why it took him so long to respond. But when he finally did speak, what he said was, 'Yes, sir, it's understood.'

'Good,' Agent Rollins said. 'Now here's your first assignment. Try not to get too drunk tonight. Take tomorrow off. Don't do a thing. Relax and get used to the fact that we're in charge now. I want you to forget about this Susanna Morgan thing for the moment. Whatever you think is going on there, it doesn't matter. Don't worry about it. I've talked to the Middleview police and the East Hampton force and they're on top of it. It's their case now. I've made Officer Meves their contact in this office.'

'Officer Meves . . .?' He suddenly realized that Rollins meant Brian. *Brian* was in charge of the Susanna Morgan investigation? 'For Chrissake . . .'

'For Chrissake *what*, Detective Westwood?'

'The girl was murdered,' Justin said. 'That's got to mean something.'

'It does. It means that it's being handled in exactly the manner I've just described to you. We have other priorities. Have I made myself clear?'

'Yes.'

'Yes what?'

'Yes, sir.'

Agent Rollins let his face relax. His eyes revealed no emotion other than pleasure in the fact that he'd just won. 'Day after tomorrow, I want you here at eight a.m. sharp. We'll have your assignment for the Maura Greer case.' Justin didn't respond, just stood silently until Agent Rollins said, 'You're dismissed.'

Justin nodded, turned on his heel, strode past Brian and Gary without looking at either of them, marched out the front door, went straight to Duffy's Tavern, told Donnie the bartender to bring him a double scotch. He proceeded to stay there for four hours. He didn't leave until he was positive he was drunk enough that for the rest of the night, until whenever he woke up the next day, he couldn't possibly speak or think or feel or, most important of all, dream.

CHAPTER THIRTEEN

When Justin woke up, he wasn't sure exactly where he was. He thought he might have passed out in Duffy's and was coming to on the floor by the bar. It seemed a realistic enough possibility that one of his first hung-over reactions was to get angry at Donnie for not getting him home and letting him spend the night sleeping on a bed of hard wood in puddles of spilled beer and whiskey.

When his brain cleared a bit more, Justin realized that he was not sprawled on a barroom floor. He was in his own home. But not on his bed. He hadn't made it that far. He hadn't even made it to the couch. He'd managed to get into his living room, take a few steps and collapse on the coffee table.

He took a deep, wheezy breath, kept his eyes open for several seconds, trying to clear the haze behind them, and forced himself to stand up. The move wasn't one of his major successes. He felt himself bob and weave and sway. But he stayed up. He took one step toward his bedroom, had to stop when he was overcome by the urge to puke his guts out. It was while he was standing there, trying to keep his balance and whatever was in his stomach in there, that he heard it. At first he couldn't place the noise. It sounded like birds squawking. Then he realized it was the buzz of a crowd. Human voices, talking. It seemed disconnected from his environment but he began to understand that the noise was close by. He managed to take several steps over to his living room window, looked outside on his small front lawn and saw that the crowd was standing in front of his house. There were several vans, all with television station logos on their sides. One had a satellite dish perched on top of it. A row of cars was parked on both sides of the street. Twenty or thirty people stood peering in at him. Several of them had cameras. When Justin's face appeared in the window, the cameras started clicking and the crowd began to vibrate.

Justin jerked away from the window, making his head feel as if it were going to topple off his neck. He took several more deep breaths, a foul odor emerging from his mouth, the taste of whiskey and bile forging up his throat. He tried to piece together what was going on. Something to do with the discovery of Maura Greer's body, that much was clear. But why the hell were the jackals pursuing *him*? He looked at the clock that rested atop the living room mantle. One o'clock. Jesus. He'd slept half the day away.

Before anything, he knew he had to clear his head. So he went into the bathroom, popped four asprin, brushed his teeth, turned the shower on as hot as he could stand it, and stepped in. As the water streamed down, he slowly turned the knob until it was ice cold. He was awake.

Toweling off, Justin went into the kitchen, grabbed a large bottle of water out of the fridge and drank half of it in one gulp. He went back to the living room, turned on the television, surfed the channels until he came to CNN. Maura Grecr was the story. And it was a big one. The media had already sunk its shark-like teeth into it and they weren't going to let go until it had been torn into tiny little pieces. He pressed the mute button on the remote control. Sat there trying to absorb what was happening. When he looked up, what he saw on the TV screen surprised him so deeply that he dropped the remote. It was Brian Meves, his fellow East End cop. Brian's mouth was still stitched and swollen, his face still puffed out from the beating Justin had given him. But he was being interviewed by some blonde woman. She had a microphone shoved up to his battered lips. Justin found the remote, fumbled with the buttons, finally got the sound back on, heard the end of the interview, heard Brian saying, 'We didn't know anything about his background. He's not much of a talker. It's all been a big shock, on top of, you know, what happened to Maura. Let's face it, the guy basically had a nervous breakdown, so that's not exactly who you want in charge of a murder investigation. His recent assault on me shows that he's not exactly stable. So yeah, I can verify the fact that he's off the case—'

What? Off what case? What the hell was the idiot talking about?

Justin clicked off the TV, ran to the front door, opened it a crack, just wide enough to pull the newspapers in off the front mat. The second the door opened, he heard questions being hurled at him from the curb. The words didn't make any sense to him, it was just one loud roar. He slammed the door shut, backed over to his couch as if he were facing down a pride of lions in the jungle.

He sat and read the front page of the New York *Times*. The entire right-hand side of the page was devoted to the discovery of Maura Greer's body. He read through to the break, didn't find any crucial details he hadn't learned the day before, other than the fact that the weekend Frank Manwaring, the Secretary of Health and Human Services, had been in the Hamptons he had several hours that could not be accounted for. It led to even more suspicion that he was involved in the murder and disposal of the body. Justin turned to page eighteen to finish reading the story. But he didn't get to continue with it. On the center of that page was his photograph. And above it was a headline: TRAGIC HERO IN THE MIDDLE OF TWO MURDERS. He read what they had to say about him. The journalist had more than done his homework. He'd talked to cops up in Providence. He rehashed Justin's history up there. He told the story of the deaths of Justin's wife and daughter. Justin stopped reading halfway through. His eyes ran back up to the headline. *Two* murders.

He skipped ahead until he read it.

Jesus Fucking Christ.

The reporter had gotten to Brian. The idiot cop had spilled his guts. He told everything he knew about Justin. Talked about his personality. His violent temper that had erupted when he'd attacked his fellow cop. And Brian said that Justin Westwood had been working on another murder case, the murder of a local journalist named

160

Susanna Morgan. Justin pictured him smiling as best he could through his injuries as he bragged that he was now in charge of the investigation and revealed that there had been a witness to that murder, a woman who had been interviewed by the East End Harbor police and who had seen everything that had happened. She was their best lead, Brian Meves said.

Justin dove to the telephone, grabbed the receiver and dialed the police station. Gary answered the phone, sounding tense and nervous.

'Where's Brian?' Justin said. 'Put him on the phone.'

'Eastwood? I mean . . . Justin . . . uh . . .'

'Get your fucking friend and put him on the phone!' Justin screamed.

'He . . . he hasn't come in yet.'

'When did he do the TV interviews?'

'What? I . . .'

'Gary, for Chrissake, I just saw him on TV, when did he tape that?'

'Last night. They talked to both of us. Around ten, I guess. I watched it last night around eleven.'

'It aired last night?'

'Yeah. They must be showing it again.'

'Did he talk about Susanna Morgan?'

'I . . . I don't know.'

'Did he say she was murdered? Did the moron say that last night on TV?'

'Yes. Yeah, I guess he did.'

'Where the hell is he?'

'I . . .'

'Where *is* he?'

'I don't know. He was supposed to be here at nine. He hasn't shown up yet. We've been calling him but there's no answer. We figured—'

'Where does he live?' When Gary didn't answer, Justin screamed into the phone: 'Give me his goddamn address!'

Gary rattled it off. It wasn't far from Justin's house. Maybe a couple of miles. Off in one of the newer developments in East End, the kind that was destroying whatever pretense the area still had of being rustic and charming.

'What's going on?' Gary asked. 'It's been insane here. The media—'

'Go over to Brian's now,' Justin said. 'If he's still alive, get him the hell out of there. If he's not, just wait for me.'

'If he's still alive? What the hell are you talking about?'

But Justin didn't wait to hear any more. He slammed the phone receiver down, pulled on a T-shirt and jeans and laced up a pair of sneakers. He looked at the folder he'd taken from his desk at the station, grabbed it. Then he saw what else he'd taken from the station and he picked that up, too. His gun. A .357 Magnum.

He fished in his pocket for his car keys and ran out the door. More questions were shouted at him but he didn't even hesitate. Justin ran straight for his beat-up Civic and turned the engine over. One of the journalist's cars was partially blocking the driveway. Too damn bad. Justin backed up at full speed, ramming it out of the way. As the rest of the reporters scrambled like mad to get to their cars, Justin put the pedal to the metal. His tires screeched, the back of the car fishtailed, and then he was on his way. Three blocks away, when he had a little daylight between

162

him and the jackals, he swerved the Civic into a dirt driveway. It led to a house he knew was at least two hundred yards further up the path. He drove another fifty feet, out of view of the road and the house, slammed on his brakes and turned off the engine. He forced himself to wait five full minutes, until he was satisfied that the reporters on his tail had to be scattered all over the place. Then he pulled out of the driveway, his wheels spinning, the car fishtailing again as he made a left, and drove back into town.

He was almost certain that the asshole was already dead. Justin wouldn't miss Brian or mourn him. He knew enough about death to know that it didn't change what you were when you were alive. The guy was a jerk. Now he was a dead jerk. Justin wasn't a romantic when it came to death. Nor was he a hypocrite.

He was also not a praying man. Nor did he much believe in happy endings. So as he sped toward Deena Harper's apartment on Main Street, he didn't pray and he didn't expect to find that things were all right. The best he could do was hope against hope that he wasn't too late and that, if he was right about Brian, he could be wrong about Deena and her little girl, and maybe, just maybe, they were still alive.

After turning the doorknob to no avail, knocking as hard as he could and yelling out her name, Justin lowered his shoulder and charged the door. It splintered open and his force carried him through into Deena's living room. He called out her name and then her daughter's, ran from room to room, but the apartment was empty. No Deena. No Kendall. But also no sign of violence, so maybe there really was a chance. Just maybe . . .

Justin heard a noise behind him and he didn't think, just reacted, whirled, reaching for his gun. He felt a sinking sensation in his stomach, knew he was dead if they wanted him dead, looked up, trembling, surprised to find he wasn't afraid, was almost relieved. But it wasn't anyone who wanted him dead. It was Deena, who was staring at him like he was a lunatic, shifting her gaze disbelievingly back and forth between him and the shattered front door.

'What the hell are you doing?' she said.

He didn't give her a chance to say anything else. 'Where's the kid?'

'Kendall? Why? What . . .?'

'Where is she?'

'At a friend's house. What's going on?'

'What friend? Someone you know?'

'Of course it's someone I know. She was at school and her friend's mother picked her up. I have a class to teach, then I'll go get her. Now what is going on and what are you doing breaking into my apartment?'

'Do you have any idea what's happened today?'

'No. What do you mean?'

'Have you seen the paper?'

'No. Not yet. I was practicing with my teacher all morning. He was out in Montauk and—'

'You got two minutes to pack some clothes. Just take enough for a few days.'

'What are you talking about? I can't just pack up and leave!'

'Two minutes. Then we'll get Kendall. You've got to get out of here.'

'What is going on?' she demanded. 'I'm not doing anything until you tell me what the hell you're talking about!'

'What I'm talking about,' Justin said slowly, 'is that whoever killed Susanna knows what you saw and knows who you are. My guess is they've already killed one person to get that information and I guarantee you they're on their way here right now, if they haven't been here already, so they can make it a doubleheader.'

She stared at him wide-eyed. 'I'll pack,' she said quietly.

'You're down to one minute,' he told her.

Art, the owner of Art's Deco Diner, placed two mugs down on the table. He had done his best to keep track of who got what, but when he set the mugs down he was too disoriented to remember. 'I gotta admit,' he said to the two blond men sitting in the booth, 'you screwed up my system. Who gets the peppermint tea?'

The blond man to Art's left raised his hand. The one to his right said, 'I get the English Breakfast.'

'I gotta say, you two guys look *exactly* alike. Can anyone tell the difference between you?'

'I'm the nicer one,' the one on the left said.

Art laughed, said, 'I'll remember that for next time,' and went back behind the counter. He didn't pay much attention as the two men sipped their tea and stared out the bay window that overlooked Main Street. He didn't hear the one on the left, the nicer one, say, when Justin Westwood's car raced up and pulled to a stop in front of

Deena Harper's apartment, 'You were right, there he is.' And he didn't hear the other one say, 'I told you we should have gotten the kid. This guy could screw us up big time now.' Art was aware that the first one lowered his voice, but the voice was too low for him to hear the customer say, 'Relax. Let's just go find out what the hell we're supposed to do now.' He certainly didn't hear the other twin's final words, which were, 'Well let's at least *try* to kill them both. We deserve *some* fun, don't we?' The only thing Art was really aware of was that when he looked up, the two identical-looking men were gone. They hadn't bothered to get a check but they had left ten dollars on the table, more than enough for two measly cups of tea.

Deena insisted that Kendall sit on her lap in the front seat of Justin's Civic. The little girl was squirming, wanted to sit in the back like a grown-up, but her mother wouldn't let go of her. She kept squeezing her and hugging her and caressing her until the girl finally said, 'Mommm, this is 'barrassing.' Then Deena let her climb over the seat and go sit in the back, telling her to fasten her seatbelt, which made her say, 'Mommmm' again because she'd already fastened it.

After picking the girl up at her friend's, Justin headed straight for the address that Gary had given him over the phone. When he pulled up to Brian's house, Gary's car was already parked in the driveway. He'd definitely heeded Justin's words and come in a hurry. His rear wheels were on the ragged gravel, his front wheels were perched on the too green sod of the front lawn. Justin told Deena and Kendall to wait where they were, to not move, then he stepped out of the car and headed toward the front door.

Gary was standing in the small entryway, by the archway that led into the living room. He was breathing through his mouth, and breathing heavily. Underneath the young cop's running shoes, Justin saw a small puddle of vomit on the green carpet.

Justin thought about telling Gary that there was no way to have prevented this. It fit the pattern. And it had been the smart play. It was time to understand that they were up against serious people who didn't make a lot of mistakes. And when they did make a mistake they fixed it. Immediately.

They had wanted information out of Brian and as soon as Justin stepped past Gary and into Brian's living room, he knew they'd gotten that information.

Brian Meves was sitting on a folding metal chair. His hands were tied behind his back; the rope that was used was also looped around the back of the chair. Brian's feet were bound together and connected to the two front chair legs. He was completely immobile. And he was naked. Not a stitch of clothing on.

The scars and wounds from the beating that Justin had given him were of little consequence now. Whoever had killed him had used matches to get what they wanted. Brian's hair, feet and testicles were burned black. When Justin looked at the expression on the dead man's face, he turned away and felt his stomach heave. It wasn't just the flavor of last night's whiskey that rose through his chest and throat. It was the taste of almost unimaginable

167

brutality and violence. And it was the taste of Justin's own past. He took a deep breath, looked to his left and saw Gary watching him. Their eyes met and Justin nodded. The nod said that it was all right to be sickened by what they saw.

He sat down on Brian's couch. Noticed small piles of matches discarded in the ugly green shag carpet. He gathered his strength, shook his head and tried to find some reserve of pity for the victim. In truth, he found none. Brian had been given a glimpse of what it was like to play with men who were out of his league. Justin had given him that glimpse just two days before and the kid had a chance to get out of the game. But Brian was a man who didn't learn his lessons easily. So he'd learned the hard way. And now he didn't have to learn anything else ever again.

Gary, on the other hand, was learning quickly. It was a lesson that would stay with him the rest of his life.

Justin Westwood stood up, walked over and touched Gary Jenkins lightly on his shoulder.

'I'm out of here,' Justin said. 'Give me five minutes, then call this in.'

Gary nodded but didn't say anything.

'You'll be all right,' Justin told him.

Gary still didn't say anything, but this time he didn't nod.

Justin went to the front door and opened it, strode back to his car.

'Did you find what you were looking for?' Kendall asked him.

He looked at the little girl, who was still in the back seat, seatbelt fastened.

'Yes, honey,' he said. 'I found exactly what I was looking for.'

Justin decided to stay on the back roads, avoiding the crowded highway, Route 27. He didn't know where he was going to go, he just knew he had to get Deena out of town and to someplace safe. He found himself heading in the direction of the ferry that would take them to Shelter Island and, eventually, back over the Long Island Sound to Connecticut. It took him a moment to realize why his instincts were leading him back in this direction and then he nodded, satisfied with the decision. What the hell, he thought. If at first you don't succeed . . .

Trying to keep everything as normal as he could, he said to the woman, 'Check out the glove compartment, will you? Why don't you put on a CD?'

She opened the compartment, picked through the musical selections. 'Tom Petty?' she asked.

'Perfect,' Justin told her.

Deena took the CD out of its plastic holder and squinted at the radio/CD player inserted into the dashboard, trying to figure out exactly how to work it.

'Give it to me,' Justin told her.

'No, no,' she said. 'I'll do it.'

She leaned over to get a better look at the controls. And the second her head bowed down, the window on her side of the car exploded.

Deena didn't seem to understand what had happened. She started to bob back up but Justin grabbed the top of her head with his right hand and shoved her back down toward the floor. Her back – along with the car seat and the entire front of the car – was covered with shards of sparkling glass. He glanced back, making sure that Kendall was all right. Her eyes were as wide open as they could be and she had a small trickle of blood on her cheek, where she'd been cut by a piece of flying glass. But she wasn't hurt badly and she didn't look hysterical, only confused.

Justin realized his foot was pushed down hard on the accelerator and the car swerved to the left, crossing over the single yellow line. A truck was coming in the opposite direction, bearing down straight at them. The truck driver had his hand on the horn and the deep, violent blare cut through the silence of the afternoon. It also cut through Justin's paralysis. He tried frantically to steer with his left hand, realized he was losing control, let go of Deena to grab the wheel with his right and turned hard. He wasn't sure it was going to hold. The back of the car hung back, for a moment it felt like they weren't moving at all, like they were simply hovering on the wrong side of the road, then they straightened out and jerked forward and Justin yanked the wheel again, hard right. As he slipped back across the yellow line, the truck roared past. The driver still had the horn pushed down, and he was screaming obscenities at Justin out the window. But Justin didn't pay any attention to him. A car had been parked on the shoulder of the road. It was non-descript. Dark color. Some kind of American boxy piece of crap. The Civic had driven by it at the exact moment the window had exploded. And he realized now that the same car had passed them by a couple of minutes earlier, sped past them at one of the few straight-aways on the curvy back road. It had passed them by just to park on the shoulder. He checked the rearview mirror. The dark car wasn't parked any longer. Now it was back on the road. It was in hot pursuit.

Justin floored the accelerator, kept it floored until he came to the first turn-off he could take. A small road leading up into the woods. He didn't know where it led, but he decided to take it. And take it at full speed. The dark car followed, its tires squealing as it made the sharp turn. Justin heard the ping of metal hitting metal. There had to be two men in the car because shots were being fired from the passenger seat, probably trying to take out a tire. He kept his foot pressed down, urging the car forward. A quarter of a mile later, he saw another turn-off and he took that, too. It led through an open iron gate. The Civic was pushing seventy and now it was slicing through the grounds of some kind of institution. Justin saw a building ahead of them and drove straight for it. In the mirror he saw the dark car appear and make the turn. He jammed his foot down on the pedal as hard as he could. When he went over the first speed bump he thought that Deena might actually go flying right through the roof. But he refused to slow down and she grabbed at the door handle for something to hold on to. He saw the dark car stop short. He watched as it quickly went into reverse, backed out of the gate, turned and disappeared. By the time Justin screeched to a full stop he realized they were safe. The dark car had called it quits.

He tried to orient himself. They were surrounded by acres of lush green grass, with patches of water and sand scattered about. Then it hit him. They had stopped in front of the austere clubhouse of the East End Golf and Tennis Club. The serenity was startling. There was no noise at this place. No movement. Certainly no sense of any urgency or that anything more crucial than a make-able three-foot putt might be happening anywhere in the world. He looked out through the windshield, which was badly cracked now, to see every caddy, golfer and pro shop worker standing in place, frozen, staring at the car.

The whole thing, from the moment the bullet had hit the window until now, had taken maybe sixty seconds.

'Are you all right?' he asked Deena.

She turned to the back seat, reached behind her and pulled Kendall back up to her, squeezing her even harder than she had before, saying, 'Are you all right, baby?'

Kendall's only response was, 'That was fun. And I'm not a baby.'

When Deena kissed the girl on the forehead, she said, 'You're bleeding!' but Kendall brushed her fear aside and said, 'I'm okay.' When Deena touched her daughter's cheek, the girl said, 'I'm okay, Mom. Really.'

Deena turned to Justin now, said, 'What happened?'

'Somebody took a shot at us. At you.'

'Who . . . How . . . Where . . .?'

'I don't have answers to any of that.'

'What are you going to do? They're getting away. Aren't you going to go after them?'

'Not with the little girl here,' he said. 'I'd never find them anyway. And I didn't get the license plate or a real make.'

'I'm not a baby or a little girl,' Kendall said. 'I'm almost eight.'

'You're right,' Justin said. 'I apologize.' And then in a stage whisper, he added, 'I'm just trying to make your mom feel better.'

The girl nodded at him, understanding. Justin reached into the left front pocket of his pants, was pleased to find his cell phone was still there. He dialed the number of the police station. Gary answered the phone and when he heard who it was, he didn't even bother to answer, he just yelled across the room, 'It's Westwood, sir. He's on the phone.'

Justin heard some vague movement in the background, then Agent Len Rollins was talking to him.

'Where the hell are you?' Rollins said. Then, without waiting for an answer, said, 'It doesn't matter. I want you to get here immediately.'

'No can do, Agent Rollins, sir,' Justin said.

'What did you say?'

'I said I can't . . . let's see, how would you FBI assholes put it . . . I can't comply with your orders. Sir.'

'Detective Westwood, we have an emergency situation here and I want you at the station immediately.'

'I'm with Ms Harper,' Justin said. 'And her lovely daughter.' He winked at Kendall and she nodded approvingly. 'My priority is getting them to a safe place.'

'This station will be plenty damn safe,' Rollins said. 'Bring them in now.'

'Maybe you haven't heard, Agent Rollins, sir. One police officer's already been killed . . .'

'I've heard. And I've seen.'

173

'But I don't think you've heard that somebody just did his best to take us out.'

'What are you talking about?'

'Somebody just took a shot at us. I'm not feeling as if East End Harbor is the safest place to be at the moment.'

'Where are you?'

'Try another question.'

'Goddamn it, Westwood! Where are you taking them?'

'Not sure yet. But when I am . . . well . . . I'd like to say you'll be the first to know, but I'd probably be lying. It's my belief, *sir*, that the reason my fellow officer had his balls burned off is because you fucked up. So I think I'd rather take my chances on my own for the moment.'

'Detective Westwood, I will personally put out a federal warrant for your arrest. Do you have any idea how much trouble you're going to be in if you don't get over here and bring your witness with you?'

'I have a pretty good idea,' Justin said. Then he added, 'Sir,' one more time. And then he hung up.

They all stayed silent in the car for a few moments. Justin saw several people from the clubhouse now start to slowly and cautiously move toward them. Justin realized he hadn't turned the motor off. He shifted the car into reverse, backed up and turned around, and slowly began heading back down the long driveway, away from the building and the golfers and East End Harbor's most visible symbol of luxury and ease.

'What are we going to do?' Deena said, her voice huskier and more tremulous than he'd ever heard it.

'We're going to find out what the hell is going on,' Justin told her.

'And once we find out?'

'Then we'll be able to do something about it.'

'Like what?'

'Get the bad guys, put them in jail, and go back to our normal lives.'

Deena looked at Kendall, who was peering at her anxiously. She forced herself to smile at her daughter and smoothed the dirty blonde hair back off the girl's forehead. 'Do you really believe that?' she asked Justin. 'About solving everything and making sure everything's going to be okay?'

'You don't know me very well, do you?'

'Is that a yes?' she asked.

The car pulled slowly out onto the street and turned left. With his right hand, his shirtsleeve pulled up over his fingers to protect them, Justin wiped some of the broken glass off of the top of the dashboard. With his left hand, he steered the car toward the ferry.

'That's a big fat no,' he said with a shrug. 'But I'll do the best I can.'

BOOK TWO

CHAPTER FOURTEEN

Thanks to the sheer stupidity and laziness of Elron Burton, it was extremely easy to break into the Growth Industries office on the third floor of the Weston Connecticut strip mall.

When the car ferry landed on the other side of the sound, Justin drove towards the mall, taking the most circuitous route possible to make certain that no one was following them. No one was.

When he finally felt comfortable enough to drive along the main road, they immediately hit a stretch of pure Americana – nothing but fast food restaurants and enormous car lots. At the second lot that they came to, Justin turned in. He told Deena and Kendall to feel free to stretch their legs, said he'd be back in a few minutes, then walked over to the white and blue trailer that served as the main sales office. Fifteen minutes later, Justin returned, holding a set of car keys. He pointed at a blue-gray 1997 Buick Regal Sedan.

'What's this?' Deena asked.

'Our new car,' he said. When her eyes widened, he

pointed to the shattered window on his battered Civic and said, 'This is not what you'd call traveling incognito.'

He opened the door to the Buick and as she stepped inside, Deena said, 'You can afford to just buy a new car?'

'It's amazing what a cop id can do,' he said. 'It not only lowers the price, it gives you good value on a trade-in.'

'I'll try it next time I'm in the market,' she said.

He pulled back onto the main road and three blocks away from their final destination, he found a perfectly acceptable looking but non-descript motel, a Hamptons Inn. He checked in – two adjoining rooms – and took the keys. He didn't bother to put their small bags in the rooms. He didn't even bother to *look* at the rooms. He just got back in the Buick and drove them all away.

Justin's next stop was the mall, where he hit a men's clothing store and bought himself a long-sleeve dress shirt and a sport jacket. Deena made a face at the tie he picked out for himself, so he let her put it back on the table and make another selection. He had to admit – actually, she made him admit – that she had superior taste in ties. He told her what he had in mind and they decided his jeans and running shoes would suffice.

Two stores down from the clothing store was something called The Ultimate Wireless Connection. Justin popped in and twenty minutes later popped out carrying two new cell phones. He got another questioning look from Deena and said, 'Anything that makes us harder to trace, that's the idea.'

The third shop was a liquor store where Justin bought a bottle of scotch.

Then it was on to Growth Industries.

As they stood in the parking lot, twenty feet or so away from the building, Justin hoped desperately that the same dullard of a security guard would be on duty, then he told Deena exactly what he wanted her to do and say. She nodded dubiously. They both looked at Kendall, who nodded solemnly and said to both of them, 'Don't worry. It sounds like a good plan.'

Then Justin headed off to another part of the mall. Deena and Kendall waited exactly fifteen minutes, as instructed, then Kendall reached out, took her mother's hand, and they started walking.

As Deena and Kendall strode up to the security guard, Deena gave him a big smile and said, 'Hi, Elron.' He smiled familiarly, nodding as if he recognized her. Elron rarely recognized anyone, there were too many people who came in and out. He knew the really fat guy who worked on the second floor and always wore a bright yellow tie. And there was an old guy he remembered because he was always complaining about something, usually Elron. Other than that, he was fairly oblivious. But he always liked it when someone said hello to him and he always made a point to respond in kind with a friendly nod or even a 'Howdeedoo.' He had no memory of ever seeing this one before, but he'd never let her know that. He was a professional, after all.

'Can you believe it?' Deena said, lingering by Elron's podium. 'Mr Hemmings is making me work tonight. He just called me, told me to meet him here. I was supposed to have the day off. Now I'm supposed to come, just like that, at six o'clock. My guess is he won't even stay. He'll just dump everything on me and head off. I'll probably be here till nine or ten! I mean, what could be so important that it couldn't wait until tomorrow?'

'Doesn't seem fair, does it?' Elron said.

'It's *not* fair. I couldn't even get a sitter. Now my daughter's got to spend her evening in the office!'

'Cute little one,' Elron said. 'What's her name?'

'Lucy,' Kendall piped up. 'Nice to meet you.'

'Well, try not to work too hard,' Elron said, as Deena and Kendall headed toward the elevators. 'Either one of you.'

As the elevator door closed behind them, Deena looked at her daughter and said, 'Lucy?'

'I always wanted to be named Lucy.'

'You did?'

'See?' Kendall said with a smirk, just as the elevator door opened and let them out on three. 'You don't know *everything* about me.'

Five minutes later, they were both back in the lobby, in front of Elron. Deena was looking as miserable as possible.

'Mr Hemmings is going to *kill* me,' she said. 'I'm supposed to open up the office for him and I don't have my key. I can't believe it. This has never happened to me before. He is *really* going to be furious . . .'

'Uh . . .' Elron said. He didn't have much more to contribute, since he didn't have any decent solution to the problem. Then he suddenly thought of something. 'Maybe he'll bring *his* key.'

'Oh, right,' Deena said. 'Like Hemmings has actually

got a key. The guy makes me turn on the *lights* for him, for god's sake.' She glanced over toward the front door, as if fearful that her boss would arrive before she'd solved the problem. 'No, I just called Mr Fromm at the management office.' She held up her cell phone, as if to verify that she'd made the call. 'It was the only thing I could think of. He said I should come back down here, that you had a skeleton key and could let me in.'

'Well . . .' Elron said, and didn't say anything else for a moment because he couldn't think of anything else to say.

'You can wait up there with me until Mr Hemmings comes in. I mean, if that'll make you feel more secure about letting me in.'

'I can't really do that. Somebody's got to be down here in the lobby.'

'If you give me the key, I can let myself in and then run it right back down to you.'

'Maybe I should call Mr Fromm, just to double check.'

'He was on his way out, so I don't know if you'll get him. But here.' She held up her cell phone. She wondered if Justin had gotten to the building manager and managed to keep him away from the phone. She remembered the final detail that Justin had told her to add. It had a fifty-fifty chance of working, he'd said. 'Just press re-dial,' Deena told the security guard. 'It's the last number I called.'

'No need,' Elron said, waving the phone away decisively then reaching for his key ring and handing it to her. 'It's not like you're gonna lie to me, are you? A regular tenant like yourself.'

'Not me,' Deena said. And looking down at her little girl, added, 'And certainly not Lucy.'

Ten minutes later, Justin strode by Elron. It was 6:30 now, time when anyone coming into the building had to sign in. Justin wrote down the time and the name Ward Hemmings. Kendall had come up with the first name of Ward. Elron glanced at the signature, then up at the man. This one he recognized, he thought. He had definitely seen this Hemmings guy before, so he took the initiative and said, 'Your secretary's already up there, Mr Hemmings. Nice lady. Very professional.'

'Glad you think so,' Justin replied. 'She can be pretty damn forgetful sometimes.'

'Not tonight,' Elron said. 'She's got everything under control. You can count on her.'

'That's good to know,' Justin said. 'That's really good to know.'

When Justin walked into room 301, he saw that Deena had an expression on her face as if to say: *What the hell is this?* When he looked around the office, he understood the expression. He had the same one on *his* face.

The Growth Industries office was one fairly large room, maybe 20 feet by 20 feet. There was one chair in the room, set up in front of a small desk. The desk had no paperwork on it. There was nothing on it – or in it; Justin immediately opened up all three drawers to check – except a blank yellow legal pad and three ballpoint pens.

Other than that the only items in the room were nine small tables. On each table were two telephone/answering machine combinations. Eighteen phones and each one was connected to a separate jack in the wall. Justin walked slowly to one of the phones, picked it up and dialed a number. A recording immediately came on and he hung up.

'Can't call out,' he said to Deena. 'These are for incoming calls only.'

'What kind of office is this?' she asked.

Justin shook his head. He went around and checked all the machines. Not one of them showed that any messages were waiting to be picked up. He went to one of the machines, pressed the menu button and followed the instructions until he could play the outgoing message. A man's voice came on and announced, 'You've reached Ed Marion. I'm not at home right now. Please leave a message after the tone and I'll return the call as soon as I can. Thank you.' He did the same on each machine. Nine of them had the same message from Ed Marion, the man who'd said he was William Miller's nephew. Nine of the phone machines had identical messages but they weren't left by Marion, they were left by a woman, Helen Roag. Justin looked up, saw the question in Deena's eyes, shook his head again because that was the only answer he had. He took a deep breath, pulled out his cell phone and dialed. In a few seconds, his call was connected.

'Gary, it's Westwood,' he said, and before the cop at the other end of the phone could sputter his name or say anything at all, he added firmly and loudly, knowing that the tone would stop Gary cold, at least for a few seconds,

'Don't say anything. Don't let on who you're talking to. You understand?'

'Yeah, but . . .'

'Just listen to me. I'm going to ask you to do me a favor. It means you're going to have to trust me. And I'm going to have to trust you. I don't want you to say anything to Rollins or even to Jimmy.'

'Why not?'

'Because I don't know who's involved in what. Or where there are leaks. And I don't want you to end up like your pal Brian.'

There was a long pause after that. Then Gary said, 'What makes you trust *me*?'

'Because of what you saw and what I think that probably did to you.' Justin then breathed out a faint laugh. 'And because you told me to stop smoking. It was a nice thing to say and you looked like you meant it. It's pretty thin but it's all I've got right now.'

There was another long pause. Justin was certain that the images from Brian's living room were running through Gary's mind.

'What do you want?' the young cop asked. And by the way he lowered his voice, Justin knew that he was going to go along with him.

'I need more phone information. Similar to what you got for me before.' He gave him Growth Industries' address and the names of Ed Marion and Helen Roag. 'There are eighteen phone lines coming into that office. I want the records of every incoming call on all of those numbers for the last three months. That's one thing. I also want you to find out who gets the bills and where they're sent. And I want you to get me as much information as you can on Marion and Roag. Check the tri-state area and Massachusetts, too. I want to get a home address and any phone numbers, including cells. I want *anything* you can get on them. I'm guessing on the spelling of Roag, but if you don't find anything, run through any variation that makes sense.'

'Yeah,' Gary said. 'I got it.'

'I meant what I said before, too.'

'About what?'

'About keeping this quiet. And about staying alive.'

'How do I get the stuff to you?'

'Take my cell number down. When you've got it, call me and we'll figure it out. Don't leave the number lying around, either. Don't let Agent Rollins see it. Or Jimmy either, for that matter. Try to be smart here.'

'What's going on?' Gary said. And suddenly he didn't sound like a cop. He sounded like a scared 24-year-old kid.

'I don't know,' Justin told him. 'But I appreciate the help. And the first day I can, I'll take you out for a drink as a little thank-you.'

'I didn't know about you.'

'What?'

'I didn't know all the stuff that's come out, that's been in the news. I mean, I didn't know what had happened to you.'

'No,' Justin said. 'You wouldn't.'

'Well, I read all about it. And Jimmy told me some stuff, too. Since it's out in the open now.' When Justin didn't respond, Gary said, 'I just wanted to say I'm sorry.'

'It was a long time ago, I guess.'

'They're pretty pissed off at you here. You watch yourself.'

'Ditto,' Justin said. 'If they know you're doing this, they'll be pretty pissed off at you, too.' And then he hung up.

'What now?' Deena asked.

Justin looked at Kendall, leaned down so they were eye to eye. 'Is there one food your mommy doesn't like you to eat?'

'More than one,' Kendall said. 'She's a health nut, you know. Right, Mom?'

'That's right, sweetie. I'm definitely a health nut.'

'Well, what's the worst?' Justin asked.

'A tie. Chocolate and French fries,' the little girl said.

Justin stood up and stretched his arms. 'I'm starving,' he told his two traveling companions. 'What say we go out and get some French fries and chocolate? I think we all deserve it.'

CHAPTER FIFTEEN

The dream came again that night.

He shouldn't have been surprised. Even as he woke up, felt his shortness of breath, Justin knew that this dream wasn't merely a gut-wrenching reminder of the past. It was a warning about the future. About the violence and danger and death that was all around them.

His instincts had dulled but they had not completely disappeared. His nostrils were filled with the scent of fear. What he didn't know – what one never knows, he thought – was whether he would be strong enough to fight off the fear and make sure they all survived.

It's why the dream kept haunting him, he understood that. It wasn't just the losses that he'd suffered. Nor was it the exposure to genuine malevolence. It was the despairing feeling in the pit of his stomach that told him he hadn't been strong enough – or quick enough, or smart enough, or tough enough or mean enough or caring enough – to protect the people he had loved.

It had been his fault, everything that had happened. His choices. His decisions. His stubbornness. His life.

Their deaths.

The dream was shorter tonight. It spared him the pleasure and brought him right to the pain. He woke up to the image of himself, lying on the floor, feeling the river of blood spread beneath him. He could feel himself turning and he could see the remarkably vacant eyes staring down at him. It was a new detail, these eyes, and it forced him to remember that they had not been hate-filled or vicious. They were the eyes of a sociopath, calm and unemotional. They were the eyes of someone doing his job. Doing what he had been bred to do.

The image of Lili's body was there, of course. Broken and crumpled. And he could see her eyes, too. Desperate and sad, in so much pain. Confused and pleading with him for help. In real life, there had been no pleading. Things had happened too fast. But in his dream, the sadness in her eyes lingered long after her life had ended.

Alicia's eyes were in the dream, too. Large and round and brown. And accusing. Staring and accusing.

Then there was the final bang, the last shot, it filled his head like an explosion, and then he woke up to find himself sweating and afraid of the violence that was sure to come.

Justin heard a door swing open and suddenly the dream didn't matter. He hurled himself toward the bed table, grabbed the gun. His hands were shaking as he pointed them toward the door, toward the figure that was standing in the shadows. He exhaled a long and quivering breath when he heard a woman's voice say, in hushed tones, 'Are you all right?'

Justin focused his eyes on Deena, peering at him from

behind the door that linked their adjoining rooms. He put the gun down.

'You cried out,' she said. 'I heard you. I thought . . .'

'I'm fine,' he told her.

'I got frightened.'

He nodded. 'Yeah. Me, too, I guess.'

'Did you have a bad dream?'

He thought for a moment, then shrugged. 'Just the usual.'

'What do you dream about when you have bad dreams?'

'Just life,' he said, putting his gun back down on the nearby table. 'That's all it takes.'

Neither of them said anything for several moments. Then Deena whispered, 'Well, I better go back to bed. Kenny's still sleeping. Nothing seems to wake her up.'

He watched her disappear and close the door behind her. He looked at the cheap, plastic clock radio by the side of his bed. It was 5 a.m. Justin decided to turn his light on. He would stay awake now.

No more dreaming today.

CHAPTER SIXTEEN

At 8 a.m., she knocked on his door. Justin cleared his throat, called out for her to come in. When she did, he could see that she was wearing shorts and a T-shirt. Her legs and feet were bare. Instinctively he tried to cover up the glass of scotch that he was holding.

'I meant to tell you this yesterday,' she said. 'I want you to tell me how much all this grandeur' – she waved her hand around the motel room – 'costs. You're doing enough for us. So I just want you to know I'll pay you back. I don't know how long we're going to have to be doing this, but whatever it is, I'll pay my way. And Kendall's, too.'

'Don't worry about it,' he said. 'I can cover it.'

'Is East End Harbor doling out six-figure salaries to their police force now?'

'I can afford it,' Justin told her. 'You've got other things to worry about. But I appreciate it.'

She looked at him curiously, and he knew she was wondering about his secrets, but she didn't say anything, then she gave her lopsided half-smile and said, 'I'm going to work out. You want to join me?'

'You mean, like . . . exercise?'

'Exactly like exercise,' she said, brushing one of the curls away from her face. 'I thought maybe I'd give you a yoga lesson.'

'I don't think so.'

'If you won't let me pay you, at least maybe I can make you feel a little better.'

'I feel fine.'

'Is that why you're drinking at eight o'clock in the morning?'

'I've already been up for three hours. So by my body clock, it's really lunchtime.'

She just stared at him. Finally, he put the glass down and said, 'Okay. Let's exercise.'

She led him nice and slowly through a series of stretches as well as various positions with odd names like Downward Dog and Upward Dog. He felt extremely awkward and strangely vulnerable; he also was embarrassed because he knew he was out of shape. She kept trying to get him to repeat the Sanskrit versions of the names of the exercises, which he deliberately mangled to annoy her a little bit. Within ten minutes, he was dripping sweat onto the motel room wall-to-wall carpet and feeling his muscles ache and his tendons stretch. She, on the other hand, wasn't even breathing hard.

'You're not in very good shape for a cop,' she pointed out.

'I haven't been a real cop for a while. I'm a little rusty.

And aren't teachers supposed to be supportive of their eager students?'

'Stop stalling and get into squat position.' When he didn't move, she said, 'I know you know what that is. We just did it.'

'I know what it is. But if I squat right now, I'm just going to warn you that several of my body parts might never return to normal.'

'I'll risk it,' she said.

So he made a face and contorted himself into a squat, his arms pointed straight up, his palms together. Then he was made to twist into two or three other positions he'd never dreamed existed. And he had to admit that she was a hell of a teacher. Using her body to gently position him, showing him what the poses were supposed to look like without showing off her superiority. She was extremely strong and extraordinarily limber. He liked listening to her, too. Her voice had a way of lulling you into a spell, so the whole session took on a kind of vague other-worldliness. It was as if she were keeping the real world temporarily at bay, which he realized was not such a bad idea at the moment.

One of his cell phones rang half an hour into the lesson. He was relieved to be able to stand up and stop working his out-of-shape body. But he instantly missed the touch of her hand, the feel of her weight against his.

'Yeah,' Justin said into his phone's receiver.

'I've got some information,' Gary said on the other end of the line. 'What's going on? You sound out of breath.'

'Don't ask,' he said. 'Where are you calling from?'

'The station. No one else is here.'

'Okay, what have you got for me?'

'Just about everything you wanted. You got a pen?'

'Go.'

'There haven't been a lot of incoming phone calls to Growth Industries. I've got three in the last month, a total of eight in the past three months.'

'Eight phone calls in three months? For eighteen phone lines?'

'Yeah. Well, seventeen now. The one that Susanna Morgan called's been disconnected. Even so, if they're sellin' something, I hope they're getting a good price for it, 'cause they ain't doing a lot of business.'

'You have the numbers of the incoming calls?' Justin asked.

'Yeah. They're all from the northeast. Massachusetts, Vermont, New York, one in New Jersey.' As Justin wrote, Gary read out each of the numbers of the incoming calls and matched them up to the Growth numbers they came in on.

'Okay,' Justin said. 'Next.'

'None of the bills for the eighteen lines go to the Growth address. Nine of them are sent to a company called the Ellis Institute and nine are sent to something called the Aker Institute.'

'What the hell are those?'

'They're research firms.'

'How do you know that?'

'I called 'em,' Gary said.

'What kind of research?'

'Medical. Ellis is in New York. Aker's in Boston.' He

gave Justin the phone numbers and addresses for both firms.

'Do we know who the bills go to at the firms?'

'Yes we do. Edward Marion at Ellis. Helen Roag at the other one. But listen to this. When I called both places, I said I wanted to talk about a bill that wasn't paid. I used the names of companies that had called in to the phone machines.'

'And what happened?'

'I got the run around. I couldn't get past Marion's or Roag's assistants. They both said that those bills weren't paid there. They're always forwarded on to something called the Lobster Corporation for payment.'

'And what's that?'

'No idea. They wouldn't give me a phone number or address. They said they'd look into it but that's as far as they'd go.'

'Son of a bitch,' Justin said. 'I'm impressed as hell, Gary.'

'Thanks. But there's more on Marion. I've got his home phone and address. He lives in Connecticut. His cell must be a company phone because I couldn't track it.' He gave the information to Justin, then did the same for Helen Roag. 'She lives in Boston. Actually, just outside Boston, in Marblehead. You did have the spelling right, by the way. It's R-o-a-g. And I've got her cell number, too.' He passed that along, then verified it after Justin read it back to him.

'You did a great job, Gary. I want to thank you.'

'Don't you want to know what else I got?'

'I didn't ask for anything else. I can't *imagine* anything else.'

'I know. But I figured you might be a little busy wherever the hell you are. So I called those numbers, the ones that made the calls to Growth Industries.'

'And?'

'And it's pretty weird.'

'How weird?' Justin asked.

'Very weird,' Gary answered. 'Every place that called? Every one of them's an old age home.'

Elron Burton had been feeling proud of himself ever since that secretary from Growth Industries had locked herself out of the office. There'd been a problem and he'd solved it. No fuss, no muss, no need to bother the big boss. So when that boss, Byron Fromm, came striding through the lobby that morning, Elron gave him a big smile and a wave and said, 'Problem solved, bossman. Everything was a-okay last night.'

'What problem is that, Elron?' the chubby, jello-like Fromm asked.

'The problem with the lady who locked herself out. I let her in, just like you said.'

'Let *who* in? And when did I ever say to let *anybody* in?'

'The lady from Growth. You know, up in 301. She got locked out and she called you and you told her to come see me . . .'

From the look on Byron Fromm's face, Elron had the sinking feeling that maybe he hadn't solved the problem. Maybe he'd created the problem. He wished he'd kept his big mouth shut.

'You'd better tell me the story from the beginning,'

Fromm said, and he looked mighty scary for someone with such a soft body.

'Yes, sir,' Elron said. And he told.

'That's amazing.'

Justin and Kendall were watching Deena finish off her yoga exercise. Justin had just seen her do something where she went from standing straight up, slowly bent over backwards and kept going down until the top of her head was resting on the floor. From that position, she slowly lifted her head up again, then uncurled her back until she was absolutely straight. Now Deena was balancing herself on her hands while her legs were bent backwards and wrapped around her own neck.

'This isn't an actual human position,' Justin said. 'I never saw anyone make herself so small.'

'The point is balance,' Deena said, not even breathing hard. 'Not size. I'm perfectly balanced.'

'You could also fit into somebody's briefcase.'

'I don't think you're grasping the finer concepts of the practice.'

'No,' Justin agreed. 'I think you're going to have to work on it with me. I'm mostly focused on the fact that your feet are in a place I can't even get my hands to.'

Deena now slowly unfurled her body and lay on the floor, rhythmically breathing in and out. She crossed her legs, bent her head forward until the crown touched the floor, told Justin that she was sealing the practice. It wasn't until she'd lifted her head that Kendall asked, 'So what do we do now?'

Justin looked at his watch and said, 'Your mom's gonna take a shower, you get to watch TV, and I'm going to start running up our phone bill.'

Byron Fromm sat in the office of Bert Stiles, the head of the Alexis Development Company. Bert had been silent for quite some time now. All he did, as Fromm sat there, was run an emery board across the tops of his fingernails. Occasionally, he would pick up a nail clipper and use it to clean a nail or pinch off an untidy cuticle. The man was obsessed with his nails, was always buffing them or polishing them or neatening them. Watching him, Fromm began to fidget uncomfortably.

'Do you want to talk to Elron yourself?' Fromm asked when he couldn't stand the quiet or the filing any longer.

Stiles shook his head, put his hands together and placed the well-manicured fingers under his chin.

'Is there anything else you want me to do?'

Stiles nodded but still didn't speak. He pulled his hands from under his chin, stared at the nails and began filing again.

'What?' Byron Fromm asked. 'What do you want me to do?'

'This Elton,' Stiles finally said.

'Elron,' Fromm corrected. 'It's Elron, not Elton.'

'Byron,' Bert Stiles said. 'I don't give a rat's ass what his name is. What I want to know is if he has any idea who these people were.' When he raised his voice, he ran the emery board a little harder and faster.

'He doesn't. But I do.'

199

'You?'

'I can't be sure. I mean, I didn't see them. But the guy, he sounds like someone who was around here two days ago. And then again yesterday. The first time he was trying to get into the Growth offices. I didn't let him in. The second time, he insisted on talking to me out of the office, said it was too confidential to discuss inside. But it was just bullshit. I decided he was a nut. But now I realize it was right around the time of the break-in. I went outside with him because he said he was a cop and I think he might be. Not local, though. He showed me his badge but it wasn't from around here.'

'Where was he from?'

Fromm shook his head. 'Long Island somewhere. He took the ferry over.'

'What about the woman?'

'I never saw her.'

'Do you remember the cop's name?'

Fromm shook his head again.

'But you can describe him?'

Fromm nodded this time. And, as Bert Stiles filed even harder and faster, Fromm described Justin Westwood as best he could. He was within two inches of the correct height, got the hair right and the body type, didn't know the eye color. When he was done, Stiles asked Fromm to repeat the description and, this time around, took notes, holding the pen very carefully and gently between his delicate fingers. Then he thanked Byron Fromm for coming to him with the information.

As Fromm walked out of his office, Stiles stared at the three-line phone on his desk. He sat there silently for quite a while, maybe ten minutes, not even bothering to use the emery board, until he decided he couldn't put the phone call off any longer. So he pushed down the button for line one, picked up the receiver and dialed, the whole time thinking he'd rather have his fingernails pulled out one by one than have the conversation he was about to have.

Justin hung up the phone, turned to Deena and Kendall, who were both doing their best to look elsewhere.

'I'll try one more,' he said.

'You're not very good at this,' Kendall told him.

'Thank you very much,' he said. 'I'm a little rusty at this kind of thing, too. And it's not easy getting information out of people when you don't even know what you're trying to find out.' He turned to Deena. 'I'm getting stonewalled. Whatever's going on, either none of the people at these numbers know about it or they know not to talk about it.'

'You still don't seem very good at it,' Kendall sniffed. 'And it's boring.'

'That's her new word,' Deena explained. 'Everything's boring.'

Justin held the phone out to the little girl. 'Would you like to try, Miss?' When she smiled a somewhat haughty smile and took the phone, Justin began dialing. Before anyone could answer on the other end, he shrugged at Deena, as if to say: *She can't do any worse than I've done.*

A moment later, Kendall was saying into the phone, 'Yes, I'd like to speak to my grandfather, please.'

Justin stopped his shrug. He looked at Kendall as if to say: *What* are *you doing?*

Next, they heard Kendall say, 'I don't really know his name. I just call him Grampy-gramps. But my daddy is Mr Edward Marion.'

Now Justin looked at Deena. This look said: *What the hell have you raised here?*

There was a pause, then they heard Kendall say, 'Yes, I'll hold.' She turned sweetly to Justin and said, 'He's getting the manager.'

Both Justin and Deena held their breath until the next thing they heard Kendall saying was, 'This is Lucy Marion. I'd like to speak to my grandpa, please.' The girl listened, then said, 'My daddy told me to call. It's Grampy-gramps' birthday.' The manager said something and Kendall responded, 'No, he's not here. I'm with the babysitter.' There was another pause while the manager said something into the phone, then Kendall broke into a huge grin. 'Yes. That's right. I guess I did know Grampy's name. Lewis Granger.'

She flashed a triumphant smile at Justin, then her eyes widened, and she looked confused. To the manager on the other end of the phone, she said, 'Yes. I'll hold.' She held the phone out away from her. 'He's getting the man,' she hissed at Justin. He nodded, said, 'You're my new hero,' and took the receiver. He waited for several minutes, then he heard an elderly man come on and say, 'Hello?'

'Mr Granger?'

'Who is this?'

'Mr Granger, my name is Justin Westwood . . .'

'What are they talking about, my granddaughter's on the phone? I don't have a granddaughter. She died years ago.'

'Mr Granger, I'm sorry, I'm afraid we lied about that. I just needed to talk to you and I didn't know how else to get you.'

'What do you want to talk about?'

Justin hesitated, then said, 'Growth Industries.'

The old man's tone got even sharper. More suspicious. 'You work for them? What happened to that Ed Marion?'

'I don't work for them. I'm trying to get some information about them.'

'What kind of information?'

'Just about anything you can tell me, sir.' There was no response from Granger. As the silence lengthened, Justin thought that the old man had hung up. 'Mr Granger? Are you still there?'

'I'm tired,' the man said. 'I'm very tired.'

'I can call you back another time, if you'd like.'

'I don't mean I'm tired right this minute. I mean I'm tired. Tired of everything. Tired of life.'

'I'd like to come see you, if I can.'

'See me?'

'Yes, sir.'

'Nobody's been to see me in years.'

'What about Ed Marion?'

'Oh yes. He comes. But he doesn't count. He just asks his questions and gives me the shots.'

'Shots?'

'I'm tired of those damn shots. I'm tired of everything.'

'Can I come see you, Mr Granger?'

'To ask me questions?'

'Yes, sir.'

'You won't believe my answers, you know.'

'Well,' Justin told him, 'I'd like to give it a try. How about tonight?'

'Tonight, tomorrow, the day after, the day after that one, doesn't make any difference to me. If there's one thing I've got,' Lewis Granger said, 'it's time.'

There was a very definite chain of command.

After Byron Fromm had passed his bad news along to Bert Stiles, Stiles made his own call, passed the same news along, and got reamed. The man who did the reaming was named Alfred Newberg. Newberg was paid over a million dollars a year to deal with bad news – to receive it and to pass it along to his employer. As expert a job as he did dressing down Bert Stiles, it was nothing compared to the verbal lashing he took over the phone. He did not defend himself nor did he offer any excuses. There were none to offer. He was paid his handsome salary – as well as given enormous loans at almost no interest rate and provided with regular use of a private jet, an extremely comfortable and luxurious Challenger – to take such abuse and then go out and solve whatever problem had arisen. So when the spew of obscenities began dying down and he heard the words, 'This is a very, very delicate situation, you do understand that?' he knew that the tirade was over and it was time for him to do his job.

'Yes, sir. I know exactly how delicate this is.'

'It's a Chinese puzzle we're involved in.'

'Yes, sir.'

'Do you know what a Chinese puzzle is, Newberg?'

'Yes, I do, sir. Boxes within boxes.'

'Exactly. And do you know what happens when one box is removed?'

'The puzzle doesn't fit together the same way.'

'It's worse than that. Much, much worse than that. The puzzle, the thing itself, is altered. It's not the same object. It becomes something different, something else entirely.'

'Yes, sir.'

'In other words, it's destroyed.'

'I understand that, Mr Kransten,' Newberg said. 'I understand what's at stake.'

'We are so close,' Newberg heard his boss say. 'We are so goddamn close. After all these years . . .'

'Yes, sir, I know.'

'I don't want to see it destroyed. I won't *let* it be destroyed.'

'It won't be.'

'Well, it might be if this goddamn policeman . . . what's his name?'

'Westwood.'

'Well, whoever the hell he is, he can't be allowed to come any closer. For god's sake, what the hell is he trying to do?'

'He's looking into what happened with Bill Miller.'

'Who?'

'Bill Miller, sir. The actor.'

'Right, right, right. What does he have to do with the policeman?'

'There was the incident with the woman. The reporter who wrote the obituary.'

'Oh, for Chrissake, it's ridiculous. Make him go away. Get rid of him.'

'I will.'

'Get rid of him *now*, before he pulls one of our little boxes away.'

'Consider him gone, Mr Kransten.'

There was a long silence and Newberg thought, perhaps, that the line was dead. But he heard the faintest wisp of breathing and then he heard Kransten say, 'You like using that plane, don't you, Al?'

'I like it very much. And you don't have to worry, sir. I like it too much to risk screwing this up. I just received a call from the manager of the Leger Home. That's the one in upstate New York, outside of Albany. He said that Lewis Granger received a call from his granddaughter.'

'Granger?'

'That's right.'

'Does he *have* a granddaughter?'

'No. I'm certain it was the little girl who's with the policeman. Her mother was the one who witnessed the . . . scene . . . in East End Harbor.'

'Careless. It's all been very careless.'

'Yes, sir. But I'm sure Westwood's going to see Granger. So we know where he'll be very soon.'

'How'd he track Granger down?'

'Possibly through Helen Roag.'

'Goddamnit . . .'

'Although it's more probable it's got nothing to do with her. He might have gotten on to Ed Marion.'

'Really?'

'Marion's the link. Between the woman in East End Harbor and now this.'

'Where'd you take it last week, Al?'

'Excuse me?' Newberg asked, momentarily thrown.

'The plane. The Challenger. Didn't you use it last week?'

'I did. Mexico. A resort south of Puerto Vallarta called Las Alamandas.'

'Nice down there?'

'Very.'

'Lot of nice places in the world, Al. A *lot* of nice places. I hope you get to see many more of them.'

'So do I. Believe me, so do I, Mr Kransten. So don't give the policeman a second thought. Or the witness. I promise you: they're as good as gone.'

CHAPTER SEVENTEEN

Ed Marion was confused and annoyed by the phone call from the manager of the Weston Mall. He was certain there was some mistake. Why the hell would anyone break into Growth Industries? And, if he did, what the hell was he going to steal? A bunch of used telephone answering machines? A cheap, fake leather swivel chair? It didn't make sense. There was nothing of value, there was no meaningful paperwork. There wasn't even any indication of what the company did. But none of that mattered now because someone had been inside and he had to go there and check things out. He hated going in to that office, stopped by only once a month, perfunctorily. He didn't really need to do it but he felt as if he should. He needed to reassure himself that things were untouched and safe.

Only now things weren't untouched. And now things might not be safe.

The best he could hope for was that this was the work of some incompetent burglar. The worst he could expect was . . .

Ed Marion didn't want to think about the worst. He knew that when it came to the realities of the game he was playing, he was in way over his head. The people he worked for were scary and they were nasty. They frightened him. They paid awfully well, though. And as long as they left him alone to do his work, he could live with what he was doing for them. His extra-curricular duties were reasonably unobtrusive and not all that time-consuming. They were also extraordinarily valuable from a professional perspective. But he knew that if they ever decided he was a liability, if, god forbid, he ever fucked up, well . . . that's what he didn't want to focus on. He didn't like thinking about his wife being a widow or his kids going through the rest of their lives without a father.

He drove his nine-month-old Lexus out of the driveway of his two-story white Colonial, turned left on his quiet suburban street and headed past a series of manicured lawns and freshly painted houses, toward the mall. Marion paid no attention to the blue-gray Buick that started up and chugged along behind him. He was so lost in thought that when he stopped at the first stop sign he came to he didn't even notice the man who was standing on the corner. He didn't see the man step toward his car and tap on the passenger-side window. The man was holding a map and looking confused, so Ed Marion instinctively touched the button to his left, the one that electronically rolled the passenger window down. Ed was still so lost in thought it took him a full three seconds to register that instead of the map, the pedestrian had shoved a gun through the open window. The gun was pointing straight at him, Marion realized, and the man, perfectly calm, there was even the hint of a reassuring smile on his face, was saying, 'It's time we had a little talk, Ed.'

Justin had Ed Marion pull the Lexus over to the side of a quiet street, about three blocks from the man's house. Deena pulled the Regal Sedan up behind them and cut the motor; she and Kendall stayed in the car, as Justin had instructed.

'Whatever you want,' Marion said, staring at the gun in Justin's hand, 'it's yours. I don't have a lot of cash but just take it. I have credit cards, a bank card, this watch is worth a few hundred dollars. Here, take the watch . . .'

'I'm not here to rob you, Ed.'

Marion studied him now, his eyes taking in Justin's posture, his clothes, the serious expression on his face. 'Oh my god,' Marion said, 'you're going to kill me.'

Justin decided to play things as they unfurled. This guy was clearly afraid. The question was, of what? Right now he was afraid of Justin. Might as well take advantage of that, give him some room and hope he'd lead the conversation somewhere worthwhile.

'I have some questions,' Justin said. 'Why don't you give me some answers and we'll see how things go.'

'I don't know anything about the break-in, I swear. I didn't do anything to cause it.'

'No? How about the fuck-up with the girl?'

'What girl?'

'The one you spoke to about Bill Miller.'

Marion looked genuinely confused. 'I did what I was

supposed to, didn't I? I called Newberg, he called . . . whoever he calls. Maybe he called you. Then he told me to call the girl back, keep her calm, he was taking care of it.'

'By having her killed?'

'Look, I don't ask about things like that. It's not my business.'

'It is now. Somebody screwed up. There was a witness.'

'I know. I saw it on the news. But that's not my fault.' Marion was sweating profusely now. 'Look, I took care of my end. I was *told* to call her. They *told* me to give out the number. What happened there, it's just not my fault. I never said a word. I mean, I'm not even supposed to be on this side of things. They said this kind of stuff would never happen. Let me just talk to Newberg. Let me talk to Kransten. I've done everything they want and I haven't said a word to anybody. I swear to god, even the people I work with don't know anything about Aphrodite. My *wife* doesn't know!'

Amfer. Or Afro. That's what Deena thought she'd heard Susanna's killer ask about. Afro. Aphrodite? It made as much sense as anything else.

Justin wasn't sure where to head next. He didn't know any of the names that Marion had just tossed out. And clearly he was supposed to. He wasn't confident of his ability to draw out information. He needed the basics – who and why and where – but he didn't have enough info to go the subtle route. And he didn't know how much longer he could keep Marion on the hook. So he took the plunge and went direct. 'Tell me about Lewis Granger,' he said.

'What?'

'What's the connection between Granger and Bill Miller?'

'What? What do you mean?' Marion's eyes narrowed.

'Do you know how old Miller was?'

'Who *are* you?' Marion asked.

'How old is Lewis Granger?'

'Jesus Christ,' Marion moaned. 'I know who you are. You're the cop on the news.'

So much for direct. 'I may not be who you thought I was,' Justin said, tapping his gun on his thigh, 'but I can still pull the trigger. So answer the questions, Ed.'

'You don't know what the hell you're doing.'

'You work for The Ellis Institute. What do they research?'

'You're the one who broke into the office. Oh my god, you don't know what you've done.'

'What's Aphrodite? Why do you think Susanna Morgan knew anything about it?'

The guy had his head in his hands now. Justin thought he might begin to rip his own hair out. 'They'll know you found me. Jesus Christ, they're going to kill me now.'

'Who?'

'You're gonna lead them right here. You're definitely dead and so am I.' Marion glanced back at the Buick. 'And so's whoever you're with. *Everybody's* dead.'

'I can get you help,' Justin said.

'It's too late now.'

'No, it isn't. But you have to talk to me.'

'I can't,' Marion said. His words were barely audible now. They were coming out as half-gasps, half-sobs. 'I can't talk to you. They'll know you got to me. You're killing me.'

'Who?' Justin asked. 'Who'll know? Newberg? Kransten?'

Marion just shook his head. His hands were shaking now. And he was biting his lower lip so hard that a thin trickle of blood was forming on his chin.

'What about the FBI?' Justin said suddenly. 'Will you trust *them*?'

Marion stopped his moaning and keening just long enough to look up questioningly. Justin continued. 'They can protect you, can't they?'

Marion seemed to regain some color. 'The FBI?'

'I can get somebody here pretty quickly.'

'They can help me?'

'Yes,' Justin said. 'But you have to tell me everything that's going on.'

'Not you. I'll tell them. I'll talk to the FBI.'

Justin raised his gun an inch but he knew it was an empty threat. So did Marion.

'Go ahead and shoot me,' Marion said. 'If I don't get to the FBI I'm as good as dead anyway.'

Justin hesitated, then reached for his cell phone. He dialed, heard Gary answer at the East End station, didn't even bother with a hello, just said, 'Get Rollins.'

Thirty seconds later, the FBI Assistant Director was on the line. 'Where the hell are you?' was his opening line.

'You know, you've got to learn to vary your questions. I'm doing you a favor, Rollins. So try not to step on your own dick for a couple of minutes while I tell you something.'

'What kind of favor?' Rollins said.

'I'm with someone who can lead us to the guy who killed Susanna Morgan. And Brian Meves.'

'Who is it?'

'Slow down a second. The guy's terrified. And for good reason. He thinks that whoever killed those two is also going to come after him. I said I could get FBI protection.'

'You've got balls, you know that, Westwood? You've got some real balls.'

'Rollins, there is some very weird shit going on which I will be happy to tell you about at some point. But in the meantime, my contact needs protection. In exchange for which, he will answer any and all questions. Those answers should lead to the capture of a man who murdered a police officer. A police officer working on your investigation.'

Rollins sighed and said, 'Where do we go?'

Justin turned to Ed Marion. 'I need to tell him where to come. I have a motel room I can stash you in. Can I give him your name and that address?'

Marion thought for a moment, then nodded.

'His name's Edward Marion. I'm going to put him in a room in a motel in Weston, Connecticut.' Justin gave Rollins the address of the motel near the mall. 'You sending someone from there?'

'No,' Rollins said. 'I'll see if I can get somebody who's closer. It'll be quicker.'

'Have your guy follow up on Susanna and Brian. My guy'll talk. Make sure he's asked about two people named Newberg and Kransten.'

'Who?'

'I don't know who they are but they're involved. Also make sure you get details about Bill Miller and Lewis Granger. And a company in New York called The Ellis Institute and one in Boston called The Aker Institute.'

'Is that it?'

'No. He's got a partner whose name is Helen Roag. She lives outside of Boston, in Marblehead.'

'Got it.'

'When Susanna Morgan was killed, the killer wanted information. Our witness heard something like Afro or Amfer. According to Marion, it's Aphrodite. Check that out, too.'

There was a silence from Rollins's end.

'You want me to spell it for you?' Justin asked. 'I know that whole "ph" for "f" thing gets kind of tricky . . .'

'Where are you now, Westwood? Are you at the motel?'

'I'm hanging up now, Rollins. It's always a pleasure talking to you.'

'Are you in Connecticut, for Chrissake? Just tell me that.'

'I'll call you tomorrow to see what you found out.'

'Westwood . . .'

'Goodbye, Agent Rollins.'

Justin hung up the phone. Turned to Ed Marion, told him the gist of the conversation. Then he said, 'Head toward the mall. I'll put you in a room and once you're inside lock every door and window. Don't let anybody in until you can see some FBI identification. You got it? I want you to see it, don't just trust voices. The guy I spoke to is named Rollins. He probably won't come himself but make sure whoever shows up knows that name.'

Marion nodded but didn't move.

'Ed,' Justin prompted. 'You've got to turn the key and start the car if you're gonna do all that.'

Marion still didn't speak. Just kept nodding. But he reached for the key and turned it. Justin rode back with him the few miles to the motel. He walked the terrified man inside, checked him into a room, closed the curtains, and told Ed Marion once again not to open the door for anyone until the FBI arrived. Then he walked outside and stepped behind the wheel of the Buick sedan, which was waiting in the parking lot. He began to fill Deena and Kendall in on what had happened. But even as he spoke, his mind was elsewhere. Another song lyric forced its way into his head. A Randy Newman lyric: *I'm dead but I don't know it. I'm dead but I don't know.*

And as he drove slowly away Justin Westwood was busy wondering, as he almost always did when his work took him too far beneath the surface, how a world like the one in which Ed Marion lived, a world that looked so clean and pure and manicured and untroubled could hold, in its heart, such violence. Such terror.

CHAPTER EIGHTEEN

Gordon Touay liked killing things.

There were other things he enjoyed, he did not consider himself one-dimensional in any way. He got great pleasure, for instance, out of looking in the full-length mirror that hung in the hallway. He had to concede, he never really tired of that. Especially when he was wearing nothing but his beige bikini underwear, the one with the little blue stripes on the front, which is what he was wearing now. He loved looking at his washboard stomach, at the ripples, the flatness. He didn't have an ounce of fat on his sides, either. At thirty-one years old, there wasn't even the slightest hint of love handles. And his chest was perfectly formed. Not like a body builder's, more like a swimmer's. Thin and tight and hard. Like Charles Bronson's used to be in those early westerns. Gordon liked to turn sideways and flex his arms, too; liked the way the muscles on his back and shoulders and even his neck bunched up and bulged and made him look so powerful. He particularly admired his hair, so very blond and straight, cut short on the sides, medium

217

on top, a tiny lock tilting forward over his forehead. He often thought he was as handsome as Brad Pitt or DiCaprio or any of those guys. He'd practice smiling into the mirror, looking cocky, and he'd think: *I should have been a movie star. I've got what it takes. I would look magnificent up there on a giant screen, looking down on an adoring audience.*

Then he'd think: *We both would.*

Wendell, his younger brother, was just as handsome. Gordon liked looking at his brother's body, too. The same hard stomach, the perfect buttocks and powerful back. Long legs, but not too long. The short blond hair. In the eyes of the world, they were identical. No one could tell the difference between them. But Gordon could, of course. He knew the small mole on Wendell's shoulder. Could see that Wendell used just a touch more mousse in his hair, that the forehead lock was slightly stiffer and shinier. Gordon was seven minutes older than his twin and he was convinced that Wendell looked younger, that the skin under his eyes was smoother, that his forehead had one less crease. He wasn't jealous. It was fine with him. He loved his brother. There was no one on earth he loved more. And he was happy to be the elder. The mentor. The decision maker.

Staring at himself in the mirror, Gordon smiled. He loved his smile. He thought it made him look elegant and mysterious. Relaxed but deep. He decided he should show it more often. Then he went back to thinking about all the things that could keep the smile on his face.

That show on Fox about animals that turned violent and attacked their owners. He liked that a lot. War movies. He loved war movies. *Black Hawk Down* was a great one. Very gory. *Private Ryan* was good. At least the first part, the battle. After that it was pretty sappy. Of the old ones, he liked *The Dirty Dozen*, particularly the part where the Spanish guy parachutes out of the plane and breaks his neck, and *Paths of Glory*, where everybody gets marched off to the slaughter. He had a collection of filmed disasters that he watched over and over again. The Challenger exploding, he never got tired of that. The Hindenburg going down. Various assassinations. He had that L.A. robbery, where the guys in masks kept firing their automatic weapons on the street and finally got cut down by the cops. He paid a lot of money over the Internet for several home movies of fiery plane crashes. And he owned several bonafide porno snuff films, which cost him a fortune. All those things were satisfying diversions. But nothing was as good as actually killing something.

Although he couldn't really take credit for it, he liked to think that his first victim was his mother. She died in childbirth, right after he and Wendell came out of her womb. Gordon never forgave her for leaving them so unexpectedly because when their father remarried it was to a woman who wanted her own children, who resented the two boys as unpleasant reminders of a past that had nothing to do with her. She didn't bother to hide her distaste for the twins; in fact, she reveled in it. And that distaste was soon championed by her husband, their own father. He saw his two sons as two beings who had destroyed his first marriage and whose sole reason for existence was to interfere with his new one. The first time

Gordon remembered their father beating them was when they were five years old. It was with a ruler that he'd picked up off the desk. He made both boys lie down on the floor while he struck the backs of their legs over and over again. After that the beatings never stopped. Sometimes he used the ruler, sometimes his fists, occasionally a belt. Once he used a broomstick. But he gave Wendell a concussion and social service workers got suspicious when the boy was rushed to the hospital, so good old dad went back to less obvious tools and other body parts.

Gordon was seven years old when he killed his first animal. It was a squirrel. In their backyard in the small house in New Jersey. He watched it scamper down the trunk of a tree, perch on a patch of grass and nibble on something, a nut maybe. The squirrel's head was cocked as he ate and the boy thought it looked cute. While he was watching, Gordon saw a rake propped up against the back of the house, had an image in his mind of the broomstick cracking against his brother's skull, and the next thing he knew, the squirrel was on its back, its head smashed in, its eyes still and lifeless. Gordon was surprised how good it made him feel.

Three weeks later he killed another squirrel. A month after that he killed a cat, a stray that was always coming into their yard looking for scraps of food. He fed it for several weeks, won its trust, then strangled it. After that, he killed on a regular basis, at least every two weeks or so. More squirrels, cats, dogs, birds. He preferred strangling, although poison was also acceptable. Stabbing was fine, too, as was fire. Methodology and type of victim didn't much matter to him. He just liked the moment when he could actually see life disappear, when movement stopped and something warm turned cold and colorless.

When the twins turned eight, Gordon told Wendell about the animals. Wendell's eyes lit up and he smiled. He said he wanted to try it, too.

A few days later, their father took them into town to go shopping. They asked if they could go into the diner and have a soda. He agreed, told them to wait there for him until he came to pick them up. The boys sipped their Cokes at the counter until Gordon looked at Wendell and nodded. In the corner of the diner, by the cashier, there was a myna bird. A big black one that talked all the time. His name was Randy and he was always saying, 'Randy wants a coffee and a danish,' which everyone thought was hilarious. The diner was pretty empty, no one was minding the cash register, so when Gordon gave the signal, Wendell walked by the myna's cage, quickly stuck his hand in and broke the bird's neck. Then he continued on his way to the bathroom. When he returned, the cashier and the waitress were standing by the cage, distraught. Wendell walked up to them, asked what had happened. They told him it was something terrible, that their bird had died. They told him not to look, that he was too young to see a dead thing. Wendell nodded, said he was sorry about Randy, he seemed like a nice bird, then went back to sit beside his brother and order another Coke.

Their stepmother had a baby girl soon after the twins' ninth birthday. When the baby was three weeks old, she died in the middle of the night. Just stopped breathing. The doctor said it was a case of Sudden Infant Death

Syndrome, a tragedy to be sure but surprisingly common. He said that the parents should go out and have another baby as soon as possible to help deal with their sadness.

They didn't. They both suspected that Wendell and Gordon had murdered their child but they never had any proof. Their father beat them more regularly and more fiercely than ever. But he never asked about the baby. And he and his wife never tried to have another. They knew that it wasn't a smart thing to do to bring another child into their household.

They were right. Dogs and rodents had become mundane victims. So in the middle of the night, the boys had gone into their step-sister's room. Wendell held the baby down while Gordon smothered her with a pillow. They watched the baby thrash around and listened as she tried to cry. When the girl stopped moving, they put the pillow back under her head, went into the room that they shared, read comic books for half an hour or so, then went back to a calm and dreamless sleep.

Over the next several years, they killed two more children. One boy they didn't know. They saw him on a street corner, lured him to an empty lot and smashed his head in with a brick. Their second victim was a girl who had made fun of Wendell's handwriting at school. They waited for three whole months, until the dead of winter. Then they went ice skating with her. Gordon found the patch of thin ice, Wendell dragged her there and pushed her through. They both watched her drown, went back home and had dinner.

When they were in high school, Gordon asked a girl to their junior prom. She turned him down. It was quite a nice rejection; she said she already had a date but perhaps they could go to the movies or something. Gordon nodded, met up with Wendell and told him what had happened. The next day, Wendell walked the girl home from school. He told her that he was Gordon, the first time he'd ever pulled that trick on his own. They walked past a barn and he asked if she wanted to see the horse that he kept inside. She did. When they got in, he waited until she realized that there was no horse, then he stabbed her to death with a knife he'd stolen from the school cafeteria.

The police interviewed both twins. They were suspicious, as, by this time, was everyone else who knew them. But once again there was no proof. There was no arrest made in the girl's murder. For several months afterward, one cop, Sergeant Joe Dankowski, followed them, hounded them, convinced he could make them crack and confess. He couldn't. Eventually his superiors ordered him to leave the boys alone. He did, but not before he promised them both that he would, at some point, put them where they belonged. 'Where do we belong?' Wendell had asked in all seriousness. Sergeant Dankowski had answered, 'In prison. And then in hell.'

Gordon and Wendell joined the army soon after they graduated from high school. They liked the physicality of the training process. They were tireless and responded well to the army's discipline. They both went off to serve in the Gulf War and they liked that a lot. The fighting didn't frighten either of them; in fact, they found it energizing. But there was a surprising amount of down time. Bored when they weren't fighting, they discovered that movie studios sent VCRs and cassettes to the men in uniform overseas. Gordon and Wendell began watching any movie they could. It kept them entertained. They found their entire war experience so entertaining that they barely felt the need to kill anyone just for fun. Their only extra-curricular activity in Iraq was when, during a brief skirmish in the desert, they decided to get rid of an Hispanic private who played his salsa music too loud and too late at night. The brothers waited until the Hispanic charged ahead of them then they both aimed their rifles and shot him in the back. He was later extolled as a hero and a tragic victim of friendly fire.

When they got out of the army, they returned to their home town. But it was a brief stopover. One day only. During that twenty-four-hour period, they robbed a 7/11, getting away with $364.27 cents and a case of beef jerky, and they murdered Sergeant Joe Dankowski. They followed him home, forced him into his own house, and carved him up the way an experienced hunter would skin a deer. It took the sergeant several hours to die and both twins agreed that it was some of the best hours of their entire lives.

The next day, they went to Los Angeles. Their love of movies motivated them to try to become actors. They had the looks for it, they decided. And how hard could it be? Six months later, they had learned that it was a lot harder than they'd thought. They had landed several jobs as extras on feature films and one other job, with no lines, on the TV show *Friends*. Jennifer Aniston was going on a date with a doltish guy and before she left she spotted the two handsome twins sitting at a table in the coffee shop.

All she had to do was raise an eyebrow to show she was considering the possibilities. It got a laugh, but it didn't get any more jobs for either Wendell or Gordon. What they did get was hired by a producer to scare the shit out of a bookie, to whom he owed two hundred and sixty thousand dollars. During the moment of the big scare they went a little too far and the bookie died. Wendell and Gordon decided to take advantage of the situation so they moved into the dead man's apartment, found his records and began to book bets. This arrangement lasted for several months before they got bored. They didn't really care about bookmaking. They didn't care about money. They cared about fun. And what was fun for them – they knew this now, it was inescapable – was killing people.

They'd been in Los Angeles nearly two years when they got the phone call that changed their lives. It was from a man named Newberg. He had talked to people in the army, he said. And to the producer who'd hired them to take care of the bookie. He'd even talked to people in their home town. He said he would be in L.A. in a couple of days and he'd like to get together with them. Two days later they met at Newberg's suite in the Four Seasons Hotel. He asked them very specific questions for almost two hours; the session was very similar to a psychological test his company gave to every potential employee. At the end of the test, he told them he wanted to review their answers and that he'd call them by the end of the week. He did. And when he called, he offered them permanent employment. Good money. A substantial relocation fee back east. And lots and lots of fun.

As Gordon Touay stood in front of the mirror now, flexing his arms, admiring his body, he saw his brother walk into the room. Wendell was wearing jeans, but no shirt or shoes. The two of them stood in front of the mirror, posing. A joyous Kodak family moment. When the phone rang, Gordon answered it. He listened to Newberg explain what it was they were supposed to do next. When Gordon hung up the phone, he went back to the mirror and stood next to his twin brother.

'Good news?' Wendell asked, twisting his left arm a bit to the side so the muscles in his triceps would pop even more.

Gordon nodded. 'We get to finish the job. Tonight.'

'The girl and the kid, too?' the younger twin said.

The older brother nodded again. They both flexed one last time, lingered in front of the glass, admiring their reflections, then went off to get dressed and pack an overnight bag. On their drive to the airport, to catch a flight to Albany, the nearest city to the Leger Retirement Home, they decided exactly how best to kill three people, satisfy their employer and get the most amount of joy out of their work.

CHAPTER NINETEEN

Justin Westwood glanced in the rearview mirror as he drove and caught a glimpse of Kendall Harper asleep on the back seat. His eyes shifted to his right and he saw that Deena was watching him, staring, as if, once again, attempting to understand what was going on inside his mind. For her sake, Justin hoped she never succeeded.

'They're not even worth a penny,' he said.

'What?' Deena asked, startled.

'My thoughts. A penny would be way overpaying.'

'I was that obvious, huh?'

'Well,' he said. 'I'm a trained investigator.'

'I thought you said you were rusty.'

'Okay, you were that obvious.' His eyes went toward the mirror again. 'She's a terrific kid,' he said.

'I know. It's a miracle, really. I mean, I don't know what the hell I'm doing.'

'Sorry to shatter your illusions, but you're doing something right.'

Deena smiled ruefully. 'Thanks. That's a nice thing to

say.' She hesitated, started to say something else but stopped. She chewed on her lip for a moment, then shrugged and said, 'You're good with her.'

'I'm glad you think so. I like her.'

'You never wanted any?'

'Children, you mean?'

She nodded.

'Yes,' Justin said. 'I wanted children.'

His words left a heavy silence in the air and she wasn't exactly sure why. When she glanced at him again, his face looked drawn and his eyes were sad. He looked as if a pain was hammering away at him inside his head. Or, she thought, inside his soul.

Before she could say anything else, they heard a stirring from the back seat. 'How much longer?' Kendall yawned.

'Another hour or so,' Justin said. 'Not too much further.'

'Do you have to go to the bathroom?' Deena asked.

'No,' Justin said.

'I wasn't talking to you.'

'Oh.'

'Do you have to go, sweetie?' she asked her daughter.

'No,' Kendall said.

'Are you sure?'

'If he can wait, I can wait,' the little girl said. And, looking straight at the rearview mirror, she nodded firmly and decisively.

Justin, eyes peering into the mirror, nodded back.

An hour and fifteen minutes later, just past 6:30 p.m., Justin pulled the Buick into the parking lot of the Leger Retirement Home. They were upstate New York, about half an hour southeast of Albany, in a small, blue-collar town called Woodlawn.

'You guys want to come in?'

'Yeah. Kenny can use the restroom.'

'No,' the little girl insisted. 'I don't have to go and I'm not using it.'

'Maybe we'll come in anyway,' Deena said. '*I'd* like to use the restroom.'

They went up the steps to the Home, a modern ranch-style building. The lobby, which also served as the reception room, was comfortable but devoid of charm. Several elderly people were scattered around the room, watching a large-screen television or playing cards. An attendant wheeled a white-haired woman past in a wheelchair. Kendall looked around curiously; she had never before seen so many old people in one room.

'Is one of these people Grampy-gramps?' Kendall asked quietly.

'That's what I'm about to find out,' Justin told her. He went up to the reception desk – it had the feel of an airline check-in counter – and he said to the woman holding down the fort, 'I'm here to see Lewis Granger.'

The woman at the desk paled and her eyes widened nervously. She gave Justin a pitying once-over, then quickly turned away, unable to look him in the eye. She said, 'I'll have to call the manager,' picked up the phone and dialed. After a brief pause, she spoke into the receiver. 'There's someone to see Mr Granger,' she said quietly.

Another pause, then she hung up, turned to Justin and said, 'Mr Depford will be right with you.'

'Is there a problem?' Justin asked.

'Mr Depford will be right here,' she said, sat back down and busied herself with what looked to be non-existent paperwork.

In a few moments, a small, fortyish-looking man in a gray suit, white shirt and blue tie came striding into the lobby. He walked directly up to Justin and stuck out his right hand. As they shook, the man in the suit used his left hand to grasp Justin above his wrist. Justin realized that this was meant to be a comforting gesture. Justin introduced Deena and Kendall as his wife and daughter, then he waited to find out why he needed to be comforted.

'Are you a relative?' Depford intoned.

'Yup,' Kendall piped up. Deena instantly grabbed the back of her shirt and pulled the girl backwards.

'I'm his son,' Justin said, trying to match the manager's solemnity.

'I'm very sorry to tell you this,' the suited Depford said directly to Justin. 'But I'm afraid your father has passed away.'

'He's dead?' Justin said incredulously.

'I'm afraid so.'

'I just spoke to him this morning. He sounded . . .'

'I know. He seemed fine up until the very end. That's often the way here. Which we're thankful for.'

'What happened?'

'It seemed to be very peaceful. He died in his bed,' Depford said.

'When?'

'Sometime this afternoon. He didn't come down for supper. Eventually, one of the nurses went to check on him and found him in bed, not breathing. He didn't look as if he suffered, if that's any consolation.'

'Yeah, that's a big consolation,' Justin said. 'Is he still here?'

'Why . . . yes, we—'

'Has he been moved?'

'No. We've called the hospital and they're going to come pick him up. I told them there was no extraordinary rush since he's already . . . well . . . I called his nephew . . .'

'Ed Marion.'

'Yes.' Depford's eyes narrowed and he stared at Kendall. 'You called this morning, didn't you? I thought you said that Ed Marion was your father.'

'This is my dad,' the little girl said, with a sweet smile on her face. 'Right, daddy?'

'Ed's my cousin,' Justin said. 'You must have misunderstood.'

'Yes, well . . . he's the only person we had on file. We were unaware there were any other . . .'

'Can I see him?'

'Mr Marion? Well, no, he hasn't responded to our call . . .'

'No,' Justin said. 'Granger. I want to see . . . my father.'

'You mean you want to view the body?'

'That's exactly what I want to do,' Justin said.

*

The four of them strode down the sterile hallway on the second floor of the Leger Home until they reached a cheap wooden door that had the number 27, in even cheaper balsa wood, attached to it.

Depford stopped in front of the door, turned and in his most sorrowful tones, said, 'Would you all like to go in?'

'Yes,' Kendall said immediately and a bit too enthusiastically. When all three grown-ups looked down at her, she said, with a little less enthusiasm, 'I've never seen a dead guy before.'

Justin nodded and said, 'Okay, we'll all go in.'

Depford opened the door and started to step inside with them. Justin put his hand on the man's shoulder and said, 'We'd like a few private moments, please.'

'Of course,' Depford murmured. He waited until they were all inside, then he shut the door and said he'd wait for them in the hallway.

As soon as the door was closed, Justin moved to the bedside and began examining the body.

'What are you looking for?' Deena asked.

'Give me a minute and I'll tell you.'

'Can I see?' Kendall wanted to know.

'In a minute.'

Justin picked up the dead man's right hand, lifted it up toward the light. He twisted Granger's head, fingering his neck and under his eyes, then he turned the body over on its side, doing some poking and probing.

'This is pretty yucky,' Kendall said. 'I don't think I want to see, after all.'

'I'm with you, baby,' Deena muttered.

Justin let Granger fall back onto the bed. When he turned around, he saw both mother and daughter staring at him expectantly.

'Look,' he said, turning back to the corpse. He picked up Granger's left hand and ran his fingers down the wrist and arm of the corpse. 'Red marks here. It looks like someone was holding him down, restraining him.' Justin turned the corpse over and showed Deena the back of the dead man's right heel. 'It's bruised. The night table over here's kind of skewed. My guess is he struggled and kicked it, that's how he hurt himself.'

'Why was he struggling?' Deena asked.

'Because somebody smothered him to death,' Justin said. 'And I'd have to say he probably didn't like it too much.'

'What's happening?' Deena whispered. He realized that she was speaking quietly not because she didn't want to be overheard. Fear was not allowing her to speak any louder. 'Why are they killing people?'

Justin wished he had an answer for her. But all he could do was shake his head. He didn't tell her what he was thinking. It was not a very comforting thought and he knew that it would occur to her soon enough. He was thinking: *Somebody beat us to Granger. Which means somebody knew we'd be here.*

When he glanced at Deena, he knew she'd just made the connection. She grabbed Kendall, drew her close, and hugged the girl to her body. As he watched Deena's eyes flicker, he knew she'd also taken the thought to the next logical step.

Which means somebody knows we're here now.

Mr Depford was waiting for them in the hallway when they stepped out of Lewis Granger's room.

'If there's anything I can do,' he said, still using his most somber and funereal tone.

'Actually, there is,' Justin told him. 'I'd like to look at any records you might have.'

'What kind of records do you wish to see?'

'My father always kept something a bit of a mystery. None of us ever knew how old he really was. I'd like to find out.'

'I'm afraid we don't have that on file.'

'Isn't that standard information?'

'Normally, yes. And, of course, we had it. But a few years ago, three to be exact . . .'

'You had a burglary.'

Depford looked surprised. 'Why, yes.'

'Right before you started the job.'

The manager looked even more surprised. 'That's right. How did you—'

'Were any other files taken, other than my father's?'

'A few. That's what I was told. But no one who's still with us, I'm afraid.'

'Thank you very much, Mr Depford. You've been very helpful.' Justin took Kendall by the hand and started walking down the hallway toward the stairs that led to the lobby. Depford did a little hop, step and a jump to keep up with them.

'What about a funeral?'

'Excuse me?'

'What would you like me to do with the body? Now that you're here . . .'

234

'Nothing but the best,' Justin said. 'Spare no expense.'

'Um . . . yes . . . of course,' Depford said. They were downstairs and almost to the front door. The prim little man looked uncomfortable now. 'But as far as payment . . .'

'The usual,' Justin said. 'Send the bill to the Ellis Institute. Just be sure to tell them I okayed it.'

Depford didn't follow them out to the parking lot. They headed quickly toward the car, until Deena pulled up short.

'I think you should use the restroom,' she said to Kendall.

'Mom,' the girl said. 'I told you. I'm a big girl.'

'I know you are, sweetie, but sometimes even big girls—'

'I know when to go!'

'But we don't know when we'll find another stop,' Deena said. 'I really think—'

'Mommmmm . . .'

'Okay,' Deena said. 'Okay. But I don't want any whining when we're in the car. Just remember I told you that, because we're not going to be able to stop in the middle of nowhere.'

The little girl tossed her head, as if to say, 'I do *not* whine,' then skipped ahead of them toward the car.

'Tell me again how I'm doing something right,' she said to Justin.

'Nobody's perfect,' he told her.

'Where do we go from here?' Deena asked.

'I was afraid you were going to ask that.'

'You don't know?'

'I've got a couple of ideas,' he said. And then, when she looked at him incredulously, he added, 'What, you thought I was kidding about that "nobody's perfect" thing?'

He got in the driver's seat, reached over Deena's lap into the glove compartment and pulled out an old Dire Straits CD. The only thing he'd bother to transfer from his old car to this one were his CDs. This one had a song on it, The Bug. Justin skipped ahead to that song, the fifth one on the album, heard Mark Knopfler twang out the line, *Sometimes you're the windshield, sometimes you're the bug.*

Yeah, Justin thought. And as he drove away, he realized that he'd spent the last six years of his life being the bug. But he never felt it quite so much as he did this very minute.

The first thing that Wendell Touay ever blew up was a rat. He was thirteen years old and caught the rodent as it was scampering over a rusty drain pipe in a construction site that had been emptied out for the July 4th weekend. The rat, struggling to escape the boy's grip, bit Wendell on his thumb, which not only pissed him off, it hurt like hell. Wendell had simply been going to strangle the animal but now that he was angry he decided it deserved a more elaborate send-off. He was carrying several cherry bombs, M-80s and M-100s, was planning on setting them off at the site, his own private celebration. He decided to ratchet the celebration up a notch. He shoved one M-100 as far into the rat's rectum as he could manage, watched in delight as the ugly, furry thing twisted and clawed and snapped, furiously trying to escape, then he lit the fuse, tossed the thing high in the air and toasted America's birthday under a rain of sparks and flesh and fur and blood.

Ever since then, he was addicted to explosions. Gordon liked to touch the things he killed. Wendell much preferred watching them blown to pieces. He read books on explosives, had late night Internet chats with fellow devotees, spent hours upon hours on the dozens of international web sites devoted to all things that explode, and he studied everything he could about homemade bombs. He'd had to buy several copies of *The Anarchist's Cookbook* and *The Poor Man's James Bond* because he'd read them both so often that the spines had broken and the pages had ripped out. He considered himself an expert and took quite a bit of pride in the scope of his knowledge. He could tell you the difference in the rate of detonation between Tetrytol and TNT and, for any Primary or Secondary Explosive, he could rattle off its color, its detonation rate and any quirks that one had to watch out for when handling it – sensitivity to static electricity, degree of water resistance, any danger that might arise from as little as a three-degree drop in temperature.

So when he and Gordon worked out their plan, he was not only pleased to have the opportunity to indulge his passion, he was confident that his skills were up to the task. Gordon's plan had failed on the back roads of Long Island. This plan would not fail. Wendell had created explosives before for them to use in their exclusive line of work and the success rate had been one hundred per cent. A small piece of Wendell was excited at the chance to surpass his seven-minute-older brother. But what excited him even more was the anticipation. When Wendell first began to picture exactly what was going to happen to Justin Westwood and his two charges, a tiny drop of anticipatory spittle formed on his lower lip and he had to lick it away. The thought of seeing the three people blown to bits actually made him drool.

While the cop, the woman and her kid were inside the old age home – just about now, Wendell thought, discovering that Lewis Granger was not going to be very much help to them – Wendell was crouched down behind the piece-of-shit Buick, busily attaching four surprise packages underneath the frame.

Each package was identical. And he was proud of them. They were not only clever, they would be devastating.

Everything had been assembled in a highway rest stop parking lot mid-way between the airport and the Leger Home. They had picked up their rental car and gone straight to a hardware store. There Wendell had purchased a kitchen timer – he picked one that was in the shape of a rooster and that crowed when the timer went off – two packages of Double A batteries, duct tape, five industrial power magnets, electrical wire, industrial-strength fast-drying glue, a plastic bucket, a two-gallon plastic jug, and a large ball of string. After that, they stopped off at a liquor store and bought five bottles of a good Bordeaux. Before paying for them, Wendell checked to make sure that the bottoms of the bottles were all dimpled in the center. He had brought his own electric blasting caps, which had required some ingenuity since they were flying and security was supposedly tighter than in years past. Still, it was no problem. He'd taken apart the DVD case in his laptop computer, removed the mechanism and inserted the caps – which were similar in size and resembled the tube of ink that fits inside fountain pens – in its stead. He then replaced the casement for the device and slipped it back into the computer, attaching it in its proper place. He was able to carry it right on the plane in his overnight bag. The caps set off no alarms and caused no special search.

After buying the supplies at the hardware store, they'd driven toward the Leger Home. Wendell directed Gordon to the rest stop parking lot, which was fairly empty. He could do everything he needed to do there and he assured his brother that the assembly wouldn't take more than a few minutes. While Gordon kept an eye out for any overly curious travelers, Wendell built his bombs. He had decided to make shape charges. For one thing, they were subtle, much subtler than something that would just total a car and blow everything around it to smithereens. For another, they required a very small amount of plastic explosives. He had decided to use C-4, a military explosive that looked like a bar of soap and was easily malleable. He could carry it, undetected, in a soap case, lumping it together with his toothbrush, toothpaste and small bottle of mouthwash. A shape charge, he knew from his Gulf War days, was capable of piercing the armor of a tank, incinerating everything inside that tank, and leaving the shell practically unscathed. Its appeal was that it focused nearly all of an explosive's energy into a very narrow, extraordinarily hot jet. And it was easy as pie to make.

The first thing he did was go into the rest stop complex and fill the plastic bucket with cold water. He also bought a five-pound bag of ice and a corkscrew. He then walked to the gas station right outside and put two dollars' worth of gasoline into the jug. Before he got in the car, Wendell opened and emptied four of the wine bottles into the bushes that partially hid the rest area from the highway. Inside the car, working in the back seat, he soaked several pieces of string in the gasoline, then tied pieces of the soaked string around four of the wine bottles, approximately three inches from the dimpled bottoms. He lit a match, set the strings on fire one by one, and watched to make sure that the bottles heated evenly all around where the string had been tied. When the string was burned down, he instantly immersed each bottle into the bucket that was filled with cold water and ice. Within seconds, each bottle broke perfectly at the point where the string had been tied and the bottles burned. Wendell now had four pieces of glass the size of small juice glasses, each with an inverted cone at the bottom.

He packed the explosives tightly into each glass, then inserted one blasting cap per container. He sealed the tops of the glasses with duct tape, allowing the wires of the blasting caps to stick through. After that, he duct taped a magnet to the bottom of each glass. The magnets were circular with a hole in the middle. This configuration suited his needs perfectly as it would create a stand-off for the explosive jet to form.

That's all it took. Wendell encased each of the packages in several feet of bubble wrap, which he'd carried in his overnight bag. He got out of the car, opened the trunk, and placed the bombs in the small niche on the side where the jack would normally be kept. He gently closed the trunk, got back in the car, told Gordon to drive very carefully – even though he knew there was no danger of the thing exploding until he attached and set the timer; he just thought he'd have a little fun at his brother's expense – and half an hour later they were at the Leger Retirement Home, where they had plenty of time to break in, smother Lewis Granger, go back to the car and wait for their next three victims to show up.

Wendell had had a little more work to do in the Leger parking lot. Once they saw Westwood pull up and go inside – 'New car,' Gordon muttered. 'This guy's not bad.' – the younger twin took the leg wires from the blasting caps in each of his four bombs and connected them together in a parallel circuit. Half of these wires were then twisted together onto another wire whose opposite end was glued to the zero point on the kitchen timer. One more wire was glued to the actual timer part of the clock, the dial that moved around and kept track of each passing minute. The other end of this wire was run, in series, to the Double A battery and remaining blasting cap leg wires. Wendell was careful not to let the wires on the kitchen timer touch. Since he hadn't bothered to include a safe arming switch, he knew that if the exposed wires came in contact with each other, the device would detonate in his hands. The last thing he did was duct tape another magnet to the base of the kitchen timer.

As he secured his bombs, via the magnets, to Justin Westwood's car, Wendell had a clear and delicious vision of what was going to happen.

He would set the rooster timer for one hour. Sixty minutes later, the wires attached to it would touch each other, completing the circuit. The batteries would supply enough energy to initiate the blasting caps and the

242

resulting shock would set off the C-4. Due to the inverted cone at the bottom of each glass, most of the explosive force would meet at the center of the cone and be directed upward, forming a molten jet of glass and energy. This was called the Monroe Effect and what it would do was cause each bomb to drill a tiny hole up into the car, through the frame, through the body of anyone sitting inside over the hole, literally drilling all the way up through the person's head, and melt whatever was in its path. It's why Wendell had decided to use four devices. Two for the front seat, two for the back. The entire inside of the car would incinerate and, except for the windows shattering with enormous force and the possible exception of the roof mushrooming out a bit, the outside would be left relatively untouched. At that point, he would open the fifth bottle of Bordeaux, he and Gordon would toast to their success, and then they would head back home.

A shape charge was a thing of beauty, Wendell knew. And, anticipating the results, he began to drool again at the thought of such beauty.

From the rear of the '97 Buick, Wendell looked up at his brother, who was sitting in their rental car, halfway across the lot. He nodded at Gordon, checked his watch, then bent down a final time to twist the timer on the plastic rooster, setting it to the sixty-minute mark. He walked back to the rental car, got inside, leaned back in the passenger seat, closed his eyes, and told Gordon to wake him up when something happened.

Something happened twenty minutes later.

Justin Westwood came out of the Home with Deena

and Kendall Harper. They headed toward their car, stopped, the mother and daughter seemed to argue for a moment, then they all got into their car. Sat there for several moments. The engine started up and they pulled out of the parking lot.

Gordon leaned over, gave Wendell a gentle two-finger nudge in his side.

'Are you just going to sit here?' Wendell asked when his eyes opened.

Gordon shrugged. 'The job's done, isn't it? We can go home.'

'I want to see this one,' Wendell said.

'That's not a good idea.'

'I want to see it, Gordon. It's going to be magnificent. You get to see your handiwork. I want to see mine.'

'It's not a good idea,' Gordon said again.

'I want to! And I deserve to!'

Gordon waited another fifteen seconds or so before he started up his own engine, pulled out of the parking lot and began to follow the Buick.

Wendell looked down at his watch. Thirty-nine minutes until the explosion.

'It's going to be so beautiful,' he said. 'Wake me up in thirty-eight minutes.'

CHAPTER TWENTY-ONE

When the knock at the door came, Edward Marion couldn't help but flinch.

He'd been sitting in his motel room in near silence, not even turning on the television, for over five hours. Every time he heard any kind of noise outside his room, he'd stiffen, wait for the knock and envision the conversation he'd have to have.

Who is it?

FBI. Open the door.

I need to see some ID.

Open the door and I'll show it to you.

Slip it under the crack. When I see some valid ID, I'll let you in.

So far, the knock hadn't come. But he'd played the scene over and over in his head while he sat there, maybe two hundred times. He had come up with ten or twelve variations. One time he'd move confidently over to the door, check the ID and verify it. He saw himself opening the door to let in someone who would stride inside and assume command, and who, without questions, could lead him out of this mess. Another time, he imagined himself picking up the photo and badge, realizing that something was wrong, and then he'd freeze, knowing they'd found him and were going to kill him. After playing out this scenario, he'd nervously scan the room, trying to figure a way out. He went into the bathroom several times, at least five or six, during this five-hour wait, and tried to imagine if he could squeeze his frame through the small window. Each time, he'd decide that it wasn't possible. But then he'd start to sweat at the thought of someone trying to force his way into the room, so he'd go back to the bathroom and try to come up with a more positive scenario. Then he'd return to his corner, re-imagine the scene and this time in his mind he'd pick up a lamp and when the door opened, he'd swing it, crash it against the stranger's skull, and race out of the room to safety.

Now it was for real.

There was the knock.

His eyes went to the bathroom door, picturing the small window. His glance flickered over to the lamp on the desk. Then he looked at the front door.

Ed Marion swallowed, tried to speak, found that he couldn't. He cleared his throat, tried again, cleared his throat one more time. He saw that his hands were shaking and did his best to steady them. No such luck.

'Who is it?'

'Assistant Director Leonard Rollins. FBI.'

'I need to s-see s-s-some identification.' Shit. He hadn't seen himself stuttering in any of his mental runthroughs.

'I've got a photo ID and badge. You want me to put them under the door?'

'Y-yes. Please.'

Marion waited, heard the scuffle of something being shoved along the floor, then something peeked through the crack under the door. Time to move. He gingerly walked across the room, reached for the ID. It looked official. But, of course, he didn't have a clue what a real FBI identification looked like. This one seemed to say all the right things. And, wait a second, he remembered the cop, Westwood, on the phone, talking to the FBI. He said that the agent he was talking to was named Rollins.

'I thought you weren't coming yourself,' Marion said to the person on the other side of the door. 'You said you were going to send someone else.'

'That's right,' the man outside the door said. 'I told Westwood I was going to send someone from a closer bureau. But I couldn't get anyone. At least not today. It was easier for me to come myself. If you're not going to let me in, would you mind slipping me out my ID? The bureau's pretty stingy with things like this and they'll actually charge me if I have to get a replacement.'

'What'll you do if I don't open the door?' Marion asked.

'Is Westwood coming back tonight?'

Marion wasn't sure. But he didn't want to admit that. 'Yes,' he said.

'I'll slip my cell phone number under the door so you can call me. Then I'll find a place to wait and when he shows up he can verify me. But I'm hoping you don't make me do that. This is kind of a busy time for me. I'm in the middle of a murder investigation.'

The guy *sounded* genuine enough. He knew Westwood and he knew the exact conversation they'd had on the phone. This guy Rollins had the right name, and he didn't seem very anxious. There was no pressure to be let in. He struck Marion as extremely professional.

Wondering how the hell he'd allowed himself to get into this situation, Ed Marion reached for the doorknob and turned it. With his other hand, he simultaneously unlocked the door and pulled it open.

Standing before him was a dark-haired man, a little over six feet tall. Not heavy but muscular. Powerful-looking upper body. He had the aura of an athlete, someone who was very confident of his physical capabilities. Marion glanced down at the photo ID, looked back up at the man. It was a match.

'May I come in?' the FBI agent said.

Marion nodded and stepped further inside the room. Agent Rollins followed, closing the door behind him. Marion sat down on the corner of the bed. Rollins remained standing by the black Formica desk against the wall opposite the bathroom. There was a phone on it and an oval mirror on the wall over it. Other than the curtains and the loud, matching bedspread, the mirror was the only attempt at decoration in the room.

'Nice place,' Agent Rollins said.

'Where are you going to take me?'

'Nowhere yet. This looks like an excellent place for a chat.'

'We have to get certain guidelines out of the way first.

I need to know exactly what you're willing to do for me.'

'What would you like me to do?' Rollins asked.

'I'm going to need immunity from any prosecution. And I'm going to need guaranteed safety for me and my family.'

'You'd better have a lot of information for that kind of deal.'

'Where do you want to start?' Ed Marion said.

Rollins pulled the one chair out from under the desk and sat facing Marion. 'How much did you tell Westwood?' he asked.

'I didn't tell him anything. I said I'd only talk to you guys.'

'Why?'

'He didn't exactly make me feel safe. He seemed like a small-timer. He doesn't know the kind of people who are involved.'

'He does now. You told him about Newberg and Kransten.'

Marion felt his hands go clammy. 'I didn't tell him. The names slipped out. I thought he was working for them.'

'You told him about Aphrodite.'

'He doesn't know what it means.'

'Do you?'

'I know some of it. I've pieced together other parts. Nobody knows everything except Douglas Kransten.'

'And Louise Marshall.'

'You already know about all this?' Marion asked.

'Like you, we know about some of it.'

'How? You've been investigating them?'

Rollins nodded.

'Why?'

'How about if you tell me what *you* know, then I'll decide if there's anything for me to tell you.'

'You don't have a cigarette, do you?'

'I don't smoke.'

'No, neither do I. I've been pretty tense waiting for you to show up. I don't know why I asked for a cigarette. I haven't eaten. And I could really use a drink. That cop, Westwood, he scared the shit out of me, if you want to know the truth. I thought he was going to kill me.'

'Why don't you just relax for a little while and tell me what you know. After you talk, you can eat and drink all you want.' When Marion nodded, Rollins said, 'You work at Ellis, right? Tell me your job, exactly. Are you a researcher?'

'I have a medical and research background. Stanford. But these guys, the people Kransten has working for him, I was never in their league. These are Nobel level minds. So now I'm a manager.'

'What needs to be managed?'

'We do medical research,' Ed Marion said. 'And we specialize in three different areas. When you're talking about this level of brilliance, there's an extraordinary amount of competition. And greed. Someone's got to allocate the funds, make decisions about various directions and priorities. That's what I do, up to a certain level. After that, it's in the hands of my superiors.'

'What are the priorities now?'

'We're biotech. We're all about genetic engineering. Kransten's been enough of a visionary to move to the forefront in three different areas. He's been there for years. We're the market leader in stem cell research derived from human embryos. There's only one other U.S. company that's even really functional at the moment. There's no funding for it.'

'But you don't have that problem.'

'No, of course not. Since the President restricted use to cells that have already been extracted, we're in the driver's seat. We're private. We don't have to worry about those kinds of restrictions.'

'And what's the emphasis in this area?'

'The same as everyone else. Stem cells are just a tool. The more we learn about basic biology, the more likely it is that we can take these stem cells, reproduce the steps inside them, and make them behave in a specific way. It's extraordinarily complicated but the embryo does it naturally. If we can learn how the embryo does it, we can duplicate the process to make something similar to what the body loses when it has certain diseases. Ultimately, the goal is to develop and market treatments for cancer and degenerative diseases.'

'You said it's a tool. A tool for who?'

'For KranMar.' He scratched harshly at the part of his shirt covering his chest, as if the conversation was making him itch. 'There's nothing illegal about this. It's why I can't understand all the precautions and secrecy. KranMar's the third largest pharmaceutical company in the world. Of course they're going to be developing products for profit. There's nothing wrong with their research program.'

'Give me the two other areas you prioritize.'

'Recombinant DNA technology.'

'Try to give it to me in English, please.'

'Essentially, that's reaching inside the body and directly fiddling with gene patterns, with DNA sequences.'

'And the goal?'

'You figure out how to change DNA, you can actually alter the species.'

'You mean, like make people stronger or handsomer or . . . whiter?'

'Agent Rollins, I don't think any of us are in this for those kinds of neo-Nazi purposes. Even if those things were possible, we're talking about altering diseases. Potentially even eliminating some of them. It goes hand in hand with the stem cell research.'

'And the third?'

Marion hesitated, then he said, 'Human growth hormones.'

'Growth as in make things bigger?'

Ed Marion laughed. 'No. Growth hormones affect the aging process.'

'Keep going.'

'I feel a little strange talking about this. We're in a very odd area here and I only know bits and pieces. The other two areas, that's hard science. I wasn't kidding when I said that there are several people working for us who could easily win the Nobel prize. Growth hormones . . . well, it's different. Some people inside Ellis, the other two divisions, really, think it's crackpot science. Kransten thinks it's the key to the future.'

'What do you think?'

'I think it's both. There's a certain logic to the

experimentation and I know enough never to bet against Kransten. The growth hormone people maintain that the key to aging lies in our pituitary gland. The theory is that once we're over twenty, the gland begins to slow down, providing decreasing levels of HGC. Human growth hormones. By around age sixty-five, most of us are producing little or none. It's this decline that leads to most of the symptoms that we associate with aging – wrinkled skin, expanding waistlines, less energy and vitality . . .'

'So you're developing artificial hormones?'

'They've been developed for years. It's how menopause is treated, for one example. And a lot of companies aren't just producing growth hormones, they're also producing something that helps the body *distribute* them. It combats the somatistatin.'

'You've lost me again.'

'The pituitary gland doesn't just produce less HGH as we get older. It produces something called somatistatin. It's a substance that inhibits the gland from distributing even the reduced levels of HGH that are produced.'

'Where does the crackpot stuff come in?'

'Basically, what's out on the market is a lot of cosmetic bullshit. All you have to do is go on the Internet and look at all the anti-aging sites. They're all selling miracle pills that keep you young. Selling growth hormones is probably already a billion dollar business.'

'But they don't work?'

'Marginally at best. They all claim that they'll improve your cardiac condition and lower blood pressure and rejuvenate your kidneys and get rid of wrinkles. It's more marketing than medicine.'

'That's supposed to be illegal.'

'It's not drugs. So it's not regulated. The FDA allows them.'

'And why is KranMar so gung-ho on growth hormones?'

'Because most companies have only been turned on to this in the last decade or so. KranMar's been researching it for thirty years.' Ed Marion sighed. 'And because most companies really do consider it cosmetic, no matter what they're saying. They'll be happy if it gets rid of a few wrinkles. But KranMar's had some extraordinary results with various experiments.'

'Like Bill Miller?'

'Yes. Like Bill Miller.'

'And how many others?'

'I don't know exactly. I only know about my group.' When Rollins waved for him to continue, Marion said, 'I have nine of them, all in the northeast. Well, eight now that Miller died. They've all lived to be over a hundred. One of them's a hundred and sixteen years old.'

'How many other groups are there?'

'I don't know. I think they're regional, so I'd guess five or six others. Maybe a few more than that. We're isolated from each other. For all I know, my group's the only one that's worked.'

'Do you know why KranMar is keeping this so secret?'

'No. That's what I can't understand. I'd think they'd be trumpeting this all over the world. I told that once . . . no, I asked it once . . . in a meeting with Kransten.'

'And what was his response?'

'He said that my job was to do as I was told and that if

I asked so much as one more question, I would be replaced. I understood the word "replaced" to mean a lot more than just being fired.'

'And why do you think he's so afraid of making this public?'

'I don't know.'

'But you've thought about it.'

'Yes,' Marion said. 'I've thought about it a lot. If there are people who've been treated who have lived to be over a hundred, there must be other people who have . . . *not* lived to be over a hundred.'

'They've killed people.'

'They've experimented.'

'And people have died.'

'I can only go by the odds. And the nature of experimentation of this sort.'

'Where's Kransten, Ed?'

'I haven't seen him in months. It's strange. He's dropped out of sight. A lot of the more serious research, particularly in stem cell and growth hormones, is done over in Europe. Fewer restrictions. I know he's got a large number of holdings over there and he spends a lot of time there. But, even for him, he's been relatively invisible.'

'How about Helen Roag?'

'What about her?'

'Where is she?'

'In Boston, I assume.'

'She's gone.' When Marion looked genuinely confused, Rollins said, 'She hasn't shown up for work. Her family says she's missing.'

'Jesus . . .' Marion trailed off.

'Tell me about Aphrodite, Ed.'

'I told you, I only know bits and pieces. It has something to do with Bill Miller and the others and the aging process.' Miller twisted his neck as if it had suddenly stiffened up. 'It's the code name we use for the program.'

'No good. You know more than that, don't you, Ed?'

Ed Marion sensed the change in Agent Rollins's voice. It had turned hard. And cold. 'Yes,' he said. 'I do. But I have to keep some things in reserve. I'm not saying anything more about that until I know exactly how I'm being protected. Until I know exactly what's going to happen to me.'

'Fair enough,' Rollins said.

'I've told you enough, haven't I? To get to the next step?'

'You've definitely gotten to the next step. Why don't we go out and get some food now?'

Marion was still uneasy. It wasn't just Rollins's voice, it was his eyes now. But then he thought, that's just the nature of the business. He's FBI, he's a tough guy, he's born with those eyes. So he nodded, got up from the bed, turned his back on Rollins to get the sport jacket that he'd hung in the closet.

As Marion turned around, Rollins pulled a .38 out of his jacket pocket, the silencer already attached. When Marion turned back to face his inquisitor, he saw the gun and he stumbled backwards.

'I don't understand,' Ed Marion said. 'You work for *them*? You work for Kransten?'

Rollins shook his head. 'I'm FBI. I'm legit.'

'But . . . I can help you guys. I know a lot.'

'That's the problem, Ed. You know too damn much.'

'I don't understand,' Ed Marion said again, and he realized that he'd just wet himself.

'I don't always understand myself,' Rollins said. 'It's a bitch.' Then he lifted the .38.

As Ed Marion lurched for the bathroom, Rollins fired. The noise was sharp but quiet, like a teenage boy playing cops and robbers in his backyard, making a sound effect with his mouth. The first bullet caught Marion in the back of the neck and he fell forward onto the floor. Rollins took two steps over to the body, pointed the gun downward and fired one more shot, straight into Ed Marion's left temple.

Rollins didn't bother to check if the man was dead. There was no need to check. He holstered the gun, turned around and left the motel.

When he got back in his car, he made two phone calls. Both were to Washington, D.C. The first one was to his direct superior, the man who was only one rung under the Director. Rollins reported that his assignment had been completed and that he would provide more details as soon as he was able. He was then told to make the second call, which he did. That one was to the White House, where he gave his name, was put through to the President's Home Front Security Advisor, and answered three quick questions.

'Yes, sir,' was his answer to the man's first question. 'He filled in several gaps and provided quite a few details. I'll come to D.C. tomorrow and provide a more thorough briefing.' In response to the second question, he said, 'No, sir. We don't know where Westwood is at the moment. But I believe we have a way to track him down soon.' The answer to question number three was a simple, 'Yes, sir. As soon as I find him.'

When he hung up the phone, Rollins sat in the car for a few moments, relishing the silence. He thought: *Sometimes my job really sucks.*

And then he thought: *I'm starting to lose my taste for this.*

As Assistant Director Leonard Rollins of the FBI turned on the ignition and broke the silence, his final thought was: *I hope somebody kills Justin Westwood soon so I don't have to do it.*

And then he willed himself to stop thinking.

CHAPTER TWENTY-TWO

'Here are the choices,' Justin said. They'd been on the road for five minutes. Deena was in the front seat, looking at him with a dubious expression, as if she'd lost some confidence in his decision making. Kendall, on the other hand, had nothing but hero worship in her eyes. Good to know, Justin thought. I haven't lost my touch with the grade-school set. 'Boston. Or just outside Boston. Marblehead. It's where Helen Roag is. She shared the phone machines in Ed Marion's office.'

'We just show up there?' Deena asked. 'What if she's . . .' She glanced back at her daughter. 'What if she's gone?'

'You mean dead,' Kendall said. 'Like Grampy-gramps.'

'Stop calling him Grampy-gramps,' Deena said back. 'You didn't even know the guy.'

'We can call first,' Justin said. 'See what we can find out.'

'I'll do it,' Kendall volunteered. When Justin grinned at her, she said, 'I mean, I was so good the last time.'

'What are the other choices?'

'New York. We try to get into the Ellis Institute and find out what the hell's going on there.'

'Is there a third one?'

'I'm sure there is. But I don't have it yet.'

'I vote Boston,' Kendall said.

'And why's that?' Justin asked her.

'The Red Sox,' Deena said. 'She loves Pedro Martinez.' She glanced over to her right as they passed a gas station. Then she looked back at Kendall. 'Honey, do you have to . . .'

'Mom,' the little girl said sternly. 'Do not ask me again if I have to go to the bathroom.' She looked up at Justin, embarrassed. 'I mean, ladies' room.'

Deena sighed. 'I vote for Boston, too.'

'Why?' Justin asked.

'Because it's closer and I'm exhausted. And New York's scary enough without people trying to . . . you know.'

'Kill us?' Kendall finished.

'Nobody's trying to kill us, honey,' Deena said. 'You mustn't even think something like that.'

'They are, too. Aren't they, Jay? Aren't they trying to kill us?'

He looked helplessly at Deena.

'If they're not, why are we running?' Kendall asked, insistent.

'We're not running,' Justin said gently. 'We're trying to solve a problem.'

'What problem?'

'Some bad people have done some bad things. We're trying to find out why.'

'Who are they?'

'We don't exactly know that either.'

'I think you need some more help from me on this one, Jay. You don't sound like you know too much.'

'Will you do me a favor?' Justin said to the girl.

'What?'

'When you're thirteen, will you call me up and remind me to stay away from you for the next six or seven years, because you are going to be some killer pain in the ass teenager.'

Kendall frowned and made a kind of 'huh' noise. Then she sat back and pouted.

They'd been on the road for seventeen minutes.

When they'd been driving for twenty-two minutes, Justin flicked around the radio dial until he got to the news. They caught the end of the sports report and a quick traffic update. Then the anchor came on and they heard, 'The top story of the hour. A man was found murdered in a Weston, Connecticut motel room just a few minutes ago, shot twice in the head. He's been identified as Edward Marion, a Weston local. Police have not revealed why he had checked into the motel or if there are any potential suspects. The man's wife has been notified and police say she is not a suspect. We will update this story as more information comes in. We repeat: a local resident was found murdered in a Weston, Connecticut motel room . . .'

Justin turned the radio off. Breathing heavily, he pulled the car off to the shoulder of the highway. The choking sensation was back, the almost unbearable weight on his chest. He sat there until his breaths came slowly and easily. Then he waited another few moments until he was sure he could speak without throwing up.

He turned to the girl in the back seat. 'Hand me a cell phone, will you? There's one in my jacket pocket.' Kendall passed the phone forward. The expression on Justin's face was all she needed to tell her that she should keep quiet. He punched ten numbers into the phone, waited until Gary answered at the East End police station.

'It's Justin,' he said.

'Jesus—' the young cop began.

'Don't say anything. Just listen. And just answer my questions yes or no. Is Rollins there?'

'No.'

'Did he go out right after I called?'

'Yeah. Yes.'

'Did he make any calls after I hung up on him?'

'Yes.'

'Did he try to contact a local Feebie bureau?' There was no answer. 'Gary, I think you're either nodding or shaking your head. That doesn't do me any good.'

'No. I don't think so. I don't know for sure.'

'Did he call in since he's been gone?'

'Yes.'

'Did you speak to him?'

'No.'

'He talked to Jimmy?'

'Yeah. Listen, I gotta tell you something.'

'Can you say it so nobody hears you?'

'Yeah.'

'All right. What is it?'

'When Rollins called Jimmy,' Gary said, his voice a harsh whisper, 'he said that you killed the guy in Connecticut. They're putting out a warrant for your arrest. You're wanted for murder.'

'Listen to me, Gary. I want you to call me later, when you can get away and can talk freely. Okay?' No answer on the other end. 'You have to trust me one more time, kid. Don't tell anybody I called. Don't tell anybody you're gonna call me back. Use the cell number I gave you earlier. Okay?'

'Yeah.'

'Gary, I know it's confusing but you can trust me on this one. Call me back later and don't tell a fucking soul.'

He hung up, slipped the phone into his jeans pocket, wiped the line of sweat that had gathered on the upper side of his neck.

'You said the f-word,' Kendall said.

'Yeah,' he acknowledged. 'I sure did.'

He pulled the car back on the highway. They'd been on the road for thirty-one minutes.

Deena was twisted in the front seat so her back was to the windshield. She was watching her daughter squirm in the back. Kendall squinted and bit her lip and looked altogether miserable and Deena shook her head.

'Mommy, don't yell at me.'

'I told you to go when we were back at the home. And do you know that you only call me "mommy" when you think I'm going to get angry at you?'

'I didn't have to go then. I have to go *now*.'

'For god's sake, Kenny, we've passed a million gas stations since we left. Why didn't you say anything?'

'Because I didn't have to go!'

'Well, you can't go now!'

'But I have to!' The girl was about to burst into tears.

'Stop it!' Justin said. Lowering his voice, he said to Kendall, 'Can you wait a few minutes until we hit another gas station or a restaurant?'

'No,' she wailed. 'I have to go!'

Justin pulled the car over to the shoulder, put the car in park. 'The bushes are all yours,' he said.

'Mommyyy . . . I can't . . .'

'Then you're going to have to wait.'

'But I can't! It's getting dark!'

'It's fun to pee in the bushes,' Justin said. 'It's my favorite thing. Even when it's dark.'

'I'll go with you,' Deena said. When the little girl's eyes welled up with tears, she softened her tone and said, 'Don't worry. Jay's right. It's fun.' She stepped out of the car, opened the back door. She reached in and unbuckled her daughter, lifting her up and out of the car. Taking her hand, they marched together into the brush and out of sight of the highway.

Justin picked up his cell phone, unfolded a piece of paper, squinted at his own handwriting, then dialed one of the numbers that Gary had given him for Helen Roag. First he called her office, got her voice mail and hung up without leaving a message. Then he called back and this time, after listening to the mechanical instructions and a woman's voice say, 'Helen Roag,' he said, 'Ms Roag, this is . . . it doesn't matter who this is. I think you're in a lot

264

of danger and you need to disappear. I'm going to say three words to show I know what I'm talking about. Kransten. Newberg. Aphrodite. If you haven't heard, Ed Marion was murdered today. Be careful of the police, be careful of the FBI. They can't be trusted. I'll try to get in touch with you somehow. But please, in the meantime, take this very seriously and please try to protect yourself.'

He tried her cell phone next, got another recording telling him to leave a message. He left the same basic message he'd just left at her office.

He hung up, dialed the number he had for Helen Roag's home. A woman answered and he said, 'Helen?'

The woman's voice quivered and she said, 'No. Who is this?'

'A friend of hers,' Justin said. 'My name's Jay. May I speak to her?'

There was a pause and Justin sensed that the woman on the other end of the phone was about to burst into tears. 'Helen's not here,' she said.

'Do you know where she is?'

'Nobody knows where she is,' the woman said. 'She's missing.'

'Who am I talking to?'

'This is her sister. Kathleen.'

'Have the police been called in, Kathleen?'

'Yes. But so far—'

'How about the FBI? Has anyone from the FBI contacted you?'

'Yes. Do you have any information, Jay? Do you have any idea what's happened to Helen? If you do—'

Justin clicked off the connection, leaned back in his

seat and closed his eyes. He opened them when he heard the sound of a car slowing down. A black American car, some kind of Ford rental, had pulled up alongside. From the passenger seat, a blond man, around thirty, stuck his head out the window. The guy's hair was perfectly coifed, dipping slightly over his forehead, and he was handsome in a boyish, asexual kind of way. Justin couldn't see the driver.

'Need any help?' the blond asked.

Justin shook his head and said, 'Pit stop,' and jerked his thumb in the direction of the bushes.

The blond man smiled knowingly. Then he looked at his watch, turned back to Justin and said, 'Bye bye.' With a jerky motion, the man pointed straight ahead down the highway and the car took off, burning rubber, tires screeching, the accelerator pressed to the floor. It was like watching a drag race. They had to be doing eighty in no time and within seconds they were out of sight.

Justin closed his eyes again, leaned his head back. *People are fucking crazy*, he thought. He couldn't help but give a rueful smile. *There I go, using the f-word again.*

The smile faded as he thought of Helen Roag. Missing and, he assumed now, dead. Ed Marion, murdered. Susanna Morgan, broken neck. Lewis Granger, smothered . . .

There has to be a connection, he thought. There has to be a pattern.

It's just another puzzle. And all puzzles can be solved . . .

And then a picture came into his mind: the man in the car, looking at his watch.

Justin's eyes flew open but the picture didn't fade.

A blond man.

Handsome.

Robert Redford hair.

Smiling.

Somebody knew we were going to see Granger.

Which means somebody knows we're here now . . .

Looking at his watch.

Speeding away.

Bye bye . . .

Smiling.

Looking at his watch . . .

Deena and Kendall emerged from the bushes just as Justin grabbed for the door handle and threw the door open. He tried to leap out of the car, forgot he was strapped in, that Kendall had insisted he use the seatbelt. He fumbled frantically to release the latch, finally got it off and rolled out of the car. When he was upright, he saw Deena and Kendall, just a few feet away now and he began screaming, 'Get away from the car! Get away from the car! Run!'

They both froze, looked at him like he was insane. He didn't bother to try to run around the front, just leaped onto the hood, scrambled over it. With one motion, he scooped Kendall up into his arms, held her as tight as he could, grabbed Deena's arm and yanked her forward. He ran as fast as he could, practically dragging Deena behind him, and he was screaming the whole time, 'Go, go, go! Faster, faster, faster!'

He got them into the woods, maybe twenty, thirty yards away, when something told him it was time. He was still screaming, and Deena was still resisting, and Kendall was still squirming, crying in his arms, when he dove to the ground, covering the little girl with his body, pulling her mother down beside him. He heard Deena scream at him, 'What the hell are you—' and then he didn't hear any more because that's when the explosion came.

It was as if a wave of flame rode over him. He did his best to shield them both. He felt Kendall struggle. Somehow he knew she was screaming but he couldn't hear anything, couldn't really feel anything now except the heat. He felt a searing pain in his left shoulder, the one that was exposed to the air, and then the heat was over. It had passed. He waited, used his weight to keep the woman and the girl pinned to the ground, then he let them go, and he sat up.

Kendall was crying, wracking sobs, and so was Deena. Their clothes were filthy and their faces were covered in dirt and scratches. Deena reached out for the girl, who rolled over into her protective arms. They hugged each other and stayed on the ground, crying. They didn't try to speak.

Justin stood up, the pain in his shoulder almost brought him back down to his knees, and he saw that a two-inch shard of glass had imbedded itself in his skin. He looked back at the road; what he saw didn't make sense. The car was intact. He'd expected it to be gone, demolished, but except for a bulge in the roof, nothing much seemed to have happened. He stepped closer, went another twenty feet or so nearer to the highway and saw that the car's windows were gone. It had to be window glass that was imbedded in his arm. The force of the explosion had sent it through the air as if shot out of a rifle. Another car was in the middle of the highway. It had been driving by at the moment the bomb had gone off and the driver had careened into the highway divider. Two men were struggling to get out. They looked dazed but relatively unhurt.

And then he saw, coming down the highway, driving back from the direction in which it had sped off, the black rented Ford.

'We've got to get out of here,' he said. Deena started to argue, but he shook his head and just insisted, 'We've got to go. Now!' He reached down to help her up and her eyes widened when she saw his arm. 'It's okay,' he told her. He grabbed the small piece of glass with his right hand, clenched his teeth, and yanked. It felt like a carving knife being removed from the soft center of a well-cooked turkey. Justin thought he was going to faint from the pain and the spurt of blood, but he didn't. His legs buckled for a moment, then they were strong.

'It's just a flesh wound,' he told Deena. 'It's okay.' He looked down at Kendall. 'She's okay, too.'

He took the girl from her mother's arms, told her to put her arms around his neck and wrap her legs around his stomach. She giggled – a weak, half-hearted giggle but a giggle – when her feet wouldn't touch, and that's when he knew she'd be fine.

'We have to get out of here before anyone comes,' he said to Deena. When she looked at him, still vacant, still in a state of shock, he said, 'It's okay. It's really okay. I know what to do now.' He began marching them through the woods, went another hundred yards or so until they were completely obscured by the greenery, then he turned and began walking parallel to the highway.

'I told you someone was trying to kill us,' Kendall said, her words muffled by Justin's chest. 'Didn't I?'

'Yes, honey,' he said, shifting her weight in his arm so she'd be easier to carry, 'you definitely did.'

'I was right, wasn't I?' She lifted her head a few inches and her words were easier to hear now.

'Yes. You were definitely right.'

'Are they *going* to kill us?' Kendall asked.

'No, honey, they're not.'

'Are you going to stop them?'

'Yes,' he told her.

'How?' the little girl asked and she didn't seem frightened now, just curious.

'Yes, how?' This was from Deena. She was curious, too. But she was also very afraid. 'How are you going to stop them?'

'I have a plan,' Justin Westwood said. 'It needs a little more work, but I have a plan.'

CHAPTER TWENTY-THREE

I t was not easy. Nor was it painless. But by midnight, Justin had their lives relatively back to normal. They walked for two hours. He carried Kendall the entire way. A half-hour into the hike she fell asleep, her arms still locked around his neck, her head drooped on his injured shoulder. He barely felt the pain.

Deena trudged along sluggishly, almost in a trance, for the first half of the trek. Then she started to put herself back together. There was almost no conversation – she uttered one 'Shit!' when she tripped and fell into a slimy patch of leaves; that was nearly the entire extent of her chatter – but he could feel her gathering herself back up. He could sense her resilience. At one point he said to her, quietly and evenly so as not to disturb the sleeping girl, 'I've seen a lot of victims, you know, over the years. Seen a lot of people after they've been attacked, after murder attempts. Most people, they're angry. I mean, really angry. Their first instinct is to strike out in revenge or rage. It's part of the process. Then they calm down. Become more rational. Sometimes. But you, I don't get that from you.'

'No,' she said.

'Are you trolling for sainthood?'

'I'm a Buddhist.'

'Buddhists don't get angry?'

'We try not to. Anger is not very productive or useful. We try to keep the world in perspective.'

'Tough thing to keep this in perspective.'

'You've got my perspective in your arms. Doesn't do me any good to get angry when what matters is keeping her safe.'

It was another minute or so before he spoke again. 'So what do you Buddhists believe in, if it's not anger? I mean, other than all those ommms and back bends and little guys with fat stomachs and things.'

She almost grinned. 'Are you saying that just to *make* me angry?'

'Kind of. But I'm curious.'

'It's hard for me to verbalize sometimes. You know, it comes out sounding a little bit like a Hallmark card. But it's not like that at all. We believe that all things are one. And that to find your self you have to lose your self. We believe that everything we do here is practice.'

'For what?'

'For something bigger. Better.'

'More peaceful?'

'More peaceful.'

They didn't speak again until he steered them back out of the woods, toward the road. They were off the highway by this point, and they didn't have long to walk until they came to a diner. It was one of the places that was geared for travelers. Near the entrance was a room off to the side filled with video games. There was a small souvenir shop that sold paperweights and T-shirts with I-heart-New York logos. There was a line of people waiting to take out food and most of the people seated in the restaurant were on stools at the counter. But there were also twenty tables or so, and eight or ten booths, many of them empty. Justin woke up Kendall, set her down, and went to the souvenir shop. He gave the woman a credit card and bought three souvenir shirts in different sizes, some aspirin and a first aid kit. By the way the cashier looked at him, he could tell his appearance was worse than he'd even thought. He gave Deena and Kendall their shirts, ushered them into the women's room, then he went through the swinging door into the men's room and did his best to wash up. It took some work. He removed his shirt, which was torn and scorched and bloody. Taking a deep breath, he cleaned his wound with hot water and soap rubbed onto a rough paper towel. He opened the first aid kit, took another deep breath, and splashed Mercurochrome onto the gash. When he looked up into the mirror, he had tears in his eyes. One more deep breath, then he went back to the paper towels and, using more soap and water, did his best to clean his face and torso and swab his armpits. He stuck his head under the faucet, rubbed a handful of liquid soap in his hair, then dunked himself again and rubbed as hard as he could manage. He bunched together more paper towels to dry himself and used his fingers to comb his hair back into place as best he could. He wrapped a gauze bandage from the first aid kit around the wound in his shoulder. It absorbed a bit of blood, but the bleeding had, for the most part, stopped. Then he put on his clean I Love New York shirt and went back to the diner.

Deena and Kendall had already taken a booth. He saw that they were both wearing their new shirts and that they'd also managed to clean themselves up to the point of respectability.

'Don't we look like the happy family,' Justin said as he eased into the booth.

They all ate tremendous meals – Kendall had a bacon cheeseburger and a chocolate milk shake over her mother's brief objection – and then, after using the cash machine and withdrawing the maximum, a thousand dollars, Justin ordered a taxi, which took them to the nearest rental car place, in the center of Albany. He rented a mid-size car, a make he'd never actually heard of, then they headed on Highway 95 toward New England. Half an hour out of the city, they pulled into a mall and bought a few essentials: toothbrushes and toothpaste, two overnight bags, socks, shirts and underwear. A mile or so past the mall, they came to a decent-looking motel and stopped. He checked them into two adjoining rooms, told them that they needed a very good night's sleep. He said that right now, whoever was after them believed they were dead. That wouldn't last long, he explained. By tomorrow, he expected that they'd certainly be checking his credit card receipts, cash machine withdrawals, and cell phone use. They'd be back on the case. He said he was too tired to explain further and that he'd fill them both in first thing in the morning. By the time he got to this part of his speech, Kendall was under the covers and sound asleep.

He said good night, went into his room, closing the connecting door but leaving it unlocked, took out his two possessions that had survived the explosion – one of the phones he'd bought and his gun, both of which had been jammed into his jeans – and put them on his nightstand. Justin lay back on the bed and before he could even get undressed, he started to doze off. As his eyes closed, he realized that Gary had never called back. He forced his eyes back open, checked his cell phone and swore – the battery had run out. He had no way to charge it, the charger had been lost in the explosion. He added that to the list of things they needed to do tomorrow, then he forced himself to remove his clothes and get under the covers. Then he was asleep. The next thing he knew, the dream was back, he was re-living his own past, watching his life being shattered, and he woke up screaming from the pain. And the next thing he knew after that, Deena was in his bed, holding him, holding him close, and telling him that he'd had a bad dream and that she was there, that the nightmare was over.

CHAPTER TWENTY-FOUR

'Will you tell me what you dream about?' she said.

It took Justin a few seconds to orient himself. He knew his hair was wet, that his sweat had soaked through the sheets and his top pillowcase. Deena was holding his head to her breast and he could feel her heart pounding against his ear. He was breathing fast and hard. His shoulder pulsed with a dull ache. Slowly, she released him, her hand stroking the back of his head until the last possible moment, until he fell back wearily against the headboard. She got up, went into the bathroom, and brought him back a plastic glass full of water, which he downed gratefully. Then he realized she'd asked him something.

'What did you say?' His mouth felt dry, his tongue thickly coated with crust.

'I asked if you'd tell me what you dream about.'

'Could I have more water, please?'

She nodded, got up again and returned with another full glass. When she handed it to him, she sat on the bed, not at all self-conscious about their physical proximity.

Her hand rested on his hip and he couldn't help but be aware of the fact that he was naked under the covers. She was wearing her souvenir T-shirt and a pair of socks. That was all. When she twisted to tuck one foot under her leg, he could see the muscles on her thigh and calf go taut. Her hair was a mess of unruly curls, which she seemed to realize just at the moment he found himself staring at her, so she shook her head and ran her hands through the tangle. It didn't do much good. She swung her head one more time and shrugged.

'I don't talk about this,' he said quietly.

'Yes, I know.'

'I've never talked about this. Not all of it.'

'Maybe it's time,' she said, matching the softness of his voice.

He shifted his weight on the bed, watched as she brushed a last, feisty curl off her forehead.

'Maybe it is,' he said.

And he began to talk.

'It's not what you think,' he began. 'It's never what people think. Even after all the publicity and the stories, no one ever really knew what happened. You didn't see the *Times* the other day . . . Jesus, was it just the other day? . . . They got some of the details right, but they didn't know what was underneath. They didn't remotely get to the truth . . .

'When we were in East End, on our way to the library, when that guy pulled up in the car, said he was my college roommate, you thought I was embarrassed, 'cause I went to a junior college or something, but that's not what it was. This is really hard for me . . . You want to know where we roomed together? It was at Princeton. I went to Princeton and then Harvard. Harvard was medical school.'

'Excuse me,' Deena said, swallowing hard. 'Can I have some of your water?'

He nodded, handed her the glass, watched her gulp what was left. She went back to the bathroom and he heard the tap run. Then she returned with two glasses, both full.

'Okay,' she said. And then she muttered, 'Harvard. Jesus Christ. I thought . . . Princeton and *Harvard* . . .'

'I lived in Rhode Island, in Providence. My father's very successful. He's . . . Oh hell . . . he's one of those really rich guys. Big house in Providence, mansion in Newport, right on the water, on the Cliffwalk, the whole deal. It's old money. My great-grandfather. He started a bank and my grandfather inherited it and then my father—'

'Your father owns a bank?'

'No. He owns several banks.'

'A Harvard rich guy,' Deena said. 'Did that bottle of scotch get blown up?'

'I'm afraid so.'

'So when you bought the car . . .' she began.

' . . . I gave the guy a check for ten thousand dollars. Five grand more than the car cost. Once the bank told him it was okay, he promised to forget we were ever there.'

She shook her head in disbelief. Then said, 'Go on. I won't interrupt anymore.'

'The whole family is pretty conservative. Stiff upper lip and all that. Very concerned with class and image. They're not very interested in your Buddhist ideal of the whole. And they're not big on denying self. So it was a major deal to them when I . . . I'm getting ahead of myself . . . Let me go back . . .

'When it was time for college, I went to Princeton. It's where my dad went. And his dad. I studied business and everyone thought I'd go back home and . . . and run a bunch of banks. But I didn't want to.' Justin took a long swig of water. 'I wanted to spend my life dealing with something other than money. So I decided to become a doctor and I switched to pre-med. Caused kind of a ruckus back home but they calmed down after a while. A doctor was a little up close and personal, too much like work, but at least . . . a doctor was respectable. And when I got into Harvard I think they actually got excited about the whole idea. They saw me running a hospital or becoming dean of a med school. Something prestigious and . . . clean. I lasted two years and then I quit. Dropped out.'

'You weren't cut out to be a doctor?'

'I was pretty good at it. The problem was that I found something else I wanted to do.' He managed a smile, rubbed his dry lips with his hand. 'You know, I wish I had a joint right now. I'd very much like to get stoned out of my gourd.'

'Finish the story, please. What is it you wanted to do?'

He shook his head as if he still couldn't believe it. 'I don't know how to explain this. When I was at Princeton, what I was good at was figuring things out. Business puzzles. I could look at a company and see where it was going. Look at the debt and inventory and the earnings potential and it was like a connect-the-dots picture, I could see the whole thing in my mind – exactly what was going to happen to this company. I absolutely could tell if it was a good investment or if it was going to tank. And I could do it in reverse, too. We'd study a business that failed and I could put the pieces together, figure out what went wrong and why. When I got to Harvard, I thought I'd find the same kind of satisfaction. You know, find someone who was sick, trace the problem, fix the problem. And I could. I did. But I woke up one day and suddenly I saw the big picture. That's not what I was going to be doing. That fixing thing. At least not fixing anything I cared about. And none of my classmates were going to be doing that either. We weren't going to be family doctors, patching people up and sending them on their way. We were going to be curing rich people's tennis elbows and staring up billionaire's rectums. I could feel myself falling into the trap.

'Then one day I was sitting in a class and I looked around and thought, "I hate all these people." I mean, my classmates, my professors, the residents. And I really did. I couldn't stand to be around them, they were everything I didn't want to be. Smug and privileged, isolated from the real world. So I quit. I went back to Providence. My parents couldn't believe it. My father is not someone who understands the words, "I don't know what I want to do." He also doesn't understand the idea of not doing anything. But that's what I did for a while. Nothing. I hung out with my buddies and messed around. And that's when I realized what I wanted to be. One of my best friends, this guy named Albie Flett, he was walking down the street in Providence, downtown, right near the Biltmore Hotel in downcity. It wasn't even late at night, and some guy came up to him, robbed him at gunpoint. Albie gave him his cash and his watch, his credit cards. He wasn't rich but he gave the guy whatever he had. The guy took it, told Albie to turn around, and when Albie did, the guy shot him. For no reason. Just for the hell of it.'

'Oh my god. Killed him?'

'No. Worse, in a way. Paralyzed him. Turned him into a quadriplegic.'

'Did they ever find the guy who did it?'

'That's the thing. It seemed kind of impossible. It was random, you know? And that's the hardest kind of crime to solve because there's no rhyme or reason. Most cops would give it a shot for a while then forget about it. But there's this cop in Providence, Billy DiPezio, he's the Chief of Police. A strange, funny guy. All squinty and leathery, drinks like a fish and smokes a ton. Very controversial up there, a lot of people want him out but he's got too much dirt on everyone, he's untouchable. Anyway, he took a personal interest in what happened to Albie. I'm not sure why. I think it just made him sad. So he decided to solve it. He wanted the prick who did it behind bars. Billy came and talked to a bunch of Albie's friends, to get any background information that might be useful. Fairly standard stuff. I told him a few of Albie's hang-outs, his habits, stuff like that. He thanked me and got ready to leave and I asked him where he was going.

He said he was going to Waggoner's, that was one of Albie's hang-outs, and for some reason I asked if I could go with him. Even stranger was that he said yes. We went to the club and I listened while Billy asked a bunch of questions – was Albie flashing any money lately, had he gotten into any heated conversations, had anybody been paying any special attention to him, that kind of thing. He just beat it into the ground, wouldn't give up. He let me tag along, figured I couldn't really get in the way and he liked talking to me – Billy likes an audience and the fact that my parents were who they are didn't hurt, Billy likes rich people, too. I spent two weeks with him and the son of a bitch solved the case. He found the guy. Did it with shoe leather, just kept pounding and pounding until one thing led to another and he got what he needed. It was amazing to me. I loved Billy's bravado but most of all I loved the fact that he brought someone to justice who otherwise would have been free to fuck up a lot of other lives. So a week after Billy arrested the guy, I went and took a test and passed and I joined the police force. Went to work for Billy and became a cop. That's what I wanted to be.'

'Your parents?'

'General hysteria. Which died down eventually, but my father never got past his anger over my decision. I no longer had the right image for the family. I wasn't someone he could parade around and talk about how successful I was.'

'Families are complicated.'

'Yeah. Well, there were other complications, too. I got married when I was a senior at Princeton. Her name was

Alicia. And . . . um . . . she liked the idea of being married to a Harvard doctor, too. It took a lot of adjustment to go from that to being the wife of a Providence cop.'

'She left you?'

'No, no. God, no. We were incredibly in love and that was what counted. At least, that's what we thought.'

He fell silent, stared away from Deena, off to the side, into the darkness of the motel room.

'What happened after that, Jay?'

'Alicia and I had a kid, that's what happened. And I turned out to be a hell of a cop. I liked being a tough guy. Took the meanest calls, got a reputation on the streets. It took me three years to work my way up to homicide. I got there because I solved a murder no one else could figure out. An academician, guy in his mid-fifties, history professor at Brown, disappeared. His wife reported him missing, said he just didn't show up one night. Everyone thought she did it, I didn't think she was the type. I spent some time with her. She was his second wife, she told me, they'd only been married a few years. Her husband had a son from his first marriage, she said he was a nice boy but had problems. She didn't tell me what the problems were. The kid was in his twenties now, he was staying with her, to help her out during this difficult period. I talked to him, something didn't seem right. So I did some checking. There was no first wife. There was no son. The kid was a street kid, and orphan. This very respectable professor, he'd been molesting the boy since the kid was ten, twelve years old. The boy lived with the professor, didn't know anything else, so he let our guy support him as an adult, too. He had an apartment that the professor paid for. They were lovers right up until the night the kid killed him.'

'Oh my god. Why did the guy get married if he was—'

'I don't know. It wasn't my job to psychoanalyze him. People are sick. They hurt in all sorts of ways. People do things that, until you actually see them firsthand, you think are inconceivable. I used to tell Alicia about some of it, but she didn't want to know. She didn't like that I knew it, either. Didn't like that I saw the things I saw. I didn't blame her. She thought she was marrying a doctor and that she'd spend her nights going to charity dinners and dances at the country club. She didn't want to know about men fucking little boys and people getting chopped up and the garbage that I had decided to cover our lives with.' He was trembling again and he knew it was time to finish the story. 'So, anyway . . . I became a hotshot. The star of the force, if you will. And when I wasn't being a cop I was a dad. We had a little girl. Lili, we called her. That was Alicia's favorite movie, the one with that French actress and all those puppets. She was a great kid. A lot like Kendall. Smart and funny . . . and sweet. God, *so* sweet. Even my dad, who's not the warmest guy in the world, he couldn't resist her. Spoiled her like crazy. He liked her so much, he could almost forget what a disappointment I was. Then, right before Lili's eighth birthday, I made a big arrest. Providence has a decent organized-crime population. There was a guy there, been there for years, basically the number two guy in the New England Mafia. Involved in a lot of union stuff and local politics. Louie Denbo was his name. He was a bad guy but everybody pretty much left him alone. Cops, politicians, no one wanted to deal with it and it was just about money, there wasn't much killing, so no one really cared. It's a separate world, the Mafia up there. He was a character, he talked funny, and he was quoted a lot in the papers, so people thought he was, I don't now, a *cute* Mafia guy or something. But then he crossed the line. He hit a banker, someone my dad knew pretty well. There was a financial scandal going on and the guy owed a lot of money and some of it he owed to Louie. So Louie took him out. Only he overdid it. He had his guys do the hit in a restaurant and they took out three other innocent bystanders. Well . . . I got him. It was three months of serious police work, Louie was incredibly well protected, but I got him. And he knew I had him . . .

'The day before the trial started, I was home with Alicia and Lili. It was after dinner. I didn't hear anything, I don't know how but I didn't. In my dream, I do. Every single time I hear them. It's like a premonition . . . but that night I didn't hear a thing. I was watching TV and I looked up and there were three guys in my house. They worked for Louie Denbo. I knew them and as soon as I saw them I knew why they were there. But the crazy thing is, what they wanted to do, it didn't matter. I mean, I was going to testify against Louie, but the prosecution didn't need me. I was the icing on the cake. So they couldn't even help him. It was just spite. I'd taken Louie down, so he was going to take me down. I was sitting in the lounge with my feet up. Lili was helping Alicia do the dishes. They were going over the multiplication tables while they were cleaning up. One of the guys, his name was Jerry, he pointed the gun at Lili and he pulled the trigger and he killed her. He didn't even say anything. He just shot her. She was standing next to Alicia and' – Justin closed his eyes now, he could see it all, picture it perfectly with his eyes closed – 'and my daughter's brains splattered all my wife's pants and shirt. I tried to get out of the chair but they shot me. Once above the knee, once in the chest, once in the back. I went down. Stayed on the floor. They thought I was dead.'

'Oh my god, Jay . . . they killed Alicia?'

'They were going to but they decided to rape her first. Jerry, he was such a sick son of a bitch, he told her they wanted her to see my face while they were raping her. They wanted her to see who'd really done this to her. So he walked over to me and kicked me, to turn me over on my back. He didn't know I had my gun with me. I'd gotten home late and hadn't put it away. I mean, I always put it away, I never wanted Lili to ever even touch it. But that night, I don't know why, I just didn't. I'd fallen on it when I went down on the floor. And I managed to put it in my hand while I was there. So when he kicked me, I turned over and I shot him. In the chin, while he was staring down at me. He died instantly. One of the other bastards shot me again, but I kept firing, and I killed them, too. Then I passed out. When I came to, a couple of days later, my little girl was dead and Alicia . . . Alicia, she . . .'

He turned away from Deena, put one hand on his throat as if to lock the words in. Deena reached over, put her hand on his. 'What happened to your wife?'

'I was in the hospital for a couple of weeks. When I got out I had a few months of rehab, I was on paid leave.

Temporary disability. Alicia couldn't bear to look at me. She just got more and more depressed. She'd cry a lot and spend most of her time in Lili's room. If I tried to say anything or, worse, to touch her, she'd just look at me, it's like she was saying, "You did this." She never said anything. Not out loud. Ever. But that's what she was thinking. And, of course, she was right. I did do it.'

'Your parents . . .'

'Not much help, I'm afraid. My mother came to see me in the hospital. My father never did. When I got out, he wouldn't take my calls. So I went to see him at his office, at the bank. His secretary let me in and my dad was sitting at his desk, working. He looked up at me and he said, "You took the thing I loved the most away from me." He meant his granddaughter. And that was it. He put his head down, went back to work. I haven't seen or spoken to either one of them since.'

'And Alicia?'

'One year to the day after the break-in and the shooting, she killed herself. I was home and she went to the kitchen, right to the spot where she was standing when Lili was killed, and she shot herself. I had put the gun away that day, but she took it out of the closet, put it in her mouth and pulled the trigger.

'I think I'm finished,' he said. 'That's the end of the story.'

Deena slid over next to him, put her head on his chest and wrapped one arm around him. 'I'm sorry,' she said.

'Bad stuff happens all the time,' Justin said. 'It just seems a lot worse when it's happening to us.'

'That's not what I meant. I am sorry for all that

happened. But I meant . . . you shouldn't have gotten pulled back into the bad stuff. You're here because of me. And you shouldn't be.'

'No one really gets pulled into something they don't want to get pulled into. Not exactly the words of the Buddha, I'll grant you, but there's my philosophy of life. When push comes to shove, people are where they want to be.'

He slid down on the bed so his eyes were even with hers and his mouth was an inch away from her lips.

'Do you want to be here?' she asked.

'Right now I do, yes.'

He could feel her warm breath on his face, feel the hardness of her body up against his.

'I know you're out of shape,' she whispered, 'and you haven't been a real cop in a while. And I know my daughter can outtalk you on the telephone.' She put her hand on Justin's cheek and stroked him gently. 'But exactly how rusty are you?'

Justin leaned in to her and they kissed. Their lips were cracked and dry and he winced when her shoulder bumped up against his. But he kissed her again, harder, and when she lifted her T-shirt over her head and tossed it on the floor, he pulled the sheet back and motioned for her to get under it.

'I think we'd better find out,' he said.

In the morning, Deena opened her eyes a few minutes after six o'clock. She thought an alarm had gone off, but then she heard someone talking, thought maybe it was a dream. She turned over, saw that he was gone. She realized it was his voice she was hearing. She looked across the room. Justin was on the telephone, speaking quietly.

'All right,' he was saying. 'You be careful. If you can get what I asked for, that's great. But don't do anything if it's too risky. Do you understand?' He listened for a moment, then said, 'Okay. Thanks for calling back. If I'm wrong, I'll let you call me paranoid. I'm sorry I woke you up.'

He hung up, saw that she was awake, smiled and slid back into bed. 'That was Gary. The kid I work with in East End.'

'Do you trust him?'

'I don't really have a choice right now. People aren't exactly lining up to help.'

She kissed the corner of his lips. 'Has anything else happened?'

'Unfortunately, yes,' he told her. 'There's a warrant out for my arrest. And yours, too.'

'For what?'

'Murder. They're saying I killed Ed Marion. And that we both killed Susanna Morgan.'

'I don't understand,' she said.

'Somebody doesn't want us to get any closer to whatever the hell is going on. And it'll be a lot harder to get close while there's a manhunt going on.'

He could feel her tremble as he held her. And he saw goose bumps raise on her arms.

'I'd better go back to my room,' she said. 'So I'm there when Kenny wakes up.'

He nodded. Ran his hand through the curls of her

hair. 'I'm not going to let them hurt you,' he told her. 'Not you or Kendall. I swear.'

'I believe you.' She did her best to smile, and then she said, 'Do you really have a plan?'

'Yes.'

'Do you want to tell me what it is?'

'We're going to Providence,' he said.

She looked surprised. 'What's in Providence?'

'Almost everything we need,' he told her. 'At least for now.'

BOOK THREE

CHAPTER TWENTY-FIVE

Deena had asked if they could do a half-hour of yoga before they all left. She said it would do them some good. Justin thought of how his body had ached after their first session and how his shoulder throbbed now. Then he thought of Deena, under the covers, and he remembered touching her smooth, perfect body. He thought of all the things they had to do and the obstacles facing them, and then he said, 'Sure. A half-hour of yoga is just what I need.'

He had to admit, he felt better afterward. He stretched and held poses, then she made him sit and do nothing but breathe deeply for ten minutes. It relaxed him and made him feel centered. After taking a shower, he actually felt pretty good.

The first thing they did after leaving the motel was stop off and buy yet another cell phone. 'It won't slow 'em down for long,' Justin said, 'but at least it'll annoy them.' Then they bought copies of the New York *Times* and the local paper. The news that they were now wanted for questioning and were suspects in two murders was on page four of the *Time*'s Metro section. They had made page two of the local.

Front page news was still dominated by the murder of Maura Greer and the burgeoning scandal with Greer and Frank Manwaring. Details were emerging daily – hourly, it seemed – that tied Manwaring closer and closer to the murder. The media was incensed by the veil of silence behind which the ex-Secretary had hidden himself. They were calling for his head. D.C. police had revealed the depths to which Manwaring had gone not to cooperate with their investigation in the months prior to the discovery of the body. And Assistant Director Leonard Rollins of the FBI, in charge of the now-Federal investigation, was quoted acknowledging that Manwaring had been on the East End of Long Island, in the nearby Hamptons, just two weeks after Maura had disappeared. When questioned about whether or not Manwaring could be tied to the attempt to hide Maura's body in the waters off East End Harbor, Rollins gave a half-hearted, 'No comment.' The dead woman's parents were insisting that such proximity to the murder scene could not be a coincidence. Public opinion polls showed that eighty-eight per cent of America believed that Manwaring was involved, if not downright guilty, in the death of Maura Greer.

Manwaring, meanwhile, had his spokesperson yet again vehemently declare his innocence. The spokesperson also said that, 'Mr Manwaring would not comment on any specifics of the investigation or any specific allegations. He is proceeding with his life as he normally would. Personally, he is dealing with the trauma this situation has caused his family. He is dealing with that privately with his wife and children. And he is continuing with his professional commitments, including attending an upcoming conference in Montauk, New York. The conference is hosted, as it is each year, by Herbert Borbidge, head of the Wall Street firm Borbidge & Company, and it brings together leaders from the media, government and business communities to discuss wide-ranging issues and problems. Secretary Manwaring is attending as a private citizen, not as a representative of the current administration. And he is attending because he is on several panels discussing topics which he considers crucial to the future of our country. Mr Borbidge has personally assured him that the Secretary's presence is not just welcome but essential to the success of the conference.' The story then quoted Herbert Borbidge giving a lukewarm endorsement at best, saying that Manwaring had been invited months ago and that, as of now, there was no intention of rescinding the invitation.

Deena read the story aloud as they drove north. She and Kendall were eating doughnuts. Justin had declined, saying that they were too fattening. When Deena looked up in surprise, he had shrugged and said, 'If I'm going to start practicing yoga, I might as well lose some weight, too.'

When she put the paper down – after reading the story of Pedro Martinez's two-hit shutout of the Yankees to Kendall – she turned to Justin and said, 'Do you think he did it?'

'Which he are we talking about now?'

'Manwaring. Do you think he killed that girl?'

Justin chewed on his lip a moment, before saying, 'I have to admit, there are too many other murders I've been concentrating on to give that one much thought.'

'It'll take your mind off other matters. Think like a cop.'

'It's hard,' Kendall said from the back seat. 'He's rusty.'

'He's not as rusty as you think, young lady,' Deena said. 'Now hush.'

Justin accepted her words with a pleased raise of his eyebrows, then he said, 'Okay, from what I've read, yes, he sounds like the absolute poster boy for guilt.'

'So he killed her.'

'Probably.'

'Not definitely?'

'When you're working homicide there are two separate and distinct points of view you constantly have to juggle. The first is that people who commit crimes really do incredibly stupid things. It's why we catch them. Every single time you think, "Well, this guy isn't really going to leave a shirt with the victim's blood lying around in his laundry for us to find," or "He can't possibly have buried the gun someplace as obvious as his front yard," and almost every time he does. Most killers either panic or just plain screw up. I'll tell you the most amazing thing criminals do, they can't resist playing around with their own names. If someone's on the run and he checks into a hotel? Well, if his name's Paul Davis, when he checks in he'll use one of three variations. He'll either keep the same first name and a different last name, usually the same initial, though. He'll use Paul Dillon or something like that. Or else he'll use a different first name but keep both initials. Phil Dillon. Or else he'll come up with some kind of rhyming scheme or pun. Saul Mavis. I swear. You find ninety per cent of the people you're looking for that way. Some of them want to get caught, some of them don't know how to avoid it. But then there's the flip side. Sometimes things are too easy, they fit too perfectly. Sometimes a cigar is just a cigar. But occasionally it's something that someone else wants you to *think* is a cigar.'

'So you're weaseling out of your answer, is that right?'

'My answer is the guy's a politician. So the odds are he's total scum and did what everybody thinks he did. But there's also a chance that he's just the unluckiest guy in the world, in the wrong place at the wrong time.'

'Like us?'

'There you go. A perfect example.'

'Am I unlucky, too, Mom?' Kendall asked.

'God, you have big ears,' Justin said.

'The biggest,' Deena said. 'And no, Dumbo,' she told her daughter, 'you're the luckiest child on the planet because you've got me as a mom.'

'I agree,' Justin chimed in.

'Yuck,' Kendall said. 'Yuck and double yuck.'

'I guess I have to agree with that, too,' Justin said.

Gary Jenkins watched as AD Rollins came into the police station, stopped just long enough to look over at him, a thin smirk lingering on his lips, then kept walking into Chief Jimmy Leggett's office. Gary's stomach clenched when, just a few minutes later, he heard Leggett call him into the office. He stood quickly, cracked his knuckles, and walked to the back of the police station. When he stepped through the office door, Agent Rollins was seated, his legs stretched out casually before him.

'Sit down, Gary,' the chief said and indicated which chair the young officer should sit in. Leggett remained standing.

When Gary settled in to the seat, Rollins spoke. There was no urgency or anger to his voice. His words sounded as casual as his posture. 'Let me get right to the point, Officer Jenkins,' he said. 'I've been tracking the calls that have been coming in and out of this office. And I know you've received several calls from Justin Westwood.'

Gary had a little difficulty swallowing the saliva in his throat but he forced it to go down and decided he was better off keeping quiet than saying anything.

'As a result of those calls, I got a tap on your office line. I also tapped your home phone, so I know you've called and spoken to Westwood.'

Gary decided he was definitely better off keeping quiet.

'Would you like to hear a tape of your conversation at six-oh-three this morning, Officer Jenkins? Or do you remember the substance?'

Unfortunately, it was time to speak. 'I remember, sir.'

'Westwood asked you to get him some information, is that right?'

'Yes, sir.'

'Phone records.'

'Yes, sir.'

'Are you going to keep yessing me to death, Officer, or are you going to explain to me what happened?'

'You know what happened, sir, if you listened to the conversation.'

'I want to hear your explanation.'

'Westwood called me early this morning. Woke me up. He asked me to get him a list of the incoming and outgoing calls for a woman named Helen Roag.'

'And why would he do that?'

'Because I got him similar information before.'

'What info?'

'When this all started to happen. Before you even got here. I got him phone records for a business in Connecticut called Growth Industries.'

Rollins nodded, as if that settled something in his mind. Then he said, 'Did you get him the records for Helen Roag?'

'No, sir.'

'Why not?'

'Because he's a criminal, and I didn't think it would be right.'

'Are you bullshitting me, son?'

'No, sir. I told him I'd do it because I didn't want to upset him. But I had no intention of getting him any more records.'

'Why didn't you report this to me or to Chief Leggett?'

Gary hesitated. 'Because Westwood's a friend of mine, sir.'

'Is that right? Chief Leggett says you never got along with him. Isn't that what you said, Chief?'

'That's right,' Jimmy Leggett said. 'He and Brian, they never got along with Jay.'

'That is right, sir,' Gary said to Rollins. 'But that was before I knew all the stuff about Westwood and his wife and daughter. I never would have picked on him the way I did if I'd known what had happened. When I heard, it made me feel sorry for him.'

'What happened in the past is totally irrelevant,' Rollins said. 'Justin Westwood's a murderer.'

'I don't believe that,' Gary said. 'He may have done some stupid stuff, but I don't think he really killed anybody.'

'I don't care what you believe. I'm telling you what I know. And what your chief now knows.'

Gary looked over at Leggett, who took a long time before nodding. 'Agent Rollins has told me things,' Leggett said to the young police officer. 'Things I doubt he's going to tell you.'

'And you believe that Westwood killed that guy in Connecticut?'

Leggett looked over at Rollins. It was Rollins who answered. 'It's worse than that, son. We think that Westwood is involved in Maura Greer's murder. And we think he probably killed your friend Brian.'

'I was there before he was. He called me to come over!'

'There's your answer, son. How else would he know that Brian was dead?'

Gary didn't say anything for quite a while. Then he whispered, 'That son of a bitch.'

'Are you sure you haven't sent him the phone records he asked for?' Rollins said now.

'I haven't even requested them,' Gary said. 'If you don't believe me, you can check your taps. I have my cell phone here, too, sir. You can check every recent call I've made on that. The last call was a call-back to that son of a bitch. Right after he called me early this morning. It's the motel where he was staying. Maybe he's still there and the number'll help you track him down. If you heard that first conversation, you'll remember that he said it was a bad connection. He thought it was from my end so he asked if I had a different phone to call him back. That's why I used the cell.'

'What was said during that second conversation?'

'It only lasted a few seconds. He made sure I had copied down exactly what he wanted to know, then he told me that he'd get back in touch with me and tell me where and how to send it.'

'But you've done nothing?'

'I haven't gotten him what he wanted and I wasn't going to. And I'm sure as hell not going to do it now. That lying son of a bitch. He let me feel sorry for him . . .'

Rollins stared at Gary, let him hold his gaze for several long seconds. 'I believe you,' the FBI agent said. 'Thank you.' As Gary turned to leave, Rollins said, 'We're going to leave the tap on your home phone, son. In case Westwood calls again. If you hear from him in any way, I want you to let me or your chief know instantly. Is that understood?'

'Yes, sir.' Gary turned to Leggett. 'Jimmy, do you mind if I take a quick walk? I'd like to get some air. I'm pretty angry about the way that cocksucker tried to use me. I'd really like to walk it off.'

'Go ahead,' Leggett said.

'Are you sure about Brian?' Gary asked sadly.

'We're fairly sure,' Leggett said. And added, 'I'm sorry about all this.'

'I'll be back in a little bit,' Gary told him, and walked, stiff and angry, out of the police station.

Gary walked at a fast pace, heading straight for the photo store at the end of Main Street by the bay. When he stepped into the store the owner, an overweight, slow-moving woman named Jayne, waved her large hand in a familiar greeting.

'Jayne,' he said, 'did that fax I asked to be sent here arrive yet?'

'Not yet,' she told him.

'When it does, just put it in an envelope and hold it. Don't call me, okay? Don't call the station and don't call me at home. I'll come by and pick it up.'

'Sounds mysterious,' she said, 'but you're the customer so you must always be right.'

'Can I make a call?' Gary asked. 'It's to a cell phone. I don't think it counts as long distance but if it does, just keep track of the bill and I'll pay you back.'

She didn't say a word, just handed him the phone and went into the back storeroom. Gary dialed. The phone on the other end rang twice before someone answered.

'Yup?' Justin Westwood said into the receiver of his cell phone.

'You were right,' Gary told him. 'They tapped my fucking phones. And you were right about the other stuff, too. I guess you're not paranoid after all.'

'What else am I supposed to have done?'

'They said you killed Brian.'

'Yeah, I'm not surprised.'

'Well, this'll surprise you. They're tying you in to the Maura Greer thing.'

'What?'

'I swear.'

'Why? I mean, I never even met her!'

'If I had to guess, I'd say they're gonna have you working with the politician, what's-his-name . . .'

'Manwaring.'

'Yeah. That's the one.'

'When Rollins was doing his spiel, did you handle it the way I told you?'

'Yeah. He totally bought the stuff about the phone records.'

'I'm sure he's checking it out now to see if you lied. No other problems?'

'Uh uh. I even improvised a little.'

'What'd you do?'

'I called you a cocksucker.'

'Great. Sounds like an Oscar winner. Where are you calling from?'

'Don't worry. The photo store. It's safe.'

'You get the stuff I want?'

'Not yet. What the hell do you think I am, a magician? My brother's working on it.'

'Your brother?'

'Yeah. You said you wanted a hacker. He's fifteen years old, he can hack his way into anything.'

'Your little brother is my hacker? Gary, we're going up against the FBI here.'

'He put another little buddy on it, too. A double team. The other kid's fourteen and he's *really* scary. I don't get it but they seem to know what they're doing.'

'Anything else?'

'Yeah. If you want me, call this number. I'm sure they're keepin' tabs on my cell now, too.' Gary gave him the number of the photo store. 'I'll come by here whenever I can. Jayne'll give me any messages. Just tell her it' – Gary couldn't help but break into a smile – 'just tell her your name's Clint.'

'Very fucking clever.'

'Take care,' Gary said, and hung up the phone.

Jayne came out of the back room. 'Sounds like cops and robbers,' she said.

'Better than *CSI*,' he told her. 'I'll be back later to get my stuff.'

Deena didn't ask any questions, she could tell that Justin was not yet ready to take them to their final destination, so she let him drive them around Providence, Rhode Island. He cruised through the Federal Hill area in the West End, pointing out the Little Italy restaurants and grocery stores and charming townhouses. He drove to the East Side, too, took the car through the exquisite and stately Brown campus, showing them the Rhode Island School of Design and the historic John Brown House. He drove slowly through the downtown area, what he called 'downcity,' staring up at the imposing City Hall, surprised at the plethora of fancy, new restaurants. It was as if he had to ease into his past by showing them the city's landmarks and gradually letting himself remember that he had a personal connection to it all.

At twelve-thirty in the afternoon, just as Kendall was beginning to complain about being hungry, Justin pulled up in front of a large, gated mansion on Benefit Street. Through the gate, what looked like a huge public park was visible. There was a rose garden, a cutting garden and a vegetable garden that was overflowing with various lettuces, tomatoes, cucumbers and squashes. There was an enormous English cottage garden, too, with brick paths winding through it that led to a picnic table and benches. There were also acres and acres of green that stretched in every direction. The house itself was turn of the century and quite austere with lots of harsh angles and intimidating columns. It was three stories and there were three distinct wings, each with four separate chimneys jutting skyward. The brick chimneys gave the house the aura of a mausoleum rather than a country home centered around hearth and warmth.

'Tell me this isn't your parents' house,' Deena said, her eyes wide.

'I'll be happy to,' he told her. 'But I'd be lying.'

'Wow,' Kendall said. 'Is your dad the mayor?'

'It's even better than that,' Justin said. 'My dad *owns* the mayor.'

Justin now drove the car past the slowly opening gates – they hadn't changed the security code in all these years – and headed up the long driveway, parking in front of the house. He asked Deena and Kendall to wait in the car, just for a few minutes. Deena squeezed his hand and he nodded that he was fine, then he went to the front door and rang the bell.

He tried to fight off the music in his head while he waited. Melancholy chords and words. Loudon Wainwright.

There's a heaven and he knows it's true.
But he's back on earth just missing you.
And it's hell on earth just missing you.
Back where he started, missing you . . .

Enough, he said to himself. Enough sadness and enough of the past. No matter what happens when the door opens, you've got to stay in the present. He glanced back at the car. *If they're going to survive, you've got to stay in the present.*

He waited maybe a minute, then heard footsteps. What amazed him was that he recognized the steps, he knew immediately to whom they belonged. So he wasn't surprised when his mother opened the door. He was surprised at her appearance, though. She had aged. Somehow gotten smaller. When he'd seen her last she'd been sixty-six years old, trim and athletic looking, attractive and vital. At the door she looked old. Haggard. Worn down by time and loneliness. When she saw him, she started to react, lifted her arms to grab him, but immediately dropped them and held herself in check. Years of restraining her emotions dictated her behavior, but in her eyes he could see the gleam. Her eyes instantly looked young again.

'It's all right if you hug me, mother,' he said. 'I won't mind.'

She took one step closer, then another. Slowly her hands raised again and she reached for him. Her arms around his neck, she pulled him close and held him tight. He could feel the soft, lined skin of her cheek resting against his. And he felt her breath surge all the way through her body.

Lizbeth Westwood released her son. She looked over his shoulder, saw the two figures in the car, turned back questioningly to the boy she hadn't seen in so many years.

'No,' he said, knowing the question in her mind. 'She's a friend. And her daughter.'

'Shall we invite them in?'

'In a minute. We need some help and before they come in I'd like to know if we're going to get it.'

'I . . . I saw the paper,' she said. 'And your father saw the news on television.'

'Is he home?'

She nodded. 'He comes home for lunch.'

'Some things never change,' Justin said.

'If only that were true of everything,' his mother said.

His father was seated at the long, eighteenth-century Spanish dining table when Justin stepped into the room. He had just dug his fork into his grilled filet of sole and was lifting a piece of the soft, white fish up to his mouth when he looked up and saw his son. Jonathan Westwood finished bringing the fork to his lips, ate the delicious, lightly seasoned sole, slowly put his fork down and took a sip of very cold Corton Charlemagne from his wine glass.

'You've gained weight,' he said, setting the glass down on the highly polished table.

'Well, you haven't. You look exactly the same. Maybe a little grayer.'

'I believe in consistency,' Jonathan Westwood said. 'Always have.'

'Yes,' Justin said. 'You have always been pretty consistent when it comes to consistency.'

'You're in trouble.'

'That's an understatement. I'm in *big* trouble.'

'Is it true, what they're saying?'

'Do you *think* it's true, Father?'

The older Westwood shook his head slowly. 'You always did what you wanted to do. Never listened to anyone. You always had a certain arrogance. But you were also always scrupulously honest. You were never the sort of boy to get yourself in trouble.'

'That's not true. I was in serious trouble once. When my daughter was killed. And my wife died. I needed help then and you turned your back on me.'

'Is that why you came back here, Justin? To accuse me? We might have grown apart over the years but surely you remember that the one thing I never allow myself is regret.'

'No.' Justin gently shook his head from side to side. 'That's not why I came back.'

'Then why?'

'To see if you'll help me now,' Justin said. 'To give you a second chance.'

Jonathan Westwood ate one more bite of fish, took one more sip of wine. Then he picked up the linen napkin from his lap, dabbed at his lips and his nearly all-white moustache. He put the napkin down on the table, signaling that he was through with his meal.

'Thank god,' he said to his son. 'Thank god and thank you.'

They didn't get invited up to the Westwood house very often. No one did. So they were all slightly confused but none of them could deny that they were also intrigued. Each of them, as they drove through the gates, was anticipating something, although none had the vaguest idea what that thing might be.

When they saw the other guests, their sense of anticipation rose. So did their bewilderment.

The first person to arrive was the one who had come the farthest, Wanda Chinkle. Wanda was forty-four years old. An attractive woman in a slightly hardened way. She was short, only five foot two, didn't have a discernible ounce of fat on her body. Her hair was dark, cut close to her scalp, not fashionably; it looked like she'd done it just to be practical. Wanda was practical when it came to most things. She was also the Special Agent in Charge of the Boston bureau of the FBI, had been for nearly seven years now. The Boston office had jurisdiction in Maine, New Hampshire and Rhode Island, so anything happening in Providence directly involved her. Wanda agreed to make the drive this afternoon because she had just begun her job – working her way up from Field Agent – when Justin was winding up his investigation of Louis Denbo. She was working closely with him when he'd been shot and she still felt guilty that she had not anticipated the retaliation and had not given the family Bureau protection. She had not heard from Jonathan Westwood in all the intervening years but when he called earlier that afternoon, said it was urgent and that he needed her, not anyone else but her, she decided she could indulge him. The news about Justin had crossed her desk first thing that morning. She suspected that the elder Westwood was looking for some strings to be pulled. She didn't think she'd be willing to pull them but she certainly was willing to hear him out. She owed the family that much.

She waited in the spacious downstairs den for ten minutes before the next guest arrived. Wanda didn't know him. He sauntered into the den, obviously as curious and clueless as she was, and introduced himself. His name was Roger Mallone and he was young, maybe thirty, with a ruddy complexion. He was solid looking, a tennis player, she'd bet, although already starting to go a little soft around the middle. He said he worked for Westwood. He was one of the bank's chief financial advisors. When she told him what her job was, his jaw actually dropped and his face turned even redder than it had been.

It only took three more minutes before the final guest came in. They both knew Billy DePezio, the Providence Chief of Police. After spending an hour with Billy and asked to guess what he did for a living, a reasonable stab would have been that he was a convict. As a back-up choice, stand-up comic would not have been out of line. But he'd been the chief for eighteen years and while he was constantly being attacked in the press and always in the midst of some kind of controversy, he was a damn good cop. Maybe not the most honest one in the world – he'd been known to favor the rich a time or two too many – but his morals were the bendable kind. As far as anyone knew, they had never broken completely.

Billy strode into the den, his usual whirlwind self, shook hands all round, looked for the most comfortable chair. Before he'd even gotten seated, Jonathan Westwood came in.

'You got a funny look on your face, Johnny,' Billy DiPezio said.

'He's in a funny situation,' Justin Westwood said, following behind his father. He had a gun in his hand and he waved it back and forth between Billy and Wanda. 'Don't do anything stupid,' he said. 'Please.' He stepped aside and Deena was right behind him. Justin pointed the gun at Billy now, and said, 'You first.' He told Deena to pat Billy down and look for his weapon. 'It's probably in a shoulder holster, but even when you find that one, keep going. Billy's a sneaky little devil and might have a spare.'

She gave him a thorough going over – Billy rolled his eyes to show he wasn't hating the procedure – but only came up with the gun in the shoulder holster.

'Okay,' Justin said. 'Wanda's gun'll be in her purse. But she also tends to be a little devious. Check around her ankle, those pants are too baggy for her superb fashion sense.'

Deena came up with two guns after searching the FBI agent. One in her purse and one in an ankle holster.

'Where's the kid?' Justin asked, and when Deena told him she was upstairs with Lizbeth, happily watching television, he took the guns, emptied the bullets into a large Lalique bowl, and tossed them into a far corner of the room.

'How about you, Roger – you *are* Roger, right?'

'Ummm . . . yeah. Who are you?'

'Your boss's son. You carrying?'

'A gun?' Roger Mallone said. 'Jesus, no. I've never even shot a gun.'

'Give him a thrill,' Justin said to Deena, 'and check him out anyway.'

She patted Roger down, came away empty handed.

'This is a huge mistake, Jay,' Wanda said.

'I know it might seem like that,' Justin said. 'But I'm out of options right now.'

'What do you think you're doing?' the Providence police chief asked.

'Oh, I know what I'm doing, Billy. Have a seat, relax, and I'll explain everything. We're just going to have a little chat.'

'No, we're not,' Wanda Chinkle said. 'I'm not having any kind of conversation under these circumstances. Put your gun down and return our weapons, then I'll consider it.'

'Oh, shut up, Wanda,' Justin said. 'Here's the deal. I'm not threatening you in any way, shape or form. You're in no danger. I'm simply going to explain something to you. Tell you a little story. I didn't think you'd listen to me

313

unless I coerced you into it. But I'm gambling big-time that you're going to believe me. When I'm done talking, you can tell me whether you do or not. I'll trust you to tell me the truth. If you don't believe me, if you still want to arrest me after you hear what I have to say, I'll tie the three of you up, take your bullets and Deena and I will leave. That should give us half an hour or so as a head start. If you tell me you do believe me, I'll give you your guns back right here, bullets included. If you're lying, you'll be free to arrest us both. If you're telling the truth, then I'll explain to you what I want and I'll ask for your help.'

'What about Johnny and Lizzie?' Billy asked. 'Are they here under duress also?'

'They are. I threatened them in order to get my father to call the three of you.'

'That's ridiculous,' Jonathan said. 'You did no such thing.'

'Billy,' Justin said, ignoring his father, 'that's the story. This is totally against their advice and their will. I forced him to make the calls. Is that understood?'

'It is.'

'My mother's upstairs in a hostage situation.'

'I thought she was watching TV with a little girl,' Wanda said.

'Well,' Justin said, 'there's hostages and there's hostages.' Turning back to the Chief of Police, he said, 'And, you know, you are the only person in the world with the nerve to call my parents Johnny and Lizzie.' After Billy shrugged cockily, Justin looked around the room. 'So do you want to listen?'

314

'I'm scared shitless,' Roger Mallone said. 'I'll listen to anything you have to say.'

Wanda and Billy exchanged glances.

'You owe me this conversation,' Justin said to Wanda. 'You know you do.'

She nodded. Looked at Billy and nodded at him. He didn't nod back.

'I worked for you,' Justin said to the Providence police chief. 'You probably know me better than anyone in this room. Do you think I'm capable of doing the things I'm accused of?'

'I've been a cop a long time, Jay. You know what I think.'

'That people are capable of anything.'

'That's right.'

'I asked you a question. What about me?'

'Okay,' Billy DiPezio said, after a long silence. 'I'm listening, too.'

So Justin began explaining.

He went slowly, occasionally referred to notes he'd made over the past couple of hours. He started with what he'd been doing since he'd left town. How Jimmy Leggett had taken him in as a small town cop. Even told them about Brian and Gary's mocking nickname. He told them about the scream he heard on East End's Main Street, and then finding Susanna Morgan's body, and discovering Deena up on the roof. He told them about the obit in the East End *Journal* and the research he did on Bill Miller. They heard about the shots taken at them in the car, about breaking into Growth Industries and finding the phone machines, about the Ellis Institute and the

315

Aker Institute and the string of old age homes. He gave them the details of the conversation he'd had with Edward Marion, repeated the names he'd heard: Newberg, Kransten and Aphrodite.

At that point in the story, Roger Mallone interrupted. 'Are you talking about Douglas Kransten?' he asked.

Justin shook his head, to show that he didn't know. 'Would it matter if I was?' He saw his father and Mallone exchange a glance.

'Yes, it would,' Mallone said. 'Kransten is one of the most influential people in the country. And one of the wealthiest.'

'Does it make sense that he'd be connected to medical research companies?'

'Yes it does.'

'Then let me finish my story and we'll get back to that.'

As Justin picked up the thread from where he'd left off, he saw Mallone shaking his head in disbelief. But now he was back reliving the events of the past few days. He listed the string of murders: Wallace Crabbe, Brian Meves, Ed Marion, Lewis Granger. He told them about Maura Greer's body being found in the bay and Agent Rollins taking over that case while sabotaging the investigation into Susanna's murder. He said that he was certain that Rollins had murdered Marion – which made Wanda Chinkle's eyes narrow and her shoulders hunch down defensively. Justin described the bomb under their car and the blond madman who said 'Bye bye.' He told them about Rollins tapping Gary's phones and the disappearance of Helen Roag and, finally, he said that the FBI was now tying him in to the death of Maura Greer, someone he'd never even *heard* of until all this started happening.

It took Justin an hour and a half to go through every detail.

'Are you finished?' Wanda asked him.

'No,' Justin said. 'I've got an update. This was faxed to me a little while ago. I had someone hack into Marblehead phone company records and Helen Roag's personal and business e-mail accounts.'

'Jesus Christ,' Wanda Chinkle said. 'Are you insane? Do you have any idea how much time you can get for that kind of stunt?'

'Yes, I do. And can we cut out the editorializing, please? Believe me, if I'm brought up for charges, this is going to be low man on the totem pole.'

'Excellent point,' Wanda said. 'How good was your hacker?'

'Good enough, Wanda.'

She lowered her eyes to the ground.

'The business e-mail account wasn't very helpful. Helen was careful. As near as I can tell, she was some kind of researcher for this Boston company, the Aker Institute. There's very little in her Aker correspondence other than standard corporate communications. But her personal account, here's where things get a little complicated. It looks like our Helen was feeding Aker's trade secrets to somebody. Actually, to two somebodies. My guy went back several months. At the beginning, the e-mails were going to someone at the FBI. You want to handle this one, Wanda?'

'Goddamnit,' the Boston AIC said. 'How'd you get those files?'

'I had to hire the best.' Justin rubbed his chin, realized he hadn't shaved in several days. 'You were Helen Roag's contact?'

'Yes.'

'Why was Helen reporting to the FBI?'

'I can't tell you that, Jay. Not right now. I need a little time to think about this.'

'But she stopped corresponding with you.'

'That's right.'

'She stopped feeding you info altogether?'

'Yeah.'

'Why?'

'I don't know exactly. I think she was scared.'

'Maybe, but that's not the reason. 'Cause she didn't stop e-mailing. She just started e-mailing someone else.'

'Someone in the FBI?' Wanda asked.

'No. There was a string of e-mails back and forth between Helen and . . . I'm glad you're all sitting down . . . Maura Greer.'

'What?' This came from both Wanda Chinkle and Billy DiPezio. And Justin thought he caught Deena's astonished voice in there, too.

'There's more. When my hacker went into the phone company, the phone records had been removed from the system. My guess is it was done by the FBI – I set them up a little bit to see how they'd respond. But my guy still managed to come up with a few interesting details. Wanda, you should know that your people are lazy. Or, more likely, incompetent. The computerized phone records were removed – but they didn't get the phone company to remove the electronic file for Helen's bill.

318

Apparently, that's kept separately. She's got an enormous number of calls over the past three months to one number in Washington, D.C.'

'Whose number?' That was Deena. She couldn't help herself.

'Don't know. Those records were blocked or erased. My guy couldn't get any more information.'

'Did you call the number?' Roger asked.

'It's a beeper. I left three messages, no one's called back.'

'But you've got an idea who it is,' Wanda Chinkle said.

'I've got a few ideas,' Justin told her. 'But I don't have a clue what any of them mean. That's why I need some help.'

'I'll take my gun now,' Billy DiPezio said. 'If I may.'

Justin retrieved all three guns from the corner of the room, handed one of them back to the chief. 'You want your bullets?' he asked.

'Not yet,' Billy said. 'I don't want to tempt myself any.'

Justin looked at Wanda, who scowled. 'You son of a bitch,' she said. 'You were always a better cop than I was.'

'Are you going to tell me what's going on?'

'I don't know how much I *can* tell you. Or how much of what I thought was going on is even true. I have to do some checking. But I will. And I won't try to stop you from whatever you're doing next.'

Justin looked at his father and smiled. He thought it was perhaps the first time in their lives that his father had ever smiled back. He glanced over at Roger Mallone. 'What about you?' he asked.

'Me? I don't have a fucking clue what's going on,' Roger

said. 'But this is the greatest thing that's ever happened to me. I am *in*.' He turned to face Jonathan Westwood. 'I'm not going to get fired for this, am I?'

'There might even be a bonus in it for you,' Jonathan said.

'All right then,' Justin told his newly formed team. 'I took the liberty of making a few lists. And I've already got a few things to add to them.'

He began handing out sheets of paper and explaining exactly what he wanted them to do. Billy had the resources to go to the old age homes that had called in to Marion or Roag's phone machines. Justin asked him to dig up the names of all the patients there who were in contact with Marion or Roag. The goal was to find something Miller and Granger and anyone else who turned up might have in common. A town, a person, a job, anything. 'We need a link,' he said. 'If we get that, we'll be able to find the next link, which I think will be to Kransten.'

Mallone was asked to gather every bit of information he could on Douglas Kransten. Roger gave Justin a brief explanation of Douglas Kransten's holdings and Justin said that he wanted the name and location of every possible company under Kransten's enormous corporate umbrella as well as what they did. He wanted the names of executives, products and development projects, as well.

Justin asked Wanda to break through the secrecy at the FBI. The most important thing she had to do was find whose phone Helen Roag had been calling. Then she had to discover whatever game it was that Rollins seemed to be playing.

'You were always a tough guy, Jay,' Wanda said. 'But Rollins isn't someone you want to take on.'

'I don't need you to tell me that,' he said. 'Believe me. Unfortunately, I don't have a choice.'

When he was done, and the three people he was now trusting to keep him alive had left, Justin went to the phone, dialed the number of the photo store in East End Harbor. They were closed, but the answering machine picked up. After the tone, Justin left his message.

'This is Clint calling for Gary Jenkins. Please tell him to buy his little brother an ice cream soda or a new body piercing or anything he wants, for that matter. And tell him it's on me.'

CHAPTER TWENTY-SEVEN

Assistant Director in Charge of the New York office of the Federal Bureau of Investigation, Leonard Rollins, had, during his nineteen years with the Bureau, been in many meetings, with many superiors, and given many briefings. None of those sessions, however, had ever been quite so high powered or quite so tense. Or, no question about it, anywhere near this fucked up.

It was his turn to be quiet now. So Rollins looked around the table and contented himself by imagining how genuinely miserable every other person at the table was.

To Rollins's left was Brewster Ford. Ford was, without question, the most revered Wall Street mind of the past forty years. He was the mentor to every Treasury Secretary post-David Stockman, regardless of party affiliation, and had been CEO of the two largest investment firms on the Street. Ford was given a huge amount of credit, by those in the know, for much of the backroom strategy that led to the remarkable economic boom of the 90s. He was now nearing 80 and was still an unofficial – but enormously valued – advisor to the current President of the United States.

To his left was Chase Welles, the recently appointed Secretary of Health and Human Services. Welles was tapping his fingers, nervously, distractedly, on the top of the conference table. He seemed out of place in this setting, out of his league socially and politically. Although he was in his early fifties and the only one in the group wearing a suit and tie, he gave off the appearance of being a child sitting at the adults' dinner table.

On Welles's other side was Fred Hoagland, the President's Chief of Staff. This was Hoagland's second but non-consecutive term in this position. He'd served twelve years ago and was considered a genius at subtly guiding, protecting, manipulating and, in general, saving the ass of whomever was serving as Commander in Chief. Hoagland was the ultimate political insider, never totally out of the Beltway loop, no matter who was in power.

Next to Hoagland was Donald Mooney, the President's old friend, ex-governor of Maryland, and current Secretary of Homeland Security. Mooney seemed uncomfortable, not restless or nervous like Welles, rather melancholy. He looked like a man who was hearing a confession he desperately didn't want to listen to.

The next two men sitting at the table were Ronald Mayberry and Patrick Arnold, CEOs of the largest and second largest pharmaceutical companies in the United States. Both men seemed confident and relaxed. They had the air of rich, powerful men who were used to being obeyed and had never in their lives been intimidated by anyone or anything.

Completing the circle was Christopher Dahlberg, Rollins's boss, the Director of the FBI. Dahlberg was quiet and conservative. But Rollins knew just how deadly he could be. The Director was a viper disguised as a common variety of garden snake.

'I want to make sure one thing is understood,' the Chief of Staff was saying. 'The President knows nothing about what is transpiring. He doesn't know about this meeting and he has not been informed of any of the events relating to this meeting that have transpired over the past several months.'

'Nor *is* he to know,' Don Mooney said. 'Ever.'

'I think you're being naïve,' Mayberry said.

'No question,' Arnold agreed. 'It's our understanding that the last three Presidents have not only known about our agreement, they've wholeheartedly supported it.'

'Well, things have changed,' Mooney said. 'You have not exactly stuck to the terms of the agreement.'

'We have,' Mayberry said. 'We all have. For years. Except Kransten.'

'That's a big fucking exception,' Fred Hoagland said. 'And it changes everything.'

'He's out of our control,' Arnold said. 'We can't possibly oversee his work. Even if we could figure out some kind of arrangement here in the US, which would be impossible considering the level of competition, his research facilities are scattered all over the world. There's no way we can keep track of what he's doing. That should be your job.'

'It *is* our job.' It was the first time Rollins's boss, Chris Dahlberg, had spoken. 'And we had things under control. Until recently.'

'What happened?' This came from Mayberry.

'I think we all know what happened,' Chase Welles said. 'And I think we all know how it was resolved.'

'Well, if it's been resolved, what's the problem?' Arnold said.

The Director of the FBI tipped his chair backward. 'There are quite a few problems. There have been some new . . . wild cards, shall we say. But they are being taken care of, largely thanks to Assistant Director Rollins.'

The Secretary of Health and Human Services began tapping the table with his finger. 'We need assurances from the two of you,' he said to Mayberry and Arnold, 'that what happened with Kransten won't happen with you and your companies.'

'I'm not defending Kransten. You know I think the man's . . . how should I put this? . . . Oh, screw it, Doug Kransten's a goddamn lunatic. Wild card doesn't begin to describe him. But you guys fucked up here, not us. You have my assurance that we'll play by the rules. But you've got to control your side.'

'That's why I'm in this meeting,' Welles said. 'Our side's been controlled.'

'Well, as long as that's the case,' Arnold said, 'you can obviously count on me, too.'

'You know, we do read the news,' Mayberry said. 'We're not idiots. You've got a few things that don't seem to be so under control.'

'Such as?' That was from Welles.

'Let's start with Kransten. If he's got what we all think he's got . . . even if he's reasonably close . . . and he makes it public . . . Do you have any idea what's going to happen?'

'Yes.' It was Brewster Ford's first word. The financial advisor and wizard followed it up with, 'We know exactly what's going to happen. It's been my job for all these years to make sure the select few involved in the decision-making process truly understand the danger.'

'And nothing's changed from your perspective?'

'Yes. Many things have changed. And they all make the situation more precarious than ever.'

'And this administration shares that perspective?'

'I would say they are more supportive than any previous administration.'

The pharmaceutical executives nodded, satisfied.

'What else?' Fred Hoagland said. 'What else seems out of control?'

'Manwaring. He won't go away.'

'He will.'

'I'm not so sure,' Mayberry said. 'He's a bulldog. And he's a fanatic.'

'And he's got no credibility. He's no threat.'

'How about the cop? Is he a threat?'

Arnold nodded. 'Yeah. What are you going to do about this cop? He seems totally out of control.'

Hoagland looked down at the notepad he had in front of him, then swiveled to face Chris Dahlberg. 'I think they have a point. This Westwood could be a serious problem.'

Director Dahlberg leaned over, gave Len Rollins a hearty pat on the back. 'I told you,' he said. 'This is AD Rollins's speciality. He's *our* wild card.'

Justin Westwood watched his mother come down the long spiral staircase into the foyer. He marveled at the fact that even at her age Lizbeth never seemed to walk down; it was as if she glided several inches off the ground. Her movements were fluid and graceful and serene. More than that, her steps were rich. His mother moved, Justin realized, as if she owned the ground in front of her. It didn't matter which ground she was walking on. She seemed to own it all.

She put her arm through his and led him into the den. His father was on the chaise longue, reading a financial report. He wore reading glasses, an added accoutrement since Justin had seen him last.

'They're both asleep upstairs,' Lizbeth said. 'I put Deena in the Blue Room. She conked out even before Kendall.'

'Thanks.'

'That little girl is something special.'

'Yeah. She's pretty special.'

'She reminds me of Lili.'

Justin felt something catch in his throat, nodded.

'I've never gotten to tell you,' Lizbeth said slowly, 'how much we miss both of them.'

'Thank you, mother. I miss them, too.' He looked over at his father, who nodded at him. Justin took the motion for what it was: a wordless acknowledgment and a silent, long overdue moment of shared grief. 'I'd like to leave Kendall here with you for a few days. Maybe longer than that.'

'Are you leaving?' Lizbeth said.

'I have to. For one thing, it's not safe for me here. Or for you. It's a natural place for them to start looking and it won't take them long to figure that out. I've got to find out what's going on before they find me and I won't be able to do what I have to do if I'm lugging around a seven-year-old girl.'

'What about her mother?'

'She'll come with me.' When Lizbeth raised an eyebrow, Justin said, 'It's the only play that makes sense. Someone is after Deena. The little girl will be safer if she's not around. I figure you can hire a couple of bodyguards while she's here. I already asked Billy for recommendations. Two good men, that should be enough security – no one's going to consider Kendall a real danger. But if Deena stays here, too, I don't think you can pay for enough security. You'll all be vulnerable.'

'And you'll be able to protect her?' Jonathan asked.

'Nothing is going to happen to this one.'

'Justin,' his father said. 'You do understand that nothing you do now is going to change what happened in the past.'

'Yes, Dad.' He felt his body go rigid. 'I do know that Alicia's dead, if that's what you're saying.'

'No. I'm just trying to make sure that you're doing what you're doing for the right reason. That it's the best thing to do, not some form of atonement.'

He forced a long breath out. And forced himself to

328

admit that his father's question was justified. 'It is,' he said. 'It's the best thing to do.'

'Good. Then of course the little girl can stay here. And we'll do whatever's necessary to make sure she's safe.' Jonathan sat back, tossed the slick pamphlet he was reading across the room. It landed on his son's lap. 'A little bedtime reading material.'

'What is it?'

Jonathan shook his head and sighed. 'Do you really not know who Doug Kransten is?' When Justin shook his head, his father said, 'With your business acumen, not to mention your medical background, it's a crime. The potential that you had . . .'

'Dad . . .'

Jonathan closed his eyes for a moment, cleared his throat as if the action would also wipe clean his thoughts. When he spoke again, his voice was gentler and his tone less aggressive. 'Douglas Kransten has been mentioned as being in contention for the Nobel Prize over the past few years. For his work in genetic engineering.'

'Kransten's a scientist? I got the impression from Roger that—'

'The impression you got from Roger was correct. Good Lord, Kransten's not a scientist. He's KranMar's founder and major stockholder. It's the second or third largest pharmaceutical company in the world. Mallone knew the implications the moment you mentioned his name. Did you see his eyes light up? When he comes back with the information you asked for, I guarantee you he'll have tied in all your various research companies to KranMar and Doug Kransten.'

'I'm sorry for being so ignorant, but where does the Nobel Prize come in exactly, if he owns a company that churns out antihistamines?'

'They do a little bit more than that. Among other things, KranMar holds the patent on several of the drugs that best combat anthrax. It's one of the reasons their stock has gone up so much while everything else is tanking. But more relevant, Kransten spent a fortune over the years – his own fortune in addition to using KranMar resources – to map the human genome. He's been one of the leading backers of research in that area. Also stem cell and almost all cell regeneration research. I've made a lot of money, thanks to Doug Kransten.'

Justin glanced down, tapped the glossy cover of the report his father had tossed to him. 'This is for Kransten's company?'

'Actually, it's for his wife's company. It's an old one, but it's interesting. I dug it out of my files upstairs.'

'Can I go back to something? Did you just call him *Doug* Kransten a little while ago?'

'Yes, I know him, Justin. You've met him, too, although you won't remember. About fifteen years ago, when Louise Marshall, his wife, was taking her company public. They both came up here for the dog and pony show, to raise money. They came to the house for lunch afterwards. You must have been home from Princeton.'

Justin indicated the report. 'What's so interesting about it?'

'You pay no attention to your financial holdings, do you?'

'No.'

'Just because we haven't spoken, your stock portfolio hasn't disappeared.'

'I haven't touched it since I left here.'

'It's disgraceful,' Jonathan said. 'The waste. The money that should have been made . . .'

'Can we please not discuss my lifestyle choices,' Justin said, 'and stick to the matter at hand.'

Jonathan nodded, took another moment to calm himself down. 'If you had been paying attention, you'd know that you own a decent amount of Louise Marshall's company. Well, you used to. Since Douglas took it over five or six years ago and they merged, it was converted and you now own KranMar.'

'I own stock in Kransten's company?'

'Quite a bit. I was fairly prescient, when I bought it for you.'

'What's his wife's end? What does her company do?'

'Beauty products. She isn't exactly the Lauders, but she isn't so far behind.'

'And what's the connection you think you've found, Father, between this report and everything I described earlier?'

'An obsession.'

'I'm listening.'

'What is the point of using the kinds of products that Louise Marshall developed?'

'You tell me, please.'

'To beautify. To eradicate wrinkles and stop hair from turning gray. To create the illusion of youth.'

'Or, rather,' Lizbeth Westwood added quietly, 'to extend that illusion as long as possible.'

Justin watched his mother lightly trace her finger over the lines in her own cheek. 'The men in the old age homes,' he said. 'Bill Miller wasn't an illusion. Neither was Lewis Granger.' He stood up, letting the financial report drop to the carpet. He spoke faster now. His voice got louder. 'I know what you're saying. I've been thinking the same thing. I couldn't bring myself to say it out loud earlier because it defies all logic, it's like science fiction . . . But if they've come up with a way to actually extend life, get people to live to a hundred or more, what's the point of keeping it secret? It doesn't make sense. My god, what would it be worth to the company? How many billions?'

'My guess is that Roger will have a precise financial answer for you, once he's made all these connections. But the answer will be staggering.'

'Then why not make it public? The stock price alone . . .'

'I don't know,' Jonathan Westwood told his son. 'But if there is a reason . . . If there is some secret that has to be kept . . . it sounds like a secret that's worth killing for, don't you think?'

Justin didn't answer. The look on his face settled into something grim and determined. 'Will you do me one more favor, Dad?' he said.

'What would you like?' Jonathan Westwood asked.

'Sell the goddamn stock,' Justin told him. 'Just sell that goddamn stock.'

Leonard Rollins tried calling Wanda Chinkle at home. When he got her phone machine, he tried her at the office. Wanda did not have much of a personal life, her existence revolved around the Bureau. She was capable of working at her desk until midnight, he knew. He made a mental note to himself that, in the future, he should always call her at work first.

Wanda's phone was answered by one of the bright young agents she'd recruited. Rollins didn't know which one he was talking to but it didn't matter. All of Wanda's recruits were good. Dedicated, clever, loyal. So when he asked to speak to Agent in Charge Chinkle and was told that she wasn't in, Rollins didn't hesitate to tell the young man why he was calling.

'You've heard about the manhunt that's on for Justin Westwood?' Rollins asked. The agent told him that he had. 'He's from Providence and his family's still there. It's a longshot, but there's a chance Westwood will return home. If other avenues are cut off from him, it just might happen. It's a bit of a cliché but people do it all the time. Tell Agent Chinkle I'd like her to assign someone to watch Westwood's father's house. Just in case.'

'I think she's already on the case, sir,' the young agent said.

'How so?'

'She was up in Providence today. At the Westwoods. She told me she used to work with the son. The one we're looking for.'

'Yes. They were quite friendly.'

'That's what she told me, sir. She was pretty upset by all this.'

'I bet she was.' Rollins stayed silent.

'Is there a particular message you want me to give her, sir?'

'No,' Rollins said, after another pause. 'Just tell her I'd like an agent in place as soon as possible.'

AD Rollins hung up the phone. Drummed his fingers on his desk for several seconds, then picked the phone back up and dialed. It only took a couple of minutes more for someone at the Bureau's 24-hour in-house travel agency to book his first-thing-in-the- morning flight to Providence.

Justin's eyes were closed, although he was nowhere near to falling asleep, when he heard the faint creak of the bedroom door opening, heard the quiet padding of footsteps, and felt the mattress dip slightly. He didn't open his eyes until he felt her arms slip around him and her body curl against his under the sheet.

'I feel like I'm back in high school,' Deena said.

'You must have gone to some high school.' He raised his right arm, and used it to pull her closer to him. 'I talked to my parents. They'll take Kendall and watch out for her.'

'Jay, are you sure it's the right thing to do?'

'I know you don't like leaving her. But you're a danger to her right now. I can't quite make the connections, I haven't put everything together yet, but I'm getting close. And I know that whoever's after you isn't going to let Kenny walk away if she's nearby.'

Deena nodded, accepting what he was saying. 'When do we leave here?'

'Tomorrow morning.'

'And where are we going?'

'It depends on the answers we get.'

'You look exhausted,' she whispered. He shrugged, not disagreeing, and she said, 'Do you want me to let you sleep?'

'Yes,' he told her. And he let her lift the sheet away, start to move out of the bed. Then he grabbed her wrist, pulled her back beside him. 'I meant eventually,' he said. 'But not quite yet.'

CHAPTER TWENTY-EIGHT

Roger Mallone was the first one to finish his initial assignment. He showed up at the Westwood's front door at 7:15 a.m. Everyone in the household was awake when Mallone burst in, carrying two large brief-cases.

He opened them, let several enormous stacks of paper, pamphlets and files spill out onto the long sidetable in the entryway. 'It's everything you ever wanted to know about Douglas Kransten,' he said. 'Can I have a cup of coffee? I've been up all night and I am *tired*.'

'How in the world did you put this together so fast?' Jonathan Westwood asked.

'Well,' Mallone said, 'your name carries a lot of weight and I bandied it about like a son of a bitch. I had financial analysts faxing, scanning and e-mailing material all night long, I had Green and Bayer pulling things off the computer at the office, and since you said that price was no object . . .'

'I don't recall saying that,' Jonathan said.

'Well, you implied it. So I paid off someone I know at the IRS up here. He was extremely helpful.'

'And how much did you have to pay him?' Jonathan asked.

'We can discuss that later.' Then decided it might be a good idea to lay on a 'sir,' so he did. He turned to Justin. 'I've been going over everything, trying to organize it and make it as understandable as possible. I'll tell you one thing, this guy doesn't have a dummy corporation, a tax dodge, a shell, a project, an employee, a goddamn dog that's not listed somewhere in all this. Can I have that coffee now?'

Deena was upstairs with Kendall and Lizbeth. She was on her knees, kneeling in front of her daughter.

'We're going to go now, Ken. But I want to make sure you're okay with this.'

'I'm okay,' Kendall said.

'Jay doesn't think we'll be away for long. And I'll call you every day.'

'Okay.'

'Kenny, it's okay to be upset. And it's okay to be scared. You don't have to pretend.'

'I'm not upset, Mom. And I'm not scared. Lizbeth said she's gonna take me shopping. And did you see the pool out back? She said I can swim every day. And they have a cook. We don't even have to go out for French fries, she said that Annabelle can *make* French fries. I didn't even know that real people *could* make French fries, I thought they were only in restaurants.' She stopped suddenly. 'I mean, not that I'm gonna eat French fries, Mom, because I'm gonna eat really healthy, you know, like normal.'

Deena leaned over and kissed her seven-year-old. 'When I come back, try to pretend you're happy to see me, okay?'

'Of course she's going to be happy,' Lizbeth said. 'Aren't you Kenny?'

Kendall cocked her head at her mother and grinned. 'Can we get a cook when we go home, Mom?'

'No, we cannot,' Deena said.

'Well, I'll still probably be glad to see you.'

Deena gave her one more kiss and another hug for good measure.

'She'll be fine,' Lizbeth said.

'I know,' Deena told her.

'And so will you,' Lizbeth added softly.

Deena shrugged, then effortlessly rose to her feet in one fluid motion. 'That one I'm not so sure about,' she said.

Roger Mallone had pulled his black Mercedes off to the side of the Westwood house, leaving it in the twelve-car parking area that had been added on several years ago. He strolled over there, got in the driver's seat, closed the door behind him. After one more solid yawn, he turned the key and started the engine. When the car got to the gate, he stopped, waited for the automatic doors to swing open, then cautiously pulled out onto the street. There was a silver Ford parked a quarter of a block away. The driver, a powerful-looking guy, had the aura of an ex-football player or a boxer. He was sipping coffee from a tall

Styrofoam cup. Roger waved to the guy, a friendly good morning wave, as he passed by, but the coffee drinker didn't wave back. Roger drove three blocks away, turned the corner, waited a few minutes, then he got out of the car and opened the trunk.

Roger leaned in, stuck his hands inside the trunk, and helped Deena Harper step out. When she was standing, he extended his hand toward Justin, who made it out, too, although a little less gracefully than Deena had. Justin reached back in, took the two large briefcases that Roger had brought over half an hour earlier.

'You were right about the house being watched.' He described the man drinking coffee in the car.

'Rollins,' Justin said.

'Do you think Wanda told him?' Deena asked.

'It's possible. But if she had, I don't think he would have been waiting outside. He'd know for a fact we were inside and he would have come in.'

'To arrest you?' Roger said.

'I have a feeling this guy's not here to make arrests,' Justin told him.

'Oh,' Roger said. Then he realized the implication of Justin's words and repeated it, with emphasis. '*Oh* . . . Well . . . The key's in the ignition. Maybe you should, you know . . . get the hell out of here.'

'One more thing.'

'What?'

'You have a cell phone?'

'Sure.'

'Can I take it? I'm sure they're not only tracking mine, they're tapping it. I can't risk it.'

'They can do that?' Roger asked. 'They can tap cell phones?'

'They can,' Justin told him.

Roger reached into his pocket, pulled out a small phone. 'It's all yours.'

'I can't thank you enough.'

'Don't even think about it. There's got to be a promotion in this for me somewhere. And don't even worry about screwing up the car. If anything happens to it, I'll make your dad buy me a new one.'

They shook hands. Roger gave Deena an awkward hug. Then he wished them both luck, stepped back onto the sidewalk, and watched as Justin got behind the wheel of the Mercedes and drove away.

CHAPTER TWENTY-NINE

'They can really tap cell phones?' Deena asked.

Justin nodded. 'There's a device called a Trigger Fish. About the size of a briefcase. It can not only tap in so they can listen to conversations, they can triangulate off satellite sites so they can get a fix on our location. That's what I'm really worried about. Rhode Island's small enough to hide in without helping them out.'

'Come on. They can tell exactly where we are?'

'Maybe not exactly. But within about a block. And if they get that close, we wouldn't be too hard to find.'

'I don't think I like the twenty-first century.'

For the next half-hour they rode in silence. Then Deena mentioned that she had never driven a Mercedes before and she asked if she could give it a shot. Justin said, 'Why not?' He pulled over and, as they were switching seats, she said, 'Oh, damn. I forgot. Your father told me to give you something after we left.' She reached into her bag, pulled out an envelope. She watched as he opened it, saw his lips curl up in the faintest of smiles.

'What is it?' she asked.

'Something we need,' he told her. 'Something I guess he didn't think I'd take from him directly.' He held the envelope out for her to see. It held about ten thousand dollars in cash.

'I'm starting to like your father,' she said.

Deena drove the rest of the way into Newport. When they were approaching the city, Justin pulled out Mallone's phone and made a call to Billy DiPezio.

'Did you get it?' he said into the phone. Then he listened for a minute, said, 'Okay, thanks,' and hung up. Deena glanced at him quizzically, but all he said was, 'A little favor from Billy. Nothing essential.'

She was hurt by his evasive answer, but she didn't want to say so. Too petty, she decided. But she sulked for the rest of the drive. Justin didn't seem to notice, though; he was lost in thought. Deena could practically hear the wheels spinning in his head, trying to put the pieces of the inexplicable puzzle together.

She forgot all about her hurt when they arrived in Newport. She was too stunned to sulk anymore. This was a town that reeked of money. Money, snobbery and faded grandeur. As they drove past manor after manor, the sea air misting over the city, she felt like she was stepping back into a Gatsby-like past that never really existed and yet still managed to dominate the present. She felt like everyone on the street should be wearing smoking jackets and sipping tea out of china cups.

Justin directed her toward the waterfront. She pulled up in front of the gates of a mansion and he hopped out of the car. Deena was proud of herself that she didn't

342

gape or go, 'Oh my god!' because this house dwarfed the Westwood home in Providence. She didn't know that houses came in this size.

Justin punched the security code into the enormous gates, watched as they swung out, then waved her through. He hopped in – she watched as the gates closed automatically behind them – and she drove up the quarter of a mile road that twisted its way to the main house. Once there, Justin walked about ten feet to the left of the front door, picked up one flower pot in the midst of several and lifted a key from beneath it. He used the key to open the door. As soon as he was inside, he raced to a green glass vase that sat on a landing by the stairway, took a key from beneath that vase, then ran back toward the front door. He inserted the key into a small silver metal box on the wall. When the door to the box swung open, he punched in another series of numbers. Then he turned to her and said, 'Come on in. All security systems are off.'

He led her upstairs, put their one small bag in a bedroom, and dropped Mallone's briefcases in the middle of an enormous king-size bed.

'Ready to start work? he asked.

She nodded and he pulled her onto the bed. They both kicked off their shoes, turned on the table lamps to the side of their respective pillows, nestled back against the headboard, made themselves as comfortable as possible, and began reading. After four hours with hardly a word being spoken, Deena finally dropped one of her files on the floor and said, 'How about some coffee?'

He mumbled a reply, never looking up from his

report, and she hopped off the bed, meandered her way downstairs. She poked around the kitchen, opening up cabinets and the fridge, checking out the well-stocked pantry. She called upstairs, 'Any ideas where your mother keeps the coffee?'

He called back down to her. 'Yup. In the house next door.'

She decided this was worth climbing back up the stairs. When she stood in front of him, hand on her hips, she said, 'Your parents own *two* houses here?'

Justin shook his head. 'Uh uh. Just one.'

'Then why would she keep her coffee next door?'

'Because that's the one they own.'

Deena's brow furrowed and she cocked her head to the side. 'Then whose house is this?'

'It belongs to the Rutherfords,' he said. 'Jane and Brandon. Old family friends.'

'And where are they?'

'In Europe. I asked my father if they were around. He told me they were in the south of France for a month. Hôtel du Cap, to be exact. I practically lived here in the summers when I was a kid. Their daughter and I used to date.'

'And they just let you stay here?' she asked incredulously.

'Well . . . no,' he said. 'Technically, we're breaking and entering.'

She moved to the bed and snatched the report out of his hands. 'Okay. Tell me what's going on.'

'It's pretty simple, really. My parents live next door. I figure that if all the various people who are now looking for us can deduce that I might have gone to Providence, eventually they'll also realize that I might come here.'

'So we came here, what, so they could just *find* us?'

'We didn't come here,' he said. 'We came next door to here. Or rather, we're here, next door to where they're going to come. This way, we can see who they are and maybe find out what they want.'

'And you don't think they'll come *all* the way next door to see if we're here?'

'No, I don't. Would you?'

Her mouth opened, then clapped shut. 'No,' she said. 'I wouldn't. I'd think that we're just a couple of normal neighbors who don't have a clue what's going on.' She frowned now, something else on her mind. 'How is anyone supposed to reach us? With the information you want. Does everyone know we're here? Or do they all have Roger's cell number?'

'No. Too risky.'

'So if Rollins is using this Rifle Trout or whatever it is . . .'

'Trigger Fish.'

'Whatever . . . to track your cell phone, how can anybody call you without the FBI knowing?'

'Nobody in law enforcement is going to think I'm stupid enough to go back to East End Harbor. I'd have to be insane.'

'So?'

'So I guarantee you that nobody's paying any attention to what's happening at my house there.'

'What *is* happening at your house?'

'I told Wanda and my parents and Roger to call my

East End number if they want to reach me. I told them someone there would tell them the next step to take.'

'Who?'

'There *is* nobody. I call forwarded that number to here. It won't fool them forever, but it will for a while. Even if somebody gives us up and they send someone to the house, it'll take them a little bit to figure out the phone.'

He smiled at her and she said, 'Is this what you were like as a homicide cop? This devious?'

He nodded.

Still frowning, she asked. 'How'd you know their security codes here?'

'I didn't. Billy's the only one who knows where we are and I got them from him. He called in a favor. The police force has access, in case they've got to get into the house when the owners aren't here.'

'Some favor. Since I met you, I don't think I like the idea of the police force knowing anything about me.'

'You might have a point.'

She stood with her hands on her hips, trying to express some form of disapproval. Finally, she just shook her head and said, 'Well, do you have any idea where Mrs Rutherford keeps her coffee?'

'Try the freezer,' he told her. Then he went back to reading his report.

A minute later, he heard her call up: 'How'd you know that? Who the hell keeps coffee in the freezer?'

They kept reading until two o'clock in the morning. Justin had pages and pages of his handwritten notes:

scribbles, facts, diagrams, links between companies and employees. Deena was concentrating on any personal material about Douglas Kransten and Louise Marshall. She'd pored over magazine profiles and newspaper stories and sifted through various corporate reports, focusing on personal information that might be gleaned from them. Justin had asked her to keep a chronology of the couple's lives together, starting from their births, keeping track of all major events. 'It's not always business or money,' he told her. 'Sometimes the answer you're looking for comes from something totally unexpected.'

At two, he tossed the business report he was reading onto the floor. He reached over, began rubbing her shoulders. She instantly melted.

'Excuse me,' he said as he kept rubbing, 'are you *purring*?'

'Mmmmm,' she said. 'Mmmmmm. That feels good.'

'So does anything strike you?' he asked.

'Uh huh. You should use your thumb a little more. Not your knuckles. Did I tell you that I used to be a masseuse? Before I started teaching yoga?'

'No, you didn't. But I was referring to what you've read, not my technique.'

'Mmmmmm. One thing. It's nothing, really. But it's strange. MMMM . . . ohhhhh. Up a little bit on my neck would be good.'

'What is it?'

She reached for her notepad, flipped over to the second page. 'They're a fascinating couple, really. Scary because there's so little about them that doesn't revolve around their businesses. When you read about their marriage, even their courtship, it's always discussed in business terms. They merged more than they got married.'

'That's what's strange? I think that's fairly common in their world.'

'No. What's strange is that there was one personal thing that seems unresolved. They had a child. Well, I don't know if they had a child. But she was pregnant. Louise, I mean.'

'You're on a first name basis now?'

She swung her eyes over at him, looked a little sheepish. 'Well, yeah, I guess I feel like I know them both' – she pointed to the stack of reading material – 'after all this.'

'That's good,' he said. 'I was just teasing. It's what happens to cops, too. When we're studying a potential perp, it becomes very personal. You really do feel like you know them. You have to. It's the only way you can get into their heads.'

'So, anyway . . . ohhh, just a drop lower . . . ohhh yeahhhh . . . ohhhhh . . . there's a mention about Louise getting pregnant.' She looked down at her notes. 'Here it is. There's a reference to it in *Time* magazine in 1974. She's eight months' pregnant. April seventy-four.'

'So?'

'There's no mention of a child anywhere else.'

'Maybe they're protective parents, worried about the kid's privacy.'

'No, no, no. No way. Too rich, too famous. Too visible. It would be like Donald Trump's kid, whether they wanted it to be or not. Page six, the whole deal. No way.'

'Maybe Louise miscarried.'

'She made it through eight months. Seems unlikely. There were no stories to indicate she was ill or having a tough time.'

'Then maybe the kid died at birth.'

'Maybe. Could be. But I don't think so,' Deena said. 'There's some reference . . . hold on . . . in an interview in *Parade* . . . here. In ninety-five. So, twenty years later. The reporter asks her about children and Louise says, 'Well, you know, our daughter died. And after that, we never felt up to having another child.'

'The daughter still could have died in childbirth.'

'I don't know. It's just a funny way of putting it. "Our daughter." It makes her sound like she was alive. More than that. Part of the family.'

'That's it?' Justin said.

Deena stiffened. 'You told me to note anything that seemed odd. Well, that seems odd to me. If there's anything that can change or define a parent, it's losing a—' She saw his head snap back as if he'd been slapped. She reached out for him. 'I'm sorry. I'm really sorry, Jay. I didn't think. I wasn't thinking about you at all, I'm sorry.'

He cleared his throat, let the tension in his shoulders relax. 'No, no,' he said. 'It's fine. You're right, though. There isn't anything quite like it. And it's worth checking out.' He reached for the phone.

'Who are you calling?' Deena asked.

'Billy DiPezio.'

'It's two fifteen.'

'He's just getting started.' She heard the phone ring, then someone pick up on the other end. 'It's Jay,' he said into the receiver. 'Where are you? . . . Nice. Does your wife ever mind that you never come home? . . . I'd like you to check something else out. I want to know if there's a birth certificate for Douglas Kransten's and Louise Marshall's baby. Should have been born in April or May of seventy-four . . . Not sure. If I had to guess I'd say New York. I also want to see if there's a record of the kid's death . . . Billy, let me ask you something? I'm stone cold sober and I'm barely going to remember talking to you tomorrow. You're in a strip club, on what, your sixth scotch . . . okay, seventh . . . How the hell are you going to remember every detail of this conversation . . . Yeah, I know you always do. I just want to know your secret . . . Oh, okay. Thanks. You know where I am.' Justin hung up, turned to Deena.

'So what's his secret?' she asked.

'"Dirty living,"' he said.

She nodded at the large bed. 'Think the Rutherfords'll mind if we join him?'

Justin smiled. 'You don't know the Rutherfords,' he told her. 'They're going to want pictures.'

The phone woke them up at seven o'clock.

'Jay?'

He coughed out a half-asleep response.

'It's Wanda. I . . . I didn't think I'd get you directly.'

'Life's full of surprises. What's up?'

'I'm just calling to say that I haven't gotten any information yet.'

'Oh,' Justin said, managing to open his eyes. 'Okay.

Maybe next time you can call a little earlier to tell me that. Like around five.'

'Have you found anything?'

'Nope. Haven't learned a thing. Until you get me what I asked for, I'm stuck.'

'I'm working on it, but it's not easy. I don't know if there's a real cover-up, but if there is it's a good one. I can't seem to break through the system.'

'I have confidence in you, Wanda.'

'Thanks. Ummm . . .'

'What?'

'I guess that's it. I just wanted to know if you'd made any progress. And how you're doing.'

'I'm doing as well as can be expected.'

'Does anyone know where you are? In case I need to find you?'

'Not a soul. And that's the way it's going to stay.'

'I'm sorry you don't trust me yet, Jay. You used to.'

He yawned slowly and elaborately. 'I'm going to hang up now Wanda. I need to get some sleep.'

'Be sure and say hello to your folks for me, okay?'

'Okay.'

'Don't forget. I'll get in touch as soon as I have anything.'

Justin hung up, poked Deena in the back. When she stirred, he gave her a gentle shake.

'So much for all my cleverness. We've got to get out of here,' he told her. 'Wanda didn't send Rollins after me, I'm pretty sure of that now. But he sure as hell went after her. That was her, and I'll bet anything he made her make that call, so they could trace it. She kept me on long enough so they'll have the call-forwarding gimmick and this location already.' He motioned to the framed photograph of a middle-aged man with his arms around a middle-aged woman and a thirty-something woman. 'Say goodbye to the Rutherfords.'

'Why didn't you just hang up?' Deena asked. 'Cut her off before the trace worked?'

''Cause Wanda went out on a limb for me. As of this second, her career's over. I didn't want to screw her up any more than I had to. It's easier for us to move than it is for her to get by without a pension. Also, I think she tried to tip me off. She told me to say hello to my parents.'

'She just saw them yesterday.'

'I know. My guess is she gave them something for me, knowing that Rollins was going to be on her ass, and that was her way of hiding it from him. But I'll find out in a minute.'

'Do I have time to shower?'

'If you can do it in the time it takes me to make one quick phone call, sure. If not . . .'

'Is it safe to make another call?'

'They can only trace us once.' He picked up the phone by the side of the bed and dialed. On the second ring, his mother answered. Justin didn't bother with any of the usual niceties, he started in with, 'Don't say who it's from or what it is, but did something arrive for me?'

'Yes. A little while ago. Why are you talking like this, Jay? What's—'

'Something you never thought would happen to a Westwood, mother – your phone's probably being tapped by the FBI.'

'Oh my god.'

'Mom, listen to me, okay? This is important. Do you remember where we used to go sometimes, just you and me? The place you never told Dad about because you were embarrassed you liked it?'

'Yes, but why in the world would you bring that up? You know—'

'I want you to meet me there. And bring the thing that came for me.'

'When?'

He thought for a moment. 'You remember my high school girlfriend? Not Portia, the one after that.'

'The redhead?'

'Yeah.' He looked at his watch. 'Think how many letters in her last name.'

'Oh god,' Lizbeth said. 'I can't remember her last name.'

'Okay, okay. Count the number in her first name and add four. Got it?'

'Yes.'

'That's the time. That's the o'clock. I'll meet you half an hour after that. Leave now, immediately, before anyone who's listening can get there. I'm sorry but you'll have to kill some time somewhere. If you remotely think that anyone's following you, forget the whole thing. Just go back home. Okay?'

'I have to say—'

'I'm sure you do. But I have to hang up. Bye bye.'

Five minutes later Justin and Deena were in Mallone's Mercedes, heading out of town. They heard police sirens and they were still close enough that they could tell the cars were nearing the Rutherford house. Justin told her they would now have to get rid of the Mercedes as soon as they could.

'Things seem to be closing in, don't they?' Deena said.

'Do you have a good lawyer?'

'I don't have *any* lawyer.'

'Well,' Justin said grimly, 'it might be time to start thinking about getting one. Especially with what we're about to do now.'

The kid looked to be about eighteen. He was white, a little bit gawky and, if Justin had to guess, he was probably driving his father's car. The car was some indeterminate make, a Subaru or a Toyota maybe.

Perfect.

He waited until the kid pulled out of the gas station and got about a block away. There wasn't a lot of traffic. He was stopped at a red light. No one behind him. It was now or never.

Justin darted into the street, ran to the driver's side of the car and flashed his police badge at the boy. In his best impersonation of a member of the LAPD, he said, 'I'm going to have to ask you to step out of the car, please.'

'What?' the kid said. 'What's going on?'

'Just step out of the car. Leave the engine running and get out.'

The boy looked like he was going to cry. 'What did I do?'

'Don't make me tell you again, son. Step out of the car before you're in even bigger trouble.'

The kid, trembling, opened the door and stepped onto the street. A car pulled up behind them now. Justin flashed his badge at the driver, an elderly woman, and waved her on. 'Making an arrest,' he told her, and she drove on, first doing the obligatory rubbernecking so she could pass on any details when she got home.

'Arrest?' the kid said. 'I didn't do anything.'

'Come with me, please.' Justin grabbed him roughly by the shirt collar, led him twenty feet away, around the corner to a white fence that had seen better days. The fence seemed to be the end of a small piece of property with a white house on it that had also seen better days. 'I want you to stand against that wall, put your hands up against it and spread your legs.'

The kid was really about to bawl now. 'But I didn't do anything.'

'Officer Harper,' Justin now said to Deena, who emerged from around the corner, after pulling the Mercedes into a safe parking place. 'I want you to search the car now.'

'Search it?' the kid wailed. 'Search for what?'

'Turn around and put your hands on the wall,' Justin said. 'Do not make me tell you again.'

The kid's back was to Justin and his hands were touching the wall. 'You're gonna find one joint in there. One measly joint. Okay, maybe two. That's all! That's not even a crime now, is it? Is it?'

'Spread your legs.' Justin kicked them apart. He pulled out his gun, flashed it in front of the boy's face. When the boy saw the steel barrel, Justin thought he'd gone too far. The kid looked like he was going to pass out. 'Now keep your eyes on the wall. We know what's in your car and we know who you are. If you so much as turn your head, I'm going to have to use this.'

Justin started backing away.

'This is an incredible mistake,' the kid cried.

'We've got to check your car,' Justin told him. 'We have work to do. I don't want to have to speak to you again.'

'You don't have the right person. I'm nobody! I haven't done anything! Really, I'm, like, a total wimp!'

Justin didn't answer.

'You gotta believe me,' the kid said. 'Don't I get a phone call? Hey, that's right, I should get a phone call. Or *you* can make a phone call. Just call my parents! They'll tell you I'm nobody! That's not even my car! It's my dad's car! Why won't you believe me?'

The boy, too afraid to turn around, sputtered on like that for several more minutes. He didn't stop until a white-haired man, walking with the aid of a cane, opened the gate in the middle of the peeling white fence and stepped out from the yard onto the street. He looked at the boy, feet spread apart, hands on the wall, chattering away a mile a minute, tears streaming down his face. Finally, the white-haired man said, 'Whatcha doin'?'

'Are you talking to me?' the boy asked, breathless.

'Yup.'

'I can't talk to you! This crazy cop's gonna shoot me if I so much as look at you!'

'What cop?' the white-haired man said.

'The cop right there! The guy in jeans. The off duty cop goin' through my car!'

'What car?' the white-haired man said.

That's when the boy pulled his hands off the wall and turned his head. He looked at the white-haired man, then back at the empty street. He stared at the spot by the stop sign where his car had been. 'Goddamn son of a bitch!' the kid screamed. 'My father's gonna kill me!'

It turned out to be a Toyota. While Justin drove, Deena went over the notes he'd made on the yellow pad, reading them aloud. Together they began to organize things and get a clearer picture of KranMar and its various subsidiaries.

'Let's keep running through it,' he said. 'I want to be able to picture this perfectly in my mind.'

'KranMar's at the top,' she said. 'That's the parent corporation. Pharmaceuticals. Everything from toothpaste and mouthwash to pills that help erectile dysfunction.'

'You love saying that, don't you?'

'Yeah, kind of,' she grinned. 'KranMar's the granddaddy of the whole shebang. Underneath they seem to own twelve research companies in America. Two in the northeast – Ellis, in New York, and Aker, in Boston. They both specialize in DNA and cellular research. I sound like I know what I'm talking about, don't I?'

'The other ten companies are in the south, midwest and west coast, right?' he continued. 'And they're mostly concerned with the less adventurous products.'

'Right. They're working on stuff for athlete's feet. The European labs are a little harder to figure out. It looks like he's got one in Switzerland, one in London, one somewhere in southern England. And there's one in Germany and one in southern France.'

'Those are their research arms. How many other companies are there?'

'Eighty-two.'

'We don't know what all of those do, do we?'

'It's incredibly complicated. I don't even know if Roger could figure all this out.'

'It could be like the Enron scam,' Justin said. 'A lot of them could be shells, set up to hide money or even purpose.' He thought for a few moments. 'How many list their officers and executives?'

'All the ones that are owned by KranMar, because it's a publicly traded company. But Kransten seems to have a lot of privately held companies, too. There's nothing but addresses listed for those.'

'Is there anyone named Newberg listed?'

'No. I've gone over it a million times. No Newberg.'

'Read the names of the companies aloud again.'

There were eighty-four spin-off companies. She named each one and when she was done with the list he threw up his hands.

'Out of all of those, we've only run across two. Alexis Developments, they own the mall that houses Growth Industries. Kransten's definitely constructed a maze that's supposed to hide his various activities. He built the mall and had his own subsidiary be the first renter. Nice financial arrangement but I don't think it ties in to all this.'

'What about the Lobster Corporation?' Deena said. 'They got the bills that came from some of the old age homes, right?'

'That's what Gary said. My guess is that Kransten uses it only for accounting purposes, to siphon checks through. Is it public or private?'

'Private. It doesn't have any names listed with it.'

'Let's run through this whole thing one more time. There have to be connections we're missing.'

'I'm listening.'

'Susanna Morgan found out how old Bill Miller was,' Justin started. 'She called Marion. Marion worked for Kransten and he called someone, maybe Kransten himself, maybe whoever Newberg is. One of those two ordered Susanna killed.'

'Why?'

'Hold on a second. I want to follow this through. Ed Marion was afraid that Kransten was going to kill him because he screwed up. I call Rollins to come protect Marion. Instead, Rollins kills him. Why would the FBI want to help Kransten?'

'Maybe Rollins is on the take. Maybe he's working for Kransten.'

'It's too much of a coincidence. If he's on the take, so are his superiors and I don't believe that Kransten's got that much muscle. Rollins couldn't have gotten himself sent to East End, he got assigned there, to the Maura Greer case, and it has to be for a reason. It's got to be connected to all this. There's a connection between her and Manwaring, that we know. And . . . wait a second . . . there's definitely a connection to Manwaring and Kransten. In that article I read, the one about Maura Greer, it said that Manwaring had done battle with the big drug companies. It was over some fake fat substance thing. I can't remember exactly what it was. But Manwaring wanted it banned. And the drug companies were pissed off about it.'

'But how does the FBI come in?' Deena asked. 'Why do they care if Kransten's happy and protected?'

'Maybe they're not trying to protect him,' he said. 'Maybe they want what he has.' Justin saw it now, the vague outline of the puzzle, one little piece beginning to fall into place. 'All right, let's think the unthinkable,' he went on. 'Kransten's researchers have come up with something that can extend people's lives. A pill, injections, some kind of formula for treatments. Whatever it is. Looking through the products that have been developed and are being developed, it actually doesn't seem that crazy. According to Roger's notes, they're really on the verge of major breakthroughs in oncology, inflammations, the ability to decrease strokes and heart attacks. So let's say he's got it. For some reason, he's keeping it a secret. But the FBI knows about it because Helen Roag, who worked for Kransten, was telling them. But *why*? Why was she telling them? And what good is it to the FBI?'

'Helen Roag'll know,' Deena frowned. 'Except she's gone.'

'Yeah. But whoever she's been calling in Washington might know, too. So let's hope that my old pal Wanda's as smart as I'm giving her credit for being.'

Deena looked at her watch. 'We only have about twenty minutes to wait.' As Justin pulled into a restaurant parking lot, she said, 'Why are we stopping here?'

Justin just smiled and Deena shook her head in amazement.

'Your mother . . . the mother I met . . . she used to like to go the House of Pancakes?'

'It was her secret shame,' Justin said. 'She loved the chocolate chip pancakes and she'd sneak out here and have them. She could never tell my father. I was the only one who knew. And that was only because I was in here with some friends, this was one of our stoning hangouts, and I saw her one day.' He pulled the key out of the ignition. 'Give me five minutes. I've got one more thing to do.'

It took him under five minutes, using the mini-Swiss Army knife that served as a key chain for the new car key, to remove the Toyota's license plates and swap them for a set on another car in the lot. 'That should buy us a little time,' he said. 'There's nothing distinctive about our car and now the license plates don't match the description. That's about as invisible as we're going to get.'

'If we ever get out of this mess,' Deena said. 'I'm giving up yoga and becoming a crook. This is very educational.'

He took her arm and they walked in together to the HOP, headed toward an inner booth away from the window. They ordered coffee, said they were waiting for someone else, and after another ten minutes a second waitress came up to them.

'This might sound kind of crazy,' the waitress said, 'but are you expecting a message from your mother?'

Justin nodded and the waitress handed over an envelope. There was handwriting on the outside of the envelope and Justin read it, shook his head in admiration, then pushed it across the table so Deena could read it, too. His mother's scrawl said:

I think someone's following me. So, since they heard you say that I had to kill time, I'm going to sit and have some coffee inside. And maybe have some chocolate pancakes. I'm writing this in the car, don't worry, no one can see anything. I'll slip it to the waitress when I pay my check. Then I'll drive around town for the rest of the day and make someone crazy, I hope.

She signed it: *Lizbeth*. Crossed that out and put: *Mother*.

Justin ripped open the envelope. Inside was a faxed note from Wanda Chinkle. This note was also handwritten. It read:

You're one smart son of a bitch. Helen Roag was calling Frank Manwaring.
    But you knew that, didn't you?
    My career's fucked. Get these guys for me, will you?
    Wanda

Deena put her head between her hands and sighed. A long, deep, hopeless sigh. 'Great,' she said. 'Now all we have to do is figure out where Frank Manwaring is and how we can talk to him. Why don't we just try to go meet Prince Charles, it'll be about the same thing.'

'Maybe not,' Justin said. 'What's today's date?' When she told him, he said, 'I know where Manwaring is. I don't know how the hell we get to him but I know where he is.'

'Where?'

When he told her, she looked at him in amazement. 'Well, I know how we can get in to see him,' Deena said.

And when she told him how, he not only gave her the same amazed look, he leaned over and kissed her. A long, celebratory kiss.

When the kiss finally broke up, Deena asked, 'Am I the first girl you ever kissed in the House of Pancakes?'

He thought for a minute, then shook his head. 'The third,' he told her. 'But this one was by far the best.'

G ordon and Wendell Touay were in the small gym in their house, the narrow rectangular space that had originally been built off the garage as a laundry room. Gordon was spotting Wendell's bench press. He was up to his eighth rep at three hundred and twenty-five pounds when the cell phone rang. The special cell phone. Gordon looked down at his brother, helped him ease the bar into a resting position. Then Gordon picked up the phone, flicked it open and said, 'Yeah.'

'They're alive,' Alfred Newberg said.

Gordon didn't say anything. The muscle in his right cheek began to twitch. It pulsed in and out. Did it again. In and out . . .

'You're fired,' Newberg said. 'You no longer work for this company.'

Gordon slapped at his cheek with his right hand. 'I don't think you want to do that,' he said.

'It's already done. You are no longer employed by this firm. Your weekly payments have been terminated.'

'We'll finish the job,' Gordon said.

'You're free to do whatever you want. But whatever you do now you're on your own. You don't work here anymore and you will never work here again.'

Gordon Touay's right hand closed into a fist now. He kept it clenched so tightly his entire hand turned red, then white as the blood supply was cut off.

'Whichever one of the idiot freaks I'm talking to,' Newberg said, 'I'm assuming you are about to fly into a psychopathic rage. So let me explain something to you. It is not an accident that you have never been allowed to contact me or know where we are. If, by some slim chance, you have been clever enough to learn anything at all, understand that we've done video surveillance on you over the years. If anything happens to me, those tapes will be delivered, along with your names, phone number and address, to the proper authorities. Your activities have been chronicled in great detail. And, believe me, there is no possibility of connecting those activities to this office. If you so much as try to contact me, you will be arrested immediately and spend a very long time in jail.' When Gordon didn't respond, Newberg added, 'This conversation is now over,' and hung up.

Gordon closed up his phone, slowly turned to his brother, who was still lying on his back on the bench, his feet planted firmly on the ground. Gordon repeated Newberg's words. Then he went back to the bench, added twenty more pounds of weight to the bar, stood over his brother and began to spot him for his next set of repetitions.

'We're going to find them,' Wendell Touay said slowly,

as he forced his first rep upward. 'That's what you want to do, isn't it?'

Gordon nodded. 'We're going to find them and we're going to kill them.'

Wendell finished his tenth rep, laid the bar to resting position. He grabbed a small towel, wiped the sweat from his forehead and then his bare chest. He smiled. 'I can't wait,' he said to his brother.

Then they were both smiling.

Justin drove the Toyota along Highway 27, past the town of Watermill, and they both saw the road sign, pointing to a turn on the left and reading: East End Harbor 7 miles. He drove past without turning.

'It's a little creepy to be back here,' Deena said. 'I used to think of this place as so normal. A nice, all-American town. Now I think of it as someplace to be running away from. It feels sinister to me. It doesn't feel like my home anymore.'

'It's like every place else,' Justin said. 'Nothing's ever as normal as it pretends to be.'

'Jay, I don't want to have that kind of dark view of life. I don't want Kenny to have it, either. It scares me.'

He didn't say anything to reassure her. He didn't have anything reassuring to say.

Deena understood the reason for his lack of response and she gave an involuntary shudder. 'What's creepier,' she said, breaking the silence, 'is Manwaring coming back here.'

'It's a conference. Media, business and politics.

Thrown by Herb Borbidge, the Wall Street guy. They've had it here the last four or five years. Manwaring was signed up to come months before any of this happened.'

'I know. But if he killed that girl, if he killed Maura Greer, to come back so close to the spot . . .' She shuddered again. 'The paper said the Greers are leading a protest against him.'

'It's going to be a media circus. Security's always tight for this thing, all the local forces are called in. I was on call for it the last few years. But this year it's going to be brutal. It's why I hope you know what you're doing.'

They drove until they drew near the town of Montauk, at the very tip of Long Island. Houses became fewer and fewer. The beach terrain turned more rugged. They passed by the popular local sandwich place, Lunch, then Justin slowed the car down as they passed the Havens Hotel & Resort, the ultra-luxurious beach and spa complex where Borbidge held his annual conference. The Wall Street mogul had a house – a compound, really – nearby, in East Hampton. He was one of the wealthiest and most dominant figures in the Hamptons social scene. He hosted charity events and presidential campaigns and sometimes threw huge parties just for the hell of it. When he asked someone to participate in his conference, that person didn't just agree. He or she came running.

Justin had seen Borbidge once, a couple of years ago, at the local breakfast joint in East End Harbor, Art's Deco Diner. He was in his early fifties, nearly completely bald, and had ears that looked like, with just a little bit of flapping, they could lift off, fly him around the town, and make a nice, comfortable landing at the local airport. He had been having breakfast with a gorgeous actress, at least twenty years younger than he was. She had made a name for herself by doing several nude love scenes in successful movies. She was looking adoringly at Borbidge as he paid the breakfast check. He paid no attention to her. He was too busy studying the check for errors.

The conference had started earlier that morning and security was out in full force. There were four police cars on the highway near the entrance to the grounds of the resort. Justin knew from experience that in addition to the eight uniforms guarding the exterior, there had to be at least that many in plain clothes inside. Depending on who was attending this year, there might also be Secret Service. Two years ago, Clinton had shown up at this thing. Heads of Wall Street, senators, cabinet members, presidents of media conglomerates, opinion makers, even leaders of foreign countries appeared to listen and lecture. This year Giuliani was one of the keynote speakers.

But the person who was clearly causing the biggest ruckus at this year's event was ex-Secretary of Health and Human Services Frank Manwaring.

The protesters were already out in force. There were probably a hundred of them, men and women, holding signs, parading back and forth outside the entrance to the Havens. Several had bullhorns and were periodically screaming out words and phrases such as 'Murderer!' and 'Tell the truth!' and 'What kind of human service is murder?!' Justin thought he recognized Maura Greer's parents from their newspaper and magazine photos. The father looked placid and out of place. The mother was one of the ones with a bullhorn.

Justin cruised by, followed Deena's instructions as she directed him to go half a mile past the resort then up to the left, into the oddly barren hills near the ocean. Soon they came to a small house, a shack clearly meant for summer living only. She asked Justin to wait in the car then she knocked on the door of the shack, opened it herself, and disappeared inside.

Five minutes later, she came out, followed by a small, thin, muscular man – lithe is the word that came to Justin's mind as he walked – with short-cropped brown hair. He wore loose-fitting sweat pants and a tank-top T-shirt. Deena had a grin that spread across her entire face.

'This is Curtis,' she told Justin. 'He's the one I used to work for sometimes, when I was a masseuse.'

'Nice to meet you,' Curtis said and shook Justin's hand.

Deena's grin seemed to grow even wider. 'I told you. If there's one thing that wealthy people always want at a conference it's a massage.'

'And you're doing the massages for this conference?' Justin asked Deena's friend.

'I'm providing all the outside work,' Curtis explained. 'They don't have enough regulars to keep up with the demand. I've done it since this thing came to the Havens.'

'So you can get us in?' Justin said.

'I can do better than that,' Curtis told him.

And when Justin gave him a look that said, *I give up, what could be better*, Deena jumped in, her words tumbling out. 'Guess who has a massage appointment for tomorrow morning? At eleven o'clock.'

That's when Justin smiled. And his smile was almost as wide as Deena's.

'And it gets even better,' Deena said.

'How can it get any better than that?'

'He wants a massage for two people,' Curtis said. 'He asked for two masseurs.'

'Is his wife with him?' Justin asked.

Curtis now joined in the grinning. 'Not according to my pals at the hotel,' he said.

Curtis was driving, Deena sat shotgun. Justin, a baseball cap pulled down low over his forehead, was in the back seat. As they made the turn into the Havens driveway, the protestors began booing and screaming. One of them even made a feeble attempt to kick the car, until a policeman came running over, and the protestor disappeared into the throng.

They drove a few feet further, inside the gate that separated the property from the road, and reached the security checkpoint. Curtis rolled his window down as a policeman approached the car.

'Oh shit,' Justin murmured.

Deena turned around then, responding to the look on Justin's face, and turned in the direction of the policeman.

'You have your passes?' the cop asked.

Curtis nodded, handed three official, laminated passes through his window. The cop examined them, glanced at Deena, nonchalantly started to hand the passes back to Curtis then swiveled back to face Deena. He stared at her for several seconds, then jerked his head to look in the window of the back seat.

Justin lifted his baseball cap, raised his head up to meet the cop's stare. He saw Gary Jenkins's mouth open, not to speak, simply to take in the rush of air he needed after his gasp. Justin said nothing, nor did he change his expression. Their eyes stayed locked. Then Gary lowered his gaze, handed the passes back in through the driver's window. Justin thought he saw the cop's lips move – a silent prayer – as he waved the car forward.

Deena exhaled a breath, the one she'd been afraid to release since Gary had approached the car.

'We're in,' Curtis said.

'Just barely,' Deena whispered.

Curtis opened the trunk, let them each lift out a collapsible massage table. He asked if they wanted him to stick around, Justin told him that it wasn't necessary. If they got caught, there was no reason for Curtis to be stuck in the middle of things. With a little luck, he said, they'd call him in a couple of hours to come pick them up.

Justin and Deena lugged their tables to the front desk, told the clerk whom they were there to see. The clerk dialed the room, got the okay, and directed them to suite 317 on the ocean side. A few minutes later, they were knocking on the door of the suite and Frank Manwaring, wearing nothing but a white terry cloth robe, was ushering them inside.

'I told them I wanted two *masseuses*,' Manwaring said, agitated, as they set the tables down. 'I didn't want a man.'

'Are you going to make me quote the words of the immortal Mick Jagger?' Justin said.

'I beg your pardon?'

'It's a good lesson for you to learn. "You can't always get what you want,"' Justin told him and, pulling out his gun and pointing it at the ex-Secretary, the next thing he told him was to sit down and shut up.

Deena went in to the bedroom, came out dragging a woman, also wearing nothing but a terry cloth robe. The woman was attractive in a plain and simple way. About five foot five, straight black hair cut off around her shoulders. She was thin and fragile looking, and right now she looked terrified.

Manwaring immediately started telling Justin that he was making a huge mistake, that there were police all over the place, that if he was part of the protest group it was all an error, that nobody knew what was really going on . . .

'We actually know what's going on,' Justin told him. 'Or at least a big chunk of it. And we're not part of the protest group. We're here to get some answers and I have to say, if we don't get them I'm going to use this gun.'

'If you pull that trigger you will never get past the lobby. You'll be committing suicide.'

'Mr Manwaring, you may be right but I can't say it scares me any. You don't have any idea of the kind of shit we've fallen into. If I pull this trigger, my guess is the only thing it can do is make me a lot more popular than I am right now.'

'I know your voice,' the woman in the robe now said to Justin. She had a soft whispery tone that Justin thought could never become too harsh or too loud. 'I recognize your voice.'

'Congratulations,' Justin told her. 'Now please sit down and keep quiet while I ask my questions.'

'You don't understand,' she said now, her voice rising to a higher pitch as she got more excited. 'I recognize your voice. You left messages for me. Warnings. I know you!' Turning to Manwaring, her soft voice as loud as it could get, she said, 'He's the policeman, Frank.' And turning back to Justin she said, 'We've been trying to find you!'

'Who are you?' he asked.

'You've been looking for me,' she told him. 'I'm Helen Roag.'

'Jesus Christ,' Justin said to Manwaring. 'Are you guys *all* the same? Does every politician think with his dick?'

'This is not what it appears to be,' Manwaring said.

'That's good. Because what it appears to be is that you're a sleazeball married guy who's being investigated for murdering his mistress, who flushed his career down the toilet, and who's now fucking an FBI informant who everybody thinks is dead! What am I missing here?' Justin knew he was on the verge of losing it. His anger was overwhelming him. He remembered the breathing exercises that Deena had taught him, part of her yoga session. He slowed his breaths down, concentrated on slowing his whole body down. He felt himself getting calmer. The anger was still there but he was in control of it. 'Why were you trying to find me?'

'Because I suspected they were doing the same thing to you that they've done to me,' Manwaring said.

'Which is?'

'Distort the truth. Destroy your credibility. Make sure you're unable to reveal the things you know.'

'We thought you could help us,' Helen Roag said.

'We thought you could do the same for us,' Deena said.

Justin walked over to a tray placed on top of the television set. He took a bottled water off the tray, opened it and took a long sip. 'I need to know what's going on,' he said. But before Manwaring could respond, the anger erupted again. 'Christ,' Justin said, and he stood up, looked around the room for something to throw, to destroy, couldn't find anything and forced himself to stop moving. 'You're one of them! Why the hell should I believe anything you tell me?'

Manwaring didn't say a word. Helen Roag reached over to him, touched his knee. He looked up at her and she nodded. Her eyes turned sad, deeply sad, and she nodded again. Manwaring patted her hand, turned to face Justin and Deena. 'I'm a married man who cheats on his wife,' he began. 'Nothing else that you think is true is even remotely true . . .'

CHAPTER THIRTY-ONE

Douglas Kransten was a bona fide visionary, Frank Manwaring said. That fact was indisputable. Almost everything else about his life could most definitely be disputed. But to understand what was going on, everything had to start with Doug Kransten.

He grew up in pre-Revolutionary Cuba. His father was American, his mother Cuban. His father, a lawyer, went down to Cuba to work for an American oil company. He wound up running the company and, knowing the money to be made in the island paradise, eventually left to become a real estate developer. The Kranstens lived the life of privileged aristocrats down there. Their splendid home was in the Miramar section of Havana and they owned a country plantation forty miles down the coast near Trinidad. Then Castro came to power. Both homes were taken away. Kransten's father was imprisoned and then killed in an uprising. Kransten and his mother escaped to Florida, leaving behind every possession they owned. They spent three months in Miami but Kransten couldn't stand it there. He didn't like being a member of the Cuban ghetto. He felt as if he had far more American blood in him, so he left his mother behind and went farther north. He settled in Georgia and started over, penniless. He was twenty-four years old.

In Atlanta, he landed a job at a pharmacy as a clerk. Fascinated by the business, he went to school, got his license and became a pharmacist. Several years after that he went to work for Maxwell Enterprises, a small pharmaceutical company, as a sales trainee. Within seven years, he was president of the company.

When he made his ascension to become head of Maxwell, Doug Kransten looked around and saw the future. What he saw was a Baby Boom generation that was young and fit and spirited. They were marching in the streets and doing drugs and defying every mode of accepted fashion. And they were getting instant gratification – sexually, politically, financially. What Kransten also saw, as he looked toward the end of the century, was that these Baby Boomers would age. They would eventually become a dominant financial power in the societal structure and they would want the same things they wanted when they were young. They were used to instant gratification, this generation, and Kransten didn't believe that age would alter that. If anything, it would intensify that urge.

He ordered the scientists working for Maxwell – its name would soon change to Kransten International – to spend their time developing pharmaceutical products that would feed into this generation's desire for youth and pleasure. They did. They began to develop drugs that would improve sexual gratification in the elderly. By the mid-90s they had a pill that gave previously impotent men erections. Three years after the pill was introduced on the market, it generated net sales of six hundred million dollars per year – and Wall Street research showed that they had managed to tap into only approximately seven per cent of the potential market. Over the years, the company made hundreds of millions of dollars easing arthritic pain with anti-inflammatories and pills that claimed to aid in cartilage regeneration. Their research department worked on creating a generic pain-relief pill. The marketing department decided to target it especially to golfers. They spent years building up brand name recognition, knowing that all the young tennis players would one day turn to the more sedentary sport in droves – and reach for the pill whose name had been drilled into their brains via commercials and billboards. Fortunes were made with weight loss and hair growth products. As early as the mid-70s, Kransten, the company, had become a corporate force to be reckoned with. By the end of the twentieth century, they were a dominant global economic power.

Kransten, the man, was also a force. And he became more of one when his life changed drastically in 1970. That was when he fell in love.

Doug Kransten was 36 years old and Louise Marshall was 28. He was living in a house very much like the one he remembered in Havana, only this one was in the exclusive Buckhead section of Atlanta. Louise was from a small town in Mississippi. She was lovely, the very vision of a blonde cheerleader, which was, in fact, what she had been all through school. Even by the time she graduated from Ol' Miss, Louise did not care one whit about politics or the underprivileged or the rumblings of dissension that were starting to sweep the country. She cared about cheerleading and staying beautiful. And not just for herself. She wanted the whole world to be beautiful. So that's what she set out to accomplish.

Like Kransten, she began in sales, for a door-to-door cosmetics company. It didn't take her long to move into the home office in Nashville, Tennessee. She became head of sales, then head of sales and marketing, and then she was made president. The company was bought by a larger cosmetics firm, based in Atlanta, and Louise was brought along for the ride. By the time she met Kransten, she was running the larger company and *Time* magazine was writing about her as the most powerful woman executive in the country under the age of 40. When she met Douglas Kransten, it was the perfect merger. She spent their first two dates telling him about her vision for beautifying the world. He spent the next two dates explaining that his mission was to keep America young. Four months later, they were married.

As early as 1970, Kransten had steered his company to become one of the first of its kind to turn its energies toward genetic engineering. They were at the forefront, too, in the extraordinary competition to map the human genome. But while others thought that the gold rush would be in the storage and sale of genomic information, Kransten knew, very early on, that it wasn't the information that was of value. Kransten staked his fortune on what he knew best: pharmaceuticals. He gambled his future on the practical applications that were now possible with the genomic miracle. And his gamble proved correct. By the mid-80s, Kransten was the third largest pharmaceutical company in the world. He had managed to buy Louise Marshall's company and they merged philosophies, products and bank accounts. They were worth several billion dollars.

In 1986, the US economy was starting to fail. At the same time, KranMar, as the new company was now called, and several other top pharmaceutical and research companies were spending hundreds of millions of dollars in the attempt to eradicate disease. They all knew that the ultimate goal was a cure for cancer. If their research could provide that, there were hundreds of billions of dollars to be made.

In September of 1986, Doug Kransten and two other pharmaceutical titans, Ronald Mayberry, CEO of MayDay, Inc., and Patrick Arnold, Chairman of Selwick International, were called to Washington, D.C. There were several people high up in the administration – not the President or Vice-President, but people who made it clear that they were representing the views of both elected officials. It was explained to Kransten, Mayberry and Arnold that the government was extremely worried about their companies' activities. They were developing products and drugs that could very possibly extend people's lives another 10, 20, even 30 years. With the developments that were certain to come in stem cell research and the final mapping of the genome, it was not inconceivable that men and women would routinely live to be a 120 years old. The pharmaceutical executives agreed that it was certainly possible, but they didn't see it happening in the immediate future. The government officials stated their position a little more clearly: it was not to happen at all. Not now, not in the immediate future, not in any future that was foreseeable.

The executives were stunned. And they demanded an explanation.

They were given one. And it was simple and obvious: the world economy could not handle it.

If the population kept exploding and people's lives were extended, the US government – all governments, in fact – could not afford to keep its infrastructure functioning. The Social Security system – which was based on the premise that each generation, as it aged, would be supported by the next working generation – could not possibly survive. It was already at the point where the post-Baby Boomer generation, the so-called Gen X, would be working harder and harder – and longer and longer – to support the huge throngs of non-working elderly among the Boomers. We were already near the breaking point. Further medical breakthroughs would bankrupt the country and the rest of the world.

The three CEOs understood the problem. They also understood that such an agreement was antithetical to the entire capitalistic system. Not to mention their dedication to science.

A deal was made. Science went by the wayside but capitalism was triumphant.

The companies – along with 7 other pharmaceutical companies that, over the following 12-month period, were brought into the bargain – were allowed to continue with their research and development. But there were specified limits. Cosmetic products could be developed – fat reducers and anti-wrinkle creams – and even certain drugs and medicines could be elaborated upon. Sex enhancers would be worth billions and the companies were encouraged to strike out in that area. In exchange for these limits, certain allowances would be made. FDA restrictions would be relaxed. Products would be let through that might not have been allowed before. They would have the opportunity to test products on a wideranging – and unsuspecting – public. There was a lot of money to be made if normal regulations were eased or even erased altogether.

A lot of money.

There was one other catch, of course. This arrangement had to be secret. Absolutely one hundred per cent hidden from the public. Yes, people cared about the economy. But if word got out that the administration – any administration – was bartering with the length of life itself, well, it went without saying what would happen. It would be very difficult for any politician to win an election if it were known that he was lopping 20 years off the lives of his constituents.

The deal was done.

And it continued for years.

From one administration to the next. It didn't matter which party, they were all politicians. They could all see the future and the same political dangers. It was a matter of their own survival.

Brewster Ford was the link, Manwaring explained. His financial acumen and his ability to interpret the world economy were legendary and near infallible. His agenda was never political, which is why he was trusted by both parties. His focus was strictly, unrelentingly on the economic picture – past, present and future. When Ford spoke about money, the whole world listened.

Some administrations were easier to convince than others, Manwaring said. Some were cynical and receptive to anything that benefited big business, no matter the consequences. Some expressed horror at the deal but overcame their moral indignation when the political consequences became so clear. Some Presidents were more detail oriented and more involved in policy decisions than others. Some didn't want to know the specifics. One insisted on an elaborate, private presentation from Ford. But the previous three Presidents had ultimately capitulated. Politics took a back seat when it came to preserving their own positions of power.

The current administration was easy. Manwaring believed that the current President had no idea about the bond between the pharmaceutical companies and the government. But it didn't matter. There had, over the past several years, been a tremendous swell against science from the religious right. Even Darwinism was under attack in several states. The President tended to share these antediluvian beliefs but, more important than embracing and spreading core philosophies, he wanted the vote from that constituency, many of whom had previously become disenfranchised from the party. His advisors – those of whom were aware of the backroom dealing – only had to steer him in the direction his instincts were already leading him. The President basically killed off stem cell research in America without even being aware that he was continuing the fifteen-year-old contract. He simply was allowed to believe that he was doing the moral and politically expedient thing. There was no problem keeping the arrangement going.

And then two things occurred.

First, he, Manwaring, was named Secretary of Health and Human Services. He was an old friend of this President and he liked him very much, even if he did not always share the man's black and white view of the world.

Several months after he was approved by Congress, Manwaring was asked to come to a meeting at the White House. There he met with the President's Chief of Staff and Brewster Ford. To his surprise, his predecessor – a liberal, from the other party – was also present. As was Chase Welles, the new head of the Food and Drug Administration. At this meeting, the arrangement with the pharmaceutical companies was explained to him and to Welles. Ford laid out the entire potentially devastating scenario. Welles seemed to have no problem with any of it. But it disturbed Manwaring. His predecessor as Secretary saw his resistance and, in answer to one of Manwaring's questions about the real necessity of the pact said, 'Necessary? Here's how necessary this is. Forget about the government trying to *ban* cigarettes. Pretty soon we'll have to make smoking obligatory, just so we can kill off a few billion people.'

Manwaring was deeply troubled by the implications of what he heard, morally and politically. But he accepted it. He understood that he was a crucial piece in this puzzle because so many of his decisions, so much of his work with the FDA, would be directly affected by what he was hearing. He weighed the pros and cons, listened to the arguments – all from people he respected and trusted – and he decided that he could live with such an arrangement. He decided that he was dealing with two evils – but one was definitely greater and more damaging to the world as a whole.

But things changed.

Accepting something in theory was quite different from accepting it in practice. The FDA, led by Chase Welles, approved several drugs and supplements that caused severe damage. Several deaths, yes, but also many recorded cases of liver damage and heart failure. An anti-depressant, released by MayDay, drove eleven people to suicide over a three-month period. A drug that was widely used in the treatment of breast cancer, released by Selwick, damaged kidneys and caused strokes. Still, Manwaring told Justin and Deena, he remained silent. The logic, he kept telling himself, was the same that applied during wartime. It was acceptable to sacrifice the few to save the majority.

After September 11, however, he clashed with Kransten. KranMar held the patent for a drug that was extremely effective against anthrax. They did not have the facilities to make enough of it – at least, enough to satisfy a public that was panicking and desperately needed reassurance. During the first few months after the World Trade Center attack, it was nearly impossible to determine potential threats. No one knew what the terrorists were capable of or willing to do. There was a legitimate fear that anthrax could be used, via mail or via our water supply, to wipe out millions of people.

Manwaring lifted KranMar's patent, allowing a Canadian company to make a generic version of the drug. The action allowed millions more people to have access to it. But Manwaring was called in to the Oval Office and told, by the President himself, that this was never to happen again. Manwaring argued – never telling the President the truth behind the pressure that was being placed on him, strictly explaining the need for such actions – but his arguments did no good. It became clear to him that the lesser of two evils could quickly become, might already have become, the greater danger.

Three months after that, KranMar introduced a pill that was marketed as one that caused fat to bypass the body's system entirely. It was an extraordinary success from the first day the television advertisements ran. Within six months, eighteen people had died after using the pills. Manwaring ordered production held up so more testing could be done. He had an extraordinary clash with Chase Welles, who publicly hinted that Manwaring was being bribed by rival pharmaceutical companies who were developing similar products. The White House did not back Manwaring, instead sided with the Food and Drug Administration chief. False information was disseminated to the media and Manwaring found his integrity and judgement attacked from both the left and the right. Still, he was a good soldier and said nothing. He kept trying to look at the bigger picture and the ramifications of going public with what he knew.

Then he was contacted by Maura Greer.

At this point in the story, Helen Roag stepped forward.

She had changed into a pair of khaki pants and a cotton blouse. Manwaring still wore his robe.

Helen said that she had been working at the Aker Institute, a subsidiary of KranMar, for several years. She had a research background but was asked to assume more of a managerial role than she had anticipated. She was stunned at the raises she was given, so she rarely argued about the responsibilities they were assigning to her. She knew she was being paid two, three, even four times the amount of money someone in her position should have been paid.

At some point, she was asked to have lunch with Douglas Kransten himself. She was stunned but, no question about it, flattered. He praised her work to the skies and then, midway through the meal, he began to talk to her about a special assignment. One that he said was a little tricky. There was some risk involved, he said, but its scientific value was incalculable. He said that as early as 1970, he had become convinced that human growth hormones were the key to eradicating many of the problems that struck the human body as it aged. He'd had a team of scientists working on it since that time. Kransten told Helen that they'd done some experiments around the country, beginning as early as 1972. They'd had astonishing success with some of their subjects. He showed her that, in the northeast region alone, 18 subjects – 10 males, 8 females – had lived to be over one hundred years old. Kransten was convinced – no, more than convinced, absolutely certain – that his people had discovered a way to slow down the aging process.

He showed her some of the experimentation. Groups

of people had been fed and injected with various combinations of such supplements as L-Arginine and Glycine and L-Ornithine and L-Glutamine. There were some miraculous results at first. Wounds healed, immune responses to bacteria, viruses and tumor cells improved. The loss of skeletal muscle diminished, as did fatigue. Gradually, the results became even more miraculous. Many of those who had participated in the experiments were living longer. The aging process had been delayed, in some cases substantially. Helen had looked at the data, agreed that it was interesting and impressive, but she disagreed with him that the proof was absolute.

It's not ready to be released to the public, he told her. There are problems. But the problems are close to being solved.

We are on the verge of doubling the life span of the normal human being, Kransten told her. *And there is absolute, undeniable proof.*

She asked to see it but he just shook his head. The proof is overseas, he told her. Someday she would see it. But not yet.

He told her what he wanted her to do and she agreed. The money he added to her salary was the main inducement, but so was the scientific value of his experiment. Everything had to be done in strict secrecy. They were doing a good thing, Kransten said, but the government did not agree. They will never allow this, he told her, until it's absolutely safe and proven. But it was a Catch-22. The only way to reach that stage was to continue with the forbidden experimentation. She accepted his logic.

She was assigned to half of the 18 survivors of the

early 70s testing. She saw each of them every three months. If they needed her they could contact her via Growth Industries, a shell corporation set up only to distance KranMar from the subjects. All of the elderly were living at different old age homes. Their expenses were fully paid for. They were given anything they needed to make their lives easier and pleasurable. When she saw them, she not only collected new data, she was charged with giving them their hormonal injections. The experiments had continued all these years. What was being injected varied, as testing and information had gotten so much more sophisticated over this period. But the ones that survived continued to survive. Several of them outlived the managers of their homes. She had one subject, in Vermont, who was now 112 years old – and healthy and vital.

But the more involved she became the more misgivings she began to have.

The original series of experiments in 1972 was given the appellation Aphrodite, named after the ancient Greek goddess of love, youth and beauty. They were administered in upstate New York, near Binghamton, in a private hospital owned by Kransten. As Helen learned more about them – from discussions with her subjects and, gradually, from files she either had access to or managed to steal – she began to realize the extent of the damage that had been done. Yes, there were eighteen survivors of the initial experiments. But over a hundred subjects had died as a direct result of the treatments.

Then something happened that forced her into action. She noticed that Kransten and his wife were spending much of their time in Europe, particularly at their house in England. She arranged a meeting with one of Kransten's researchers, a young and attractive man named Lonnie Parker, who had been spending time in the English lab. It wasn't anything out of the ordinary. It was part of her job to remain current on research matters. But Dr Parker was – and here Helen hesitated, had the good sense to blush slightly, before continuing on with her story – interested in her. Romantically interested. Well – and Helen blushed again – sexually interested. She saw him several times. He would only give her minor details about the experiments taking place in England. She learned that the main lab was actually in Kransten's home, which she hadn't realized. But, although she sensed he wanted to talk, he shied away from revealing anything substantive. On their third date, however, he had too many margaritas and he began to talk about what he'd seen in England. He still wouldn't come out and tell her exactly what was going on, but he used a strong word for a scientist. He used the word 'ungodly' when he described the program known as Aphrodite.

The next morning, when Lonnie Parker sobered up, he begged her not to repeat anything he'd said. He told her it would be dangerous for her if any rumors were traced back to her. 'Dangerous?' she asked, and she remembered laughing. Parker didn't laugh. He told her he was going to resign. That he was not able to deal with what he had seen and done over the past few months. He was going to resign that very day.

'What happened to Dr Parker?' Justin asked. 'Where is he now?'

Helen Roag shook her head. 'I never saw him again,' she said. 'We were supposed to have dinner that night. After he resigned. He never called.'

'Did you call him?'

'Of course I did. I left messages on his phone machine for two days. Then it stopped picking up. I went by his house one afternoon. There were two men in there. I only talked to one of them, he opened the door, but I could see the other one, off to the side in the den. He was looking through Lonnie's bookcase. The man I spoke to said that Lonnie didn't live there anymore. He asked if I wanted to leave my name, that he'd be speaking to Lonnie and would give him a message.'

'Did you?'

She shuddered. 'Something told me that I didn't want them to know who I was.'

'And you never heard from Parker again?'

'No.'

'What do you think happened to him?'

'I think they killed him,' Helen said. 'I think they couldn't let somebody walk away from Aphrodite, not someone who they sensed might talk about it. So they killed him.'

She went to the FBI after that, she said, to the Boston bureau and told her suspicions to the agent in charge, Wanda Chinkle. Wanda spoke to her superiors. She asked Helen to remain in Kransten's employ, to keep doing exactly what she'd been doing, but to report in regularly to the FBI and to keep them informed of anything that happened with Aphrodite.

She did exactly as they asked. Partly, she said, out of

fear. She was afraid to leave after what had happened to Lonnie Parker. But after a year of passing along information, of keeping her eyes open, her suspicions all began to seem foolish to her. Maybe Lonnie really had simply left town. Maybe she'd just become paranoid because of the odd nature of her job and the strange area of experimentation she was involved with. Then, her fear and suspicions rose again. Several of her subjects – and those tended to by Ed Marion – died. But that wasn't all. There were other deaths, and many of those she was certain were connected to the Aphrodite project. People at the old age home suddenly died in their sleep. Friends of the subjects were in fatal car accidents or fell down the steps of their homes. She became certain that not only was Kransten protecting his secret, by killing those who discovered it, she began to realize that the FBI was also protecting his secret. They were not using her information, she realized, to put Kransten in jail. The info she passed along was disappearing down a black hole. When she pressed her FBI contacts, they turned evasive, even threatening. And she noticed another pattern emerging – drugs developed by KranMar that were not yet ready for public consumption were being approved by the FDA and released into the market place. She tried to tell herself that she was being paranoid but couldn't talk herself out of her conviction that some kind of huge web of deceit was being played out.

Helen had a close friend from college. They were two years apart, Helen the elder of the two, but had still become close. She got an e-mail from her friend saying that she was interning at the FDA. The friend came up to

Boston for a weekend, a reunion of college pals. On Sunday night, Helen got very drunk and told her friend all about her suspicions. The friend said that she might be able to sniff around and see what was what. She had access to a lot of people as well as a lot of information. She was just an intern, she told Helen, so no one took her seriously. She might really be able to find the truth and stay under the radar.

The intern was Maura Greer.

That's when Manwaring took center stage again. He explained that he had met Maura several times when he'd gone to meetings at the Hubert Humphrey Building, the home of the FDA. She was flirtatious, she was attractive. They'd begun an affair several months before Maura had spent the weekend with Helen. After a while, Maura came to Manwaring and told him about the conversation she'd had with Helen. This was exactly at the time that he was struggling with his own conscience and suspicions. He encouraged Maura to become Helen's contact and to pass all information on to him. He didn't know what to do with it, he didn't know exactly to whom he could turn. But he knew he had to do something. And he knew he had to turn somewhere.

Then all hell broke loose. Maura was killed. He, Manwaring, was set up and his credibility destroyed. He explained that the powers that be even managed to provide women who told the media that he'd been having affairs with them, that he'd become violent when they had discussions about leaving his wife. He'd never even met any of those women, he told Justin and Deena. Never met them, never heard of them. They were complete and utter fabrications. But they were smart fabrications. Manwaring had been unfaithful, and with women other than Maura. It was his weakness and they were able to exploit it to their advantage. He knew that the more he denied these specific affairs, the more likely it was that other women would step forward to denounce his credibility. Once the media jumped on board and he became the favorite topic of talking heads and tabloid headlines, he was fairly helpless to combat the smears. Everything was a brilliantly executed ploy – organized by masters of manipulation – to remove him from office, stop him from talking, and to install Chase Welles, who would go along with any and all cover-ups.

Helen was now close to panic mode, she said. She wasn't sure who she could talk to next. She waited for two days, then went to one person. One of her college professors. A mentor. His name was Joseph Fennerman. She showed him files she had stolen and notes that she had compiled. He was the only person she knew who might have the scientific knowledge to perceive what was happening and the connections to do something about it. She was afraid he would laugh at her but after listening to her and studying the material she gave him, he didn't laugh. He told her he had people he could see in Washington and that he would look into it. He called her to say that he had made two appointments. One was with a scientist who worked for one of the top pharmaceutical companies. It was someone Fennerman trusted. The second appointment was with the head of the FDA. He would get to the bottom of this, he told Helen. Don't worry.

Three days after he told her not to worry, Dr Fennerman was mugged and murdered after a lecture in London.

'I felt trapped,' Helen said now. 'I couldn't prove that Dr Fennerman's death was connected to Aphrodite. But I knew that it was. I felt responsible for the deaths of three people. Two people I cared about.' She sipped at a glass of water, her lower lip trembling at the memory. 'Also,' she said, putting the glass down, 'I was afraid that somehow they'd find out what I'd been doing. And that I'd be next.'

'I'd say you were right to be afraid. What did you do?' Justin asked.

'Maura had dropped a lot of hints about her . . . relationship . . . with Frank. I knew that she trusted him. So, despite everything that was in the press, that everyone was saying about Frank, I decided to go with Maura's instincts.'

'She got in touch with me,' Manwaring said. 'I didn't really know how to help her, so I urged her to stay at Aker and to keep reporting to me. Directly to me, this time.'

'Which you did,' Justin said.

'Until Maura's body was discovered. Then I got too scared. So I ran. To Frank. I didn't know anyone else I could trust. Or who'd even believe me.'

'How the hell,' Deena spoke up, 'could this possibly get so out of hand? It's insane!'

'It's the nature of business and government,' Manwaring said. 'This is the reality now. It's the way things play out.'

'No more rules?' Deena asked. 'Just greed and chaos.'

'There are rules,' Manwaring said. 'But both sides broke the rules. That's why it all happened. And then it became a race against time. Kransten needed to keep his new product under wraps until it was perfected – because if it was announced to the public and it didn't work, the damage would be irreparable. Unless he could prove that what he'd developed was legitimate, and make that proof as visible as possible, the FDA would shoot it down and destroy it because of the financial danger it presented. If that happened, his company would go under. The government – using the FBI – eventually understood that Kransten was ignoring their longtime agreement and they were determined to prevent his experiments and product from ever being revealed. It's why Kransten disappeared. He wasn't only protecting his formula, he was trying to stay alive until he could go public. Both sides had been successful for so long playing their little game. Both sides had stopped outsiders from interfering or discovering too much. Or if they *had* discovered too much, they were stopped from revealing it. Both sides have played to a draw so far. But now the game's coming to a close. And both sides are determined to win.'

'At any cost,' Justin said.

'Now, you've got it,' Frank Manwaring said. 'And now you know most of the story.'

'Most?' Justin was sitting in a chair across from the Secretary. 'What's the rest?'

'You're the rest.'

Before Justin could ask exactly what he meant, there was a knock on the door. Everyone froze, then they heard the words, 'Room service.'

Manwaring glanced at his watch, relaxed and nodded. 'I ordered lunch for twelve-thirty. After our massages were supposed to be over.'

'Just leave it outside the door,' Justin called out. 'We'll get it in a minute.'

They waited five minutes then, as Justin kept his gun in his hand, Manwaring went and opened the door. All that was there was a serving cart.

Manwaring wheeled it in. 'I only ordered for two,' he said. 'I didn't realize we'd have company.'

'What did you mean, we're the rest of the story?' Deena asked.

'I mean that I'm a middle-aged bureaucrat given to intellectual obfuscation. I'm fairly helpless when it comes to transferring my knowledge to action. They've also rendered me impotent. My access to the White House is gone, the media has turned me into a pariah and the police consider me a murder suspect. I wouldn't be believed by anyone, even if I could get anyone to listen to me.' He nodded in Justin's direction. 'You, on the other hand, have managed to beat them so far. Or at least equalize the playing field.'

'So far. The closer I get, the more they're going to turn up the heat.'

'Probably. But now that you know what's really transpiring, maybe you can do something about it.'

'Such as?'

'Find Doug Kransten and stop him.'

'Stop him how?' Deena asked.

Manwaring stared pointedly at the gun in Justin's hand. 'However you can. You've got both sides after you.

The government will do anything to keep the Aphrodite project secret. And Kransten will do anything to prevent it from being sabotaged. Right now, both of them see you as their number one enemy. That's my definition of a rock and a hard place. But if Aphrodite is . . . abandoned, shall we say . . . you've eliminated any reason for either side to keep squeezing.'

'And just coincidentally,' Justin said, 'you'll manage to escape their squeeze, too.'

'I'm not pretending I don't have a personal interest in this,' Manwaring said. 'But I've done quite a bit of thinking about this and I don't see any other choice.'

Justin was shaking his head as if trying to clear it. But also to show that he was resisting what he'd been hearing. 'There are just too many connections I can't get my mind around.'

'Such as?' Manwaring asked.

'I'm as cynical as the next person about politicians. But this . . . Democrats and Republicans can barely be civil to each other. How the hell can they join forces for a conspiracy like this?'

'I've spent most of my life in politics,' Manwaring said. 'People don't understand what really motivates those of us who run this country. Not just politicians but business and financial leaders, too.'

'So tell me.'

'Two things. One is simple and practical: demographics. Even before Kransten's Aphrodite project began, the elderly were the fastest growing segment of the population. Their political and buying power can't be underestimated. If there's one sacred trust, for the left and the right, it's Social Security. Screw around with that, you're out of public life. But now think if the elderly, who are facing death and frightened as hell about it, get a chance to escape it. For twenty, thirty, forty more years. Screw around with *that*, you'll be crucified. The classic rock and a hard place.'

'What's the second?'

'Fear. And it's even more powerful than the first. We're all afraid of failing. Of losing our power or our access to power. Of public humiliation. Of becoming . . . insignificant. Fear is a much greater force among these people – me included, I'm ashamed to say – than any kind of political philosophy.'

'Why haven't you done anything up till now?'

'Because when I finally realized how desperate the situation was, I didn't have the means.'

'And I'm the means?'

'It's why we wanted to try to find you,' Helen Roag said.

'It's a sick and deadly game they're playing. But you seem to know how to play it using their rules,' Manwaring said, lifting the silver covers off the two serving dishes.

'Why do you think he's doing this?' Justin asked, half to himself. 'Kransten's made his fortune. Why break the agreement and risk everything?'

'If you stumbled onto the fountain of youth,' Manwaring said, 'what would you do? Jump in or board it up so no one could find it?'

Justin didn't answer. Wasn't sure he could answer. He ran his fingers through his hair, pulled tight at the ends. When he put his hands down, the expression on his face was set and determined. All he said was, 'Do you know how to find Kransten?'

Manwaring and Roag shook their heads.

In the ensuing silence, the aroma of the food began to fill the room.

'I hate to sound gauche,' Deena said, 'but I'm starving.'

'You're welcome to it,' Manwaring said. 'It's Lobster Newburg. It's their speciality here. Absolutely delicious.'

He began doling out a portion onto a plate for Deena but Justin stood up and grabbed his hand, stopped him.

'What did you say this was?'

'What we ordered?'

'Yes,' Justin said. 'Say it again.'

'Lobster Newburg,' Manwaring told him. 'Is something wrong?'

Justin turned to Deena. 'Remember what I told you about criminals, how they always make one stupid or arrogant mistake? How they can't resist word play?'

'Yes,' she said.

'Well, we just found our mistake. I can't believe I missed it.'

'What the hell are you talking about?' Manwaring asked.

'Make sure you enjoy this lunch,' Justin said. 'Because it just told me how to find Kransten.'

CHAPTER THIRTY-TWO

According to the report that Roger Mallone had provided, the address for the Lobster Corporation was in Manhattan at 289 Park Avenue. Justin parked the stolen Toyota in a garage on 47th Street, half a block away.

By 5 p.m., Justin and Deena had been to a florist, a bookstore, a stationery store and an American Express mailing office and returned to the shimmering glass Park Avenue office building, supplies in hand. Deena went in first, checked out the directory in the large glass-enclosed case, then went back out to meet Justin on the sidewalk. She told him what she'd found, he nodded, then they went in together.

Justin held an enormous potted plant. Under one arm was an unfolded, flat American Express carton. Deena held an equally large and elaborate bouquet of flowers in a heavy glass vase. 'For Carol Schlossberg at Bailey and Potter,' Deena said to the security guard. She checked the envelope that held the gift card. 'It's room 2210. Must be her birthday.'

The guard called up, said that flowers were being delivered, and waved Deena and Justin on through to the proper elevator bank.

'Packages usually go through the mailroom,' Justin said. 'But flowers are almost always allowed to go straight up.'

'I'll remember that,' Deena said. 'Next time I have to break into an office.'

They went up to the twenty-second floor, dropped off the plant and the flowers at the Bailey and Potter law offices, caught a glimpse of the very confused Ms Schlossberg as she collected her gifts, then they took the same elevator up to thirty-three. On that floor, Justin found the men's room, went in, checked it out. Seconds later, he came out, told Deena it was empty. They went in together.

'How long are we going to have to wait?' she asked.

'Building probably closes at seven,' he told her. 'I'd say eight, eight-thirty should be safe.'

They went into one toilet stall, the middle one of three, closed and locked the door, sat and got as comfortable as they could.

'If anyone comes in, pick your feet up and keep quiet,' he said.

She nodded, opened the book she'd bought. It was the true story of some guy who traveled around the world with his cat.

'I never would have thought of bringing this,' she said, tapping the cover of the book.

'I've been on stake-outs,' he said. 'I know how boring it gets.'

'The glamorous criminal life,' she muttered, and started reading.

At 10:15 that night, the cleaning crew stepped out of office suite 3310 and made their way along the gray, tightly woven industrial carpet until they came to the next stop on their usual trek – the men's room.

They did the toilet stalls first, from left to right. The middle door had swung shut. One of the crew members jabbed at it with his mop and the door opened. He stepped in, found nothing unusual, began to swab the floor. It didn't take them long to clean the sinks and toilets and tiles. Neither the men's room nor the women's room – which they'd cleaned half an hour earlier – got much use on this floor. When they finished, their next stop was office 3325 – the beveled door with the elegant gold lettering across it that read The Lobster Corporation. In front of the door was a medium-sized American Express carton.

'Mailroom shouldn'ta left it here overnight,' one of the crew members, a black man in his early fifties, said and the other two nodded their agreement.

'Careless,' the only woman in the crew said. 'They're gonna get in trouble.' And this time it was the two men who nodded.

The man who was the first to speak now took his skeleton key and opened the door to the office. The other two pushed the carton inside, into the waiting room.

'Heavy,' the second man said.

'Bet it's a computer,' the first man told him.

'Shouldn't leave no computer in the hallway,' the woman said, still angry that the mailroom had been so lax.

It took them fifteen minutes to clean the entire office space. They vacuumed the carpets, emptied every waste-basket, and swept off the tops of the ventilated air conditioning ducts. They also dusted the doors that led to the two offices in the suite and cleaned the glass partition in the reception area as well as the top of the reception-ist's desk. Then they left to get to work in the next office on their route.

Fifteen minutes after the crew left the Lobster Corporation, Deena sliced her way out of the small card-board box, using the box cutter they'd bought at the stationery store. She slithered out and took a couple of minutes to unfurl and stretch her legs, which had been tightly wrapped around her body so she could fit into the Am Ex package. It had been Justin's brainstorm to put her in there. 'How long can you keep yourself that small?' he asked. When she told him she thought she could stay like that for two to three hours, he cackled and insisted she give him a high five.

While she stretched, Deena took in the entire office. There were two soft leather couches in the waiting room. On the wall opposite the reception desk was a genuine Warhol Mickey Mouse. It was huge and dominated the space. There was a door that led past the waiting room and into a hallway. Off the hall was one small office, plain and impersonal, and at the end of the hall was an enor-mous office, decorated in chilly chrome and black steel. As soon as she felt limber, Deena went back to the phone on the receptionist's desk and dialed.

'Come on up,' she said and waited, tapping her fingers on the desk.

Two minutes later the receptionist's phone rang. It was the security guard in the lobby, saying that there was someone there to see Mr Newberg. She told the guard to send the visitor up.

'Workin' late,' the guard said.

'Always,' Deena told him, hanging up.

Several minutes later, Justin was in the office with her.

'The couches look a little more comfortable than the toilet stall,' he said.

'Why don't we test them out,' she said.

'We can't sleep later than seven-thirty,' he told her.

Deena took him by the hand and led him over to the first large couch. 'As far as I'm concerned,' she said, 'we don't have to sleep at all.'

At three-thirty in the morning, they were wrapped around each other, arms and legs entwined. She could hear his rhythmic breathing, feel his chest rise and fall. The rhythm shifted and Deena sensed that he was now awake. She put her hand over his heart, pressed down lightly, felt the pumping against her palm. His eyes opened and she could feel his lungs taking in a deeper supply of air.

'Thank you,' she whispered.

'For what?' he said, his voice low and hoarse.

'For everything. For saving my life.'

'I think you've got that backwards,' he said.

She smiled, put her head on his chest.

They both stayed silent until Justin said, 'It's not over.'

'I know that.'

'No,' he said. 'It's going to be . . . different . . . from now on. The stakes are higher. The endgame is starting.'

'I understand,' she told him. Lifting her head, twisting it so she could see his eyes, she said, 'I trust you.'

'I'm glad. And I want you to trust me. But it's going to be different now.'

She nodded, put her head back down on his chest. 'I understand,' she said.

He put one hand on the back of her head, drew her even closer to him. Justin closed his eyes and smiled sadly because he knew she didn't understand at all.

She couldn't possibly.

At nine forty-five in the morning, Al Newberg walked into the reception room of the Lobster Corporation. He started to walk past the reception desk, as he did every morning, with nothing more than a brusque nod. Today, he stopped mid-nod. Gloria, his regular receptionist, wasn't there. Instead, there was a woman with streaked blonde, curly hair. Before Newberg could say anything, he felt another presence behind him. He turned, saw a man with a gun. The gun was pointed at Newberg's chest. The man's eyes told Newberg that this was someone who was more than capable of pulling the trigger.

He quickly ran the calculations through his mind. It was instinctual with Newberg. He was not a physical person. He never had been. At five foot two and a hundred and fifteen pounds, he was incapable of intimidating anyone on a physical level. Nor could he make himself appealing in any sort of visceral way. He was a rat-like man with thinning dark hair and a scratchy beard and thick horn-rimmed glasses and a nose that was twice too big. He had two things that carried him through life, had since he was quite young. Money and intellect. Passion had never ruled his life. It was possible that he had never even experienced genuine passion other than his lust for the possessions he'd managed to acquire over the years and his desire to defeat anyone who could possibly interfere with his climb toward success and thus thwart his acquisitive nature. Newberg was, by necessity, a logical, practical man who saw all existence in terms of problems and solutions. Life was, for Al Newberg, one lengthy list with prioritized items waiting to be checked off. So that's how he dealt with his current situation. He knew no other way. He shifted his gaze to take in the woman at the reception desk, then swung his eyes back to the man holding the gun. He mentally checked off item after item as he ran through his potential choices. There was no question who these two people were. He had no idea how they'd found him – he had felt very secure that he had insulated himself from those on the outside – but he absolutely knew who they were. Why they were here was another matter. The most logical possibility was to get information. Something specific, possibly. Or an attempt to get a general sense of what they'd stumbled into. It could go either way. The first question Newberg asked himself was: Could he bluff them? Could he feign ignorance, pretend to be what he was not? The answer was: No. It was too late for that.

The cop was no idiot. If they were here, they knew too much to be bluffed. Next attempt at a solution: Could they be bought off? Maybe. People's responses to money were often amazing – they took enormous risks, they sacrificed lifelong ideals – but his instinct told him that in this instance such a solution was unlikely. What was left? Get them talking. Find out what they wanted. Then find out what they'd settle for. It was all about negotiation.

Everything was about negotiation.

'Congratulations,' Newberg said. 'You're obviously much cleverer than anyone gave you credit for.'

'Shut up,' Justin said.

'And much more dangerous.'

Justin didn't speak again. He took one step forward and backhanded the grip of his pistol into Newberg's mouth. Deena gasped as the man went down on one knee and blood began to gush from his lip and gums. The expression on Newberg's face was one not just of pain but of shock and fear. Justin learned what he'd needed to know: this was someone who had other people commit violent acts. He was a stranger to real violence and to pain.

'There's no need for—' Newberg began but he didn't get to finish the sentence because Justin hit him even harder. This time the little rodent-like man's eyes rolled back in his forehead and the color in his face – a rich man's smooth tan – drained and was replaced by a sickly green.

'Justin . . .' Deena said, but he turned on her, a ferocious expression on his face, and she cowered back from him. When he was satisfied that Deena was not going to say anything more, he turned back to Newberg, who was still crumpled on the floor, but his hand was groping at his side, trying to find a position to help support his weight as he tried to sit up.

'I'm sure you're a smart guy,' Justin said to the little man on the floor. 'So you should be able to absorb what I'm telling you. From this point on, I don't want you to say one fucking word unless it's to tell me what I want to know. Don't ask a question, don't try to tell me anything you think might interest me because it won't. If you say anything that I don't want to hear or if I think you're lying to me, I will hurt you beyond anything you can possibly imagine. If you make too many mistakes, I'll probably hurt you so badly you'll die right here on this floor. If you wait too long before telling me what I want to know, my guess is you'll wind up crippled for life. If you somehow think that the two women who work for you can possibly help you, they're locked in the closet over there. They're bound and gagged. They can do you no good. I hold you personally responsible for everything that's happened to us. And for a lot of other deaths. So I have no qualms whatsoever about reciprocating. Is that understood? You can answer me now.'

Newberg nodded, weakly.

'Okay,' Justin said. 'This is going to be very simple. I only have one question. Give me the right answer and we're out of here. Where is Douglas Kransten?'

Newberg did his best to lick his lips, to get some moisture in his throat so he could speak. He had no luck. All he could do was croak out the words, 'I can't tell you that.'

'That's the wrong answer.' Justin took a step forward,

then he looked up at Deena. 'I think you should leave,' he said to her.

'Jay, don't.'

'The best thing is probably for you to go to the ladies' room. I don't think this will take very long. This guy uses other people's balls, he doesn't have any of his own. I'll come knock on the door when I'm done.'

'Jay, please don't do this.'

'Deena, I told you it was going to be different now. I'm doing what has to be done. Go to the ladies' room and wait for me.' His tone was like ice. Cold and even and remote. 'There's no other alternative right now. If we don't find Kransten we're dead. And so are a lot of other people. So I'm going to find him. I'm not going to let what happened to Alicia happen to you. So go outside. Now.'

She didn't argue. She didn't say another word. Deena nodded sadly. She didn't look at Justin or the broken man on the floor. She stepped out of the office and went down the hall to the ladies' room.

Justin stood over Alfred Newberg. 'Where's Douglas Kransten?' he asked again.

'I don't know,' Newberg whispered.

And then he began to cry.

Twenty minutes later, Justin tapped on the ladies' room door. He heard Deena's voice, quiet and far-away, say, 'Come in.' He stepped inside.

She was crying, too. Trying not to, but unable to stop. Looking in the mirror and using brown paper towels to soak up her silent tears.

'I'm sorry,' Justin said. He reached out to touch her shoulders, to pull her close to him but she recoiled. He watched her shudder as if she was repulsed by his touch and he said, trying not to cry himself now, 'I'm sorry. I'm truly sorry. But I didn't have a choice.'

She nodded, still didn't speak.

'Deena,' he continued softly. He started to reach for her again, stopped himself. He didn't want to see the revulsion in her eyes. 'I can't let them hurt you. I can't. You have to understand.'

'Did you kill him?'

'No.'

'Did you find out what you needed to know?' she said. Her voice was barely above a whisper.

'Yes.'

'About Kransten?'

'Yes. And other things.'

'If you didn't kill him . . . Newberg . . . won't he talk? Warn somebody?'

'No.'

'Why not?'

'Because he knows if he does, I *will* come back and kill him. Or worse, I'll hurt him again the way I just hurt him now. People like Newberg, they understand one thing – fear. And he's now much more afraid of me than anyone he might want to warn.'

'Where's Kransten?' Deena asked, still speaking softly.

He didn't answer. When he did, he first told her that he wanted her to come with him. One more time, so he could keep her safe. Then it would be all over.

Deena took a last sniffle, used a paper towel to wipe

her nose. Then, the tears no longer in her eyes, she looked at him. 'You have blood all over you,' she said.

'It's not mine,' he told her.

She nodded. Turned on the hot water tap for him. 'You'd still better clean up,' she said.

As Justin washed his face and then used paper towels and soap to dab at the blood spots on his clothes, Deena said, 'Jay?' When he turned toward her, she said, 'When you have your nightmares, what is it that scares you? Is it only the things that happened? Is it only what they did to Alicia and Lili? Or is it something else? Is it more than that?'

He didn't answer right away. It was a question he'd often asked himself but one he'd always refused to answer. 'It's mostly that,' Justin said. 'It's the loss and the waste and the guilt. But it's also the things I feel now. It's the things I want to do them. The things I know that I *could* do. That I *would* do. It's what you just saw,' he told her. 'Or what I didn't let you see. That's what scares me more than anything.'

She took a damp towel and wiped it across his forehead.

'I'm sorry,' he said. 'I don't know whether it's what they turned me into or whether it's what I always was. But I'm sorry.'

'I guess there's no way of ever knowing the answer to that. But I'm sorry, too.' She put her hands on his shoulders, stood on her toes and gave him a gentle kiss on the lips. 'So where's Kransten?' Deena asked. 'Where are we going?'

411

They were a few blocks away, on Park and 54th, standing outside an office building, in an alcove under a marble overhang. Deena was reading that morning's New York *Post*, which had their photos on page three, with the headline: Bandits On The Run. Underneath the photos was a caption. *Renegade cop turned killer and sexy yoga moll are still eluding a nationwide dragnet.* While Deena read and averted her face so passersby wouldn't recognize her, Justin was using Roger Mallone's phone to call Billy DiPezio.

'So how are your underworld connections these days?' Justin asked the Providence Chief of Police.

'You've been paying too much attention to the papers, again, Jay. Goddamn scandalmongers. You know I don't have any connections in that area.' Justin could hear Billy light a cigarette on the other end of the phone. 'But if I did, what is it you might need?'

'Two passports.'

'That's all? Two passports for people about to hit the FBI's Ten Most Wanted List? No counterfeit money? No bags of cocaine or semi-automatic weapons?'

'Two convincing passports. And driver's licenses.'

'All done?'

'And a credit card.'

'Any particular kind?'

'I'm open to surprises.'

'Well, as I said, I don't know anyone who does that sort of thing. But I'll tell you what I'd like, just for my desk, you understand, a sentimental thing – four passport-size photos. Wait a second – you want a photo credit card? 'Cause then I'll need five.'

'Not necessary. I'll overnight them within an hour.'

'Good. I'll add 'em to the little shrine I've got set up. And as long as we're gabbin', I got some other info for you, *mio compagno*,' Billy said. 'You wanted a link between the geezers in the old age homes? Well, my boys found one.'

'They all spent time in upstate New York, around Binghamton, in the early seventies.'

Billy sighed. 'I forgot how annoying you can be.'

'Kransten owned a hospital there. It's where the initial experiments were done.'

'But I can still top you. You wanted to know about Kransten and Marshall's baby. Louise Marshall did give birth. They had a daughter. April seventy-four. April tenth to be exact. There's no record of the kid's death but you know that doesn't always mean anything. But there *is* something you don't know. Care to guess what the daughter's name was?'

Justin held the phone away from his ear for just a moment. He took a deep breath, brought the phone close again. 'Yeah,' he said to Billy DiPezio. 'I'll give it a shot.'

'So I'm waiting. Let's hear it.'

'Aphrodite,' Justin said. 'The kid's name was Aphrodite.'

By the silence at the other end, Justin knew he'd gotten it right. It was confirmed when Billy said, 'Send the photos, you lucky fuck. I'll have the passports in forty-eight hours.'

Justin clicked the phone shut.

'Jay,' Deena said. 'Even with fake passports, how are we going to get out of the country?' She held up the *Post*, then quickly pulled it down behind her back. 'Somebody's going to recognize us. We'll never get to the gate.'

'We might not have to.'

'*Now* what do you have in mind?' she asked.

'One last favor,' he told her. 'Remember the guy in the blue Jaguar?'

'Your college roommate. With the house in Southampton.'

'Yup. He also lives in the city. Or at least his office is here.'

'And he's going to help us how?'

'He's rich,' Justin said.

'Yeah?'

'He's *really* rich.'

And as Deena stared at him, puzzled, he pulled out the phone again, dialed, and made yet another foray into his long ago past.

CHAPTER THIRTY-THREE

Justin and Deena sat on one side of the table in a corner of the Harrison restaurant in Tribeca. They both faced away from the door and kept their heads bowed as much as possible.

'Chris's father started Jordan's,' Justin said as he munched on the restaurant's curry spiced French fries.

'Jordan's the stores? The office supply stuff?'

'When we were in college, we got completely bombed one night and Chris actually wrote their TV ad line. "The law of supply and demand: You demand, we supply."'

'They're everywhere, those stores.'

'That's right. Chris is always traveling. He and his entire real estate department are always flying around the country. For my wedding, his gift to me and Alicia was the company plane. It flew us down to the Virgin Islands.'

'The Virgin Islands is one thing but we're going to fly across the Atlantic on a tiny, little private plane? I don't know about this. It feels too much like Snoopy flying on top of his doghouse.'

A voice behind her said, 'It'll be a little more comfortable than Snoopy's doghouse. And it's not exactly a tiny, little plane.'

Chris Jordan slid into a chair on the opposite side of the table.

'It's all worked out,' he said. 'You leave in four days from Teterboro, it's right across the river in Jersey. The pilots'll fly you to London and wait for you there. You've got them for up to a week.'

'Jordy . . .' Justin said.

'Yeah, I know, you don't know how to thank me.'

'That's right.'

'First of all, it's almost enough just knowing that you're fatter than I am. But if you really want to thank me, you can have dinner with us when you get back and this is all over.'

'What happens at dinner?'

'You mean, like, do I make you paint my living room or stand on your head for twelve hours? No. It'll be like the old days, that's all. You'll come out to Southampton and sit around with me and Jenny and we'll drink very good wine and . . . God, I hate this kind of male bonding crap, but I've missed you.' When Justin didn't say anything, just looked suddenly uncomfortable, Chris said, 'Yes, Jay, I understand it won't really be like the old days. It can't be. Not with what happened to Alicia. What I mean is . . . it'll be like the old days . . . except it'll be new days. Nobody wants you to disappear again.'

Justin shook off his melancholy and nodded. 'You drive a tough bargain,' he said. 'But I guess I can put up with spending a whole night with you.' He glanced over at

Deena and jabbed his thumb in her direction. 'Besides, she's never seen me beat you at pool.'

'I've been practicing,' Chris Jordan said. 'You're gonna lose your entire salary.' The waiter brought over another round of beer. The three clinked glasses and Jordy said, 'Is there anything else I can do for you?'

'Actually, there is,' Justin told him. 'We have to stay out of sight. We need a place to stay until we get our passports.'

'Same old Jay.' He drank half his beer in one gulp. 'To the old days,' he said. 'To the new old days.'

Four days later, they were on the Jordan's company jet flying across the Atlantic.

Jordy's driver picked them up at 7 p.m. and took them to Teterboro Airport, to the Jet Aviation terminal. There they were led on board a dark blue Gulfstream III with the words 'Jordan's: You demand, we supply' written across it. The inside had six leather swivel chairs and two built-in sofas. The trim was burl maple and much of the interior fabric – carpets and sofa coverings – matched the deep blue of the exterior. There were two pilots, who introduced themselves before the plane took off as Dreux and Buddy, and a flight attendant named Katerina who smiled and said she was at their disposal. After serving them coffee, Katerina pointed out the DVD player, the video tape player, the video game player and the CD player. She showed them where the wine was kept and said there were lobster, cracked crab and omelets whenever they wanted to eat. Justin said that they would probably sleep most of the way but he thanked her profusely. All three crew members made a point of saying that they loved flying for the Jordans and Justin made a point of saying that he'd be sure to pass it along.

There was no security – no metal detector, no bag search – flying non-commercially. There was a checkpoint a quarter mile before the terminal where a guard asked for passenger ID and the flight number for the plane. After that, the driver put the car a few feet from the runway, a Jet Aviation employee appeared, took their luggage and put it on the plane, and as soon as the two passengers were ready and comfortable the plane took off.

Deena was asleep soon after the plane left the ground. She hadn't slept much in the four days they'd spent in Jordy's Manhattan apartment, waiting for the ID documents to arrive. She was nervous about the impending trip and had now been apart from her daughter for a long enough time that she was having child withdrawal. Justin had asked her not to call Kendall because of the danger of phone taps. She was missing the little girl and that made her edgy. So did being around him, Justin knew. Over the four days they'd spent shut in the apartment – not wanting to risk being seen wandering the city streets – Deena had been polite and thoughtful and they'd had long, intimate conversations. He learned more about her first marriage, which was brief and never very satisfying. She talked a great deal about Kendall, about being a single parent. She told him about her broken hearts and her insecurities and the fact that she once wanted to be an actress but she didn't have the ego or the confidence. He did yoga with her for two hours each day and he knew he was stronger, already getting into the kind of shape he should be in. They slept in the same bed but as soon as they got physically close to each other her discomfort was obvious. By nature she was a toucher but she made no move to touch him during this period. He sensed her guilt. And her desire. But he could also sense her fear. She was afraid of him now or, rather, she was afraid of what he was capable of doing. So he never forced the issue. He made sure she understood how much he cared for her and he decided that was all he could do. After that it was up to her.

On Jordy's plane she sat next to him rather than across from him. Deena didn't like to fly and Justin was glad that he could be beside her, holding her hand, taking care of her in some way. When she began to doze, her head dropped onto his shoulder and her arm wrapped around his chest. For the two hours she slept, he did his best not to move or sigh so she could rest undisturbed.

When she woke up, her eyes opened slowly. She must have felt him against her, and she smiled. Her hand squeezed his . . .

And then she remembered. He could see it on her face and he could feel it in the tension in her hand. She tried not to be too obvious but soon her head was upright and her hand was in her lap. And soon after that she was sitting across from him.

Justin didn't sleep at all during the overnight flight.

He knew what was going to happen when he arrived at his destination, knew that the violence of his dream was about to cross over, irreversibly, into real life. He did not want to lose the reality he was in – the luxury of the plane, the peace and silence surrounding him, the softness and the beauty of the woman sitting near him. He wasn't ready to give that up yet. It was going to disappear, all on its own, soon enough.

At some point in the middle of the night, Justin eased himself out of his leather seat, walked to the small bathroom at the rear of the plane. He splashed some cold water on his face, wiped himself dry with a color-coordinated blue towel. He started to open the door to return to the main cabin, stopped, leaned down to rest his hands on the rounded porcelain sink. Justin forced himself to look in the mirror, let his eyes lock into the eyes that peered back at him from the glass. He knew how much he'd kept frozen inside in the years since Alicia and Lili had died. Knew how much of himself had died with them. But, for the first time in years, he acknowledged how much of himself was still left.

He reached out, his fingertips grazing across his reflection.

In the glass he saw the man he'd been and the man he was. He didn't have to see the man he was about to become. He knew.

Private jets fly into Luton airport, slightly north and just west of London. When they landed at Luton it was ten o'clock in the morning. Their bags were removed from the plane as they were greeted by a customs inspector who came on board, asked them a few perfunctory questions and then welcomed them to England. They took a courtesy van to the airport's Hertz rent-a-car, used Justin's new driver's license and credit card – he was, while he was in England, someone named Lee Scheibe; Deena was Virginia Donnaud – to rent a small but surprisingly powerful Ford. It took him about ten minutes to get used to driving on the wrong side of the road. Deena did her best not to scream or curl up with her eyes shut while he banged into a median divider and made a right turn directly into oncoming traffic. After a lot of horn honking and some serious sweating, he began to get comfortable behind the wheel. Eventually, he found the M25, followed the signs that said 'To the West' and, after stopping for a quick pub lunch of shepherd's pie somewhere outside of Oxford, they found themselves, several hours later, in Devon. He steered the car off the highway and along lovely, idyllic backroads until they came to the small thatched roof town of Lower Wolford.

As he drove out of the town, Justin passed several of the landmarks that Alfred Newberg had finally told him about and managed to write down – the sign that advertised a home built in the 1630s that was now a cozy B&B, a wildlife preserve, an antique store with a sign in the shape of a rocking chair. Eventually, after winding their way into the desolate and magnificent moors, he came to an ancient and inviting pub. The sign posted out front said that they served the best hot chocolate in the world and also announced that the fire burning in the fireplace had not been allowed to die out since 1846. Justin pulled the car over to the side of the road across the street from the pub. He looked across Dartmoor, to a hilltop perhaps a mile or two away. At the top of the rugged hill was a stone building that Justin knew to be an early sixteenth-century castle. He also knew that the castle had, over the past thirty years or so, been modernized and refurbished to the cost of tens of millions of dollars. He knew there were state-of-the-art laboratories set up in one wing and the plushest of living quarters, with luxurious amenities befitting a twenty-first-century billionaire, in the others. Justin squinted up at the castle for one more long moment, then stepped out of the car, opened the trunk and unzipped a small suitcase that Dreux, the pilot, had taken on board and told the customs people belonged to him. Justin reached into the middle of the bag, underneath several shirts, and pulled out his gun. He felt around for a pouch, found it, untied it and pulled out the bullets that he'd stashed there. He loaded the gun and tucked it into the front of his pants. He went around to the passenger side of the car, asked Deena if she wanted a hot chocolate. Even at this time of year, in the middle of the afternoon, it was cold in Dartmoor. The dankness in the air chilled to the bone, although the sun was out and shining. Deena said that she wouldn't mind a hot chocolate, it sounded good. So they went in, sat by the historic fireplace and while Deena talked about the beautiful countryside and the charming barroom, Justin Westwood thought about the castle on the hill and how that's where he expected to find Douglas Kransten and what he was going to have to do when he found him.

CHAPTER THIRTY-FOUR

There was no point in being subtle now.

They had analyzed every possible way of getting into Kransten's English home. It was impossible to anticipate what would be waiting for them inside but Justin didn't expect overwhelming resistance. Somebody like Kransten would have a bodyguard, maybe two. There'd be no need for more than that here. Exterior security was reasonably lax. Understandably so. The castle's isolation was security in and of itself. It had been built in an era when there were two classes of people – landowners and serfs – and its geographical location was for one reason only: protection. From its position atop the highest point in the area, it was possible to see anyone and anything that was coming within several miles. No surprises were possible. Not from warring armies or lower-class uprisings.

Certainly not from a mid-size rental car with two desperate people inside it.

So Justin went the no-surprise route.

They drove up to the top of the hill. Justin didn't know

how close he could get; it turned out to be not too close. A high stone wall surrounded the grounds and the only break in that wall was a metal, spiked gate that opened into the driveway leading to the house. Climbing over the wall did not seem practical or effective. So Justin pulled up in front of the gate, went to the intercom that was attached to the stone post, and pressed the buzzer. He rang twice and there was no answer, so he just kept his finger on it, pressing down. After thirty seconds or so, a man's voice, with a brittle English accent, spoke through the intercom.

'Who is this and what do you want?'

'My wife and I thought this was a museum or something,' Justin said in the most cracker-like voice he could assume, 'but we can't get in.'

'It's not a museum, it's a private home. Now please stop ringing.'

The man clicked off. Justin immediately put his hand on the button again and kept it there.

'I told you to stop ringing. Go away,' the voice said after several seconds.

'I'd like to,' Justin said, 'but now I got a problem. My car's overheated. Looks like it's ready to blow up. Can we come in to use the phone and call some kind of garage?'

'No, you cannot.'

'That's not very friendly of you. We're stuck and this place is in the middle of goddamn nowhere.'

'That's not my problem.'

'Well, if we can't come in, could someone bring out a cell phone or something? All I want to do is get someone to fix my car.'

'No. Now, stop bothering us.'

He clicked off again and Justin immediately put his finger on the buzzer. He left it there for several minutes. Then he got the result he wanted. The front door of Kransten's retreat opened and a man stepped out carrying a rifle. As he approached the gate, Justin could see that it was a shotgun.

'There's no need for guns,' Justin said as the man approached. 'I'm just trying to get some help for god's sake.'

The man walked up, stopped maybe two feet from the gate, lifted the shotgun and pointed it straight at Justin's chest.

'Get the fuck out of here,' he said.

Justin did his best to look terrified, which was not, in fact, all that difficult. 'I'm s-sorry,' he stammered. 'My car's overheated.'

'Then push the fucking thing,' the man said.

Justin nodded nervously, scurried to the rental car, opened the door and got behind the wheel. The man stood directly on the other side of the gate, the rifle now pointed at the front of the car. Justin shifted the gear into place, turned to look over his shoulder to check that nothing was behind him as he backed up.

'You're not in reverse,' Deena said. 'You're in first.'

'Put your seatbelt on,' he said as he turned the key in the ignition.

'This guy's got a rifle pointed at my head and you're worried about an accident?'

'Put it on,' he told her, never turning to face front, 'and duck.'

Her eyes widened but she managed to click her seat-belt on just as he jammed his foot down on the accelerator and the car sped forward. The bodyguard didn't even get a shot off as Justin slammed the car through the gate. The bodyguard ricocheted off the right fender and he screamed in pain.

Justin screeched the car to a halt, leaped out of the car, saw the bodyguard on the ground, the man's face contorted in pain, on his hands and knees trying to drag himself over to the shotgun several feet away. Justin beat him to the rifle, picked it up. As the man looked up pleadingly, Justin jabbed the butt down hard into the side of his head and he lay still and silent.

Justin dragged the man's body into the bushes, shoved him in so he wouldn't be easily visible. He went back to the car, told Deena that she should get behind the wheel and drive out of the grounds. She started to argue but he said, 'It's dangerous now. Too dangerous. I want you to take the car, drive about half a mile away and wait for me. If I don't show up in two hours, go back to Luton. Go to Jordy's plane, tell them to take you home.'

'I'm not going to leave without you, Jay.'

'If I don't meet you in an hour you're not going to have much of a choice 'cause I won't be leaving.' She started to shake her head, he could see the stubborn resistance in her eyes and the set frown on her face, so he said, 'You can't help me now. You can only hold me back from doing what has to be done. You know that's true. Please. It's almost over, Deena. Let me end it. I brought you with me so I could keep you safe. *Let* me keep you safe.'

He watched the tip of her tongue snake out to lick her lips. Justin could see that she was torn. Part of her wanted to stay with him, felt she *should* stay. But she couldn't hide the fear, the desire to escape. Or the fact that she didn't want to see and have to take responsibility for what was about to happen. Her eyes met his and she nodded once, curtly. She lowered her gaze, got behind the wheel and backed the car into the road. Justin waited until he couldn't hear the car's engine.

Then he reached into the front of his pants, pulled out his gun and started toward the house.

It was eerily still.

He reached the thick and ancient front door, pressed down on the cast-iron latch and the door swung open. Justin wiped the sweat off his right hand onto his jeans, made sure he had a tight grip on the pistol, and stepped into Douglas Kransten's house.

The foyer had stone floors and exquisitely carved wood paneling. The detailing along the floor and ceiling was elaborate and formal. An enormous grandfather clock stood in the corner to his left. The ticking echoed throughout the room. A circular stairway, also stone and probably ten or twelve feet wide, dominated the space, leading upstairs. Against the curl of the stairway was a massive carved wooden couch. A huge, rough candle chandelier hung down from the ceiling, which was a good thirty feet high. There were doors to the right and left leading to other rooms. The door to the left was shut. The door to the right was ajar. Justin took a cautious step inside into the foyer. Then another. When he was in the middle of the room he stopped, hesitated, then took one more step in the direction of the closed door.

He heard the click – a double click really, but he was moving after the first one – and without thinking, without turning, without hesitating, he dove headlong behind the couch. His arms were scraped raw as he slid along the stone floor and his shoulder slammed into the base of the stairway. He heard the roar of the shotgun blast and above him saw the stairway railings explode and splinter. Justin heard the double pump again, rolled away from the couch onto his side, his gun ready to fire. Another blast from the shotgun and this time the wooden couch was blown apart. Justin fired twice at the figure in the open doorway, saw blood spurt from the man's shoulder and then watched as the man's chest turned red and he dropped the shotgun and fell forward onto the foyer's cold stone floor.

Slowly, Justin stood into a partial crouch, his gun raised and aimed.

Nothing.

There didn't seem to be any movement at all from anywhere within the centuries-old house. He forced his breathing to slow down, waited until he was certain his legs would support his movement and walked over to the man he'd just killed, picked up the shotgun. The open door led into a plain, non-descript office. Several desks were set up with computers, phones and faxes. It seemed deserted, not just shut for the day. Justin had the strong sense that no one had worked here for some time. It was too neat. There were no papers on the desktops, nothing was out of place, not even a pen or pencil. He walked to the door at the far end of the office, leading further into this wing of the house. The door was also open and it led to a mammoth laboratory. The room was sterile; the desks and tables were steel and aluminum, the chairs were wood or plastic. There were more computers set up and one wall of bookshelves filled with medical and scientific reference books. One wall was nothing but vials and bottles and canisters. Built into a third wall was a deep restaurant-style refrigerator/freezer, the size of a walk-in closet. He turned, went back to the foyer, stepped to the closed door across the room that led to the opposite wing.

Justin turned the knob and, as expected, found it locked. He held the shotgun up to the lock, turned his head and pulled the trigger. The force of the explosion blew the door wide open and, dropping the empty shotgun on the floor, Justin stepped through.

This was a formal dining room. One wall was dominated by a large fireplace and carved, dark wood mantle. No fire was burning and its absence made the room feel cold and harsh. There was a heavy oak dining table with fourteen oak chairs around it. There were three place settings arranged at one end of the table. He checked the door that he'd shot open, saw that there was no lock from this side of the room. It could only be locked from the outside.

At the end of the room was another door. Closed. He crossed to it, moving quickly now. He turned the knob and pulled but the door was locked.

There was a rustling noise. He spun, handgun up, extended and ready.

He was pointing his gun at a middle-aged woman wearing an indistinct white uniform. She could have been a nanny or a nurse or a housekeeper or a waitress in a diner. Her skin was very pale with a touch of red in her cheeks and her hair was white. She was trembling as she stared into the barrel of the gun.

'Where's Kransten?' he said.

'Not here,' she managed to get out. She sounded vaguely Irish.

'Where is he?'

She shook her head tightly, as if too much movement would be dangerous.

'Who else is here?'

'No one.'

'Nobody else in this whole place?'

She shook her head again. The same tight movement.

'What were they guarding, those two guys, if there's no one here?'

'Nothing. They weren't doing nothing.'

'What's behind here?' Justin said, indicating the locked door.

'Just another room,' the woman said.

'Open it.'

'I don't have a key.'

Justin moved the gun several inches closer to her head. 'Get the goddamn key,' he told her.

The woman, her expression revealing nothing, reached into the front pocket of her uniform shift, pulled out a key.

'Open it,' Justin said.

She stepped around him, put the key in the lock and opened the door. He waved her forward and he followed her inside.

The room made his jaw drop open.

It was like stepping from the Middle Ages into the twenty-third century. The room was two or three times larger than the foyer and the ceiling was at least as high. It was all decorated in sleek chrome, thick glass and light, modern wood. There was a balcony that ran around the entire room, extending out uniformly about ten or twelve feet, beginning perhaps twelve feet below the ceiling. All the furniture was angular and minimalist. The lighting was modern and bright white. A giant flat-screen television hung on one wall. Stereo speakers were mounted in each corner of the room. Built-in shelves were filled with thousands of CDs, video tapes and DVDs. On a chrome and glass desk was a computer with an LCD flat screen. As he surveyed the space, Justin realized that the walls of the balcony above him were lined with books, from its floor up to the ceiling.

He motioned the woman to open the door that led to the next room. She went to a key ring that hung on the wall by the television, selected a key, went to the door and opened it. Again, Justin waved her through and then followed.

They were standing in the first room of an enormous bedroom suite. The décor was decidedly feminine. The sweeping, quilted curtains were woven in lush flower patterns that matched the quilt, bolsters and pillows on the king-size four-poster bed. The carved wooden headboard was also quilted with the same fabric. This floor was carpeted, a thick, deep burgundy weave. Fresh flowers were in vases scattered throughout. Books were stacked high on both end tables by the bed and on the desk positioned in the middle of the room. Another large-screen television was mounted on a wall. At first glance, it looked like a room fit for a queen. But as Justin stood there, he began to think there was something prison-like about it. Despite the flowers and the bright colors, the room felt lifeless and stifling.

'Whose room is this?' he asked. 'Who lives here?'

The frightened woman didn't answer.

'Who lives here?' he asked again, waving the gun in her direction.

This time there was an answer. But it came from the doorway that led to a bathroom off the second room of the suite.

'It's my room,' the voice said. 'I live here.'

The speaker stepped out into view. Justin realized she had been hiding in the bathroom.

He also realized that she was a little girl, perhaps eight years old.

'Who are you?' the girl asked.

'My name's Jay,' he said. 'Don't worry. I'm not going to hurt you.'

She was staring at him with a sense of wonder. He couldn't help but feel as if he was an alien whose space ship had just crashed on a strange planet.

'It's okay,' the girl said now to someone Justin couldn't see, and her voice was soothing and strangely adult, as if she was used to explaining things to people. 'I think it's safe to come out now.'

He heard another movement and then, from the bathroom, another woman timidly stepped out. She was also in a white uniform, also middle aged, with graying hair.

'Are you a new doctor?' the little girl asked Justin.

'No,' he said. 'I'm not a doctor. Are you sick? Do you need a doctor?'

'Don't talk to him,' the first woman in white snapped at the girl. 'Don't say nothing.'

Justin waved the gun in her direction. He didn't have to explain to her what he meant. The woman stopped talking immediately.

'That's a gun,' the little girl said and there was the sound of genuine astonishment in her voice. There was no fear. Just the opposite. Almost a feeling of joy at seeing something new and amazing. 'Why do you have a gun?'

'Because people are trying to hurt me.' Slowly, he stuck the gun back into his belt. 'I've put it away now. I'm not going to use it anymore, okay?' To the women in the uniforms he added, 'Unless I have to.'

'Why are you here?' the girl asked.

'To find someone.'

'Me?'

'No,' Justin said. He did his best to smile. 'Not you.'

'I thought everyone was looking for me,' she said.

He started to say *No, don't worry, no one's looking for an eight-year-old girl*, but before any words came out, his eyes narrowed and they gazed around the bedroom. The little girl's room. He saw the books on the table nearest to him. *Manifestos of Surrealism* by André Breton. Proust – *Swann's Way*. Next to her bed were copies of *Madame Bovary* and *To the Lighthouse*. And *A History of*

Mathematics in America. The Structure of Evolutionary Theory and The Power of Myth. He turned back to the little girl, who now took her first step out of the doorway. She moved closer to him. Her movements were wary and tentative as if moving toward an uncaged lion in the center of a circus ring. She was thin, he saw, with no hint of baby fat. Strongly muscled for someone so young. Her hair was dark and perfectly straight and hung down to her shoulders. Her skin was perfectly white and smooth, her eyes were strikingly blue and clear. She was wearing a light blue dress, a shift with thin straps over bare shoulders. The dress came down to several inches above her knees. She wore no shoes or socks. It was all perfectly appropriate for her age but Justin suddenly shivered. He stared into her eyes now and in addition to her extraordinary beauty he saw something disquieting and disturbing. He saw a sadness there that belied her youth and a hunger that was frightening.

'You're looking at me funny,' the girl said.

'I'm sorry,' Justin mumbled but he didn't stop staring.

'It's okay. I don't mind. You're the handsomest man I've ever seen in person,' the girl said and the hunger spread from her eyes all across her face.

'I'm not so handsome,' he said.

'Yes,' the girl whispered. 'You're very beautiful. I've never seen anyone like you.'

'Hush!' the second woman said.

'Oh my god,' Justin said quietly. Then he said it again and the words rang with a strong sense of wonder and horror and shock. And of pity and fear. Facing the small girl, looking at this exquisite little creature, the perfect eight-year-old girl, he suddenly understood. Maybe it was in the girl's eyes. Or maybe he was looking into her sad soul.

Justin remembered the word that Helen Roag's doctor friend had used: 'ungodly.' And now he understood who he was looking at. He didn't know how it was possible but he was absolutely certain that it was.

'You're here to find my father, aren't you?' the girl asked him.

'Yes,' Justin said, his voice barely audible in the room.

'And my mother?'

'Yes.'

'They'll be here soon. They're coming today.'

'You be quiet!' the first woman in white hissed at the girl.

'No,' the girl said. 'I won't be quiet.' She turned to Justin. 'I've never spoken to anybody before, not real people, not strangers, and I'd like to talk to you.'

'I'd like to talk to you, too,' Justin breathed. And then he knew he had to say her name. Just to be sure. Just to know that he hadn't gone mad. 'I very much want to talk to you . . . Aphrodite.'

She smiled. 'Everybody wants to talk to me. I know a lot of things.'

'I'm sure you do.'

'Would you like me to tell you everything I know?'

'Yes. I would like that very much.' He knew he was speaking very quietly. He was almost afraid to look away or even breathe too loud, as if the slightest disturbance would cause this fragile thing to shatter as if she were made of glass.

'Will you do something for me?' she asked now. 'If I ask you nicely and then I tell you everything I know?'

'Yes,' he said.

'Anything?'

'If I can,' he told her. 'I'll try to do whatever you want me to do.'

'Then I want you to find my mother and father,' she said. 'I want you to wait here until they come back.'

'I will,' he said.

'And then,' Aphrodite said, 'I want you to kill them.'

CHAPTER THIRTY-FIVE

They were outside walking down the path that led to the gate. The girl kept twirling around in delight and amazement.

'I've never been outside without supervision,' she said.

Justin nearly began to cry. He couldn't help himself. He wished he hadn't sent Deena away now. He wanted her to be there so he could grab onto her arm, needing an anchor to a different reality than the one he was suddenly confronting.

They stepped over the broken gate and Aphrodite crossed over the property line. She turned back to him and smiled hesitantly.

'I've never been here before. Never been outside these walls.' She reached out to take Justin's hand. 'It's frightening.'

'Everybody's got walls that keep them somewhere they don't want to be,' Justin said. 'And it's always frightening to go someplace you've never been before.'

She let go of his hand now, bent down to pick a yellow

wildflower from alongside the road. 'I don't want to go in,' she said. 'Ever.'

He let her wander and gawk and touch. She kept reaching out and stroking tree trunks, picking up rocks and fondling them in her palm, kneeling down and stroking the grass. Justin knew she'd talk when she was ready and soon she was. She stood in the middle of the road, turned and lifted her face toward the sun, and he listened while she told him her story. As he watched her, Justin had to tell himself over and over again that she wasn't what she appeared to be. He was not looking at a fragile eight-year-old girl. He was looking at a woman. A woman who was born in 1974, who had been kept locked away, an unholy experiment, for her entire life.

'It was my mother's idea,' she told him as they strolled. 'She'd read Skinner back in the sixties. He was the psychologist who talked about raising his children in a cage so he could control their environment and study the effects. My mother liked that concept. I think she gave birth to me so she would have someone to put into a cage.

'My father started his experiments in seventy-two. You said you know about them, the ones in New York. When they began to come to fruition, they needed someone they could study from a very early age. He's told me often how they used to long to experiment on a newborn baby, how they thought they could double the human life span if they only had the opportunity to get someone early enough. He's always told me that no one ever wanted a child more than he and my mother wanted me. He says that no child in the history of the world has ever been loved so much or so valued by her parents.'

438

'What about friends?' Justin asked. 'Did you ever have any friends?'

'Not allowed. At first, I was too young to know what I was saying so they couldn't take a chance that I might reveal something without realizing the consequences. Eventually I was old enough to understand what they were doing to me and, of course, then they really couldn't let me in a room with strangers. I might say something *knowing* the consequences. I've seen the doctors and scientists, of course. The house was filled with them up until a month or so ago. And I've had caretakers over the years. Those two women, the ones you locked in the bathroom, they're the latest. One of them's been there eight years. They keep me company but mostly they're there to make sure I stay behind locked doors. I've been locked inside that house since I was born.'

'Jesus . . .'

'I've got almost everything I could possibly need,' Aphrodite said matter-of-factly. 'I'll bet I'm the best read person you've ever met. And I've probably seen more films than anyone my age in the whole world. I can speak four languages, too. Well, five, counting English. French, Italian, Russian and German. I spend a lot of time on the Internet, although always under supervision. They can't take a chance that I'd contact someone or get into a chat room that might expose them.'

'Why did they leave?' he asked her. 'You said the house was filled with doctors and scientists until a month ago. What happened a month ago?'

'They finished.'

'Finished?'

'With the experiments. The formula.'

'What do you mean, finished?'

'They're all done. The treatments they started administering thirty years ago. They've come to fruition. They don't need to do anything else. They've got what they've always wanted.'

'And that is . . . ?'

'They can do to other people what they've done to me. They can provide a fountain of youth for anyone who wants it.'

The sun had moved along in the sky now and she walked slowly to the far side of the road so she could remain in its warm stream of light. 'I'm almost thirty years old,' she said now. 'Mentally and emotionally, I'm an adult. Physically, outwardly, I'm a child. I can't talk to anyone who looks like me because we're not remotely on the same level. And I can't talk to anyone my own age because they'd view me as a freak and a monster. I see the way you look at me while I'm talking. You think I'm a freak, too.'

'I'm sorry,' Justin said. 'I don't mean to. I just can't reconcile what I'm hearing with what I'm seeing.'

'It's all right. I *am* a freak. I've never been in love, I've never had sex. I'm probably twenty years away from even menstruating. I have no pleasure in my life and none to look forward to. I think about almost nothing but killing myself but I have never even been given that opportunity. If I keep taking the drugs and supplements and hormones I've been given my whole life, I will probably live another hundred and thirty years.

'That's why I want you to kill them. So I can finally

escape from what almost every other person on earth would pay millions of dollars for.'

'What happens if you stop taking the treatments?' he asked quietly.

'I don't know,' she said. 'That's the one thing no one knows. I could go on as I am or . . .'

'Or what?' Justin said, when she didn't finish her sentence.

'Or my body will stop functioning on its own because it's forgotten how.' She cocked her head now, and she looked across the horizon. She crossed back to his side of the road to stand directly in front of him. 'Listen,' she said. 'Do you hear it?'

Justin cocked his head, too. Heard a familiar whirring noise off in the distance.

'His helicopter,' Aphrodite said. 'They're back.' She took Justin's hand now. 'You should be in the house. It'll be easier if they're inside.'

He let her lead him back toward her prison. Her hand felt warm inside his.

'They're going to offer you anything you want,' she said. 'I know them. And they've got a lot to offer.'

'I'm not for sale.'

'My father has kept the scientists separate. They all know pieces. He thinks that no one has access to the final formula but him. He thinks that no one can really put it all together but him.'

'But that's not true?'

'I know everything they've done to me. I've kept track of everything since I was fifteen years old. Every medication, every injection, every pill. I've read and studied the

441

exact same materials and experiments that my father's scientists have read and studied. They talk to me, they've explained things to me. I've had nothing to do my entire life but learn what it is I am and why.'

Justin saw the helicopter now. It flew into view and headed for the landing strip several hundred yards behind the house.

'I can give you anything and everything that they offer,' Aphrodite said. 'Anything at all.'

'There's only one thing I want,' Justin said, and he told her what it was.

They were at the front door now. She told Justin how Kransten and Marshall would enter, where they would go. She told him exactly where to wait for them. Then she asked him to bend down.

When he did, she reached up and put her hands around the back of his neck. She stood on her toes and she kissed him. Her lips grazed his and lingered, pressing against him. Justin didn't move. Stood absolutely still until she released him.

'Thank you,' she said. 'I've been dreaming about a kiss for almost twenty years.'

Justin watched her go into the room to the left of the foyer. She came out a minute later and handed him a floppy disk.

'I have a friend,' he told her. 'She's in her car, parked, half a mile down the road. Her name's Deena. I'd like you to go to her and wait for me.'

'Leave here on my own?' she asked.

'Yes. Can you do that?'

Aphrodite nodded. 'I've dreamed about leaving here

on my own. I've dreamed about it my whole life.'

'Did you dream about what you'd do when you left?'

She smiled a deep, inward smile. 'Yes,' she said. 'I definitely dreamed about that.'

'You go wait with Deena. Then we'll help you do whatever you dreamed about. Okay?'

She smiled again, nodded, turned and walked out the front door and headed back toward the gate. Justin watched as she walked the path that would take Aphrodite outside the walls that had so long imprisoned her.

Aphrodite never turned around to look back. Justin saw her step past the wall. He saw her smile brilliantly right before she turned, heading toward Deena, and then disappeared from view.

Five minutes later, waiting exactly where Aphrodite had told him to, he came face to face with Douglas Kransten and Louise Marshall. Kransten was tall and rigid, with long, wavy, silver hair and deep crags in his tanned face. His fingers were long and elegant. Justin was surprised to notice such beautiful hands on an old and despicable man. Louise was younger, but the years didn't really matter because her age no longer was discernible. She had had too many face lifts. Her skin was unnaturally smooth and wrinkle free. Her breasts were too large and firm under her sweater. Her hair was too dark and her features seemed frozen, cast in something that only resembled human flesh. Neither of them made a sound when they saw him.

Justin didn't say anything either. There was no point. Words meant nothing now. The only thing that had any meaning was that now he could finish what he'd come halfway around the world to do.

Ten minutes later, it was done.

Louise Marshall didn't utter a word before she died. Douglas Kransten said only one thing. He looked straight into Justin's eyes and whispered, 'Aphrodite?'

Justin understood the question. The old man was asking if his experiment had survived. Would continue to survive.

Justin let him die without ever finding out the answer.

When he reached Deena, she was sitting in the car, parked off the narrow dirt shoulder of the road. She was sitting there alone.

'Is it over?' she asked as he walked over to her side of the car.

'It's over,' he said. He peered into the car, checked out the back seat. Then he glanced around at the quiet countryside. 'Where's the girl?'

Deena looked at him questioningly. 'What girl?'

He didn't know how to tell her, couldn't begin to explain, so he just said, 'A little eight-year-old girl. Dark hair. Very pretty. Didn't she come find you?'

Deena shook her head, said, 'Who is she?'

Justin shrugged, his eyes focused down the road, half-expecting Aphrodite to simply appear. 'The daughter of one of the servants, I guess.'

'And she just left on her own? Will she be all right?'

Now Justin nodded. 'I think she will. She seemed to have some kind of plan.'

'An eight-year-old girl with a plan?' Deena said. 'Should we go look for her?'

'No,' Justin said. 'We should let her be.' He smiled, opened the car door and slid in behind the wheel as Deena moved over to the passenger side. 'And we should go home,' he said.

CHAPTER THIRTY-SIX

Kendall came rushing up to Deena and threw her arms around her. Despite all the homemade French fries she'd devoured over the past week, she was definitely glad to see her mother. Deena hugged the girl tightly and planted kisses all over her face until Kendall began to protest and squirm. When she finally escaped her mother's arms, she made her way over to Justin and, with a bit more decorum, kissed him on the cheek. He couldn't help himself – he grabbed her tightly, too, and hugged her to him. The girl didn't squirm this time. She seemed instinctively to understand Justin's need to hold her.

'You're lucky,' he said to Deena's daughter.

'I am?' she said. 'Why? Because I got to stay here and go swimming every day?'

'No. Because you get to grow up and experience all these great things that life has in store for you.'

'But there's a lot of bad things, too, Jay. I know there are 'cause I heard you telling my mom. It scared me.'

Justin gave her a mock scowl. He chewed on the inside

of his lip, wondering when and how kids got to be so smart. 'You're right, as usual,' he finally agreed. 'There are a lot of bad things. But you can't let them scare you.'

'But what if they're *really* scary?'

'Well, for one thing, your mom and I are here. And one of our jobs is to make sure the really scary things don't ever get to you.'

'But what if you're not here? What if they do?'

'Then,' Justin said, 'you just have to realize that all those scary, bad things don't really matter. They're just part of life. Once you know that, they're not so scary.'

'I don't want them to be part of my life.'

'I guess nobody does. But you know what? There are so many good things that are also part of life, they make up for all those scary things. They more than make up for them because they're so much more important.'

'What kind of things?'

'You know what the good things are,' he said. 'You don't need me to tell you.'

'You mean stuff like how much my mom loves me and all of that?'

'That's exactly what I mean.'

'So you don't think I should worry?' the girl asked.

'No, Kenny,' Justin said. 'I don't think you should worry one bit. Why don't you leave that part to me.'

Kendall looked at him for a long time. Then she grinned and said, 'Okay, Jay. I believe you. I won't be scared anymore and I won't worry, okay?'

'Okay,' he said, as his mother and father came out of the den and walked up to them.

'She was a pleasure,' Lizbeth said, touching Kendall on

447

the small of her back. 'I'm going to miss her. We both are.'

Jonathan Westwood nodded his agreement.

'I'm sure she's going to miss you, too,' Deena said.

'Lizbeth said I can come back any time I want, Mom. I bet you could too, if you wanted to.'

'You both can,' Lizbeth said smiling. 'You're both welcome.'

'Can you stay for a few days?' Jonathan Westwood asked.

'No,' Justin told him. 'There are some loose ends that need taking care of. We've got to get moving.'

'Will we see you soon?'

'I hope so,' Justin said.

'I hope so, too,' his father told him.

Deena turned to both of Justin's parents. 'Thank you for taking care of my daughter,' she said.

Lizbeth reached over and, to Justin's astonishment, took his hand and squeezed it. 'Thank you for bringing our son back home,' she answered.

CHAPTER THIRTY-SEVEN

Gordon and Wendell Touay were all packed.

The plan was simple. Nothing remotely fancy. They were going to drive to East End Harbor. They were going to wait until Justin Westwood and Deena Harper were together and they were going to kill them. If possible, they would hurt them first. Hurt them badly. But that would be a luxury. All they really cared about was putting an end to their lives. Putting this whole unpleasant situation behind them. The bonus, they hoped, would be the little girl, Kendall. Her they'd let live for a while. A little while, anyway.

They went out through the small workout room, into the garage. They took no luggage; they weren't planning on staying overnight. When this was all done they had decided they were going to put their luggage to good use. They were going to take a long vacation. Maybe down to the Islands. Spend a few weeks on the beach, soaking in the sun, drinking margaritas. Looking for some new and different kinds of fun.

'I've been meaning to ask you,' Gordon said as he opened the car door.

'What?'

'Did you drink my Diet Coke?'

'What? No.'

'Well, somebody did.'

'Gordon,' Wendell said, 'I don't drink Diet Cokes. I have never in my life had one of your Diet Cokes.'

'I'm just saying, I had one in the fridge this morning and now it's gone.'

'Maybe you drank it and forgot.'

Gordon shook his head. 'I didn't drink it.'

Wendell looked at his watch. 'Can we discuss this while we're on the road?'

Gordon was certain Wendell was lying – who the hell else would have been in their house, been in their refrigerator – but he sucked back his annoyance, nodded at his younger brother, opened the door to the driver's side of the car and stepped in. Wendell got into the passenger's seat, reached into the glove compartment and pulled out the automatic garage door opener. He pointed and clicked and the door began to slide up and open.

'Oh, for god's sake,' Gordon said as he put the key in the ignition. 'Look.'

Wendell turned his head. On the floor of the driver's side, by the gas pedal, was a hand grenade. Wendell had a collection he'd brought back years ago from the Gulf. Gordon reached down and picked it up, handed it to his brother.

'For god's sake,' Gordon said again, then snapped,

'How the hell can you leave this thing in the car? Have you lost your mind?'

'I didn't leave that in the car,' Wendell said quietly.

'Well, who else do we know who has toys like this?'

'I'm not saying it's not mine. It is. I have two of them left. I'm just saying I didn't leave it here. And I didn't drink your Diet Coke, either.' Then they both fell silent.

The silence was broken when their cell phone rang. The twins looked at each other. As far as they knew, Alfred Newberg was the only one who had that particular number. And he'd made it clear that he would not be calling anymore.

'Hello?' Gordon said tentatively into the receiver.

'I got your number from Newberg,' a man's voice said.

'Who is this?'

'Also your address.'

'What the hell do you want?' Gordon asked.

'I just want to tell you two things,' the voice went on.

'Fuck off,' Gordon said. When the man didn't say anything in response, Gordon put a little bit of a sneer into his next words. He was getting angry. Whoever this guy was, he was going to suffer. 'Okay, here's your big break. What do you want to tell us, asshole?'

'First, thanks for the Diet Coke.'

Before the man could continue, Gordon and Wendell both heard the noise at the same time: a rolling noise, like a bowling ball slithering down a lane. The noise ended when whatever the object was came to a stop, bumping against something. The rear right tire, it sounded like.

'You want to know the second thing?' the voice asked. ''Cause I'd really like you to hear it.'

Gordon swiveled around, saw a man standing outside their garage. The guy looked familiar. He looked like . . .

'Shit,' Wendell said. And when Gordon turned to face him, the younger twin said, 'The other grenade.'

'Bye bye,' the voice on the phone said. 'That's the second thing.'

They both reached desperately for the door handles, Gordon to his left, Wendell to his right. Wendell got his fingers wrapped around the metal handle. Gordon didn't even get that far.

By the time the fire trucks arrived, Justin Westwood was over a mile away, driving back north, heading out of New Jersey on the two and a half hour drive toward East End Harbor.

When he reached the sign on the side of the highway that welcomed him to Long Island, he realized he was whistling and had been whistling for quite some time.

CHAPTER THIRTY-EIGHT

FBI Assistant Director Leonard Rollins thought he was having a bad dream. In this dream, he was suffocating. He couldn't breathe. It felt so real, as if something was stuffed down his throat, cutting off his air supply. At some point, the pain in his throat deepened and that's when he realized that he was awake. This was not a dream. He was in his queen-sized bed in his room in the not very swank East End Motel, naked under one sheet. His eyes were open and above him he could see Justin Westwood. Westwood was holding a gun. The barrel of the gun was jammed into Rollins's mouth. He could feel it pressing against the back of his throat and he could see Westwood's finger on the trigger.

'I'm here to give you a message,' Westwood said. 'And I want you to tell your boss exactly the way you hear it from me.' Justin tossed that morning's *Times* on the bed. It landed on Rollins's chest. Justin eased his finger off the trigger then slid the barrel of the gun out of Rollins's mouth. He motioned so the agent knew it was okay to move, to sit up.

Justin flicked on the bedside lamp and Rollins squinted at the sudden brightness. He waited a moment to focus his eyes, reached for the newspaper and angled it so he could read the front page story Justin wanted him to see. The story told about the discovery of the bodies of Douglas Kransten and Louise Marshall. The bodies were found in a room in their remote estate in the English countryside. One gun was found in the room. British police had ruled it a suicide pact. They determined that Kransten had shot his wife of over thirty years, turned the gun on himself, and pulled the trigger. Although there was no suicide note, the Justice Department had already issued a statement saying that Kransten and Marshall had been investigated for the past several months for illegal financial manipulations of their company, KranMar. The transgressions were of Enron-like proportions. Chase Welles, the head of the FDA, said that Kransten had been falsifying medical research reports on many of KranMar's products that had recently been released on an unsuspecting public. According to the *Times*, the company was about to declare bankruptcy and the couple faced, in addition to public disgrace, charges that ranged from fraud to murder.

'I know all about this,' Rollins said. 'Who the hell do you think formulated the Justice Department's response?'

'The threat's over,' Westwood said. 'Nobody has anything to worry about from Kransten or from the Aphrodite experiment. It's over.'

'I told them it was you. They didn't believe me. They couldn't figure out how you got out of the country.' Rollins gathered himself under the sheet, propped

454

himself up further and stuck his hand out. 'You did pretty good. I told them they shouldn't underestimate you.'

Justin ignored Rollins's hand. Wouldn't shake it. He waited until the agent slowly dropped it back by his side. 'I did better than you think.'

'And I'm sure you're going to tell me about it.'

'As a matter of fact, I am. Here's the first thing you have to know. And here's the first thing you have to tell your boss. Kransten had what you were so worried about. The formula was finished. He had the fountain of youth in his computer, along with marketing plans and a multi-million dollar launch. The government's worst nightmare come true. It exists.'

'What's the second thing?'

'I've got it. The complete formula. All the details of the years of experimentation. It's enough to perfectly recreate it.'

'Then just turn it over,' Rollins said, 'and the whole thing'll be forgotten.'

'Not a chance,' Westwood told him.

'You don't want to be in that position, Jay. As long as you have it, they're going to come after you.'

'As long as I'm the *only* one who has it.'

'Oh, Christ. What are you telling me?'

'It's been distributed. To quite a few people. Everyone I trust has a copy.'

'You fucking idiot. You don't know what you've done.'

'I know exactly what I've done,' Justin said quietly. 'I've made sure you bunch of lying psychopaths leave me, Deena Harper and her daughter Kendall alone.'

'You've done just the opposite. You just signed your own death warrants.'

'I don't think so. You pass all this along: The people I've sent copies to . . . no one knows what he's got. They don't know its purpose. Everyone knows one thing only: over the next ten years, starting today, if anything happens to me, Deena or her little girl, they're all to make the notes and the formula public. They've got instructions exactly how to do it. And you'll never be able to stop all of them.'

'Why ten years?'

'Less than that, you people hold grudges. You'd kill us out of spite as soon as you think it's safe. More than that didn't seem realistic. After a decade, I'll take my chances. I figure by then you'll be old and I'll be able to take you in a fair fight if you decide to come after me.'

Rollins sank back in the bed. 'How many people have copies?'

'Too many for you to go after. And in case you decide to, they've all got the names of three other people who have the disks. Anything suspicious happens to any of them, someone's going to release the formula and spread the word.'

Rollins stayed quiet for the longest minute of his life. Finally, he said, 'And all we have to do is leave you alone?'

'No. I want news coverage clearing us. Me, Deena, Frank Manwaring. I want a plausible explanation for Maura Greer's death made very public. I want Wanda Chinkle to get credit for solving the case so you can't fire her. You can link it to Kransten or Newberg or whoever you want. But we're absolutely cleared of any suspicion in

456

any of it. Same for the murders of Ed Marion and Brian Meves. Solve those cases and make sure we're cleared. Wanda can get credit for everything, if that makes it easier for you. But I want to read about all of it in the New York *Times* and see it on every television news show in the country within forty-eight hours.'

'I don't know if that's possible,' Rollins said.

'I do. You want me to run down the list of murders the government's been involved in that have never come to light? How about just a list of supposed suicides?'

'I have to check with my superiors.'

'Fine. While you're at it, check and see how they'll like it if CNN gets proof of the conspiracy that's been going on for fifteen years with the pharmaceutical companies.'

'All right. Let's assume you've got a deal.'

'I want to make it even clearer. I want to make absolutely certain you understand the way things stand, you little shithead. If anything happens to me, Deena or Kendall over the next ten years, and I mean anything, you're fucked. If any of us get hit by a car crossing the street or choke on a chicken bone in a restaurant or get cancer, the Aphrodite formula is made public and the conspiracy's revealed. So you might not just want to leave us alone, you guys might want to hire crossing guards for us and make sure we've got really good medical insurance. You got it?'

'I've got it. Anything else?'

'Yeah. Get out of East End Harbor. After tomorrow, if I see you within two blocks of where I am, anywhere in the world, I'm going to kill you without even asking a question. You got that, too?'

'I got that, too. You have anything else?'

'No.'

'Then I have a question for you.'

'Okay. You can have one.'

'We heard there was a daughter. Kransten had a daughter.'

'I heard that, too. Apparently she died a long time ago. As a child.'

'So you didn't see anyone? There was no trace of a daughter living there?'

'Absolutely no trace,' Justin said. And then he said, slowly, almost incredulously, 'You people. You fucking careless people. You think you can do what you want, hide the things you don't want people to see. Why'd you go along with it? What makes you so sure you're right about things that you'll let so many people die?'

'I work for the government,' Rollins said. 'I work for people who see the big picture.'

'There's always a big picture with you guys, isn't there? There's always something that justifies all the damage you do.'

Their eyes met and locked. 'Congratulations,' Rollins said. 'You won.'

Justin shook his head. 'Everybody lost,' he said. Then he turned, walked out of the motel room without ever looking back.

CHAPTER THIRTY-NINE

They had dinner at Sunset. Sat outside and watched the moon's reflection glide over the water of East End Bay. They had oysters and then grilled fish, with a good bottle of chilled white wine. Neither one of them wanted coffee or dessert but they had an after-dinner drink, thin cordial glasses of a vin santo.

Justin walked Deena home after dinner. They strolled along Main Street, which was still busy with the mid-summer tourist crowd, desperate to pack in as many evenings of carefree fun as possible before Labor Day. They reached the front of her building, went inside, up the stairs into her apartment. They paid the baby sitter, looked in on Kendall who was asleep, then they went into Deena's room and they made love. There was no conversation, he just reached for her and she responded. It started simply enough, with a kiss, but then her nails ran down his back and she bit his lip until he yelped in pain. He grabbed her hair and kissed her hard. They undressed each other, yanking their clothes off in jerky, spasmodic movements, and fell on the bed. They made love for a long time and

459

they both knew there was something desperate, almost violent in the way they were kissing and touching and writhing and moaning. When they were done, they were both sweating and breathing hard, both of them stunned at the emotions and the release they had just experienced.

It took Justin a long time before he could speak but finally, his chest still heaving, he said, 'So what happens now?'

Deena wiped the sweat off her forehead. She got up from the bed, grabbed a blue silk robe off the hook on the back of the bedroom door. She wrapped the robe around her, sat back on the bed, one leg tucked under her. She reached over and put one hand on his arm. 'My whole life, the last few years of it anyway, has been spent trying to achieve some kind of spiritual balance. That's what I believe in, Jay. Balance and peace. Your life . . .'

'I know. Not too spiritual or balanced. And not too peaceful.'

'It all just scares me so much. And it's not just me. Okay, I know it all exists, all the ugliness you choose to see. But I don't want to have to face it. I'm sure you think that's hypocritical or cowardly but I *don't* want to face it. And Kendall, maybe she can get through the rest of her life without having to see some of these things. Maybe her life can be different.'

'But not if I'm around it can't.'

'No.'

He nodded, turned and started to move away. She reached out for him, hooked his arm with her hand, pulled him back closer to her.

'I know what you think. You think it's what happened

with Newberg. The violence. But it's not just that. It's more than that. It's all of it.'

'It's what my wife used to say. Alicia. She used to have that same look in her eye that you have.'

'What look?'

'I used to point it out to her and she'd say I was crazy. She said the only look she had was one of love.'

'And what did you say it was?'

'Oh, it was love. But it was something else, too. It was fear.'

'I'm not afraid of you, Jay.'

'No. Neither was she. It's a different kind of fear. It's a fear of life. Of my life. Of what I'd bring into *our* life.' He smiled at her, leaned over and kissed her lightly on the lips. 'You want to tell me that the only look in your eyes is one of love.'

'No,' Deena said sadly. 'I can't do that. But there is love in there, too.'

'So what do we do?' he said.

'I don't know,' she told him. 'Maybe we just go on and see what happens. See which is stronger, the love or the fear.'

He thought about that for a while, then he nodded, smiled a brief flicker of a smile. They made love again, this time slowly and gently, and she fell asleep in his arms.

At two o'clock in the morning, he untangled himself, slipped out of her bed and got dressed. He leaned down, kissed her lightly on the cheek. She stirred in her sleep and gave a satisfied sigh. He turned, left her bedroom and then her apartment, headed down the silent, deserted street, back to his small Victorian house half a mile away.

461

When he opened the door, stepped into his living room and felt the solitude envelop him, Justin Westwood waited for the familiar roar of music to take over as it had done so often over the years. He expected something sad or harsh or cynical to fill him up. But no music came just now. He was restless, he realized, thought about having a couple of scotches, but that didn't seem right somehow. He stood in the darkness of the living room, not bothering to turn on the lights, and he closed his eyes for a moment, remembering how easy it was for him, not so very long ago, to disappear within his own head and shut the world out.

But after a few seconds, his eyes opened. The world was quite visible, if cast in late night shadows.

Justin turned the light on. He walked to his built-in bookshelf. He removed three books from the middle of the shelf, reached behind them. His hand came out holding a floppy disk for a computer. The disk was protected in a thin paper sheaf. Justin stared at the disk in his hand for quite a while, then he went to his laptop, inserted the disk into the A drive. Justin studied the formula on his screen, read the notes and history well into the night. It was dawn when he was done and he clicked on 'close.' A box came up on the screen asking him if he wanted to save the document. He clicked on 'no,' and watched as the words disappeared.

Justin removed the disk, put it back in the thin paper covering, walked over to a wastebasket at the other side of the room. He held the disk over the basket, picked up a book of matches that was lying next to a candle on his window sill. Justin lit a match, held it up to the disk and set it on fire. He held it between his thumb and forefinger until he couldn't hold it anymore, then he let it drop into the wastebasket. He watched as the disk began to melt and curl and disappear.

Justin realized that he had an early and busy day tomorrow. He was back at the East End Harbor police station and there was a lot of work to do. He was suddenly overcome with exhaustion, he knew he should try to get a couple of hours' sleep.

Justin decided that before he went to the station in the morning, he might go see Mrs Dbinsky on Harrison Street. After the raucous weekend, she'd probably be complaining about the traffic again. About all the trucks that had driven past her house in the last two days. He liked the idea of heading her off at the pass, not even waiting for her to call.

But first he'd get into bed and try to sleep.

Even if only for an hour, he'd have a peaceful, quiet, dreamless sleep.

GIDEON

Russell Andrews

When they asked him to be a ghost writer, he didn't realise they wanted him dead.

Struggling writer Carl Granville is hired to turn an old diary, articles and letters – in which all names and locations have been blanked out – into compelling fiction. For this, and for his silence, he will be paid a quarter of a million dollars. But Carl soon realises that the book is more than just a potential bestseller. It is a revelation of chilling evil and a decades-long cover-up by someone with far-reaching power. He begins to wonder how his book will be used, and just who is the *true* storyteller.

Then – suddenly, brutally – two people close to Carl are murdered, his apartment is ransacked, his computer stolen, and he himself is the chief suspect. With no alibi and no proof of his shadowy assignment, Carl becomes a man on the run. He knows too much – but not enough to save himself . . .

'A fast-moving thriller in the Grisham genre' *Sunday Telegraph*

ICARUS

Russell Andrews

ICARUS. The boy who flew too close to the sun. The boy who fell to his death. It is a story that captured the imagination of ten-year-old Jack Keller, but one that is also eerily prescient. For a vicious assault resulted in the murder of Jack's mother, sending her plummeting seventeen storeys to her death – right in front of her son's eyes.

Thirty years later, and history is repeating itself in the same horrific manner. Kid Demeter, a physiotherapist Jack helped raise as a teenager, has fallen to his death. The police think it was an accident, but Jack doesn't believe them. For Kid had confided in Jack about his ongoing relationships with a string of women, women he gave a series of intriguing nicknames. The Mortician. The Mistake. The Destination. The Murderess.

As Jack delves into Kid's world, and realises just how high the stakes really are, he knows only one thing for certain: he must find the killer before the killer finds him, and makes him the final victim . . .

'I defy you to figure out who dunnit, why they dunnit, or how they dunnit' Janet Evanovich

Other bestselling Time Warner titles available by mail:

☐ Gideon	Russell Andrews	£6.99
☐ Icarus	Russell Andrews	£6.99

The prices shown above are correct at time of going to press. However, the publishers reserve the right to increase prices on covers from those previously advertised, without further notice.

———————— **timewarner** ————————
paperbacks

TIME WARNER PAPERBACKS
PO Box 121, Kettering, Northants NN14 4ZQ
Tel: 01832 737525, Fax: 01832 733076
Email: aspenhouse@FSBDial.co.uk

POST AND PACKING:
Payments can be made as follows: cheque, postal order (payable to Time Warner Books) or by credit cards. Do not send cash or currency.

All UK Orders	**FREE OF CHARGE**
EC & Overseas	25% of order value

Name (BLOCK LETTERS) ....

Address ....

....

Post/zip code: ....

☐ Please keep me in touch with future Time Warner publications

☐ I enclose my remittance £ ....

☐ I wish to pay by Visa/Access/Mastercard/Eurocard

☐☐☐☐☐☐☐☐☐☐☐☐☐☐☐☐☐☐

Card Expiry Date ☐☐☐☐